THE EXPER

THE EXPERIENCE BUYER

Alexandra Hampton

PAN BOOKS
LONDON, SYDNEY AND AUCKLAND

First published 1994 by Pan Books

a division of Pan Macmillan Publishers Limited
Cavaye Place London SW10 9PG
and Basingstoke

Associated companies throughout the world

ISBN 0-330-33087-X

1 3 5 7 9 8 6 4 2

A CIP catalogue record for this book is available from the British Library

Typeset by CentraCet Limited, Cambridge
Printed by Cox & Wyman Ltd, Reading, Berkshire

This book is dedicated to
the man on the 7.47 train from
Brighton to London.

No man's knowledge can go beyond his experience.

JOHN LOCKE

Morality weighs heavily upon me
Like unwilling sleep.

JOHN KEATS

Homo sum; humani nil a me alienum puto.
(I am a man; I count nothing human alien from me.)

TERENCE, *c.* 195–159 BC

Experience One

'Listen, let me tell you what I know. I'm not that good with words so you'll have to bear with me. I'll just talk. All right? I'll just talk. I'd been sick, heart trouble – the doctor said something about my left ventricle, or something like that. Anyway, he said I'd die unless I had the operation, so I did. Not die – I had the operation. Only after it I went into remission, then a coma, then nothing. Well, so they thought. They *thought I was dead to the world. Out of it, as the Americans say. I was just lying there, comatose.*

'Only I wasn't. Comatose, I mean. I was listening, clever as you like. Listening. I could hear every word and knew they didn't expect me to live. My relatives came to see me. They stood by the bed.

' "He's looking better."

' "Whatever do you mean? He's awful. Just awful."

' "Oh, Ivy, don't. He can hear, you know."

' "Never! He's out like a light."

' "Someone told me he can understand every word."

' "Well, if he can, it's a bloody miracle. He was never that smart before."

' "He looks handsome, though."

' "He looks dead."

' "Yeah, dead handsome."

'You had to hand it to her, she was trying. My wife, pretty once, long ago. Pretty once, slim once, witty once. All those onces, mounting up. You could reach the stars on the pile of onces in just one life . . . Anyway, I wasn't dead, handsome or otherwise. I was just sleeping, and listening. But that was when it happened – my experience. Suddenly I was dying. I knew that. I'd seen something in the paper about near-death experiences, and here I was, living it. Well, dying it, anyway. There was the tunnel, my dead parents, the white light and that peace they tell you about.

'Heaven. Or so I thought. Heaven . . . Only it didn't last. The good

feelings went. All the people I loved who had come to meet me went too. It was awful. Ghastly. I've never felt such a sense of unbearable loss. I just stood there, deserted, and then I was transported into this room. A white room – white furniture, white curtains – and when I looked out of the window, a white landscape. Imagine it if you can – white sky, white trees, white grass. Whiteness, as cold as pure loneliness. As cold as desertion, as utter loss. There was no one there, and the only colour in the room came from a box high up on the wall.

'The box ticked, but no numbers came up. Just photographs. One after the other. Photos of people I'd never seen before. All kinds, all ages, all colours. On and on. Click, click, the pictures kept coming, and then suddenly someone was talking to me. I couldn't see them, just hear them, and they explained.

'They said that soon I would be taken from that place and stripped. Then I would be forced into a machine naked – the Mother Womb, they called it. The words terrified me, but I couldn't escape because there was no way out, and nowhere to go. The room had no doors . . . I was to be reborn, you see, only this time I would be in full possession of my faculties, and would know and feel everything. The blood, the pain, the final, rupturing expulsion from the womb. I didn't know if I was to be born crippled, or mentally impaired, I just knew that outside that damned and damnable room a steel womb waited to give birth to me.

'Not everyone made it, they explained. Some panicked in the birth canal. Some had to be taken out because they'd injured themselves struggling, had broken limbs against the sides of the machine. Some went insane. Forced down the narrow passage, covered in blood and slime, gasping for air and light, not knowing how you would come out, or if *you would come out! Jesus, help me!*

'I'm sorry, I'm finding this very difficult . . .

'The voice went on, explaining. I had to wait, you see, Mr Taverner. I had to wait in that empty, silent, unearthly white room and watch that bloody box, with its unending stream of faces gawping out at me. I had to watch and wait. I had to sit there hardly able to breathe, as photograph after photograph clicked over. I had to wait, knowing what was coming,

until finally the picture on the box was no longer a stranger's but my own . . .

'I came back to life screaming hysterically. Or so they told me afterwards at the hospital. They said I'd been lucky, that I'd begun to fight and rallied. They said I'd struggled so much I'd pulled out my tubes. They said I'd escaped death. But I know better, Mr Taverner. You see, I know that I might have escaped once, but there'll be another time. One day or one night I'll go back to that white room with its white landscape, and I'll hear that box and see its reel of unending faces ticking over and over and over . . .'

EXPERIENCE TAKEN FROM *Mr William Hunt*
FEE PAID: *£600*
SIGNED: *Aubrey Taverner*

Experience Two

'So I had this accident, you see, I fell off a building, about thirty-odd feet – not that far really. Well, I lie, it felt a bloody long way, especially when you're panicking and trying to grab hold of a passing pigeon, but it wasn't that far really . . . At the time I was working on a site for this architect, some American geezer who was supposed to hurry things along. Well, he did, he hurried us all along. Me in particular – hurried me right off the edge of a building and nearly into the next world . . .

'Not that it was all his fault. I'd been having some trouble for a while, but kept quiet. You know how it is? What with work being hard to find, you learn to keep your mouth shut. Anyway, a blackout was what made me fall, but when I was admitted to the hospital they discovered that I had this virus on the brain . . . Yes, that's the word for it, a virus. Such a posh name, isn't it? Well, the "virus" took hold and I was hospitalized – not for long, just a week or so – and then I was allowed home. So far so good, hey, Mr Taverner? But, you see, the thing was I also got this autoscopy *as a result of the "virus" – a-u-t-o-s-c-o-p-y. It's a condition, very rare, which affects some people after a virus. Not everyone, just some.*

'Well, I didn't even know I had it until I left hospital. Then one morning I was walking along, minding my own business, when there I was – walking towards myself*!'*

'Walking towards yourself?'

'Yes, I was walking along without a care in the world and all of a sudden I saw myself in front of me, walking towards me. *Large as life. Gave me a bleeding turn, I can tell you. So I sort of narrowed my eyes and stared at myself and watched as I came closer and closer . . . Then I* passed *myself. Walked past! Can you believe it?'*

'Then what?'

'Well, I was mystified, wasn't I? I mean, who wouldn't be? I thought I was crazy, but I couldn't have been that crazy or I wouldn't have recognized the person as myself, would I? So you know what I did? I

followed him – or rather, me *– I followed myself. All over London. Well,* we *– or rather, I – went up Charing Cross Road, along Tottenham Court Road and I finally ended up in bloody Highgate. Jesus, did my feet ache. And then d'you know what happened?'*

'No, tell me.'

'I walked through myself. Can you believe it? I walked through myself. *I was suddenly seeing myself, then drawing level with myself, then walking on towards myself and then . . . then I walked through myself. Christ, it hurt. I mean,* hurt*! I thought it would kill me, the pain. Far worse than falling off a building – any bleeding building. Well, when I came out of myself – at the other end, so to speak – I mean, when we had parted company, so to speak, I was left with this . . . I'll show you, if you just hang on a minute whilst I take my shirt off. Now, look at that. Can you believe it?* I'd walked right through myself. *Right through . . .*

'I know what you're thinking, and you're right. I've got the backside of a man on my front. And yes, that's right, on my chest I've got his back, and on my genitals, his bloody arse . . . You may smile, Mr Taverner, but it's a hell of a way to end up. A hell of a way, especially when you're not expecting it. He walked right through me, he did, and then jammed, sort of locked himself in . . . Funny, isn't it, how things turn out?

'Worth money, though, hey? Worth a good fee, Mr Taverner? Well, what d'you say? Hey? What d'you say? I'd say that was worth anyone's money. I said so to the wife this morning. I said, this is an experience worth money, enough for a fortnight in Spain . . . You wanted an experience and it's certainly that. Oh, yes, it's certainly that. So what d'you say, Mr Taverner, what d'you say?'

EXPERIENCE TAKEN FROM *Mr Terry Peacock*
FEE PAID: *£500*
SIGNED: *Aubrey Taverner*

Chapter One

WANTED Intelligent young man
to assist in research for author.
Excellent salary in return for loyalty
and integrity.
Tel: —

entry in the Personal Column of *The Times*,
21 September 19—

THERE had been a thunderstorm over Greek Street. Rubbish littered the pavement and smothered the drains, leaving greasy puddles which would lurch through the grilles with the sound of an old man gargling – a disagreeable old man, disturbed by the thunder, wheezing awake in Soho. Edward Dadd read the advertisement twice and wondered about the real meaning of the words. Then, deciding he had just the right amount of integrity and loyalty to merit an excellent salary, he dug out a coin from his pocket and phoned the number.

It was engaged. Thwarted, he decided there and then that the position was entirely what he needed to withdraw himself from a situation which was becoming increasingly complicated, and with the ferocious determination of a fanatic he dialled again. The number was still engaged.

Feverishly he redialled. The number rang twice before being answered.

'Hello.'

No question in the tone. Direct statement.

'I . . . saw your notice in *The Times* this morning.'

'How old are you?'

Edward frowned. 'Twenty-seven.'

'Too young—'

He interrupted quickly. 'The advertisement asked for a young man.'

'Not so young.'

'Twenty-seven isn't that young,' Edward insisted.

The voice was without animation. 'Why do you need work?'

'I have no money.'

A laugh. Almost a laugh behind a hand. 'Oh, I understand . . . Come round to see me at four o'clock this afternoon. I'm at number six Cook's Alley.'

Edward repeated the directions carefully.

'That's correct. Ring the second bell and I'll come down to greet you. What is your name?'

'Edward Dadd . . . And yours?'

There was only the slightest pause before the man answered. 'My name is Taverner; Aubrey Taverner.'

For the remainder of the day Edward wandered. It was an occupation he had perfected since occupying a bedsit in Ealing with a shared bathroom. The depression that four walls and pre-war wallpaper inflicted on his senses forced him out into the capital early in the morning, where he stayed until darkness forced a reluctant return late in the evening.

During the day he gambled – and lost. And as every drunk insists each drink is his last, so Edward kept believing that his luck would change. It never occurred to him to stop gambling. There was an eroticism about the cards which sucked him in; a juiced belief, full-bellied and willing, which shifted in his hands. The shuffle of number and picture cards, the swish of mumbled paper endearments – they all lied and promised everything, but exchanged only the deep-throated death of desire for the barren cold mouth of bad luck.

Only the night before he had lost all that remained of his

money and his possessions, including a gold watch inscribed: 'To Edward, on his twenty-first birthday. Father.'

When the shock faded, bewilderment set in. Driven by his obsession, Edward had pursued the wheel grimly. Then, stupidly, he had tried to wheedle his way out of his difficulties, pleading with the men who ran the clubs, grovelling for a loan or for one last try. He was met with stolid resistance. They were immune to his coaxing and his plaintive threats. Their interest never extended beyond their hands: picking up the money Edward had lost, their eyes remained remote and their voices curiously free of triumph.

All they wanted was repayment – the one thing Edward could not guarantee.

Cook's Alley was so firmly tucked behind the knotted streets of Soho that to the uninitiated it remained hidden and undiscovered. On each side of the alleyway, tall buildings rose up and nudged one other, some red-bricked, others white-fronted, although the paint was peeling in places and the window frames were scuffed with rot. Only occasionally was there some evidence of money: a couple of the buildings well tended, smug little newcomers nestling amongst their pensioned neighbours.

Most of the buildings were slumped into old trades, doors opened to display the business behind or resolutely shut, the terms and hours of work stated on notes stuck carelessly on to the scratched glass. Nameplates worn illegible by time and Brasso told of dead solicitors, and two ash trees stood guard on the street, their trunks bearing the passing epitaphs of the long-departed. No one could remember who 'G' and 'H' were, or why the date 12/6/49 was so important, but someone had scarred their glory days on to the trunks and the trees continued to bear them up to heaven by inches.

The afternoon drowsed under an unexpected sun. The alley,

smelling of paper size and drying rain, seemed fixed oddly in the past. Edward glanced around, taking in the steaming air, the wet city moisture of a past shower. The atmosphere was cloying; the buildings, with their open windows and doors, winded in the still air. Nothing moved, nothing shifted; only time scuttled around him like a climber grubbing for purchase on a rockface. Then suddenly Edward felt as though he had moved backwards, as though he was half remembering an old dream of an old place in an old time. A dank smell sneaked up on him, the buildings mould-spotted, the cobbles oily. The place took the breath from him; it shimmered darkly in front of his eyes, the chimneys gridding the skyline.

Giddily, he stretched out his hand and touched the wall next to him, struggling for breath as his fingers lingered on the cool stone. Cook's Alley was real, he knew that; logic affirmed it. The buildings were real, the trees real, the iron railings sharp under his touch. All real – and yet all unreal. His breath came from the top of his chest, quick and uneasy, giving little oxygen as he paused on the greasy cobbles. He gulped avidly at the thick air, then finally moved, stepping heavily on to the pavement.

The noise startled him – the sound of his footfall, unusually loud. It was then that he realized why the alley was so threatening. The silence, the utter lack of noise. Beyond this place, only yards away, Greek Street clashed under London traffic, the drumming of feet and the clatter of plates through open restaurant windows drowning the passers-by. But not here. Here there was an *absence* of noise, a suspension of all sound.

Under the still sun the buildings defied Edward to stay – they ostracized him, cold-shouldered him. There was welcome from neither window nor door. All were closed to him, and for an instant Edward had an overwhelming desire to run, as the trees grasped upwards with their impoverished limbs and the silence tingled spitefully in his ears.

'What are you doing?'

The impression of evil vanished as a girl spoke. Startled,

Edward glanced up, hearing at the same moment the unexpected hum of a sewing-machine coming suddenly from No. 3.

'Well, what *are* you doing?' she repeated, leaning further out over the windowsill, a half-eaten apple in her right hand.

'I'm looking for Aubrey Taverner,' he called up to her. 'At number six.'

Her arm extended outwards, across the alley. It came from the house like a disembodied limb, a white pointer.

'Over there, at the end. The buildings aren't in any order. None of the numbers makes any sense. It drives the postman mad.' She dipped backwards suddenly, a voice calling her from behind, and the window slammed shut fiercely.

No. 6 bellied out slightly at the front, old and much renovated by many different hands. It was like a rag rug put together from disparate bits and pieces. Mottled stucco adorned the front, whilst a wrought-iron balcony, rusted from neglect, jutted its chin over the alleyway. On the second floor the windows were grilled, sickly ivy suckling the discoloured metal and a pale rectangle of brick showing where a plaque had once been. Nothing was in order. The windows here were not related to those on the first or third floor, and the shadowed basement yard was cordoned off completely by spiked ebony railings, the gate manned by a lugubrious black dog.

'What's the matter? What do you want?' a voice called out suddenly.

Edward glanced round, saw no one and then peered down into the minute basement yard. An old woman stood there, hair dyed henna red, her eyes narrowed against the light, one hand extended towards the dog.

'I've come to see Mr Taverner. I have an appointment.'

'Appointment,' she repeated, obviously amused. 'All the others just walk up. What makes you so special you need an appointment?'

Her hand closed round the dog's tail and gave it a sharp tug. The animal turned its head and looked at her balefully.

'I've come about a job—'

'I clean his rooms for him,' she said, ignoring Edward's words. 'Been cleaning for him since he came. Two years now.'

Nodding politely, Edward leaned forwards and rang the bell.

Immediately the woman's head tilted to one side. 'Oh, I shouldn't do that. If he's got someone upstairs, he'll be angry if you disturb him . . . Hey, Dr Wells?'

It took Edward an instant to realize that she was talking to the dog.

'Never seen Mr Taverner shout, mind you, but he can be peevish. Chooses his words . . . makes sure you know your place.' She tugged on the dog's tail again as though signalling the end of the sentence. 'Old Dr Wells, now there was a gentleman. Good as gold . . . fixed up my legs a treat. That's why I named the dog after him.' She gave one final wrench. 'Good as gold, both of them.'

Edward smiled half-heartedly. The sky was clouding over and it was getting dark. Soon it would be raining again, he thought, as he glanced upwards to a window where a light burned.

The old woman followed his gaze. 'Yes, that's the place. Streams of people coming in and out at all times of the day and night. That's why I have the dog . . . You can't be too careful, what with living in the basement. Anyone could break in.'

A perfunctory drop of rain fell on to Edward's face. The dog stretched itself and gazed at him patiently, its heavy tail thumping the stone step.

'I'd walk on in. I really would. Go up the stairs to the second floor and it's on the left. His name's on the door.' She watched Edward hesitate. 'Well, go on then!'

He walked in with an air of fake confidence, well aware of her eyes following him. The hall was cool and smelled of paper size. Noises were coming from a room at the back as several voices called out instructions to a young boy no more than sixteen. He ran past Edward without a glance and banged the front door, Dr Wells barking as he moved down the street.

The first floor was silent, although a light shone out from underneath one door and illuminated the depressingly dim landing. What had once been cream paint had soured to dull ochre; the banister and stairs were varnished wood, the dried-out veneer lifting in places. A large circular table fought for space on the half-landing, its brass claw feet gripping the cracked linoleum beneath, as Edward manoeuvred past it and walked to the next floor.

The musty gloom was lifting. An overhead skylight let in some illumination, whilst a few paintings lent a jaded air of prosperity. Curious, Edward leaned forwards. On closer inspection he was amused to find that each picture was screwed to the wall – apparently to discourage any passing connoisseur from enjoying further study off the premises.

The nameplate on the door stated simply 'Aubrey Taverner'. Edward took a deep breath and knocked. No response. He was just about to knock again when the handle turned and he was confronted with the owner.

'I . . . I'm Edward Dadd.'

Aubrey Taverner was standing against the light. For an instant the advantage was his.

'Come in, please,' he said, stepping back.

The room glowed, as incongruous in Cook's Alley as the jewel on the head of a toad. The high walls were hung with silk from the ceiling to the floor, the colour as soothing as the skin of a washed pearl. The carpet was defiantly dark, acting as a subtle backdrop to the main focus of the room: two sizeable display cabinets which contained a selection of teeth, bones, plaster casts of hands and letters – the bizarre collection carefully portioned off with lengths of red ribbon, the glass shimmering in the alternating light.

Mesmerized, Edward blinked. The light was definitely

changing, he realized, as he glanced around and saw that every window was blinded with silk to create a shaded, and suffocating, atmosphere.

'You seem intrigued by my office,' Aubrey Taverner said softly.

Aware of his bad manners, Edward turned round and looked at him for the first time.

The sun came out that second, throwing a hot light through the silk and turning the corporal body of Aubrey Taverner into a momentary ghost. Supernaturally blond, his hair acted as a nimbus to his face; his eyes were devoid of colour, his skin angel white.

For an instant Edward was overawed.

'Please, take a seat,' Taverner said easily, moving behind his desk just as the sun dimmed. The light shifting through the curtains made his skin colour unreal, first greenish, then pale amber, altering him in the way that sunlight filtering through water colours the fish beneath.

'What prompted you to telephone me?'

'Your advert,' Edward replied.

'Just the advert?'

'It was an intriguing notice. I expect you had a great response.'

Taverner sat down behind a heavy walnut desk. Beside him were two phones, a tape-recorder and a couple of immense ledgers. He sighed shortly, the light altering again, taking away the angel and leaving behind a man. Relieved, Edward studied him, noting the blond hair, the manicured appearance and the expensive clothes. He seemed no longer celestial but conservative, and it was only when Taverner moved that Edward realized his hair was drawn back from his face in a pigtail which rested on the back of his collar. Instead of seeming absurd in comparison with his attire, the effect was one of eccentric refinement.

'There were some replies. Mostly unsuitable.' Taverner leaned across the desk, offering Edward a cigarette, which he refused. Without taking one himself, he slid the box into a drawer. 'I need someone who is reliable and trustworthy.'

Edward tried hard to look both.

'You said on the telephone that you had no money. Why is that?'

Edward's hesitation gave him away immediately.

'I'm broke.'

Aubrey Taverner raised his eyebrows. 'Why?'

'I've lost my money.'

'Were you robbed?'

'No . . .'

Taverner was no longer smiling. Indeed, he was sharply curious. 'A business venture which failed?'

'No.'

He rose to his feet and walked over to one of the display cabinets. Opening the glass doors, he reached in and brought out a piece of bone no longer than the first joint of a finger.

'This specimen originally belonged to a Chinese boatman. They lived on the water all their lives. Originally stealing to make a living, they became known as the water gypsies.' He turned to Edward. 'Have you heard of them?'

'Vaguely.'

'Well, this is the toe of a water gypsy,' he continued, holding out the piece of bone. 'Fascinating, isn't it?'

Edward swallowed with difficulty. Knowing he had ruined any chance of getting the job, he decided that he could afford to be truthful.

'I lost my money gambling.'

'Gambling,' Taverner repeated thoughtfully. 'I've never met a real gambler before. Or should I say a failed one?'

The tone was bland, the words exact, just as the woman in the basement had said: '. . . Chooses his words . . . makes sure you know your place.'

'Some make fortunes out of gambling,' Edward said stubbornly.

'But not you, I take it?'

He shrugged. 'No, not me.'

'So now you're penniless and need a job?' Taverner paused and replaced the bone in the display cabinet. His movements were precise and rather slow as the glass door closed noiselessly over the macabre contents.

'Whatever made you think that I might hire you? A gambler, of all people. Someone quite obviously feckless.'

Edward bristled. 'All right, you've made your point.'

Smiling, Aubrey Taverner turned back to him and leaned against the table. 'The advertisement asked for a young man with integrity and loyalty. Hardly your strongest points, I would imagine, Mr Dadd. Gamblers would sell anything for another turn of the wheel. Their houses, cars, the clothes off their backs, prized possessions . . .'

Edward remembered his gold watch and shifted in his seat uncomfortably.

'Yours is hardly a trustworthy character, is it?'

Smarting, Edward stood up. The rain was falling heavily and through the coloured blinds the bleak light sketched indigo shadows on the dark carpet.

'Mr Taverner, perhaps I should go.'

Taverner looked both concerned and surprised. 'You appear to be a little upset. Have I offended you?' he asked slowly, without giving Edward sufficient time to answer. 'Forgive me if I have. Do you really want to know about the job?'

Wrong-footed, Edward blustered, 'But I thought—'

Taverner interrupted. 'You thought *what* exactly? Mr Dadd, I have a belief that to think is folly unless one has some idea of what to think about. So much time is wasted in thought which is random – about what *may* happen, or who *might* say *what* to *whom* . . . Chance thought, chance reasoning.' He raised his hands languidly. He had an air of sudden listlessness, his energy failing as the light did. The room and he seemed oddly in rhythm.

'It is such a "gamble" to think continuously in the hopes that one might think of something worthwhile.'

'Descartes said, "I think, therefore I am."'

Taverner smiled as though the argument was an old one. 'And what was he? *He thought, therefore he was* . . . what? He never really clarified the statement. Does thinking make me human? Or does being human make me think? Descartes was a clever man, but a careless thinker.'

Edward hesitated. He had been walking the streets for much of the day. He was tired and anxious and unwilling to enter into a discussion about philosophy. His return to London had been the return of a failure, and had resulted in further defeat: his money was gone, his hopes were lower than at any time in his life. He missed the advice his sister would have given him; he missed her company and her support. The world seemed bleak and he was weary and alone.

So he plunged in, looking up at the figure in front of him. 'Tell me about the job, Mr Taverner.'

The words darted out, then hung for an instant, ignored. Apparently deep in thought, Taverner walked round the desk and drew a paper out of the top drawer. It was that day's copy of *The Times* – the paper in which Edward had read the advertisement for a research assistant. Carefully, Aubrey Taverner turned to the Personal Column and circled an entry, then passed it across the desk.

Experiences bought by author
for research. Payment according
to story. Anyone may apply.
All replies considered.
Tel:—

Edward read it and looked at him, dumbfounded. 'You *buy* people's experiences?'

Taverner smiled elegantly. 'I have a great many on my files – which is why I need an assistant.'

'People come here and tell you what's happened to them, and you *buy* the stories?'

'You seem astonished, Mr Dadd.'

The whole idea seemed beyond belief, but Edward was careful in his response. 'It's just that . . . What do you want all these experiences for?'

Taverner straightened up and walked behind his desk, pointing to the ledgers and the recording-machine next to him. 'Research.'

'Research,' Edward repeated woodenly. 'Research for what exactly?'

'A book.'

'On what subject?'

Taverner frowned, momentarily annoyed. All listlessness was gone, in its place a quick frisson of irritation. 'Mr Dadd, there was one point I omitted to mention in my advert. I said I needed an assistant, someone trustworthy and discreet. I forgot to add that the same person should also be incurious.'

Although Edward was twenty-seven, the words actually made him blush. Embarrassed, he glanced down at his hands. 'Sorry. I didn't mean to pry.'

Aubrey Taverner regarded him thoughtfully for a long moment before continuing. 'You will need to read and listen to a great many experiences. Some are strange, others harrowing, and some owe more than a little to embellishment.' He was smiling again. Edward's head swam with hunger. 'I want everything in these ledgers and on these tapes . . .' He flipped open the recording-machine and dropped a small tape on to the desk. '. . . to be filed on computer. Every word. I make some salient notes whilst my clients talk, but obviously, as I do not do shorthand, I take the precaution of recording the complete conversation on the tape. Your job is to combine my notes with the recordings, and put all the information on the computer, with the name of the person, the date the story was related and the fee, all in precise detail. Some of my visitors have been coming to see me for quite a while.'

'But you haven't begun the book yet?' Edward saw his mistake immediately and tried to redeem himself. 'Not that it's any business of mine. Listen, I can do what you ask, in return for a good wage. Although the amount wasn't specified in the advertisement . . .'

Taverner picked up the cue like blotting-paper sucks up spilt ink.

'I thought . . .' He mentioned an extremely generous fee. '. . . would be fair.'

'More than fair.'

'One buys loyalty, Mr Dadd. Or so I am told, although I've found that the generalization doesn't include everyone. Some women, for example, are immune. A man will sell his dreams for money; a woman will sell some but keep back a few secrets. It's the difference between a dog and a cat: a man can be bought for money like a dog for bones; a woman will choose who buys her and how much she will sell – just like a cat chooses its company.'

'Does that mean that most of your clients are male?'

'Sixty per cent are male. Forty per cent are female. Some need money, like yourself. Some come for other reasons.'

'Such as?'

'You're being curious again, Mr Dadd.'

Edward smiled uneasily. 'Sorry. It's just that I thought people were supposed to ask questions at interviews, to make the employer think they're highly intelligent. You know the kind of thing . . .' Aubrey Taverner looked mystified as Edward went on. 'They usually like people to show an interest, then they think they'll be enthusiastic.'

'You're poor. That's all the enthusiasm I need.'

Stunned, Edward lapsed into silence as Aubrey Taverner continued.

'Mr Dadd, you have no money, so you need the salary I'm

offering. I need someone bright and quick to learn. You seem adequate. You won't find the work difficult, merely painstaking. The arrangement should work well. You will be earning a good wage, whilst I will have the benefits of your services.'

'How long do you think the job will take?'

He smiled, immensely amused. 'As long as you continue to gamble.'

Edward hesitated, regarding Taverner thoughtfully. The man was more substantial than he at first appeared, his body larger, the well-tailored suit masking a certain muscularity of limb, his careful movements denying his size. As though he was unaware of being watched, Taverner glanced through some papers, his left hand resting on the desk, his head bent down. For an instant Edward had a shuddering sensation of *déjà vu*, and spoke without thinking.

'Have you and I met before?'

Taverner glanced up. The rain had passed over outside and the sky had lightened, making the room a pale ochre.

'Pardon?'

'You seem familiar,' Edward persisted.

The gold light shimmered over Taverner's hair. It made an angel out of him once more.

'I am known to you?' Taverner asked eagerly, his voice firm. Again, his mood had altered, energy sparking out of him as the sun filled the room.

'No . . . I just thought, maybe we had met. Once . . .'

Edward floundered, feeling suddenly foolish. How could he have met Aubrey Taverner and not remembered it? How could he have even seen this man without the image being burned into his memory for ever?

'Do you know me?' Taverner asked again. The question seemed to hiss in the warm air as his eyes fixed on Edward, his left hand on the top of the desk, the pale fingers spread wide like the rays of a white sun.

'No, I was wrong,' Edward said finally, surprised by the

sharp undercurrent of menace which had suddenly taken shape in the room. For God's sake, get a grip on yourself, he thought angrily. You're just tired, tired and hungry. 'I'd like to see the rest of the offices, please.'

Taverner hesitated, then slowly closed the fingers of his left hand. The action was a small one, but it seemed oddly benign and Edward relaxed.

For the next fifteen minutes he spoke of his clients, but gave nothing away about himself and had to be persuaded to show his new employee his office. The reason was obvious when Edward saw it. It was a dull little place, with none of the chameleon fascination of Taverner's room, being narrow, functional and surprisingly modern. Edward wondered, not for the first time, why someone like Aubrey Taverner should choose to stay in Cook's Alley. Finally he plucked up the courage to ask.

Taverner seemed to have anticipated the question. 'Mr Dadd, if I had an apartment in Mayfair, some people would come and see me, but not many. The address would intimidate them. This is neither a palace nor a slum. It would not be too grand or too modest for most tastes. It suits my public.'

'I see,' Edward said simply, but remained unconvinced by the explanation. The alley had its own atmosphere and was suspended in time: it belonged neither to the past nor to the present, and, unless Edward was very much mistaken, its very eeriness was the true reason why Taverner had chosen to work there.

He changed the subject deftly. 'What hours would you want me to work?'

'Twelve noon to midnight.'

Edward was surprised and showed it. 'Isn't that rather strange?'

'I sleep badly and work late. I shouldn't think the times will be a problem for you. Gamblers hardly keep regular hours.'

Immediately Edward bristled. 'I'm not gambling at the moment.'

'Not at the moment.'

'I can't afford to lose any more money.'

'That's what you say now, when you have none. Maybe your philosophy will alter with your first pay cheque.'

Hungry and tired, Edward was unreasonably nettled. 'You have very little faith in me.'

'Why should I have?' Aubrey Taverner replied evenly. 'I have no desire to convert you, Mr Dadd. It has been my experience that people are seldom willing to take advice or to act upon it. You are a gambler. At present you are out of funds. When you have funds, you will gamble. Your instinct has not changed your habits; a lack of means has.'

Edward shrugged and then put out his hand to finalize the deal. Aubrey Taverner did not take it.

'Forgive me, I mean no offence. I never shake hands with anyone.'

Clumsily, Edward's hand dropped down by his side. 'When do you want me to start?'

'Tomorrow. At noon. I don't suppose you have any references?'

He shrugged. 'None.'

'Good, I despise the things. They tell you less about a man than one glance at his face.'

'Are you never wrong about people?' Edward asked coldly.

Taverner remained smoothly confident. 'No, not that I can remember.'

Only moments later, as he made his way downstairs, Edward passed a wasted man with a package. He was walking with his head bent down, the surface of his bald scalp exposed like a bare knee through a torn trouser leg. When their paths crossed, he brushed into Edward and apologized, his accent Middle European.

'No harm done,' Edward said easily.

The man stopped and put his head on one side. A large red muffler was pushed into the neck of his coat and the wire from his hearing-aid hung down.

'What?'

'I said, "No harm done." '

'He's gone! What d'you mean he's gone?'

Edward frowned and leaned towards him, raising his voice. '*I said there was no harm done when you bumped into me.*'

The man blinked. A white arcus surrounded the pupil of each eye and his breathing was irregular.

'He can't be gone! I've got to see him. He knows I'm coming. I always come same time every week.'

'*Who knows you're coming?*'

'Mr Taverner,' he snapped, looking at Edward in exasperation. 'That's who you said had gone.'

'*You misheard me,*' Edward shouted, pointing upstairs. '*Mr Taverner's waiting to see you now.*'

'I know that,' the man said, walking off, muttering. 'Stupid . . . stupid.'

Edward was nearly at the bottom of the stairs when he heard him call out. As he glanced up the dim stairwell, the old man's bald head loomed eerily over the banister rail.

'You shouldn't tell lies. You shouldn't worry people.'

Burning with irritation, Edward turned and walked out into the daylight.

Chapter Two

AT TEN to twelve the following day an optimistic Edward Dadd arrived outside 6 Cook's Alley. The black dog saw him and barked, its tail lashing backwards and forwards in the sharp air.

'Morning, Dr Wells,' Edward said, stroking his head. Two eyes the colour of mustard watched him. 'Cold today, isn't it?'

The basement door opened quickly and the same old woman Edward had seen the day before came out.

'What are you doing with that dog? That's my dog!' she snapped, apparently not recognizing him.

'I'm just stroking him, that's all,' Edward said patiently, peering though the railings.

'He bites.'

'No, he doesn't.'

'Bloody does!' the woman insisted. 'You leave your hand there and he'll prove it.'

Naturally cautious, Edward withdrew his fingers from the dog's ears as Dr Wells gave him a long-suffering look.

'You saw him, then?' she asked, tugging the dog's tail.

'Who?'

'Mr Taverner, who else? Wasn't that who you wanted to see yesterday?'

'You remember me then?'

Her face was a study of irritation. 'Of course I remember you.' She turned to the dog and tugged his tail again. 'We remember him, don't we, Dr Wells?'

The creature made no comment.

'You going to work for him, then?'

Edward nodded. 'Begin today.'

'As what?'

'A kind of secretary.'

She screwed up her face. 'That's a woman's job. What d'you want with a woman's job?'

'It pays well.'

She smiled and buttoned up the green cardigan she was wearing.

'Yeah, I'll give him that, he does pay well,' she agreed, walking up the basement steps and nudging the dog with her foot. 'Move over. That's it. Good boy.' Smiling thinly, she extended one dry hand towards Edward. 'My name's Tunbridge, Mrs Tunbridge – although I'm a widow now. Good name, isn't it? Me and Dr Wells . . . Tunbridge Wells, get it?'

He smiled tactfully. 'Oh, yes. Very good.'

Although Edward had not asked for any money, Aubrey Taverner had extended a small loan to him the previous afternoon, and a good dinner followed by a sound night's sleep had restored some of his spirit. Yet as he had walked into the alley, his optimism had felt suddenly threatened, the quiet buildings bearing down on him oppressively once again.

'Odd, my having a doctor called Wells, wasn't it?' Mrs Tunbridge continued, impervious to Edward's unease. 'Like an omen, I always thought.'

Edward glanced at his watch. 'I should be going now,' he said, moving towards the front door.

She hurried after him. 'Just a minute! What's your name?'

'Edward. Edward Dadd,' he said, pushing open the door and walking in.

Her voice rose up behind him from the street. 'Dadd – not much of a name, hey, Dr Wells? Not much we could do with that.'

Aubrey Taverner was writing at his desk. The cold day made the room blue and silver, the raking light cooling the reds and golds and forcing its soulless mood on to the place. As he heard Edward's footsteps, Taverner looked up and smiled.

'Are you ready to begin?'

He nodded. 'Ready and willing.'

'Excellent. Here is a list of the people coming today. From now on you will attend to this, answer the phone and make the appointments.'

Edward took the paper from him, counting seven names.

'Are there usually seven appointments?'

'It varies. Sometimes more, sometimes less. Some people take ten minutes, others two hours. Your job is to placate the people who are waiting and arrange the appointments. Everyone must be made to feel special. I insist on that. No one is to feel unimportant or rejected.' He glanced towards the far wall, frowned and walked over to a painting hanging against the silk. 'This will have to be altered. Ring Mr Walters at the Loucells Gallery and ask him to exchange it.'

Quickly, Edward scribbled down the name on his notepad. 'For what?'

'Another painting.'

He smiled without conviction. 'Yes, but what? What do I ask for?'

'Use your initiative.'

'But I don't know the value of this painting,' Edward said. 'How could I begin to know what to exchange it for?'

Aubrey Taverner considered his words carefully. 'You are not an uneducated man, Mr Dadd. What would you choose to hang there?'

'A Herring,' Edward said quickly – rather too quickly. Herring was a horse painter, the kind of artist who would naturally occur to a betting man.

'You suggest horses?' Taverner asked with some amusement. 'You think a horse study would suit this room?'

A picture of a horse would have suited the room like a

leather jacket would have suited the Queen. Edward shifted his feet uncomfortably. 'Well, maybe not. What about a landscape?'

'Too tame, too unremarkable. Think, Edward, what would *you* like to see here?'

He thought frantically, then blurted out, 'Egon Schiele.'

'You haven't disappointed me,' Aubrey Taverner said, walking back to his desk and turning to the ledger. 'Arrange it with Mr Walters.'

The first few minutes followed in such a fashion. Aubrey Taverner asked for Edward's opinions, Edward hesitated, then made crashing blunders after which Taverner waited patiently for him to collect his thoughts. A private education had developed Edward's intelligence in his youth, but the lazy years in his father's firm had all but smothered his intellect. His sharpness had gone, and although his particular brand of bluff would have passed in most circumstances, the glaring faults were apparent to Taverner, who was merciless in exposing them. Little cracks in Edward's knowledge yawned into chasms, lack of detail suddenly making him sound superficial, and the difference in their ages, not to say positions, reduced Edward to a resentful nonentity – exactly as Taverner had intended.

'You haven't seen the waiting-room, have you, Edward?'

Shaking his head, he followed his employer meekly, watching as Taverner opened the door and allowed Edward to pass through. Nothing could have prepared him for the place. Approximately twelve feet by fourteen, it was painted deepest green, with a tracery of gold figures along the walls and several gilt-framed mirrors. On the floor a Chinese carpet languished under several deeply cushioned chairs, and at the flick of a switch music washed over them, Eastern temple music, complementing perfectly the heavily scented atmosphere.

Edward turned to find his employer looking at him.

'Well?'

'It's . . . unusual.'

'Atrocious.'

'No! I said unusual.'

'I know you did,' Taverner said evenly. 'I was the one who said it was atrocious.'

'So why did you have it like this?'

'A theory. I find that it gets the best out of my clients.'

Edward hesitated, unwilling to show any curiosity.

'Go on, you can ask me.'

Unnerved that Taverner seemed to have read his mind, Edward said cautiously, '*How* does it get the best out of them?'

'Drama!' Taverner replied, picking up the cue and walking into the middle of the room.

He was dressed that day in a navy-blue suit, white shirt, navy shoes and a plain tie. His white-blond hair was tied back as usual, his heavy ivory brows low over the changing eyes. In the clear light of the waiting-room, he was ready to spring into middle age, his youth left hanging with the drapes in the outer room. He seemed no longer familiar. In fact, he seemed totally different from the man Edward had met only the day before.

'Drama?' Edward repeated, tossing the cue back to him like a shuttlecock.

Taverner nodded. 'Yes, drama. They feel obliged to amuse, shock or annoy me. Anything other than *bore* me. If they bore me, they disappoint me . . . and I don't pay them. They know that. This room forces them out of themselves. Do you feel a malice here?'

'What?'

'A malice,' Taverner repeated, tracing his left eyebrow with the tip of his finger. 'This building, does it disturb you? Does the alley give you a *feeling*?'

'Why?' Edward countered. 'Does it have an effect on you?'

He saw his mistake too late.

Taverner was suddenly quick with anger. His whole body stiffened. 'I don't like being questioned, Mr Dadd! I've already told you that—'

'It has malice, yes.'

Taverner blinked slowly, mentally wrong-footed. He regarded Edward thoughtfully and then smiled. The anger slid away from him. It peeled off his clothes and he stepped out of it.

'Hundreds of years ago there was a church on this site. One priest was the victim of a violent assault. He didn't die from his injuries, but he was brain-damaged and lost his reason. He turned from God and cursed Him. He cursed what he had loved most and fell from grace . . . Can you imagine anything lonelier than that?' His glance moved towards the window. 'They say that at night you could hear him howling like a dog howls. He died alone, of course. Sometimes I hear Dr Wells below and think of the priest . . .' He paused. The room was limp with despair. 'Mrs Tunbridge cleans for me. She also reads my letters.'

Nonplussed by the sudden change of mood, Edward tried to sound nonchalant. 'Then why don't you fire her?'

'For what reason?' he asked, vastly amused. 'One of the chief joys of her life is to read my post. She works hard and well for me. If I dismissed her, I would be losing a good cleaner.'

'But what about your letters?'

'All fakes.'

Edward blinked. 'You mean that you write yourself letters and then just leave them lying around to appease her curiosity?'

Aubrey Taverner nodded. 'I have to create my own amusements too.'

Unsure of what to say next, Edward was relieved to hear the sound of feet on the stairs and moved towards the door to greet the visitor, Taverner returning to his room without saying a word.

A moment later a tall man of approximately thirty-five walked into the waiting-room and regarded Edward suspiciously.

'Oh, I thought I was the first.'

Edward smiled. 'You are. I'm Edward Dadd,' he said,

extending his hand and getting his fingers mangled for his trouble. 'I'm Mr Taverner's new assistant.'

'What happened to Lilian?'

This was unfamiliar territory to Edward. 'I don't know. Did she work here?'

'For the last few months. I never thought she'd leave.'

He seemed irritated by the change in staff and sat down without glancing at Edward again. His accent was northern, bald in the vowels, his clothes modern and well worn. In a sharp way he was attractive, although when Edward looked at him closely his fingernails were bitten to the quick and the dull cynicism of the melancholic coloured his eyes.

'If you're the twelve-thirty appointment, you must be . . .' Edward looked at the list. '. . . Alan Painter.'

The man nodded.

'I'll just go and see if Mr Taverner's ready for you.'

Mr Painter did not reply.

Tapping lightly on the office door, Edward walked in to find Taverner trying to pull his bulky antique desk further towards the window.

'Can you manage?'

He glanced up and nodded. 'Just help me push this another six inches over.' They heaved it along the carpet. 'All right, that will do.' He stepped back and looked at the new arrangement. 'Well, what do you think?'

'I preferred it the way it was before,' Edward said honestly. 'Like this you would be sitting with your back to the light, so you couldn't see what you were doing – and anyone facing you couldn't see you clearly.'

'Excellent!'

'So we move it back?'

He frowned. 'No. Ask Mr Painter to come in, will you?'

Edward turned to go and then paused. 'Do you want me to start putting the notes on the computer?'

Hurriedly, his employer pushed a vast ledger across the desk towards Edward.

'Enter everything in there, if you would, and type up all my previous notes. From now on I'll record what the clients say and then you can put everything on disk afterwards.' He pulled a smaller volume towards himself, wrote something on the fly leaf, then glanced at Edward again.

'Yes?'

He was taken aback. 'Oh, I . . . I just wondered if I should show Mr Painter in now?'

Taverner nodded once briefly.

Alan Painter was with Aubrey Taverner for over an hour. Edward could hear nothing from the office and set about the computer with forced enthusiasm. It wasn't difficult. Apparently Lilian or some other departed aide had programmed the machine and it was merely waiting for Edward to begin. So, after he had typed in some details on the blank screen, he opened the ledger and turned to the first page.

In florid, rather old-fashioned italic, Aubrey Taverner had written:

EXPERIENCE TAKEN FROM *Mr Michael English*
FEE PAID: *£400*
SIGNED: *Aubrey Taverner*

'I saw your advertisement in The Times. *It caught my eye – well, I suppose it was meant to. Someone advertising for experiences is pretty unusual . . . I can't say that this is easy for me. I've been wondering all week how to tell you my experience. It's all in confidence, isn't it?'*

'Entirely.'

'Well, that's all right, then. I need to know this will go no further,

you see . . . and I need to talk. That's why your advertisement sounded like a godsend.'

'Go on.'

'What are your rates? I mean, what will you pay me for what I tell you?'

'It depends on the quality of the experience.'

'On the quality? I see . . . perhaps this wasn't such a good idea after all, Mr Taverner. I should go now. I'm taking up a lot of your time. I should go, I suppose . . .'

Edward stopped reading and listened. There was no sound from the office and for some reason he felt embarrassed, even though he had been invited to pry. He also thought that Mr English would have been distressed to know that his life was about to be picked over by a stranger. With a tight feeling in his chest, Edward continued to read.

'Oh, what's the use? I have to tell someone . . . I served in the Second World War, Mr Taverner, and we'd been posted to Holland, where, for a time, the regiment was housed in a large country manor near Delft. On the second night we were stationed there, some of the men went for a drink in the village, returning late and in something approaching semi-stupor. Although they had permission to take time off, I was disgusted by their behaviour and took a very firm line with them. I was supposed to. It was my job. Well, one man in particular, a private called Rogers, received the full brunt of my anger and I made him do extra drill the following day. Then I gave him extra duties, and before long I found I was persecuting him—'

'Pardon? Could you speak up?'

'I said that I persecuted him. *That's the truth – no point lying about it any more. The boy was about twenty and rather slow-witted. I knew I was being unfair, but I couldn't seem to stop myself. He was so irritating, so bloody weak. I kept picking on him, and pushing him, and finally he became ill, losing weight and developing a nervous twitch. It was the twitch which did it. That flaming ticking by his left eye, like he was just doing it to annoy me! Anyway, no one stopped me. Even though they all knew what was going on. So naturally I thought that meant it was all right . . . No, that's a lie! I knew what a bastard I was. It wasn't all right at all.*

'Well, one night the inevitable happened. I'd bullied the boy too much, pushed him too far. Rogers retaliated and hit me, splitting my lip. Look at this photograph, Mr Taverner. That's Rogers. Nondescript, isn't he? I had him court-martialled for striking a senior officer – that was the way the Army did things – but whilst he was waiting for trial he . . . he . . . hanged himself.'

Edward stopped reading and glanced over to the office door. Alan Painter was obviously still occupied with Aubrey Taverner, yet not a sound came from the room, just as no noises came from the other offices. Edward realized then that the premises must be sound-proofed. Discomforted, he tried the window. It was locked.

With a cloying sense of unease, Edward returned to his seat and reluctantly continued to read. He had no real desire to know any more about English or the unfortunate private – the story disturbed him – but it was his job to transfer the experience from the book to the screen, so slowly he turned back to the page.

'None of the officers blamed me. They said it was the boy's fault, that he had been simple-minded and unable to tolerate discipline. But I knew different. I began to sleep badly, although I never had nightmares, and my work deteriorated. Only a reprimand from my senior officer pulled me into line. Soon, incredibly, I managed to put the whole incident to the back of my mind.

'The war ended shortly afterwards and I left the Army for a life in the City. I never completely forgot Rogers, but I put the past behind me and married late in life, fathering two sons. Then, eighteen months ago, a woman came to see me at work, where I do some bits and pieces part-time. She was about sixty and said she had come for payment. Naturally I asked her what the payment was for, and she said that she had been acting as my conscience and that for years she had prevented me from

being plagued by the memory of Rogers. *I was dumbfounded. I thought the suggestion was ridiculous, and then realized, with horror, that she was the only person outside the Army who knew about Rogers. I was frightened then, and had her thrown out, convincing myself that she must have heard about the story from someone in the regiment and tried to use it to scare money out of me. I believed that was the truth . . . yes, I actually believed it . . . and even dismissed the incident.*

'But the incident didn't dismiss me. From that day on, the memory of Rogers was with me day in and day out. Every face looked like his, every voice was his. I couldn't think of anything other than him and, forced to remember, I finally admitted to myself what I'd done – that I'd driven the boy to suicide. But admitting it didn't help, and within weeks I was almost mad with guilt.

'So I began to try and find the woman. I made enquiries about Rogers, but apparently he had had no family apart from a sister, and no one knew where she was. I spent most of my money searching for her, hiring investigators and walking around London in the hope that I might catch sight of the woman. My wife and sons were mystified by my behaviour, and, having never been told the story of Rogers, they were completely in the dark.

'I was haunted. I lost weight, my marriage failed and I was forced to leave work. People who had known me previously thought I had gone mad or been reduced to a senile old man. Of my two sons, only the younger one, Timothy, stood by me, and after he had found me in a third-rate boarding-house in Battersea, he forced the truth out of me . . .

'That was three days ago. Timothy was marvellous and promised that he was going to do everything in his power to help me. And you know, Mr Taverner, after only a day, he found traces of the woman. I was almost crazy with relief. You can't imagine how it felt. And when he suggested a meeting, I made him promise to go with me . . . He agreed. He wanted to help, you see. He really wanted to help.

'That day, at six o'clock, we arranged to meet outside the woman's block of flats. There was a small garden and a bench where we could sit and watch for her. But because of a hold-up on the Underground, I arrived late, to find Timothy's coat on the bench but no sign of my son. When I

asked at the flats for the woman, I was told that no one of her description had ever lived there.

'Timothy never turned up. Neither did the woman. I walked round and round that garden for hours, well into the early hours, waiting, hoping – against logic, against sense. You see, I knew he wouldn't, but I couldn't stop hoping that my son might suddenly materialize, tell me that there had been a mistake, that he'd got the wrong address . . . But he didn't come, and neither did she. Or rather, she did *come, but not for me – for my son.*

'When I finally returned to my lodgings with Timothy's coat, I searched it. But there was nothing there except a picture in the pocket. A photograph of Rogers in uniform. This photograph, the one I showed you a moment ago . . .

'Now, you tell me, Mr Taverner, what's that experience worth? Come on, tell me, I'd like to know. What's it worth?'

Totally absorbed in the story, Edward jumped nervously when the door of Aubrey Taverner's office opened and his employer walked over to him.

'Here's a new experience for your collection,' he said, passing it across the desk. Shaken, Edward dropped the tape on to the floor and had to bend down to retrieve it. When he straightened up, his employer was reading the open ledger.

'So you've discovered Mr English? A very interesting experience. I found it so anyway,' he said, turning back to Edward and scrutinizing his face. 'You look ill. Are you all right?'

'I was unnerved by the story—'

Taverner's voice severed his sentence. 'These are not stories, they are *experiences*.'

'And you believe them?'

Taverner's eyebrows lifted. 'What else should I do?'

'But, it's impossible,' Edward stammered.

'What is?'

'The woman being his conscience.'

'Why is it impossible?' Aubrey Taverner asked calmly. 'Because you've never heard anything like it before?'

'No one has—'

'Really? How can you be so certain, Edward? For a gambler, you seem curiously devoid of imagination.'

'Gambling is chance,' Edward replied hotly. 'Imagination has nothing to do with it.'

'You must see yourself winning, becoming rich when you gamble – that is a feat of imagination.'

Defeated, and having no desire to argue with the man who was paying his salary, Edward changed the subject. 'Has Mr Painter left?'

'For now,' Taverner replied coolly, looking down at the list of clients. 'Florence is due at any moment.'

'Florence?'

He smiled at Edward, delighted to watch him fall so readily into the trap. 'I see that although you have limited imagination, you have plenty of curiosity.'

The remark was still stinging Edward as Taverner left the room.

'Edward, if we were ever parted . . .' His eyes opened with shock as he looked at his twin sister. '. . . how would we get in touch?'

'Hennie, what are you talking about? No one's going to part us.'

'Oh, I know that,' she said briskly, seeming suddenly much older than her eleven years. 'But in the future, in that great big future everyone keeps telling us about, what happens if we get parted? How would we stay in touch?'

'By letter?'

She struck the top of his head.

'*Hennie!*'

'I'm being serious, Edward,' she said fiercely. 'We must have a code. A secret method of communication.'

'Like what?'

She studied him for a long moment, then rested her head against his. Her ear to his. Softly, she whispered to him, 'Sometimes, Edward, I can hear your thoughts.'

He was sure he had misheard. That the words, accompanied as they were by a sudden scattering of birds, had been distorted.

'What did you say?'

'I said that I could hear your thoughts.'

He tried to smile but couldn't, and gingerly stole a glance at his sister, who had moved and was now staring straight ahead. Was she lying? No, he knew she wasn't – Hennie never lied. She *had* heard his thoughts.

'You just think you did,' he said firmly. 'Like people hold a shell up to their ear and think they hear the sea.'

Her eyes flickered. 'People pick up shells on the beach, so no wonder they hear the sea – it's only a yard away from them!'

He laughed, but she had already returned to her previous train of thought. 'I *heard* what was going on in your mind, Edward. I knew what you were thinking.'

He stiffened suddenly, because now there was a distance between them, a chasm widening to leave him on one side and his twin on the other. Hennie was different from him now. She knew more and was moving away . . . Edward frowned, dry with despair. What else had she said? Something about parting . . . His heart-rate accelerated, a vacuum of anguish pushing the air from his lungs. Don't go, Hennie, don't go.

She turned and looked at him steadily.

She stared at him.

She picked her way into his thoughts like a thief picks a lock.

Then she sighed and stroked the back of his hand. 'We won't be parted for a long time, Edward. Don't worry,' she said, giving the perfect answer to his unspoken question. 'But one day, we will, and for that day we have to be prepared.'

She clicked her fingers suddenly three times. The noise flickered in the high trees.

'Now, you answer me.'

And he did, clicking his own fingers. One, two, three. The sound followed hers, found hers, matched hers perfectly and then continued on together.

'We are each other,' she said carefully. 'Remember, Edward, whenever we are parted, you can call me and I can call you.'

Then she clicked her fingers again, and laughed for both of them.

'I don't pay you to daydream.'

Edward blinked and glanced up at Taverner. 'I wasn't. I was thinking, that's all.'

His employer studied him for a long instant and then looked out of the window. 'Florence is always late,' he said simply. 'It's an affectation of hers.'

'I can't find her notes,' Edward said.

There was no response. Taverner just walked back into his room and closed the door behind him. Infuriated, Edward searched the office for Florence's details, but soon gave up. Apparently there was nothing on file about this client, no clues at all. Idly, he found himself creating imaginary scenarios. What kind of woman had such a name? Who was she? What type of work did she do?

But no answers came and, after another ten minutes, Edward walked into Taverner's office. It was shaded deep amber by the afternoon sun that bled through the drapes covering the windows. He was writing and looked up when he heard Edward.

'Yes?'

'I wondered if you had the key to my window. It won't open.'

'Won't open?' he repeated. A shadow passed the window, probably a bird, but it looked threatening, only half seen.

'The window's locked.'

'Lilian had all the keys.'

Edward ran over the information a couple of times. What next? Certainly not a question. Cautiously, he shadow-boxed.

'Do you know where she left them?'

Taverner was pleased, Edward could see that. Lesson number one, learned: do not ask questions about people, or, in fact, anything else. Smiling winningly, Taverner rose to his feet and presented Edward with a large ring of keys.

'Have copies made, will you? One set for me and one for yourself. And one spare.'

Edward nodded. 'Whatever you say.'

It took him several moments to find the key which opened his office window and when he finally inserted it, he had to use considerable force to turn the lock. After breaking his thumbnail and cursing, he pushed the window open, a thin strip of paint peeling off the inside of the ledge and tumbling down on to the street below.

Gulping in the thick London air, Edward leaned out – and then he saw her. She was walking close to the railings, her stick tapping every third one, the noise scattering upwards. The movement was neither hesitant nor pitiful. If anything, she looked at ease, and when she stopped and glanced upwards Edward jumped back, not realizing for an instant that she was blind. Her face was not pretty – too pink and white for prettiness, too much like the sugar mice Edward's mother used to bribe him with when he was small – but there was a shrewdness in her expression which was unexpected and a certainty which denied the dark wells of her eyes.

Alerted, Edward ran down the stairs two at a time, wrenching open the door just as Florence passed Dr Wells. The dog didn't bark. His tail merely thumped on the flagstones, his eyes following her.

'Florence Andrews?' Edward said, by way of greeting.

She paused, the stick motionless in her hand. 'Yes. Who are you?'

Edward had not been prepared for the voice, the astonishment of which struck out at him like a fighter's glove and made pity difficult. From the dead eyes, somewhere in the seething brain, came a voice of potent and heavy sensuality.

'I'm Edward Dadd,' he said finally.

She moved towards him. A scent of her, not expensive, in a way at odds with her voice, wafted to him – the scent of lilac.

'I'm pleased to meet you, Edward Dadd,' Florence said, extending her hand, the glove pulled off, the fingers short, functional, the nails unvarnished.

'Welcome,' he replied, taking her hand. The grasp was unremarkable; apparently all Florence's power was in her voice. 'Would you like to come upstairs for your appointment?'

She followed Edward easily, talking now and then, before pausing outside Aubrey Taverner's door and waiting for Edward to announce her.

'Wait just a moment before you knock. How is he?'

Edward frowned. 'Who?'

'Aubrey,' she said, her voice faintly puzzled.

Edward found himself transfixed by the undulating promise of passion in her tone and took an instant to rally.

'Has Mr Taverner been ill?' he asked, cursing himself immediately. If Florence had been asked to test him, he had fallen at the first hurdle. With surprise, Edward was beginning to realize that curiosity was too large a part of his life to be easily suppressed.

'He is ill periodically,' she volunteered. 'When we met – a few months ago – he was just recovering. How long have you been with him?'

'I started today.'

Her head turned in Edward's direction as she considered the reply. There was no expression on her face but he felt in some inexplicable way that he had disappointed her.

'In that case, Edward,' she went on, 'you couldn't be expected to know.' Smiling, the voice and the person suddenly matched. 'Shall we go in?'

Taverner was ready for her. He rose to his feet and moved across the room to take her hand.

'Florence, my dear, it's good to see you. Very good indeed.' His eyes flicked from his visitor to his employee. 'Coffee, please,' he said.

Dismissed, Edward made the coffee and then went back to his office. He sat down heavily in his chair, his chin cupped in his hand. He wondered idly what Hennie would have made of Aubrey Taverner, knowing instinctively that she would never have been able to resist the challenge to test him. Had she still been alive, he could have predicted what she would have done. She would have visited Taverner and made up some story – sorry, *experience* – and she would have laughed with Edward later about having duped him. Or would she? Edward wondered suddenly . . . Perhaps she would have *wanted* to talk to him, perhaps she would even have offered to share a little of the magic she too possessed.

His thoughts shunted back several years to the time Hennie and he had lived together in London, having left their home in France. He thought of her quickly, without effort, seeing her as she walked into the restaurant that afternoon. She came in without smiling, wearing a short black skirt, opaque tights and suede boots. A white blouse, with the collar turned up, framed the familiar face: skin always lightly tanned, even in November, eyes shadowed with grey, the mouth rich with colour. She came in without smiling, several of the men looking at her curiously . . .

'We don't want to be disturbed.'

The words startled Edward and he turned quickly to find Taverner standing in the doorway.

'Do you hear me? We don't want to be interrupted.'

Nodding, Edward watched Taverner go back to his room and waited until he was sure the door was closed.

Then he returned to his memory.

*

It was urgent, bringing with it a numbing sense of grief as he thought of his sister: mercurial, mischievous, funny. Her moods had no rhythm to them, but he always sensed them coming, like hearing a train in the distance before seeing it. Her irritation was sparked by little irrelevant things; anguish she took in her stride – their father's illness, their mother's dependence. The big tragedies she shouldered, but mundane angst incapacitated her.

Effortlessly Edward saw her. As though he had passed back in time, he watched her through the restaurant mirror all those afternoons ago, noticing how her jacket had creased at the back and how she paused to talk to a friend. A clever woman, educated at the Sorbonne, wise with words, stupid in her affections. Older men loved her, finding in her that devastating combination of intellectual ability coupled with an unlined face. But they never stayed, married or otherwise. Lovers came, lovers went – in and out of both their lives. Only the two of them remained constant. They felt for each other and loved for each other, and, like the parasitic mistletoe, each took on the life of the host body.

Turning, Hennie saw Edward and moved over to his table, clicking her fingers three times beside his ear.

He was ungracious. 'You're late.'

She pulled a face. 'I came as soon as I could. What's so desperate that couldn't wait until tonight?'

'I need some advice, Hennie, I've got a problem—'

'Female?'

'No, it's more serious than that.'

She rolled her eyes melodramatically. 'Nothing is more serious than love . . . Unless it's money.' Her interest quickened. 'Have you done something dishonest? No, you couldn't, could you, Edward? You haven't the heart – or the balls.'

'Delicately put,' he replied drily.

'So tell me what the matter is.'

'I've been gambling.'

Her eyes watched his.

'I've lost a lot of money. My savings.' Edward continued. 'And I still owe a thousand pounds.'

'Which game?'

Edward frowned. 'What?'

'Did you lose it playing cards or roulette?'

'What the hell has that got to do with it!' he countered meanly.

'Quite a lot I would have thought,' Hennie replied. 'I mean, if you'd been playing cards and kept playing cards and kept losing, well, that would tell me you were a bloody idiot. But if you'd been playing cards, then roulette, that would show a vague plan of action – some kind of application. I hate to think of you as a right chump.'

He sighed. 'Hennie, I need a thousand pounds.'

'I've never been in a casino,' she went on. 'Is it glamorous and full of men who keep their hats on indoors?'

'*Hennie!*'

Her hand tightened over his. 'Oh, I'll give you the money, dear love,' she said simply. 'But don't be a mug, Edward. Get in a mess again and you're on your own.'

She made him promise to give up gambling, forcing him to swear to it. Without having the benefit of a Bible, she made him take the oath on her cheque book, insisting that God was an accountant anyway – *on account of the fact that he was supposed to know everything*. She laughed at her own joke and he swore silently to be there for her always. Always . . . But as he looked at her, at the shadowed eyes and the familiar face, as familiar as his own, he stopped laughing. Because somewhere between knowledge and anticipation, he saw tragedy.

Edward shook his head, his thoughts hurtling back to Cook's Alley. No, he decided, Hennie wouldn't have liked Aubrey

Taverner, and she would never have exchanged some of her own past for the price of a pair of Manolo Blahnik shoes.

The intercom sounded next to him and he jumped as Taverner's voice came into the room.

'Edward, phone Kirovski and have some lunch brought round for myself and Florence.'

'Lunch?' Edward repeated. 'What should I ask for?'

'Alexander knows,' Taverner responded. 'Just ring him. His number is in the small, brown-leather notebook by the phone.'

Edward looked round and found the notebook.

'Got it?' his employer asked patiently.

'Yes.'

'Now ring him, Edward,' he continued, 'and ask him to bring something for you too.'

Uncertainly, Edward dialled the number, and was rewarded by a man's heavy voice barking a brusque welcome.

'What!'

'Is that Alexander Kirovski?'

'Yes.'

'I'd like to order lunch for Mr Aubrey Taverner and a guest.'

There was no hesitation on the other end. 'Fine.'

Edward paused. The man's answers were monosyllabic and his accent was hard to decipher. 'Can you bring it over?'

'Don't I always?' Kirovski replied curtly.

'I don't know. I only started here today,' Edward replied coldly.

Apparently the news was of little interest. 'I'll be round in about twenty minutes,' Kirovski replied, slamming down the phone before Edward had a chance to order his own lunch.

Dr Wells prepared Edward for the arrival of Alexander Kirovski, barking continually as he pulled savagely at his chain. Alerted by the noise, Edward glanced out of the office window in time to see Kirovski struggling with a large container, his clumsy hands clasped around the box like a man holding on to a reluctant woman at a dance. Instinct told Edward that this was not a man to appreciate any offer of help, so he merely waited until Kirovski arrived at the top of the stairs.

'Lunch,' he said flatly, banging down the container on the hall table.

No more than five feet three, he was ill-proportioned, his shoulders and arms over-developed in contrast to the stunted legs. A look of established defiance blazed out of his eyes and what appeared to be four days' growth of beard stubbled the belligerent chin. Edward was suddenly grateful that he hadn't ordered lunch from him.

'Could you bring the food through into the office?'

The suggestion was met with something less than delight.

'I have other customers waiting,' Kirovski replied, showing an impressive set of peg teeth.

'But it's only next door.'

'So, if it's only next door, you take it,' Kirovski replied, turning round and making for the stairs.

Hurriedly Edward leaned over the banister. 'What about payment?'

The man stopped and looked up at him. 'Taverner pays at the end of the month. You should know that . . . Who are you anyway?'

'Edward Dadd. I'm working as his assistant.'

For the first time, some interest showed on Kirovski's face. 'You're his assistant?'

Edward nodded.

'So what do you think of him?' Kirovski asked slyly, pushing the sleeves of his shirt higher up his bulky arms. 'You tell me, what do you think of Aubrey Taverner?'

Edward hesitated. 'I haven't been here long enough to form a judgement.'

Without another word, Kirovski shrugged and walked off down the stairs, the outer door banging closed, Dr Wells barking as he passed him on the street.

The food wasn't good, it was superb. Edward could tell that

much the moment he lifted the lid from the box in the kitchen. Filthy, disagreeable Alexander Kirovski cooked like a master chef. Drawn by the aroma, Aubrey Taverner soon materialized by the kitchen door.

'Food, excellent,' he said happily. 'Get the plates out, Edward.'

He glanced round as Taverner's index finger pointed to a cupboard over the sink. Obediently, Edward opened the door in front of him and then paused, transfixed. A Sèvres dinner service stared back at him, plates piled high, tureens and serving dishes, all in immaculate condition, resting imperiously on the Formica shelves.

'Shall I use this?' Edward asked his employer disbelievingly.

'Naturally. Hurry, please, Edward, or the lunch will be cold.'

Nervously, Edward deposited equal amounts of Kirovski's masterpiece on two plates and walked to the door with the loaded tray. Even holding the porcelain made his hands shake and he walked stiffly, taking uncertain steps.

Taverner smiled wryly. 'Relax, Edward. Whatever is the matter with you?'

'I'm not used to serving food,' Edward replied peevishly.

'You'll learn,' his employer responsed without a trace of malice. 'Tell me, Edward, what did you think of Alexander Kirovski?'

Thinking it strange that both men should ask the same question of the other, Edward was cautious in his reply. 'His appearance doesn't match his culinary skill,' he said tactfully.

Florence laughed, the sound as provocative as her voice. 'Well done, Edward! I had no idea how Aubrey's chef looked. I only know that in the summer I can smell him before I hear him.'

'Don't you find that off-putting?' Aubrey Taverner asked her as he laid a knife and fork beside her plate. The gesture was tender, familiar.

'I know I should,' Florence replied honestly, 'but it seems only curious. Where did you find him?'

'Oh, I never find anyone. People find me,' he replied, watching Florence as she ate. 'Is that good?'

She chewed thoughtfully, swallowed and considered her verdict as he waited. 'Superb. A little too much seasoning perhaps, but I'm only quibbling.'

Satisfied by her reply, Taverner also began to eat and Edward, becoming used to his various means of dismissal, left the room.

His own lunch was eaten in a sandwich bar off Greek Street. It hadn't the piquancy of Aubrey Taverner's repast, but Edward was glad of that. He had developed a dull headache, partly through concentration and partly through disbelief. He had expected the job to be unusual – the buying of experiences was, after all, not a common occupation – but the atmosphere of the alley had depressed his senses and the curious gallimaufry of people who visited No. 6 appeared to be as eccentric as Taverner himself. Obviously like did attract like, the clients as willing to sell their experiences as Aubrey Taverner was to buy them . . . But to what end? Edward wondered. Oh, yes, Taverner said he wanted them for a book, but was that the real truth? And if it *was* for a book, what kind of book would need such information?

He saw suddenly an image of Taverner, his hand reaching into one of his display cabinets, his fingers brushing the red ribbon which separated the exhibits. Where did such objects come from? From whom were they taken? Edward shook his head, surprised by the unexpected power of his own imagination – just as he was surprised by the sudden recurring memories of Hennie. Hennie and Cook's Alley. His dead sister coming back . . .

But why now? Why, after all the longing for her, was she suddenly so real again? Edward sighed loudly, angered by his lack of understanding. Hennie would have already known the answer, but he didn't. They might have been twins, but his mental processes were laborious, the quickness of her brain denied him. Half-heartedly, Edward chewed on his sandwich and then paused, an uneasy thought needling him. For all their closeness, he had never managed to contact Hennie since her death, the signal they had agreed upon – the secret code, the finger-clicking – falling on dead ears. But then again, maybe Hennie *had* heard and responded; maybe she had been calling for him but he hadn't heard her . . . The thought locked in Edward's head and made his palms clammy as he dropped the sandwich and glanced to one side.

His eyes fell on a discarded newspaper. They focused as his breathing regulated suddenly, the panic lifting. Then with shaking hands Edward turned to the sports pages, dismissing all thoughts of Aubrey Taverner and Hennie as he looked up the runners in the three-thirty.

When Edward finally re-entered Cook's Alley, Dr Wells heard him and came dashing up the steps, teeth bared, although the savagery melted into immediate ingratiation as Edward stopped to pat him on the head.

'It's me, boy, just me.'

Upstairs, the office door was open and Florence was sipping a brandy as Taverner beckoned for Edward to come in.

'Where have you been?'

'Lunch.'

His ivory-coloured eyebrows rose. 'I told you to get something from Kirovski.'

Edward shuffled uncomfortably. 'He hardly gave me the chance.'

'Upper hand,' Taverner muttered.

'Pardon?'

'Don't let him get the upper hand, Edward.'

'I wasn't—'

'Of course you were!' he responded vehemently. 'He intimidated you, so you had to go out and buy yourself lunch when you could have eaten here for nothing.'

Florence stared straight ahead as Edward squirmed with embarrassment.

'I meant to order—'

'*Meant* to? That means nothing. *Insist, insist.*'

Crimson-faced, Edward stood up to him. 'Now, just a minute.'

Taverner interrupted him again. Edward wasn't sure whether his employer's performance was for the benefit of Florence or if he was simply trying to humiliate him, but his fists clenched with the effort of keeping his temper. He knows I need this job, Edward thought angrily, that's why he's goading me. He knows I can't retaliate.

'Alexander Kirovski deserted from the Soviet Army during the last war,' Taverner explained, his voice honeyed. 'He is a lying, deceitful traitor of a man. His only saving grace is his ability to cook. When he cooks he is with the gods – otherwise his life is pointless. I despise him, Edward, and he despises me. But I pay for his services. Check every bill he sends us. Every couple of months he tries to cheat and every time he fails. Tomorrow, order what you want, Edward, and make sure Kirovski brings it upstairs and carries it into the kitchen. Master the man.'

Humiliation made Edward reckless. 'So Alexander Kirovski cheats you and Mrs Tunbridge reads your mail . . .' His tone was provoking. 'Why surround yourself with people who dislike you, Mr Taverner? What's the point?' His fists were clasped so tightly they were bloodless and he could sense that Florence had stiffened in her seat.

His employer responded smoothly. 'I have no belief in anyone, so if I hire them knowing their faults, I have no illusions and they can't disappoint me.'

'Am I classed in the same category as the others?'

Taverner wiped his mouth with a napkin and then laid it down on the tray beside him. 'Why should you be different, Edward?'

'I—'

Taverner seemed suddenly to lose patience and changed the subject. 'Did you speak to Mr Walters at the gallery? When is the Schiele painting coming?'

'Tomorrow,' Edward said, before returning stubbornly to the previous topic. 'Mr Taverner, I want to say something else to—'

Hurriedly his employer stood up. 'Say nothing. Please, Edward, don't promise me faithfulness, loyalty, integrity. If you fail – *when* you fail – you will feel far worse than I will.'

'Fail?' Edward echoed hoarsely. 'Fail at what?'

Taverner was turning away from him, moving towards the draped window, through which he could see nothing.

Childishly frustrated, Edward was about to follow him when Florence caught hold of his sleeve.

'Edward, will you please get me some more coffee?'

He paused, staring at his employer's rigid back, the tall figure against the silk drapes, the white pigtail lying on the collar of his immaculate suit. The overwhelming desire to win his approval made Edward gauche.

'Mr Taverner?'

Florence tugged at Edward's sleeve again, forcing his attention on to her. 'Edward, please. The coffee . . .'

Reluctantly, he walked out of the room.

Never in Edward Dadd's life, on no occasion in his childhood, had he wanted anyone's approval so desperately. Aubrey Taverner's power, he realized, lay not in his wishing Edward to do well but in his expectation of failure. The first signs of his control over Edward were apparent as soon as he asked nothing of him. Without logic, tears burned in Edward's eyes as he walked into the kitchen, and as the kettle began to boil he felt a sense of shame which no one had ever managed to provoke in him before.

Chapter Three

FLORENCE had no story to tell – at least, not one that Edward was permitted to read. Apparently she was merely a friend, and over the next two weeks she called at Cook's Alley several times, always to lunch with Aubrey Taverner, always to be courteous, charming and sympathetic to Edward.

'How are you getting on?' she asked one day, leaning against the side of his desk whilst she waited for Aubrey. 'Is he a very hard taskmaster?'

With perfect honesty and some feeling, Edward could have said that Taverner was a mendacious bastard, but she seemed fond of him, so he was tactful. Since he had begun the job, his employer's attitude had veered between cool aloofness and chilling humour. Money made Edward stay with him, money and curiosity – the one trait Taverner abhorred.

'He's . . . difficult at times.'

'Temperamental?'

'Hard to please.'

'Isn't that the same thing?'

'No,' Edward replied evenly. 'Temperament implies histrionics, and hysterical is one thing he isn't. He's just . . . demanding.'

She thought for a moment, feeling round the side of the desk for her stick. It wasn't a white stick – nothing so obvious – it was just a carved walking stick, the kind an old man would use. Her fingers closed round the handle easily.

'He's been ill, you know. And he finds people . . . perplexing.'

'Perplexing?' Edward echoed, with a trace of humour. 'Well, he's more than a little unusual himself.'

She laughed.

God, Edward loved to hear her laugh, loved to feel the reaction inside himself as the sound came freely from her, without strain, bolting out from the heart – as Hennie's had done. But his sister's laugh had fitted her personality; Florence's did not. Hers was another woman's laugh, a woman he would have liked to know.

'Stay with him, Edward, he needs someone to rely on,' she said as the door opened. 'Is that you, Aubrey? I was just talking to your assistant.'

Taverner glanced over to Edward momentarily, and then turned back to Florence.

'Come through into the office,' he said kindly, guiding her with his hand. At the door, he turned. 'Order lunch, please.'

Automatically, Edward picked up the phone.

'Incidentally, we have an extra client today. You'll like him. He's a regular visitor, young Martin . . .' He squeezed Florence's side with his fingers. Edward could see the flesh soften under his touch. 'Martin is a remarkable young man,' he continued, smiling innocently. 'I think you'll enjoy him enormously.'

When they walked out they were both laughing.

As Edward was to remember, Martin's first words were memorable.

'*Go screw yourself!*' he shouted, delivering a swift fist to Dr Wells's snarling face. '*Bloody dog!*'

'Martin Binns?' Edward asked sarcastically, going through the motions, although it could hardly have been anyone else.

The figure in front of him stopped and screwed his eyes up against the sun. 'Who the bleeding hell wants to know?'

'I do. I'm Mr Taverner's assistant.'

It was a bad mistake: an assistant meant a prize nerd in Martin's book. 'An *assistant*! Bloody hell!' He laughed loudly and for far too long.

'One joke goes a long way with you, doesn't it?' Edward asked drily when Martin paused for breath.

'An *assistant*,' he repeated helplessly. 'What do you assist him with?'

'Corporal punishment,' Edward answered coolly, pushing himself away from the wall where he had been leaning and standing full square in front of the redoubtable Martin Binns.

He was thirteen or fourteen at most, and quite tall for his age – thin, with that kind of lanky gaucherie all pubescent boys have. His hair was thick and in poor condition, lying on his small head like a doormat which had endured the passing of too many visitors. Under the unprepossessing hair, his face was sparsely featured, and saved only from plainness by an expression of ferocious confidence in the hazel eyes.

'You a bleeding comic or what?'

Edward ignored the question. 'Mr Taverner's waiting for you. We'd better get a move on.'

In a deliberate attempt to be awkward, Martin trailed about ten paces behind, forcing Edward to wait on the top landing for him to catch up.

'Pissing assistant,' he said finally, opening the door of the office and walking in.

He was with Aubrey Taverner for nearly three-quarters of an hour. As usual, Edward could hear nothing from the other side of the door, and after entering some notes into the computer he leaned back and contemplated the doorway of the opposite building. He was just watching a dispatch rider deliver a parcel when his employer walked in.

'Could you show Martin the cabinets?' he asked.

'The cabinets,' Edward repeated, glancing at the odious youth behind Taverner. '*Your* cabinets?' he asked.

His employer smiled patiently. 'Who else's? I'm just going out, I'll be back soon.'

He disappeared then, leaving Edward with Martin.

'You want to see the cabinets?'

'No.'

Edward's limited patience was fading. There was a two-thirty race and he wanted to place a bet on a dead cert. He had discovered that, being paid weekly, he could live cheaply, pay off part of his debts and still have some money left for life's necessities. Like gambling. He was even moving up-market again, away from Ladbrokes and back to the West End casinos, his addiction providing a useful amnesia. When he gambled, he forgot his emotional barrenness, he forgot his disturbed mother and Hennie, and soon began to feel a pathetic gratitude to the one activity which gave him some serenity. It never occurred to him that the peace was bought, and that the soothing effect was as ephemeral as the mayfly.

He gambled, and in gambling forgot. He forgot how his father had left his mother when Hennie died, forgot how Antoinetta Dadd had shuttered herself into the house in France, curtailing her life as a way of punishing herself for the death of her daughter – the child she had not wanted. Whilst gambling he could depress the remembrance of her dependency, how she had clung on to him greedily as the only surviving child.

With his sister, there had been complete understanding; with his mother there were merely recriminations, guilty secrets and the dull weight of the future, which terrified her. Even the house in France took on her dwindling personality. Soon the outside walls at Misérie needed repointing, the woodwork around the windows was rotting and the garden overgrown, and as the house went to seed, stray farm cats invaded the empty outhouses and the dry yard.

Only Hennie's bedroom was kept in pristine order – even from a distance Edward saw to that. No decay was allowed into her red and gold shrine – the curtains drawn in the daytime, the quilt as glaringly crimson as it had always been. And at night, whilst his mother slept, Edward would lie on that bed and talk to his lost sister until his throat was dry, lying with his eyes wide open, his body rigid. He told Hennie every detail of his day and sometimes, just sometimes, he had managed to suspend disbelief long enough to imagine a sound in the room, or a faint impression of a body breathing beside him.

In the dark it was possible to believe she was alive, possible to hear her voice.

In such a way he had existed between the living and the dead, between mother and sister, and all the time he had waited for Hennie to return. He had waited whilst his mother clung to him, and as the months passed he had grown to resent both Antoinetta's guilt and his father's desertion, seeing himself forever damned to pay for the actions of others. He wondered then if his mother realized how much more he wanted to be with Hennie than with her, seeing in the older woman's face constant flickers of a young woman lost to him.

He had tried to conceal his feelings, but Antoinetta knew his thoughts and slid further backwards into an emotional senility, the two of them existing in a fantasy land shored with guilt, grief and burning resentment. Too kind to leave, Edward had stayed, becoming gradually too weak to risk further injury – his mother's or his own. He was kind because kindness became him, and when he finally left it was after an argument, using anger as an excuse.

'Do you think you were the only one who loved her? Hennie was my child, *my* child!' Antoinetta had shouted, rising to her feet.

As ever, he had been surprised by her height.

'But she was my twin. We shared a life—'

His mother had been cruel with despair. 'She had more of you than you ever had of her. Hennie bled you, Edward—'

'*Hennie loved me!*' he had howled.

'She loved the control she had over you. She loved the power. You were the mirror in which she saw herself reflected – beautiful, clever, without fault.'

He had moved towards her. He could almost smell the scent of her anger and for once he was immune to reason. In that moment he saw only an ageing woman, neglected and ugly in a dressing-gown, a woman whose guilt was corrupting both of them.

'You never wanted Hennie and you never wanted me,' he had said viciously. 'And now it's too late. You were always jealous of her when she was alive and now she's gone you can grieve all you like, Mother, but your guilt won't bring her back.'

As he had moved to the door, his mother's voice followed him: 'Your love won't bring her back either, Edward! Remember that. Remember *that*. Hennie was a bitch in life and she'll be a bitch in death. Be careful when you call for her, or one day she might answer you.'

'What the bloody hell's the matter with you?'

Startled, Edward blinked, surprised to see Martin standing in front of him and not his mother. The shaded room crowded down on him, the draped windows cheating the daylight, the shimmer of the glass display cabinets blurring before his eyes. Disorientated, he snapped at the boy.

'Well, do you want to see the collection then or not? If not, don't let me keep you.'

'The boss said you were to show me, so you'd bloody better.'

Edward breathed in deeply, exasperated. 'Martin, have you ever thought of trying to say anything without swearing?'

A look of profound indignation crossed the boy's face. 'Listen, swearing's my way of expressing myself. I never swear really bad, not like some. No four-letter words for me. No fucks.'

He said it with real pride, Edward realized with astonishment.

'You see, I'm "selective in my vocabulary",' Martin went on. 'Nothing really crude. Never liked the "F" word . . .' He screwed up his face. 'It takes no imagination to use that. Besides, everyone uses it all the time. No, I like to test my brains, think of something a bit different – but not effing, that's real shit.'

Edward turned away. His thoughts kept wandering, swinging uncontrollably from the past to the present. At that moment all he wanted was to be left alone. Then, when he had composed himself, he could get out, go down to the bookmakers, take his mind off things.

'Listen, Martin, do you want to see the cabinets or not?'

The boy thought for a moment. 'What's in the poxy things?'

'Human remains.'

'Like guts?'

'Only bones, I'm afraid,' Edward said bitingly. 'We're fresh out of guts at the moment.'

Martin was immune to sarcasm. 'Well, let's have a look, then. I haven't got all bleeding day.'

He actually spent all of three minutes looking at Aubrey Taverner's collection. Frowning over the more gruesome objects, he found nothing that really fired his imagination. Straightening up, he stuffed his hands into his pockets and told Edward so.

'It's crap.'

'It's unique,' Edward responded evenly.

'Bullshit.'

'If you say so, Martin. You would seem to be an authority on that subject.'

The barb missed its target completely as the boy walked to the door. 'I'm off now. Tell Taverner I'll be back at the end of the week.'

'I'll be breathless with anticipation until then,' Edward

replied, resisting the impulse to help him downstairs with the toe of his boot.

With little time to spare, Edward hurried to the betting-shop, placed his wager for the two-thirty race, then sat watching TV and waiting for the result. It was an exhilarating run but, having led for half the way, his horse, Belly Dancer, came in fourth. More like Belly Flop, Edward thought ruefully as he tore up the slip and walked out.

The sun was high and he blinked momentarily in the harsh light before his eyes adjusted to the glare. Across the road, Aubrey Taverner was looking in the window of an electrical goods shop. Aware that his employer might at any moment turn and catch sight of him – and, seeing the betting-shop, would be sure to put two and two together – Edward's first instinct was to beat a hasty retreat, but the longer he stood there the more it became apparent that Taverner was so preoccupied he was unlikely to notice anyone.

Fascinated, Edward crossed the street and then paused a few yards away, watching his employer. Taverner was standing perfectly still, the daylight outlining his figure against the shop front, his ethereal hair godlike. His silence and immobility were hypnotic. He seemed for an instant to have fallen, fully grown, out of a myth, and by his very presence enchanted the London street. On the pavement, his figure cast an elongated shadow, and Edward was surprised to find that, away from the macabre surroundings of his office, Taverner was even *more* impressive – as though he carried within him some quality as potent and haunting as the memory of a ghost.

Slowly Taverner lifted his head, his face tilting upwards to the sun. The light bleached his skin as his eyes closed, his left hand touching the line of his throat. Feeling uncomfortably voyeuristic, Edward was about to move away when Taverner turned suddenly. His lethargy and stillness were gone at once and his energy restored as his eyes fixed on the window beside him. He stared, frowned momentarily, then continued to gaze at an object before him.

There was a video screen in the window in which passers-by and the people looking into the shop were reflected – just as Aubrey Taverner was at that moment. Edward smiled, amused by his employer's vanity, but, as Taverner remained transfixed, he became uneasy.

Studiously, his employer stared at his own image. Yet instead of this being the scrutiny of something familiar, Edward had the creeping impression that Taverner didn't know *who* he was looking at, and that the reflection was unknown to him. The white-haired man looked *in* at the white-haired man looking *out* from the screen, but neither recognized the other.

Edward shivered involuntarily and moved away, just as Aubrey Taverner turned and saw him.

'Edward!' he called out.

Reluctantly Edward walked over to him. It seemed for a fleeting instant that someone had turned up the day's brightness by remote control. Aubrey Taverner's hair was burningly white, the eyebrows almost albino fair over the brilliant eyes.

'Well,' he said simply. 'Gambling again?'

So he *had* seen him come out of the betting-shop, Edward thought sourly.

'I just had one bet.'

'Did you win?'

'Yes,' he lied.

'Good,' Taverner replied, walking off. Edward kept step with him. For a while they continued in silence. Taverner apparently didn't want to talk and Edward had nothing to say. Finally, as they rounded Old Compton Street, Taverner asked, 'What did Martin think of the cabinets?'

'He said they were bullshit,' Edward reported with relish.

'Bullshit,' Taverner repeated thoughtfully. 'He really does have a splendid grasp of the vernacular.'

'Did you pay him?'

'Don't be absurd, Edward.'

He was getting breathless. His employer walked quickly, too quickly for an out-of-condition twenty-seven-year-old.

'Did you pay him for his story?' Edward persisted.

'*Experience*,' Taverner corrected.

'Sorry, his experience. Well, did you pay him?'

'Don't be tiresome.'

They paused at the traffic lights, waiting to cross. 'He always has such intriguing things to tell me. Today was no exception,' Aubrey Taverner continued as they walked on towards Frith Street. 'People talk to Martin.'

'You surprise me.'

'Things happen to him.'

'Things should.'

Aubrey Taverner laughed. 'Oh, Edward, you don't like him! You will. Wait until you hear what he said. Wait until then to judge him.' He stopped, glanced round and sniffed at the air. 'It's autumn, the leaves are turning.'

Edward could smell nothing but car fumes.

'Tell me, what kind of an upbringing would you say our Master Binns has undergone?'

Frowning, Edward considered his reply. 'Poor family, disagreement between parents, lots of other children, no money. Quarrels, no affection.' He gave his employer a sidelong glance. 'Close?'

'Not really. Martin's father is a preacher—'

'A *what*?'

'A preacher, Edward. A man of the cloth.'

'Martin's *father*?' he repeated stupidly.

'He belongs to a church near here. In fact, he's a much-loved man. And he loves his only son.'

'So why doesn't he have his mouth fumigated?'

'I imagine that Martin doesn't swear at home. Or if he does, his father possibly makes excuses for him.'

'What about his mother?'

'Dead.'

'Since when?'

'You're asking questions again, Edward,' he said, as they turned into Cook's Alley. 'I ask the questions. Not you.'

Stinging, Edward followed his employer up the stairs.

The next client arrived late, hurrying into Taverner's room without exchanging a word with Edward. The door slammed shut violently. Making himself a mug of coffee, Edward reached for the tape on which was recorded Martin's interview, pulled on the headphones and leaned back in his seat to listen. He expected little as he turned on the machine and pressed the play button, but within minutes his eyes were fixed disbelievingly on the twirling spool, the boy's voice curling into the room as he told his tale.

'I met this man on the Underground a few weeks back. He was pissed, you know, right over the top, and he'd been up West all night. So I asked him if he was OK, and he said he'd been walking the streets. Would you credit it? He was filthy but his clothes . . . real Giorgio Armani stuff. Money, real money, and here he is, rolling bloody drunk with nowhere to sleep. I took him down to the little Italian café, fat shit serving, same as usual, and poured about three pints of coffee down him. They say it helps. I dunno, but he seemed better after a bit . . .

'So he says he had this job, City stuff, like the old yuppies in the eighties – on top of the shit heap – and then he gets some flash bird, and some tarty flat in Docklands, set up nicely . . .

'Well, he gets ill, doesn't he? Puking, a snotty nose, the works . . .

Tells me all this and says he went to the hospital that morning. Or was it the morning before?'

Edward took a gulp of coffee and carried on listening.

'Some special poxy clinic and they said he had Aids.'

The coffee burned Edward's throat. It gagged him, hearing a death sentence. He knew the route too well.

'Well, there's only one outcome, isn't there? It's a one-way ticket. Cheerio, my deario . . .'

Edward closed his eyes. He thought of Hennie and the disease which had crept up on her. He thought of the medication she had refused and the way she had slipped to her death, like someone falling down a flight of stairs. He felt mortally cold, chilled with remembrance, the headphones pressing heavily against his skull. But he didn't turn off the tape.

'He starts crying and saying that his girlfriend's left him, and his parents won't have anything to do with him, and he's getting sicker and sicker, and he . . . Well, you know, he wants to pack it all in.

'So, he'd piled together all these pills, hadn't he, and a bottle of bloody booze, and was about to top himself, only he can't make up his mind where to do it. Well, he starts drinking, and thinking. Bloody thinking! *And he reckons that it would be a kindness not to kill himself in the flat – after all, it would be some kind of flaming mess for some daft sod to clear up – so he thinks, in a rush of spite, that he'll drive over to his parents' house, at night, park outside, and do it there . . .*

'Did I tell you how he got Aids? From some woman abroad. He kept saying he wasn't a queer, and that he hadn't got it from one – not that it matters in the end, it kills you either way – but some bloody woman gave it to him! He seemed to think that mattered, you know, like a betrayal. I said

that people used to die of the pox in the olden days, and that Aids was just a modern version of the same thing . . . not that it cheered him up at all. I'm not heartless, but what do you say?

'Anyway, I couldn't just up and bugger off, could I? So I spent the rest of the day with him, and come evening he starts bloody whingeing and asking me what to do. Me! What the bleeding hell would I know about it? Anyway, it was Errol who finally made up my mind for me. Up he swaggers – now, he is *queer – and starts asking me who my friend is. I could see him, he had his eye on the clothes, so I told him to piss off. Just like that . . . I hate the bastard, he runs a string of rent boys up West, some of them only ten, eleven years old. He goes up to Euston and catches them off the trains. I'd heard about him before and about the runners—'*

'What are runners?'

'Runners! Jesus, you know. Kids who skip off from home. Mostly from up North or Scotland . . . Well, as I said, Errol picks up these kids, and some of the runners, and rents them out for all the filthy rich sods in W1 . . . Pimping with women's enough, but boys – bloody disgusting . . . So I hauled Geoff—'

'Who's Geoff?'

'My mate . . . I hauled him to his feet and we got out of there just as fast as we could go, considering that he's leaning on me like a ton of shit. We hadn't got to the corner before I thought of the boat up by – no, never mind, better you don't know. But it's quite nob, now that the bleeding estate agents have put their oar in . . . My grandma used to have it, before the bad winter last year. Then she died, so it's just been empty. My dad goes down when he's got time and checks it out, but there's nothing to steal on it anyway.

'So what with both of us weaving and bobbing, we finally gets there, and I couldn't find the key, so I climbed in through the window. Phew . . . what a stink. Been a cat in there, hadn't there? Cat pee everywhere. Anyway, I get Geoff in and light up the lamps and pull some old blankets out of the cupboard, making him half-way comfortable anyway. He fell asleep soon after, and before it got really dark I brought some food in and lit the heater. Almost cosy, really. Not like my grandma used to have it, but not bad. Better than topping your bleeding self outside your folks' place . . .

Before long it was really black. When I looked out there were lights on the docks and I could hear someone's radio playing off another boat . . .'

Edward could hear it too, the sound of music over the inky water, the man asleep, whilst a boy, hardly more than a child, watched over him.

'I left a note and sodded off home. My dad was still up when I got in, asked me what I'd been doing.

' "Does everyone really get to heaven?" I asked him, 'cos that bleeding Geoff had got to me.

'Grinning like a Cheshire cat, 'cos he thinks I've finally got religion, my dad says, "Everyone."

' "Whatever they are? Whatever they've done?"

' "Whatever," he says, real sure.

'When I went to bed I keep thinking about that – Geoff, getting to heaven, after all . . . Then I remembered Errol and suddenly started wondering why a shit like that got forgiven too.

'The next day Geoff looked better. He even managed to go out and get some stuff – you know, razor and the like. He'd cleaned up his suit and drawn some money out of the bank to pay me for what I'd gone and done. Bloody hell! If I hadn't've liked him, I'd never have bothered. Still, I took the money. That was a few weeks ago. He's still on the boat, but he's a bit sick. I go over most afternoons, and every night until it gets too flaming late to stay, then I go. But he starts getting real upset now, begging me, pleading with me. And when I get back on land I can sometimes hear the sound of him crying out from the boat . . .'

Edward's hand hovered over the STOP button – hovered, but never pressed the switch. His eyes had misted, the machine blurring in front of him.

'He'll get worse, won't he? He can't recover, I know that. I read the bloody leaflets the bleeding Government stuff through the letter-box. I've seen the telly. But he'll die, won't he? He's almost like a brother really . . . I can't

face him when he gets sick. Not the mess, that's no shit – well, it is some shit! But I don't want to pigging lose him . . . Seems, well, I dunno, but it seems creepy.'

'Have you told your father?'

'Why should I? He'd get him put into hospital, or in some home. He'd say he has the money to be properly looked after, not bobbing about on some half-arsed boat on the freezing bloody Thames.'

'He might be right.'

'Geoff wants to be there! It's home. Besides, no one else wants him. I'll look after him.'

'He'll get too ill for you to be able to someday.'

'Someday! *So? That's* someday, *Mr Bloody Shitting Taverner, not now. Now he's safe—'*

'But it might not be safe for you.'

'You mean he might be contagious? Cut fingers, blood and all that stuff? Bullshit! I read the blurb at that shit hospital, and it's nothing I can't handle. Some people nursed victims through the plague, never caught it. Like Nostradamus . . . Well, I think it was him. They were immune. Like me. I'm immune, *I know it, I can feel it. There's nothing going to happen to me . . . Why all the questions, anyway? You promised me you won't tell no one! You wouldn't go back on your bleeding word, would you?'*

'No.'

'Listen . . . When he gets real sick, I'll get my dad, honest I will. I'm not stupid. But not now, now we're OK, just the two of us. Anyway, he's better, and he's eating well. He's not a bloody murderer, for God's sake! He's just sick . . . he's just bleeding sick.'

There the tape finished. Swallowing, Edward glanced over to the corresponding entry in the ledger. Beneath the notes, a sum was written in at the bottom, a sum of money his employer had paid the boy. No doubt most of it would find its way to the weary little boat on the Thames, to feed a man who was already dying, who cried out in the dark, and who hung on to life as grimly as the Thames water ebbed and flowed under his feet.

Edward glanced away, his eyes resting on the tapes and the great ledger he was to transcribe on to the computer. The office seemed suddenly choked with the experiences of people's lives – the debris of trauma and horror, snippets of times gone, people losing others and themselves – all the words mingling haphazardly like a dream from which one struggles to escape. Why keep all these experiences? Edward thought blindly, his hands pulling off the headphones and then loosening his tie. Why? For what? Why would any man buy another person's misery or happiness? To what end?

The people leaped up around him suddenly, crowding into his room like souls from which something infinitely precious had been stolen, and they pressed down on Edward as he struggled to his feet and threw open the office window.

The ten o'clock night snapped at him, the autumn chill Taverner had identified that afternoon making its presence felt. Across the alley the buildings were silent and dark, except for one window where a light burned and silhouetted the outline of a bird – a mobile bobbing crazily on a rusted spring. Taking greedy breaths, Edward gulped at the air and realized that he would never be satisfied until he knew what Aubrey Taverner was up to.

His head thumping, he turned away from the window and leaned forwards towards the tape-recording machine, about to press the STOP button. His finger depressed the switch, but for some reason it jammed and, instead of turning off, it clicked loudly. Once, twice and then again. Three times. It clicked into the room and the noise echoed. One, two, three.

Edward stared at the machine and heard the sound of clicking fingers. Hennie's fingers . . . So she was finally back, walking into Cook's Alley, standing beside his chair, egging him on. But why? he wondered, suddenly suspicious. She hadn't come back before, so why now? Because of Taverner? An illogical jealousy swamped him. His sister had not returned for her dull brother; she had been enticed by Taverner – just as he was.

But he would beat her at her own game. He would find out what, and who, Taverner really was. He would take on both of them.

It was a decision he would come to regret.

Chapter Four

FOR A few long minutes Edward watched Florence without her being aware of him. She sat down and crossed her legs, her shoes low-heeled and sensible, her clothes unremarkable. Who chose them? Edward wondered. Did she have a family? If she had been blind from birth, how did she know what she looked like? And if not, did she resent someone else inflicting their style on her? She coughed, reached into her handbag and took out a lipstick. Edward frowned, waiting for the second inevitable action a woman always makes. But Florence did not pull out a mirror. Instead, with touching hesitancy, she traced the line of her lips with her fingers and then slowly, achingly, applied the colour.

The action was so brave and so pitiful at the same time that Edward felt ashamed for spying on her and walked in quickly.

'Florence, how are you?'

She turned her head towards him. The lipstick was perfectly applied. It shone on her lips and had the poignancy of all small triumphs.

'Edward, so good to hear you,' she replied easily. 'Come and talk to me. I think Aubrey's going to be delayed.'

He knew better than to pry into the reason, and pulled up a seat next to her. 'Are you well?'

'Very. And you?'

'Fine,' he replied, scrutinizing her face. 'Florence . . .'

'Yes?'

He took in his breath, then launched forth. 'How long have you known Mr Taverner?'

'A while, Edward.'

'When I first came to work here, you said that he had been ill.' He paused, anxious not to alienate her, and yet aware that he was about to deceive her. 'Listen, I don't want to be curious – he hates that – but I just thought, if I knew more about him, I could understand his moods better.' He paused again, waiting for a response.

When it came, it was not what he expected. 'What was your childhood like, Edward?'

'I . . . I was brought up in France. Mostly in the country. My father is English, a broker.'

'And your mother?'

'French.'

She nodded, apparently satisfied. 'And your education, Edward? What of that?'

'My mother was well read, so we learned a lot from her. We had private tutors too—'

'We?'

Edward shifted in his seat. Far from prising secrets out of Florence, he was being interrogated by her.

'I had a sister. A twin sister.' He was surprised how the words hurt: *sister*, *had*.

Florence frowned, but her eyes remained blank, without life. 'Was she very remarkable?'

'I thought so.'

'Clever?'

'Oh, yes.'

'They say it's difficult to lose a twin. Like losing a part of yourself. Was it like that, Edward?'

Her sympathy caught him out and he hesitated before replying. 'I lost the only person who understood me completely. There *is* no greater loss.'

He hesitated, his thoughts uncoiling. He had watched his sister die, seen her personality dissolve – portions of Hennie sliding away from her, the leukaemia taking hold, all her little selves drugged and washed, her spirit sterilized in disinfectant. The disease wasted her more quickly than anyone had expected, her gums bleeding, her loss of weight so drastic that she found walking difficult – even to the bathroom.

So she remained mostly in her bedroom, that red and gold shrine – red as the womb in which she and Edward had first met; red as the blood in which they were born; and gold as the light they had shared. Gold for power and status. Hennie had not had enough time to achieve a spectacular life, so she was going to have a spectacular death. It was to be the last concession to her sense of humour, the last joke she would play on herself.

'Remember, Edward, I am you and you are me.'

He found speech difficult. Her bravery beggared him.

'Don't go, Hennie . . .'

Her hand moved across the quilt. Red as blood. Whilst her own blood thinned, it seemed to Edward that the coverlet deepened in colour, as though her veins were emptying into the quilt and it was soaking away her life, washing her out to the dead sea.

'Edward, don't be so bloody morbid,' she said sharply. 'I'm relying on you.'

He nodded, dumbly bereft. 'I don't know what to do.'

'Stay with me,' she said simply. 'Until it happens . . .' She paused. 'I want to be buried here.'

He stood up, moved away from her, and her temper snapped. 'Don't do that! Don't distance yourself from me. It's not fair, Edward, it's not my fault.'

Ashamed, he regained his seat beside her, reaching out his hand, his head resting against hers on the pillow.

'You're so weak,' Hennie said gently. 'Here I am, quite prepared to go first and sort things out for you, and this is all the thanks I get.'

His eyes burned, his throat closing.

'I won't leave you, Edward, I promise you that. And I always keep a promise . . . We have secret powers. Do you *know* how magical we are?'

He said nothing. Her skin seemed to blister his, her voice was hypnotic.

'No one can separate us, Edward. Not death, not God – we can only separate ourselves. If you doubt, you'll lose me. If you believe, I'll only ever be an instant away.' Her hand rested on his forehead, forcing the words into his head. 'There's nothing more powerful than belief. Remember that. When I'm gone, each time you doubt that I'm near you, you'll be pushing me away.'

'No!' he said violently. 'I would never do that.'

'You will, Edward, you will,' she said with certainty. 'Because you're weak. So listen to me, listen to what I tell you. And remember . . . Believe me gone and I'll be exiled from you. *Don't do that.* Let me stay with you, Edward,' she pleaded, suddenly helpless. 'Let me stay. When I'm buried, never think of me as a body underground, think of me next to you. *Imagine me back to life, Edward.* Keep me alive.' Her voice rose. 'Believe, for my sake. Believe in me . . . Dear God, I would have done the same for you so willingly.'

'Hennie, don't—'

She interrupted him violently. 'I never had a chance, Edward. I never met the people I wanted to, nor did the things I wanted to. People live every day without wanting to live, they don't use their lives. I could have done. *I could have done!*' Her temper faded, her voice swooping downwards, taking him with her. 'But I can start again, Edward. *We* can start again. Imagine me back to life, and I'll come.'

She died two weeks later, when the snows began to melt, one morning just after eleven. She died silent, and when Edward leaned over her body and clicked his fingers three times he expected, beyond reason, to hear her response. But for once she didn't answer him: only her body remained in the great bed, her eyes closed, her mouth as full as a child's in the wasted face.

'Did she look like you?'

'What?' Edward asked, startled by the question, the image of Hennie fading as his attention turned back to Florence.

'I asked if she looked like you, Edward?'

'Yes,' he replied quietly.

'So tell me, what do you look like?'

The room was suddenly silent. Edward did not respond immediately to the question, he simply leaned back in his seat to widen the distance between them. For some inexplicable reason, he did not want Florence Andrews to know about his appearance, even though his employer could have answered the question for her. As her blindness gave her a secret, so Edward wanted to keep something of himself hidden too.

'If I tell you, will you answer me a question?'

She nodded. 'Of course.'

'All right. Well, I'm tall and fair-haired—'

'Strange, I would have thought you were dark.'

'With grey eyes.'

'Are you handsome?'

Edward smiled. 'I don't know.'

'But I can't see you, Edward, so you have to tell me the truth. I rely on your eyes.' Her voice was as liltingly sensual as it always was. 'If I asked you to tell me the colour of the carpet you would at once. You would say, "It's green"—'

'It's dark blue.'

'Blue then,' she said, smiling, 'and I would have to trust you and believe that what you said was not a lie. You have no idea how frustrating it is to be so dependent on other people's honesty.' She leaned towards him. 'Especially as most people are natural liars.'

'Were you born blind?'

She seemed not in the least perturbed by the question. 'No, I lost my sight when I was fourteen.'

'Was that difficult?'

'Oh, no,' she said, laughing. 'It was due to an accident and happened overnight. It was very easy really and required absolutely no effort on my part.'

Edward paused, unsure how to continue. 'I wondered . . . No, perhaps I shouldn't ask.'

'Go on.'

'How do you know when you're alone?'

She considered his words carefully. 'When I was first blinded, it was difficult. I knew that everyone could see me and I couldn't see them. How do you know you're not overlooked, spied on? Does the toilet window have frosted glass? Is there someone in the room when you undress?' Her voice deepened. 'I felt vulnerable. I thought that there was always somebody watching me. But they weren't, of course, and after a while I developed a second sense and *knew* when someone else was in the room.'

Edward felt a dark nudge of guilt. He had watched her and she hadn't known. How much that knowledge would have undermined her and shaken her confidence, he thought, feeling suddenly protective.

'Do you live alone?'

'Yes, Aubrey has been very kind.'

The information was unexpected. 'He's helped you?'

'For a while,' she answered, her hand reaching out to him. He took it and she held it between her own. 'Tell me more about yourself.'

'But I wanted to know about Mr Taverner—'

'Don't be impatient to know,' she said quickly. 'Let things unravel in their own time. We move too recklessly towards conclusions, Edward. Be careful.' She paused. 'I have learned *not* to be curious. Aubrey wants to know everything about people.

He digs and listens, he draws out all their secrets. He has to *see* everything, just as I see nothing.'

Edward frowned. 'But he hates anyone else being curious.'

'About *him*,' she replied firmly. 'His life is concealed from all of us, just as ours are open to him. I've become used to a handicap, so his secrecy doesn't bother me.'

'But it must!' Edward said heatedly. 'You must be curious about him.'

'I am curious about this room and the street outside, Edward, but it does me no good. Curiosity will not bring back my sight.' She sighed quickly. 'I've adjusted. Now I take what's offered and ask no questions.'

But Edward wanted more. 'Just tell me how long you've known him.'

'Nearly a year.'

'And you said he had been ill,' Edward persisted. 'How ill?'

'*Ill! Ill!*' she said, suddenly irritated as she let go of his hand and shook her head. 'Enough, Edward. Aubrey was ill, now he's well. That's all.'

'But what was wrong with him?' he urged, staring into her blank eyes and hazarding a guess. 'Did he have a breakdown? A nervous breakdown? I mean, that would make sense. He's always so changeable, so moody.'

'Let it rest,' she warned him.

'I can't, Florence! Just tell me a little—'

'A little is never enough!' she said furiously.

'Just a little,' Edward persisted, 'then I'll stop asking questions.' He caught hold of her hands. 'Oh, come on. Tell me what you know. It can't hurt anyone. I could understand him better if I knew more, and I would know how to avoid upsetting him. I might even be able to help him.' He paused, his curiosity outweighing his caution. 'Where does he come from? What do you know about him?'

Florence stiffened in her seat, her hands fluttering in

Edward's. 'He has trouble with his nerves,' she said finally. 'That's all I know.'

'So he had a breakdown?'

Her head turned, and in that instant Edward turned also – to find Aubrey Taverner watching him from the doorway.

His expression was unreadable, his appearance as immaculate as it always was. In his right hand he held a copy of *The Times*, in his left, what appeared to be a small, transparent box. Without uttering a word, he walked over to Florence and opened the parcel, taking out a gardenia and holding it an inch under her nose. She smiled, breathing in and drawing on the scent, the white flower, with its waxen petals, glowing against its dark oily leaves.

Gingerly Edward rose to his feet, moving towards the door, his eyes fixed upon the back of Taverner's head. He was just turning the handle when his employer spoke.

'Who had a breakdown?'

Edward flinched. 'I . . . I . . .'

'We were talking about a friend of Edward whose car broke down last night,' Florence said smoothly.

The lie jolted Edward. So she too was a natural liar, just like all the others, even though she was lying to save him.

'Yes, the poor man was left stranded in Blackheath.' Her melodious voice rang out clearly, defying contradiction.

Taverner hesitated, glancing towards Edward. But Florence, sensing the tension, distracted him by taking hold of his hand and carefully lifting the gardenia out of his fingers. Knowing then that she was watched by both men, she sensuously stroked her cheek with the flower, the petals bending against her skin.

'Edward was telling me about his sister. He had a twin, you know, Aubrey.' she continued.

The atmosphere was still humming with malice. She could sense it, just as she could sense the colour of the flower. 'A twin,' she continued. 'Isn't that interesting?'

Taverner's eyes were still fixed on Edward – ash-coloured, wary.

Florence persisted. 'What was she called, Edward?'

'Hennie,' he replied, his voice breaking. He coughed, then repeated it more loudly. 'Hennie,' he said, bringing her into the room, introducing her. Her very name made him stronger. She wouldn't have been intimidated by Taverner for an instant.

Incredibly, her name seemed to have some effect on his employer too and Taverner glanced away, walking behind his desk and handing the morning's ledger to Edward. His voice was serene when he spoke, calm, without emotion.

'Mr English will be coming to see us again next week,' he said simply.

'Good,' Edward lied, thinking of the ex-Army man and his story.

'But his son is dead.'

The words clattered against the walls.

'Dead?'

'He drowned,' Taverner went on. 'Apparently it happened after he and English met up and he told his father he had found the woman—'

'Which woman?' Florence asked eagerly.

'The woman who acted as his conscience,' Taverner replied, his eyes turning back to his employee. 'Although Edward never believed it, did you? You thought it was far-fetched. Well, Mr English seemed to think it was all very real. Very real indeed. I've just attended his son's funeral,' he continued, his eyes mesmeric. 'There were only a few people there. When I left I passed his grave and there was a woman standing beside it . . .' His voice held just the faintest suggestion of triumph. 'You don't suppose for one instant, Edward, that it was her?'

'Who?' he asked stupidly, although they both knew.

'*The* woman. English's conscience,' Taverner replied, leaning his elbows on the desk, the tips of his fingers joined together, shielding his chin. 'Well, if it was, he'll have a very interesting story to tell next week. *Won't he, Edward?'*

Edward jumped at the unexpected loudness of his voice.

'I shall look forward to hearing all about it,' Taverner continued softly, his change of mood unnerving. All the coldness gone, he was suddenly smiling. 'I'm so sorry about your sister, Edward. It's such a tragedy when people die young.'

The words shuddered.

'I never said she was dead,' Edward replied, his throat dry.

Taverner nodded sympathetically. 'No, you didn't, but Florence used the past tense – Edward *had* a sister – so naturally I presumed she was deceased.' He stared at his employee. 'Well, *is* she dead?'

'Yes.'

'Then I'm sorry.'

Nodding his head briefly, Edward walked out.

Closing the office door behind him, he leaned against it heavily. No noises came from Taverner's room. All Edward could hear was the sound of pigeons outside and the panicked drumming of his heart. Reluctant as he was to admit it, his employer had frightened him. Something in his expression and in his voice had suggested violence, an instability barely controlled under an elegant fleece of respectability. Taverner's interest in Hennie had alarmed him too. For some inexplicable reason, Edward had not wanted his employer to know about her. Yet he did, and he had commiserated, offering condolences whilst his voice implied something altogether different.

But what? Pleasure at the death of Hennie? Edward shook his head. Taverner wouldn't care whether she was alive or dead. He had no interest in Edward. Indeed, in the months since he had come to work for him, Taverner had shown *less* interest rather than more. Edward Dadd was his employee, nothing else. He paid him to perform a service and had no curiosity about him otherwise. If his work was adequate, Edward was tolerated. But he wasn't liked by his employer, and as Taverner's interest decreased, Edward's increased.

Pushing himself away from the door, Edward felt growing resentment. He didn't enjoy being bullied, even if Taverner had every right to be annoyed. He had overheard himself being discussed and hadn't liked it. He was angry, and in his anger he had humiliated Edward to prove that he was strong and in control.

So why didn't he just pack the job in? Edward wondered. Walk away from Cook's Alley and Taverner. Forget the place . . . But he knew he wouldn't. And it was no good trying to pretend that he stayed just because of the salary, even if it was large enough to support his gambling. Edward wasn't a stupid man, and he knew the real reason was far more complex. He was being enticed by Aubrey Taverner into a world which fascinated him. He was being seduced by his employer into dangerous waters, and found that the danger excited him. Cook's Alley sucked him in, it cradled him as it cradled all its unlucky children, and at that moment Edward Dadd felt oddly and malignantly at peace.

Chapter Five

''Bout time. I've been waiting ages.'

'Sorry, Mr Painter.'

'Yeah, sure. It happened sixteen years ago. Up in Bolton. I had a bike, Honda. Big one. Black with chrome. Took it everywhere. Pulled the girls. A real bird-catcher . . . I was nineteen then. Worked at the factory. Panel-beater. Shit bad job. But who likes work? It paid the bills. Just. At the weekends I had my bike.

'Women liked it. I loved it. Felt like a king on that bike. Drove it hard too. Went miles. Up to Manchester. Down to the Smoke. Sometimes country. But not often. Don't like greenery. It's boring. Anyway, fifteen years ago I'd fought with this bird. Good-looking, but pushy. You know the type. Wanted marriage! Don't they all? At nineteen too, silly cow. We'd scrapped and I just buggered off. On the bike.

'It was hot. Shit hot. But when you get moving it's cool. Even in leathers. Wind going past. I left Bolton and headed way out. To the moors. Up Saddleworth way. It was a great day. Hot. And I had some food and beers with me. I was thinking about that – the food and beers – when it happened. I'd gone round a bend. Road was empty. No other traffic. Then suddenly a van comes from nowhere. Nowhere. My guts knotted. I swerved. I was nineteen but I knew how to drive that bike. I was ace. Quick reflexes. I swerved. The wheels went from under me. I hit the deck. My helmet came off. It shouldn't have, but I never fixed the strap.

'Jesus, I can feel it now. The way my head slammed on the road. My eyes blurred. I could see the van pass. Bastard! And the heat haze on the road. There were insects too. Buzzing. Humming. And I was sweating in my leathers. Hot as fire, it was. I didn't remember anything else. Knocked out.

'You listening?'

'To every word. What happened next?'

'I came round. I moved my head. It hurt like God knows what. The

road was empty. Same heat haze. Same insects. Humming. Like my head. I remembered what had happened. I could see the helmet next to me. So I reached out . . . I reached out.

'But it wasn't my hand. Well, it was. But it was older. Not as it had been that morning. I stared at it. Another hand. I swear, it had aged. In the time I'd been knocked out, my hand had aged! Bloody hell, I was scared. I panicked. I don't mind telling you. I scrambled over to the bike on all fours. Then I looked in the wing mirror.

'It wasn't me. Well, it wasn't me as I'd been that morning. But that's the point. Isn't it? When *was that morning? I'd aged. I was looking at a man fifteen years older. Like I am now. But what had happened? How* could *I have been on that road all that time? Why hadn't anyone helped? Bastards! People must have gone past! They must have! But they didn't help. Pigs!'*

'What happened then?'

'I passed out. That's what happened. When I came round, I was nineteen again . . . *I went back home. Drove dead slow. Even apologized to the girl. Made up with her. I was shaken, you see. We married. Didn't last. Didn't expect it to. Kept riding the bike. She didn't like it. So I left her. Moved down here.*

'Then last week I went back home. By bike. I knew. I knew what I was doing. Took the old machine up the moors. Same road. Same heat. Same van. Saw it coming and swerved. Expected to be knocked off. Like the last time. Only I wasn't. The van *ran into a tree instead.*

'Have you got it, Mr Taverner? No? You surprise me. I ran across to the van. The bloke was slumped over the wheel. Dead. I knew that. Stone dead. But I couldn't help myself. I touched him. Pushed him back in his seat. Looked at his face. My face. At nineteen.'

Experience taken from *Mr Alan Painter*
Fee paid: *£450*
Signed: *Aubrey Taverner*

'You're running behind.'

Hurriedly Edward pulled off his headphones. The computer

glowed in front of him, Alan Painter's words green on the black screen.

'I've only got English's tape left to put on disk.'

'You're getting slower,' Taverner said, deliberately provoking him.

'That's not true and you know it,' Edward replied calmly. 'We've had more clients this week than ever before.'

'Don't make excuses,' Taverner retorted, glancing at the screen. 'I think he's mad.'

'Who? Painter?'

'Who else?' he replied evenly. 'I don't like him.'

The admission hung on the warm air, but for once Edward didn't respond. Instead, he pulled on his headphones again, reaching out for the next tape, and after another second Taverner left the room. The headphones blocked out all sounds, the leather pressing over his ears as he paused and gazed out of the window. Nothing stirred. No birds, nothing. The very deadness of the alley was heightened, a silent, unearthly world made real only when he pressed the PLAY button and Mr English began to talk.

'Listen to me, Mr Taverner, I want to explain and I know you want to listen. I know, I can see it in your face. You try not to make it too obvious, but it's there. Your curiosity. So many people are greedy for information. Don't you think so? It's funny, but only yesterday I was wondering about the other people who come to see you . . . Do they tell you interesting things? Or do they lie? I don't lie to you, Mr Taverner, never.

'You know all about Timothy's death. Of course you do, you came to the funeral. Thank you for that. I didn't expect it. It was kind of you, Mr Taverner, especially when people spend all their time pouring their problems over you. Does it help them to confide? Or do they keep coming to see you, month after month, talking on and on? Do they get reliant on you? I could see how they might. If they were lonely—'

'Mr English, do you have something for me today?'

'You know I do. You know I have something very interesting to sell. Something absorbing, about the woman. You know who I mean, the woman

who acts as my conscience. She has driven me beyond hope, you know. She's always there, always everywhere, even at the funeral. I know she was responsible for my son's death. Not directly, but then it doesn't have to be directly – people can do terrible things indirectly. From a distance people can inflict horrors.

'Funny thing is that when I saw her, I was relieved. Even though I knew she had taken my son, I thought that in her I could find forgiveness for the boy I once persecuted. Maybe my absolution for my cruelty to one man was to be secured by the death of my own son. I believed that, and I believed she would tell me that, because she had acted as my conscience for so long, taken on my sins and my anxieties, felt all the remorse I never felt.

'She was my redeemer, my guardian angel. Surely. Or so I thought. So I believed . . . After the funeral, when I saw her standing in the graveyard, I excused myself and went over to her. I remember thinking how ill-fitted she was for the part of saviour. A middle-aged woman in a cardigan, a woman with a cough which was sure to keep her awake at nights.

'She saw me coming and smiled in welcome. I felt such relief! Surely now I could finally repair what I had done, and this woman would show me how. With her help I could make amends for what I had done to the boy, and for the death of my son. She watched me approach and put out her hands, and I took them so eagerly. But as her palms rested in mine I felt the skin change, her flesh furring over. I snatched my hands back, certain I was imagining things, desperate to believe it was only imagination.

'But then she extended her palms, turned upwards, and showed them to me. There was dense fur covering the skin . . . Then, almost in the instant that I saw it, it was gone.

'"I've worked for you for years," she said. Her voice was pleasant, and it confused me. "Now it's your turn."

'I nodded, still eager to agree with whatever she suggested. Surely I had just imagined the business with the hands? After all, this was the woman who would help me, deliver me.

'"I need a holiday."

'"Abroad?" I asked, baffled.

'"No, not abroad!" she laughed wheezily. A middle-aged woman with a bad chest. Benign. "I want to go away, Mr English, but without taking *any baggage. I want to have a break from my work. I carried all your guilt for years, whilst you led a happy life, so now you can carry mine."*

'She said it simply, so I wasn't prepared. But as soon as she stopped talking my mind was immediately full of images, sounds, sights, a cacophony of hysterical noises. God, I saw things no one would want to see or hear. A million secrets crowded into my head: pictures of death, torture, betrayal. A whole world – a million worlds – of evil took root in an instant.

'I can't tell you what I saw and heard – what I still *hear and see. It is beyond description, beyond words . . . Do you know how it feels to bear the conscience of a mass of people? Do you know, Mr Taverner, what real wickedness can do? It takes the colour away from the world, it silences everything, it feeds itself on misery and depression. There's no opportunity for redemption, because all hope has gone. And where there's no hope, there's no chance for love or peace of mind . . .*

'She's gone away. Disappeared. I don't sleep now, of course not. I can't. I have a job to do. I listen and watch constantly, taking on the conscience of God knows how many. She said she would return, but I don't know when, Mr Taverner, I don't know when . . . She left me something, you know. An address. Hers . . . Of course, I've tried to write to her, to beg her to release me, but the funny thing is that although I can write the letter, every time I begin to write the address it changes. *As I write the house number and the street, the words alter on the page, they change as I write them . . .*

'I wondered if . . . I wondered, Mr Taverner, if someone else could write it for me?'

'No.'

'No . . . No, of course not . . . I was foolish to ask.'

EXPERIENCE TAKEN FROM *Mr Michael English*
FEE PAID: *£125*
SIGNED: *Aubrey Taverner*

Exhaling painfully, Edward thought of Michael English, a man with a military bearing and a loud voice. He had sat in the waiting-room, ignoring the magazines and taking a crossword book out of his pocket instead, filling in the clues quickly, almost irritated that the puzzle wasn't more taxing. He had said nothing, but he coughed repeatedly, a dry cough, like the one he described to Aubrey Taverner. The woman's cough, the cough which would probably keep them both awake at night.

Edward looked at the words on the screen, then rewound the tape and listened, again closing his eyes to concentrate. The story unwound as the tape did, English's voice controlled and businesslike, in direct contrast to the tale he told. Over and over the phrases repeated themselves, Edward pressing the REWIND button, then listening, then running the tape on. The sun came through the window and made the little office hot. His head, encased in the headphones, bent down, his concentration absolute.

So engrossed was he that the sudden touch on his shoulder made him jump, the wire of the headphones catching against the side of the desk and jerking them off his head.

'Jesus wept!'

'You get more like Martin every day,' Taverner said coolly, his eyes moving to the screen.

'Well, what did you think of English's tape?'

The words left Edward's mouth before he had time to check them. 'She's a succubus.'

The ivory-coloured eyebrows rose. 'English's woman, a succubus? A nocturnal demon in a cardigan?' He laughed, and Edward felt chronically foolish. 'Dear God, what a lurid thought! Your imagination's improving daily. I can remember a time when you would have laughed at such an idea.' He leaned back against Edward's desk, his long legs crossed at the ankles. 'Are you happy here? I should have asked before, I know, but I've been so busy.' His glance flicked back to the computer screen. 'Your work is better than I expected, even if you are slow. But then, you do have the benefit of a good education.'

Edward made no response, simply cleared his throat.

'Aren't you going to ask me anything?' Taverner went on.

'Usually you can't resist the odd question or two – or perhaps your curiosity is fading as your imagination is flourishing?'

Baited, Edward gave in to temptation. 'Don't they affect you?'

'Who?'

'The people, the stories.' He pointed to the tape. 'English is barking mad. Shouldn't you tell him to see a doctor?'

Taverner smiled. 'Don't be absurd, Edward.'

'Why is it absurd? The man's mentally ill.'

'That is your professional opinion, is it?' Taverner asked slyly. 'I hadn't realized I'd employed a psychiatrist.'

'Sarcasm doesn't change the facts,' Edward replied with considerable coolness. 'Many of the clients seem . . . odd.'

'Not to me, they don't.' He paused. 'You're very nervous, Edward. I did warn you before you began working here that some of the experiences people had to relate were unnerving.'

'You never said they were sick.'

'Oh, so you've set yourself up as judge and jury of them all? For someone who doesn't like responsibility, that's quite a feat.'

Edward ignored the remark. 'Doesn't it strike you as strange that no one tells you about love? I mean, apart from Florence, no one who comes here is happy.'

'And you think Florence is happy?'

'In a way,' Edward said hesitantly. 'When she comes here, she's happy. *Because* she's here.'

Taverner's expression was blank. 'Why?'

It was obvious to Edward. 'She's in love with you.'

Taverner's face changed again. For a moment it seemed to fall between expressions, an unexpected bewilderment fluttering in his eyes.

'*In love with me?*'

'Well, she didn't say it in so many words, but it's pretty apparent,' Edward said uneasily.

'*In love with me*,' Taverner repeated.

He said the words without gloating over them, simply with

the air of someone who had missed a vital fact and was made suddenly aware of it. 'How bizarre. Ah, now I see.'

'Does that happen a lot?'

'What?' Taverner replied distantly.

'Women falling in love with you?'

The question was too intrusive. Edward knew it as soon as he spoke.

'Do you like your work?'

Edward nodded.

'Then stop asking questions,' Taverner said, leaving the room.

Chapter Six

THE LIST of hospitals in the inner London area was daunting, a rota of saints' names in unsaintly places, the last remnants of religious fervour emblazoning the titles of martyrs under which the capital's sick continually passed. Whilst Brompton Oratory shimmered under a coating of prayer and polish, the gloomy relics of the Victorian medical halls dulled under the weight of feet and the curling poster warnings of infectious diseases. Even the names depressed Edward and, after listing all the National Health hospitals, he was glad to write down the bland names of the private clinics before finally turning his attention to the grim litany of psychiatric hospitals.

When he had completed the list, Edward studied the names and then glanced over his shoulder. The door of Aubrey Taverner's room was closed, the last client having been ushered in ten minutes earlier. Frowning, Edward scanned the names of the hospitals, wondering where to begin. He had some facts to go on, but only a few. After all, Florence had virtually admitted that Taverner had had a nervous breakdown, and when they had first met she had said that his last illness had been some months before that.

Edward's hand hovered over the telephone. His palm itched to lift the receiver and yet he hesitated. What was he going to ask the person at the other end? Whether a Mr Aubrey Taverner had been admitted with a nervous breakdown approximately nine months ago? The plan was ill-considered and he knew it. No one was going to give out information over the phone to a stranger. No, if Edward was going to discover anything he had to prepare a story, a plausible link with Taverner.

He toyed with various ideas and dismissed all of them, finally settling on the simplest. He would tell the hospital that he was

Aubrey Taverner's cousin and was trying to find him because a member of the family was seriously ill. He would say that they had been estranged, due to a misunderstanding, but now family tragedy was bringing them together again and he was desperate to find his missing cousin. Glancing furtively towards Taverner's closed office door, Edward rehearsed his speech in a whisper, a few added inflections in his voice making it sound more convincing.

Finally satisfied that no one could resist such a poignant story, he folded the piece of paper and tucked it into his pocket. It was nearly midnight, far too late to begin making enquiries, and, besides, using the office line would be dangerous. Taverner could walk in at any time and overhear his conversation, or he could already be tapping the phones. After all, if he went to the trouble of writing fake letters for his cleaner to find, it would be perfectly in character for him to spy on his employee.

The door of the office opened a moment later and Mr Glaxman, the old bald man with the hearing-aid, walked out, giving Edward a sour look.

'You still here then?'

'I always stay until we finish, whatever the time.'

'I didn't ask you that,' Glaxman said impatiently. 'I asked if you always stayed late.'

Realizing that he had completely misheard him, Edward raised his voice. '*I stay until the last client's gone.*'

Glaxman nodded. The cuff of a thick thermal vest hung beneath the sleeve of his shirt. It was frayed, the white dulled by myriad washings and slow dryings on steaming radiators. 'So you should. Young people don't know the meaning of hard work these days.'

Noiselessly, Taverner emerged behind him, looming over the small figure. His face was impassive, but his actions were quick, as though he was eager to be gone. But gone where? Edward wondered.

'Well, Mr Glaxman, we'll see you soon.' Taverner's voice

was pitched more loudly than usual, the more clearly to be heard.

The old man smiled broadly. 'I've enjoyed it, Mr Taverner, and the money's always welcome. I can't tell you how much. Well, you know how it is, with just the pension coming in . . .' He kept talking, without realizing that he was being gently guided to the door. 'Money goes nowhere, not these days. When I was younger—'

'Tell me about that another time, Mr Glaxman,' Taverner said, with surprising kindness. 'You don't want to be giving away information for nothing, when I could be buying it.'

Glaxman paused, then began to laugh, genuinely amused. 'There's not many men who would say that, Mr Taverner. You're a gentleman,' he said, shooting a surly look at Edward before leaving.

Both of them heard his slow feet descending the stairs, Taverner sighing with relief when the front door closed. He seemed tired as he smoothed back his immaculate hair, fingering the pigtail for an instant before turning to Edward.

'You can go now, I'll lock up.'

Feeling guilty as he thought of the list of hospitals in his pocket, Edward was unusually docile. 'Fine. I'll see you tomorrow.'

Something in his tone made Taverner suspicious. 'How's the gambling, Edward?'

His employee stiffened. 'Under control.'

'And everything else is all right?'

'Of course,' Edward replied, unable to meet his gaze. 'Should anything be wrong?'

'No,' Taverner responded, his eyes narrowing for an instant. 'Nothing should ever be wrong.'

*

At the end of Cook's Alley, where it emerges into Greek Street, Edward waited. From his doorway he could see the entrance of No. 6 and he had plenty of time to conceal himself when Aubrey Taverner walked out twenty minutes later. Holding his breath, Edward pressed himself against the door as Taverner's tall form passed, the collar of his overcoat turned up against the damp London night.

Counting to five, Edward slid out of his hiding-place and glanced down Greek Street. There were possibly two dozen people milling around, but no sign of his employer as he looked down the street, cursing. Several men passed, a group of Australian tourists crossing the street in front of them, a taxi blaring its horn. Glancing around repeatedly, Edward turned his footsteps towards Chinatown, passing the New World restaurant and pausing under the red China Gate. The smell of stale fat slid down the street, together with the scent of burning candles, and under a torn awning a man stopped, lit a cigarette and then moved on.

Edward was so surprised to see Aubrey Taverner there that it took him an instant to react before he followed him. The white-blond hair and the plume of cigarette smoke made him an easy target to track, and although he seemed unaware of Edward he walked less hurriedly than usual, almost to allow for his follower's slower stride. Doggedly, Edward crossed London behind Aubrey Taverner, his steps in time with his employer's, his eyes never leaving his back. They walked for nearly an hour, the older man never glancing round, only walking on, apparently with some purpose in mind.

Although he had expected Taverner to be returning home at that time of night, Edward soon realized that his employer had another motive for his walk – just as he suddenly realized that Taverner knew he was there. He didn't know *how* he knew, only that he did, and that his protracted excursion was his way of teaching Edward a lesson. He was not going to lead his employee to his home – he wasn't going to give himself away so easily – instead he was going to take Edward on a long tour of London by foot.

Feeling increasingly foolish, Edward found it easy to imagine what Hennie would have said . . .

Oh, Edward, you are a bloody fool. He's making a complete prat of you. You'll have to do better, you really will.

He stopped walking just as Taverner did, a few yards ahead of him. They had reached the Embankment, and the liquid Thames was speckled with streetlights as Taverner sat down on a bench staring straight ahead, his hands deep in his pockets. Exasperated, Edward leaned against a wall on the other side of the road. He could see his employer clearly, and although Taverner's face was emotionless, he seemed for an instant to shudder with suppressed laughter.

Knowing that he had been duped, Edward should have given up, but he couldn't. Instead he waited, knowing that Taverner *had* to go home at some point. Cold to the bone, he watched the still, seated figure, his fingers tingling with the night chill, the damp swath of the river making inroads into his clothes.

He waited, and on the bench opposite Aubrey Taverner did the same.

The quick feet darted up the stone steps to the front door of 6 Cook's Alley, one hand pressing the bell urgently. As though released from reluctant silence, the sound pealed out cheerfully into the dark house and the still of the three o'clock hour. It darted out into the quiet and looked for company, but, finding no one to take charge of it, lost heart and faded.

The hand pressed the doorbell again, the second sound picking up where the first had begun to die. They seemed almost to join forces, to catch on to each other, hurry up the dark stairwell, twirl under the moon looking down through the skylight, and hold their breath. Then mischievously the sounds slid further upstairs and curled under Aubrey Taverner's door. They rubbed themselves against the draped walls and tickled the leather chair where he had sat only hours before.

The sounds became animated, took on shapes. They scuttered in amongst the cupboards, turned brilliant eyes on the paintings, poked curious noses amongst the ledgers and then began to fade. When the bell wasn't depressed again, the sounds began dying, the glossy pelts of their mischief moulting against the dark walls, their clever clawed feet losing their grip on the stairs. Finding no home for themselves, they lost will and then breath in the shadow-bound hall.

The figure outside would have continued playing music with the bell had not Mrs Tunbridge been woken downstairs. Pulling on a worn candlewick dressing-gown, she peered blearily out from the basement door, her hennaed hair as red as wax against the tired face, her hand tugging Dr Wells's tail.

'Who's that, at this time of night?'

There was no reply, but the dog slipped from her grasp and ran up the basement steps. At the top, Dr Wells crouched, his hysterical barking giving way to a dull growl.

'Come back! Come back, boy. Come on!' the old lady cried from the basement below. Her heart was beating quickly, fear making her voice shrill. 'Come home. Come on, boy!'

But the dog would not return and remained on the street outside No. 6, growling, its eyes fixed on the stranger. Reluctantly, the old woman edged her way further out into the basement yard, the warm yellow glow of the room behind following her timorously.

'Who's up there?'

Hearing her voice, the owner of the footsteps ran back down the stairs and then paused by the black railings, looking down into the yard below. Automatically, Mrs Tunbridge stepped back, but after screwing up her eyes to focus them, she realized with surprise that she was looking up at a pair of black-tighted, miniskirted legs.

'Who is that?' she asked more confidently. 'Answer me!'

Suddenly the top half of a female figure bent over the railings above, a heavy fall of blonde hair obliterating all sight of the face.

'Is Mr Taverner here?'

'*What!* Are you mad?' the old woman replied, infuriated. From the pavement she could still hear the dark rumble of the dog's growl. 'Who would ask such a damn fool question at three in the morning?'

'I thought he worked late.'

'So he does,' Mrs Tunbridge replied, staring beadily up at the figure above and cursing herself for not having brought her glasses out with her. 'But they don't work that late.'

'*They?*'

'Mr Taverner and his assistant. They work until midnight, but no later.'

'What's he like?'

Mrs Tunbridge wrapped her dressing-gown around herself tightly, her fingers chilling in the night air. She was not eager to continue the conversation but, as the dog refused to come in, she had to find a way to get rid of the stranger herself.

'He's all right. Not that some of his clients aren't a bit odd.'

The woman laughed. The sound was huge, vast in the empty air of the small hours.

'And what's his assistant like?'

'Oh, Edward Dadd's a nice boy,' the old woman said sincerely – then remembered having been woken from her warm bed. 'But neither of them are here now, Miss, so you'd better just go home and come back tomorrow around noon.'

The figure suddenly straightened up, the feet running back up the steps of No. 6 and pausing. Then, with a flourish, the stranger pressed the bell again.

Cursing, Mrs Tunbridge hurried up the basement steps as fast as she was able to, Dr Wells barking furiously behind her, the alley throbbing with sound. The figure did not run away, but merely slid back into the doorway so that only the blonde of her hair and the white of her shirt were visible.

'What did you go and do that for? You'll wake everyone.'

'There is no one else here but us,' the girl replied.

A quick rumble of fear jolted the old lady. 'I've told you. Come back tomorrow—'

'But I do *so* want to see him. I *have* to see him,' the stranger replied, her voice lilting with laughter.

'Then you'll have to come back tomorrow!' the old woman repeated angrily, approaching the doorway with some curiosity. She was no longer afraid, and felt even a little sympathy for the girl. After all, she didn't sound drunk or drugged, just silly. A silly girl out late at night alone. Silly, nothing more.

'You shouldn't be wandering about at this time. Especially not round here. It's not safe.'

'Oh, I can take care of myself,' the young woman replied easily. 'Just let me in.'

'I can't do that! It would be more than my job's worth.'

'But I do *so* want to see him.'

'I dare say you do, but you'll have to wait until morning, like the rest,' the old woman replied, her eyes narrowing. 'Have you come to sell something? He buys experiences, you know. Sounds damned odd, I'll grant you, but it's true. That's what he's called, the Experience Buyer. Have you got an experience for him?'

The young woman nodded, the blonde hair sliding further across her face.

'I have an experience he's never heard of before.' Her voice shuffled with humour. 'I have something unique.' She took on a coaxing tone. 'Oh, let me in. Please. Let me in.'

The old woman stepped forward, suddenly compelled to see the girl's face. But the instant she did so, a cloud screened the moon and the stranger moved quickly away from the doorway. In the deep darkness she pushed a piece of paper into Mrs Tunbridge's hand, her voice lowered, even.

'Give this to his assistant – the nice boy, Edward.'

The old woman couldn't see her face, but she could swear she was smiling.

'Tell him that I kept my promise, and that I'll be back.'

'He'll want a name. You'll have to give me a name!' Mrs Tunbridge called out as the girl began to hurry away.

But she never replied, and all the old woman could hear were her quick feet on the cobbles, the sound disembodied in the dark air.

The following morning Edward arrived early for work. He had watched his employer from the Embankment for a further hour and a half, the time creeping round to one-thirty in the morning, the heavy chill dulling his thoughts and his enthusiasm. Almost as though he had been sculpted and placed on the Embankment for all time, Aubrey Taverner remained staring out at the oily Thames, his pigtail looking like a frosted twig, his body apparently impervious to the evil cold.

But Edward's was not. As the minutes passed, he found his eyes closing and his focus blurring, his employer melting into the bench, his coat becoming fluid as the Thames mingled with Taverner, and Taverner with the Thames. Incredibly, leaning against a hard brick wall, Edward fought sleep. But it fought back viciously. Each time his eyes closed, it required a greater effort to open them again; each time his attention wandered, it seemed to slip further away on an ever extending lease of abstraction, his good intentions giving in to his weakness and bolting, like an unharnessed pony, down the Embankment and home to Ealing . . .

He woke with a start, knowing before he looked that there

would be no figure on the bench. He was right. The bird had flown.

'Bloody hell!' he said, turning round and kicking the wall with irritation. 'Bloody, bloody hell.'

For the next couple of hours he walked the streets, haunting familiar night cafés before finally returning to Ealing despondent, his season ticket sticking in the machine at the Underground station, a morose Indian spending fifteen minutes arguing with him before agreeing to rescue it. Bleary-eyed with exhaustion and irritation, Edward walked the twenty yards from the station with his eyes fixed on the pavement, the yellowing street lights giving way to a maudlin dawn.

He fell on to the bed heavily and slept fully dressed, waking around eight-thirty with a dry mouth. Still unusually irritable, he pulled off his clothes and ran a bath. What infuriated him most was that Aubrey Taverner had duped him. He had known Edward was watching him and had simply waited until he had a chance to slip away unobserved. Exasperated, Edward closed his eyes and sank below the surface of the bath, a slop of water pooling over the rim. Then slowly he resurfaced, squirting a jet of water from his mouth, his eyes fixed on the steamed-up mirror over the wash-hand basin. His whole body tingled with heat, just as it had done in his childhood when Hennie and he had played outside the house in Misérie. Whilst her skin would darken to the colour of toast, his would shade to pink and peel along the shoulder blades.

Winter was his season, Edward thought. In winter he looked good – a tall, blond man who responded to fine suiting, just like Aubrey Taverner. He groaned slightly, ignoring the rattling of the door handle. How *could* he face him today? How could he walk into Cook's Alley and pretend that nothing had happened?

The rattling of the door handle began again.

'Go away!' Edward shouted.

'I want to come in. You've been in there nearly fifteen minutes,' came back the muffled reply.

'Use the bathroom downstairs.'

'I can't. The basin's cracked.'

Edward took a deep breath, pulled himself out of the water, then peered around the door. His body steamed with heat. 'Listen, didn't I give you that tip last week?'

The man outside shuffled his feet. 'Well, yes . . .'

'And you made a good few pounds out of it?'

'But—'

Edward's tone hardened. 'Well, if you want any more favours I suggest you stop trying to get a tune out of the door handle and leave me alone.' Then he shut the door again and got back into the water.

Remorse set in within minutes. Feeling guilty for his bad temper, Edward sank further under the water, the skin of his fingers wrinkling, his neck bent at an unnatural angle against the end of the bath. How was he going to face Aubrey Taverner? he wondered. If Taverner would choose to face him at all . . . Maybe even now there was a note pinned to the front door of 6 Cook's Alley, saying: 'Thank you for your services. Here is the money I owe you. Goodbye.'

Edward cursed his stupidity. The job had been easy and the wages had been excellent. He had actually managed to save a little money, and with his recent winnings at the roulette table he was hopeful that he could soon leave Ealing and move back to town. His fantasy was always the same: a flat in Kensington, a car, clothes from Turnbull and Asser, membership of the best clubs . . .

But not now, now he had ruined his chances. He had thought he was as clever as his employer and had been wrong. He should have known better. He had never been good at deception, that was more in Hennie's line. If cornered, she could lie without a flicker, her expression guileless. She remembered everything too. If either of them had ever been wronged, Hennie would wait for her revenge. It might take a day or a year, but she never gave in – and if she was ruthless for herself, she was even more protective of her brother. Any injury inflicted on Edward was felt by her. Yet whilst he would walk away from trouble, Hennie would always confront it.

Her strength of will was formidable, as was her courage. But what Hennie could do naturally, Edward found difficult, and he realized with despair that the fiasco of the previous evening would have belittled him in her eyes. He felt nothing strange about his belief that she was watching him. Indeed, her presence was growing stronger, and if he thought about it, he could date her return to his arrival at Cook's Alley. Day by day Hennie was becoming real again, Edward thought, getting out of the bath and drying himself, his conscience only momentarily troubled as he spent the remainder of the morning picking out the bets for the two o'clock race at Epsom.

But his light mood altered and his feet dragged as he made his way back to Soho just before noon. His legs seemed to slow down, to gain poundage as he entered Cook's Alley, the familiar smell of size coming out from the ground floor of No. 6. Unsure of the reception waiting for him, he hesitated on the pavement. A couple of pieces of paper were flapping aimlessly in the letter-box and a Labour candidate's poster was going up in one of the windows opposite as Dr Wells hurtled up the basement steps towards him.

'Hello, old boy,' Edward said, sitting down on the step outside the front door. 'How's things?'

'Mr Dadd! Mr Dadd!' came a voice from below.

Edward peered through the railings. Mrs Tunbridge was waving a piece of paper at him, her hair, newly dyed that morning, was the colour of a Guernsey tomato.

'Mr Dadd! You had a visitor.'

Edward scrambled to his feet, the dog following him as he made his way down the basement steps. The smell of cabbage cooking crept uninvitingly out from the front door of the flat.

'Who was it?'

'A lady,' Mrs Tunbridge replied archly, teasing him. 'She

came after three in the morning to talk to you . . . Well, she seemed to want Mr Taverner too, but I think it was you she really wanted to see.'

Edward frowned and extended his hand for the piece of paper.

'Oh, yes, she said to give you this. She didn't leave a name, just walked off. Oh, she was a sly one, all right,' the old lady went on. 'All on her own at that time of night too. Then young women wonder why things happen to them . . .' She stopped, watching Edward as he looked at the paper in his hand.

It was an old piece of newspaper, *The Times*, folded to show Aubrey Taverner's advertisement:

Experiences bought by author
for research. Payment according
to story. Anyone may apply.
All replies considered.
Tel: —

It was the same advertisement Edward had seen many times before, but as he looked at the paper he noticed that the white newsprint had faded and that the date on the top of the page was 18 February 1989. Dropping the page from his hand, Edward rocked backwards, nearly losing his footing as he gulped at the air.

Stunned, Mrs Tunbridge gripped his arm as he sat down heavily on the stone steps.

'Dear God, are you all right?'

'What did she look like?' Edward asked hoarsely.

'Well, I couldn't see her face properly, dear, but she was wearing a short skirt and black stockings, like we used to wear when I was a girl. The stockings, not the skirts – oh, no, we'd never have worn anything like that.'

'What else? What else did you see?' Edward persisted.

'Not much, I'm afraid,' the old lady replied kindly. 'It was dark at the time, and she seemed to keep to the shadows, and ever since that blasted streetlamp was busted it's impossible to see your hand in front of your face at night—'

'Mrs Tunbridge, did she speak?' Edward paused, his voice sounded hoarse. 'What did she say? What did she say?'

'She said . . .' The old woman frowned to concentrate better. '. . . to tell you that she kept her promise, and that she'd be back.'

Far away, somewhere over his head, Edward could hear a sound like ice cracking. It exploded in his head so loudly that he winced and put his hands over his ears, his chin tucked down towards his chest. The stone steps under him seemed to separate from the wall, to drift untied away from reality, just as the few hopeless daffodils in the basement window shuddered under the daylight and turned their faces towards him accusingly. Every one of their fluted heads seemed open-mouthed, admonishing him for his fear.

You wanted her back, they seemed to say, *and now she is. Hennie is back with you. Your Hennie . . .*

Finally Edward lifted his head. The stone steps were firm again, fixed to the basement wall, the daffodils only flowers. But when his eyes moved back to Mrs Tunbridge, his focus blurred and, as he looked up at her face, her red hair became the red quilt in Misérie, the quilt under which Hennie had died on 18 February 1989.

Chapter Seven

CLUTCHING the newspaper clipping in his hand, Edward crept silently up the stairs to Aubrey Taverner's offices and slid into his own room. Once there, he resisted the temptation of looking again, tucking it into his jacket pocket and beginning to type out the list of clients due that day. There were six, and Florence was expected for lunch at one o'clock, Taverner having scored out appointments until two-thirty.

His ears straining for any sound of his employer's usually punctual arrival, Edward was surprised when Taverner was late, especially as he had to spend several minutes trying to placate an irritable Alan Painter in the waiting-room.

'I've never known him to be late before.'

'So what? He said twelve. I came at twelve.'

Edward's voice was even. Painter was frequently difficult, alternating between morose depressions and vicious attacks on anyone within striking range. Apparently unconcerned about the effect this temperament had on others, Painter indulged his capricious nature to the full.

'I'll stay, but only five more minutes,' he said, chewing the nail of his third finger, his eyes suspicious.

Edward looked at the ugly hands. The nails were bitten down to the quick and were puffy at the finger ends, the skin around the nail beds ragged, years of oral abuse leaving their indelible mark.

'If you'll just be patient, Mr Painter, I'm sure Mr Taverner won't be long.'

'D'you hear the stuff?'

'What?'

'The *experiences*!' Painter snapped, the index finger of his left hand already *en route* to his mouth.

'Yes. It's my job to put them on to the computer.'

'How d'you feel about that? *Snooping?*'

Edward bristled. 'It's my job—'

'You said that already. Does it give you a kick? Listening?'

The green waiting-room bore down on Edward, the bilious walls closing in. He felt threatened suddenly.

'I don't think about it.'

'Oh, I bet you bloody do!' Painter responded shortly. 'I bet you love it. Listening, imagining.' He paused. 'Do people talk about their sex lives?'

'That's none of your business.'

'Perhaps I should liven up your dull life,' Painter said maliciously. 'Pep you up a bit. Add some spice. You wait, next time I'll *really* give you something to listen to.'

Considerably nettled, Edward walked out in time to see Aubrey Taverner gliding out of his private cloakroom, obviously having been in the building for some time. His hair was meticulously neat, his suit pressed, his face bearing no sign of a long night or exposure to a chilling walk in the small hours. In fact, he looked invigorated and smiled widely at Edward.

'Oh, so you *are* here. Florence is coming for an extended lunch today, so you might like to take a couple of hours off.' It wasn't a suggestion, it was an order. 'Go for a walk or something.' His tone was provokingly genial. 'The fresh air will do you good, it might pick you up. After all, you look as though you had a bad night. Were you late in this morning?'

Edward hesitated. Having expected immediate dismissal, he was uncertain how to behave and found himself unusually aggressive.

'Actually, I've been here a while,' he snapped, 'and Mr Painter's waiting.'

'You know, I am told that he was quite a good jazz pianist, so I went to listen to him play once,' Taverner confided, leaning against the side of his office door. The room behind was shaded with a cool light. It looked almost moonlit. 'He was very good, surprisingly so. It's always refreshing to realize that despicable people have talent. It makes up for so much.'

'So only despicable people are allowed to be talented?' Edward replied, perplexed by his employer's attitude and still uneasy about the message Mrs Tunbridge had passed on to him.

'I didn't say that. If a person is good and gifted, so much the better, but if a person is loathsome and talented one forgives the worst parts of their nature in deference to their ability.'

'I have no talent,' Edward said coldly. 'But I can appreciate it in others.'

'How lovely for you,' Taverner replied drily. 'But is it enough?'

'It depends on what you want from life,' Edward responded, his face impassive. 'I never wanted to be famous or fêted—'

'That's fortunate, since you are unlikely to be either.'

Bridling, Edward held his temper. 'You know, I just said I had no talent. Well I was wrong.'

He could see his employer's interest flicker and felt a dark moment of triumph. In all these months, this was the first inclination of curiosity Aubrey Taverner had ever shown in him.

'I was a gifted twin. Not gifted like Alan Painter, but I was gifted in sharing.' His thoughts ran on, almost unaided. 'Hennie – my sister – was clever, but she didn't know how to live as well as I do, or how to be content.'

'Gamblers are not usually content.'

'I didn't say I was *always* content, just that at times I knew how to be. At least I know the difference,' Edward responded calmly. But Taverner's interest was already slipping. Edward could feel it and he threw out a mental net to hold him.

'You see, my talent was understanding.'

But his employer was not Hennie and he slipped the net. His momentary attention faded and he straightened up at the doorway before moving into the shaded room.

'Show Mr Painter in, will you, Edward?'

The disappointment almost winded him.

In the house in Misérie, Antoinetta Dadd was standing listlessly by the drawing-room window, one hand on the brass latch, the other raised to her face. She hesitated, wondering whether she should phone her son, or if Edward would resent her call. Her hand remained on the latch, her fingers cooling as they brushed against the glass. The window through which she looked was dulled with grime, the outside ledge bearing traces of decay and the droppings of sparrows, the paint crazed like the surface of an Old Master.

She no longer cultivated the energy required to sustain an interest in life – the effort was too wearying and with too little return. Besides, bitter reality had obliterated all hope. Her daughter was dead, her husband had deserted her and now her son had left, taking with him her emotional balance. So, as though to punish Edward and herself, she gave up, falling willingly and rapidly into old age.

It was her way of saving face. To her, the *grande dame*, the cultured socialite, failure was too huge to condone or to admit. So illness became her excuse. With phenomenal will-power, she allowed a cunning brain to deteriorate and gave everyone reason to abandon her by embracing the long-winded suicide of senility. She let go by centimetres: she spoke little and walked less, her body adapting to the stoop of decline. Gradually her skin tired, her eyes assumed a bland expression and only a few things, inexpressibly precious, survived the decay.

Hennie's room was one. At Misérie, it became a place of retreat, and there Antoinetta played her old blues records and thought of Paris, and then of her husband, Theo. In the secret world of her inflicted senility, she pretended she had lost her intelligence and her memory, recalling only the things she wanted to retain. Like Edward.

Yet much as she wanted to hear his voice, she couldn't make the call, and stood with her hand on the window latch, sly with despair.

'He's busy,' Edward said coldly, looking at Martin on the top of the stairs. 'You haven't got an appointment today.'

'Don't bugger me about, I want to see him,' the boy replied truculently. 'I got a story for him.'

'An experience.'

'Huh?'

Edward repeated the word carefully. 'An *experience*, Martin. You're not supposed to come here selling Mr Taverner stories, just experiences.'

'Same thing.'

'Not quite,' Edward retorted. 'If I were, for example, to throw you over the banister rail, that would be an experience – especially for you. But if I were simply to tell you a story about another boy I had treated in a like fashion, that would be a story.'

Martin's face was a study. 'What the hell are you talking about?'

'Stories, as opposed to experiences.'

The boy narrowed his eyes, digesting the information. 'I want to see him.'

'Then we'll make an appointment for you tomorrow.'

'Can't come then.'

'So, hard luck.'

Martin glanced over the banister rail. 'Did you really throw a kid over this rail?'

'He was a plump child, I feel sure that the experience did

him little harm,' Edward replied, watching with some pleasure as Martin backed off.

'You're bleeding crazy,' the boy said, making his way downstairs without Edward's help. 'I'll come back, but I'll tell him what you said. I swear I bloody will.'

The threat was lost on Edward. After having waited for some kind of confrontation with his employer, he realized when Florence arrived that there was to be none. Apparently Aubrey Taverner was not going to dismiss him, or even reprimand him. But why? Edward asked himself repeatedly. How could he possibly let the events of the previous night pass without comment? It went against everything he had ever said, especially as Edward had displayed the one trait his employer abhorred above all others – curiosity. He had tracked him, followed him, watched him, and yet Taverner had said nothing.

He kept asking himself the same question all the way to the phone-box on the corner, and the more he asked the question, the less he saw the answer. The afternoon light was full of sunshine as Edward pulled open the door and walked in, laying down the sheet of paper on the metal ledge in front of him. The list of hospitals looked up at him as he laid the faded newspaper page beside it.

Glancing at the first hospital on the list, Edward dialled the number, asking to be put through to Information.

The person at the other end was suspicious.

'What d'you mean, Information?'

'I want to trace someone who might have been a patient of yours about nine months ago. They were admitted—'

Her hostility was palpable. 'So you want Admissions?'

Edward blinked. 'I do. Yes, I do,' he said firmly. 'Can you put me through?'

'It's their lunch-hour.'

'But surely there must be someone there?'

'There've been cuts,' the voice replied defiantly.

'Cuts?'

'This is the National Health, not private practice. We do what we can, and that's as much as we can do.'

Edward began to bluster. 'I just wanted to ask some questions . . .'

'Did they die?'

'What?'

The voice on the other end was hard with impatience. 'Did the patient die here?'

'No, he's still alive!'

'Shame, if he'd died, I could have put you through to Records. They have a list of all the people who died here, and there's usually someone in that department.'

Edward took in a deep breath. 'He didn't die, he just had a nervous breakdown.'

'We don't do mental cases.'

'He wasn't mental, he just had a breakdown.'

'A breakdown comes under mental,' the woman insisted.

'But it was only temporary,' Edward persisted. 'He recovered.'

'So try the Psychiatric Department.'

'I thought you said that you didn't have mental cases there?'

'We don't now, but we used to. Before the—'

'Cuts!' Edward said, finishing her sentence for her.

'Listen,' she replied coldly, her tone injured, 'I'm doing my best to help you. It's very difficult here and I'm on my own, taking all these calls. They've been laying off people left, right and centre. We're all worried sick about our jobs, and whilst I've been trying to help you, there've been dozens of other calls. I've got lights buzzing all over the switchboard.'

'Perhaps I should just phone back later and ask for Admissions,' Edward suggested patiently. 'Unless you think they might all have been fired over lunch.'

The line went dead.

He had even less success with the following two calls.

Apparently there was little chance of raising anyone at lunch-time, so Edward left the phone-box and began to retrace his steps to the office. As sometimes happened, Cook's Alley had temporarily thrown off its stillness and was shuddering with activity. The hazy sunshine had drawn a gaggle of printers out from the ground floor, the errand boy was eating an orange on the steps of the building opposite No. 6, and a young girl from the dressmaker's was flirting with him. Her hair was tied back in a scarf, her face flushed with animation, her legs crossed, her arms wrapped round her knees as she leaned forwards to talk to the boy. Embarrassed and yet flattered by her attentions, he offered her some of his orange and pulled thoughtfully at his ear, his eyes avoiding Edward's as he passed.

Taking advantage of the weather, Mrs Tunbridge sat on the basement steps with her arm around Dr Wells in a parody of the lovers opposite. Her hair, red as fire, glowed under the sun as she patted the step beside her.

'Come and have a chat, Mr Dadd. I'll get us a nice cup of tea.'

He hesitated, then sat down. The stone steps were warm to the touch.

'Lovely day. Spring's here.'

Edward glanced up. A lone pigeon winged its way over the jagged skyline of Cook's Alley. The girl was chasing the printer's boy back to No. 6, their feet clattering noisily up the steps, the smell of size seeping out through the open door as they ran in.

'Here you are,' the old woman said, handing Edward a cup of tea and rearranging her cushion on the step. 'You're not cold there, are you? I could get you a cushion too. No trouble.'

'I'm fine,' Edward replied, grimacing when he tasted the tea.

She mistook his reaction for pleasure and nudged him. 'I put some Carnation milk in that for you. Makes it good, doesn't it?'

'Very,' Edward lied.

'My late husband, Mr Tunbridge, swore by it. Said Carnation milk did you a power of good. A regular cure-all. His mother used to make something like it, and she lived a long while.' Mrs Tunbridge nodded her head wisely. 'My husband swore by it.'

'When did he die?'

'Oh, he's been gone thirty years now.'

Edward stared fixedly at the curdling tea and fought a ghastly temptation to laugh.

'He didn't live long, but he had marvellous health.'

Utterly defeated by her lack of logic, Edward swallowed the tea manfully and rose to his feet. The day had been wearisome and all he wanted to do was get back and absorb himself in his work. After thanking Mrs Tunbridge, he began the walk up the stairs, his thoughts jumbled with phrases about hospital cuts and Carnation milk as he walked into the reception area and then on into the waiting-room.

Having forgotten that his employer had told him to stay away from the office until two-thirty, Edward was baffled to find the curtains drawn and, without thinking, moved over to the window to open them. He tugged them apart, the quick sunlight splashing into the room in a tidal wave – and deluging the two figures on the couch. Transfixed, Edward stood with the curtains still clutched in his hands, his mouth opening as though he was about to speak.

But no words came. Instead he remained unmoving, his eyes fixed on Aubrey Taverner's naked body and on the white line of Florence's extended left arm. Having heard him come in, she moved slightly. Knowing that she could not see him, Edward was tempted to slip from the room, but he was incapable of movement, and realized with a mixture of relief and incredulity that his employer was asleep.

Knowing that there was someone there, Florence's face was pinched in an agony of embarrassment and distress as Edward moved towards her.

Silently he knelt down, his lips to her ear. She felt his breath and flinched.

'It's me, Edward. I'm sorry . . . I didn't realize.'

She nodded, her eyes filling.

Distressed beyond measure, Edward turned away from her and stood up. He wanted to redraw the curtains and leave, but her body, half obliterated by Taverner's form, fascinated him and he found himself staring. The green walls rose up around them, the two supine figures and the watching man. They shimmered with their gold frieze of dancers, the heady smell of incense reaching deep into the room, the mirrors reflecting Edward and the couple intertwined. And still he could not move.

Florence's breasts, depressed by the weight of Taverner's right arm, were full, her stomach the colour of milk. As though protecting her modesty as he slept, Taverner's right leg was bent, shielding her pubic area, his foot resting against the back of the settee. He lay deeply asleep, his hair for once untied, the savagery of its whiteness surrounding his face like frost.

But there was no sexuality in him. The naked body was utterly without emotion. Physically handsome, he lacked the reality of feeling, and from him emanated no kindness, only the electric force of something primeval, devoid of tenderness. Without knowing why, Edward felt hatred for him, just as he felt pity for Florence. Her face, her eyes now closed, was turned away from him, her cheek resting against Aubrey Taverner's neck, her profile laid against the hoar frost of his hair.

Edward was imprisoned, his curiosity making him a voyeur, his own sensuality awakening with unwelcome force. Taverner's image trapped him. It netted him, fascinating him in a way that turned his character, and in its power it corrupted him, just as Edward was sure it would corrupt Florence.

She lay unmoving and whimpered, and *still* he did not move. He stared at Taverner. He swamped his memory with the image of the man; he drew from the sleeping figure some of its burning coldness and he saw then the absence of heart. The room chilled and, for an instant, Edward had the impression of such bleakness that it seemed as though he looked not at people but at a bas-relief, some half-created hybrids in a winter garden, half human, half formed, without blood or life . . . And even as he watched, Florence was transformed in front of him. He saw her change and tried to reach out, not knowing what he reached for, only that she had fallen and, in falling, would suffer.

The moment held the three of them, and in that moment Edward had a vision of her sinking into the frozen pallor of the man who held her, the man with whom she had made such unseeing and unlucky love.

Chapter Eight

IN THE week which followed Edward avoided Aubrey Taverner. He did his job efficiently but without enthusiasm, his eyes constantly averted from his employer's gaze. Not that Taverner seemed to notice any difference in him: he continued as before, arriving at noon, seeing his clients and then leaving around midnight. He did not comment on Edward's reserve – indeed, he might almost have welcomed it – and made little conversation as he passed his employee the tapes to be transcribed. His thoughts were fixed upon his work, nothing else.

Edward's thoughts were not so easily channelled. Avoiding any direct communication with Taverner, he did, however, find himself watching his employer avidly. The image of the man's sleeping figure was impossible to dislodge from his memory, as was the pitiful image of Florence, blind and pinioned under Taverner's sleeping weight. But it was more than that. Edward's involvement with their love-making had put him into an invidious position: it had tainted him and made him an unwilling observer. For an instant, Edward saw himself as others might see him – a snoop, a man deriving his satisfaction, sexual or otherwise, from spying on others.

The knowledge that they were lovers made Edward uneasy, and the realization that he was somehow tied into their affair made him awkward and ashamed. But his first thought was not for himself, it was for Florence. He felt that she had been abused; that in the solitude of her blindness her seduction had been not a tender act but something infinitely more terrible – an act not of love but of control.

She was limited. In being blind, she lacked the full knowledge of her lover, and missed all the nuances others took for granted. She might hear Taverner's words, but she could not see his face or catch the changes of expression by which to read the depth of his affection. She had to guess and hope for so much.

Her vulnerability aroused Edward's pity, and a fierce desire to protect her, as he had protected his sister. In Florence he saw many shadings of Hennie. But whereas his sister had been whole, Florence was lacking. His sister had been powerfully attractive, and though there was a beauty in Florence, her blindness negated her sexuality. Hennie had hurried through life; Florence tapped along, feeling her way. And some routes were more dangerous than others – none more so than the one she had taken with Taverner.

Edward glanced over to his employer's office door and, knowing that he would be fully occupied for a while, slid into Taverner's private cloakroom. He was not allowed in there, as he had been told repeatedly, and yet he went in, pausing in the doorway. It was a compact room with a toilet and wash-hand basin, nothing else. The walls were white, the floor also, but the window was covered with a shutter, the back of which was mirrored. Edward glanced at his reflection, surprised at the sour look on his face, and then hesitated.

He tried at first to convince himself that it was a trick of the light, but it wasn't. For an instant, one brief instant, there had been a similarity between himself and Aubrey Taverner. He could not imagine why it had not occurred to him before. They were both tall and muscular, both fair-skinned, light-eyed, and exceedingly blond. There was an age difference of perhaps twelve years between them and obvious differences in their manner of dress, but there was definitely a likeness – not good enough for them to be mistaken for each other, but sufficient for them to pass as brothers.

Discomforted, Edward stepped back and pulled the door closed behind him, returning to his office. The likeness to his employer made him uncomfortable, although he realized it might well turn out to be an advantage. If he had to visit any of the hospitals and they remembered Taverner as a patient, how easy for him to pass himself off as a relative when there was obviously a lucky resemblance. Luck? he wondered uneasily. What kind of luck?

All luck's lucky, Hennie would have said, chiding him for being nervous.

Do get on with it, Edward, phone some more hospitals. You never know what you might find out.

He had wanted to impress her whilst she was alive, and he still did even though she was dead. Nothing had changed, Edward thought dully, nothing at all.

I could have a life between lives, she had said, and he hadn't doubted her. He hadn't dared to.

If you doubt, you push me away. Believe me gone and I'll be exiled. Imagine me back to life . . . imagine me back to life . . .

And he wanted to, more than he wanted anything.

That lunchtime Edward enthusiastically phoned the rest of the hospitals on his list. He persisted, cajoled, pleaded, but to no avail. No one had heard of Aubrey Taverner. There had been no patient of that name. No mental breakdown, no admission. No, no, no. Fiercely disappointed, Edward then pursued a different line of enquiry. Perhaps Taverner had used another name, he reasoned, describing his employer in an effort to jog a reluctant memory.

'He's about six foot three, with white-blond hair tied back in a pigtail.'

'We don't have photographs on the files, sir,' came the reply.

'But someone *must* remember him,' Edward persisted.

'From nine months ago? Listen, he could have looked like a silver-backed gorilla, but no one would remember nine months later. We need facts,' the voice insisted. 'Find out dates and names and then come back.'

But there were no facts. No dates, no names, nothing. Only what Florence had told him. When he telephoned the last hospital on the list without success, Edward leaned against the glass side of the phone-box and slowly tore up the paper. If Aubrey Taverner had been hospitalized, he had covered up his tracks as thoroughly as he covered up everything else. To all intents and purposes he had no home, no family, no past. Perhaps he had merely slid, unseen and unobserved, into Cook's Alley, and perhaps one day he would simply slide away, leaving no trace.

The idea unsettled Edward. He didn't want Taverner to escape, because he didn't deserve to. He couldn't prod around in people's lives and give nothing back. He couldn't make love to a blind woman and walk away. There were responsibilities to be shouldered, Edward decided. No one was supposed to have the luxury of total selfishness.

There *had* to be some solution, some way of unpicking the lock. There was *always* a way. Hennie would have known, but Edward didn't. He could ask Florence for more information, but that idea seemed both embarrassing and unwelcome. If Taverner had been hard to face, Florence would be doubly so. His employer did not realize that he had been seen; Florence *knew* she had. And such knowledge would put anyone on the defensive.

Another idea presented itself. Perhaps Edward should question the other clients, ask them for information? The notion was speedily dismissed. He had heard the tapes and read the experiences. The people who visited Cook's Alley knew less about Aubrey Taverner than he did. There was only one person with intimate knowledge, and that was Florence Andrews. If Edward wanted to know more, he had to ask her.

Reluctantly he turned his feet back to Cook's Alley. Walking up Old Compton Street, he saw a familiar figure a little way ahead of him. She was moving quite quickly through the crowds, although she kept close to the wall and away from the traffic, her stick tapping against the pavement like the ticking of an irregular clock.

Hurriedly Edward ran up to her, catching her arm lightly.

'Florence, it's Edward.'

She stopped, turning her face upwards. Her eyes carried the same vacant look as they always did, like a person newly awakened, caught in that instant before focusing. Except that Florence never focused.

'Edward.' Her voice slid round his shoulders like an embrace. It held no acrimony or embarrassment, just a tired welcome.

'I wanted to talk to you,' Edward said quickly, 'and I wanted to apologize. I'm so sorry.'

Her hand moved upwards and covered his mouth. Edward was surprised both by the movement and by the dexterity of the action.

'Sshhh . . . It's forgotten.'

'Do you forgive me?'

She remained glancing up at him, expressing no surprise that he should ask the question. Obviously she had known he had watched her, seen her and enjoyed, for an instant, the body she could no longer see for herself. What had she to forgive? she wondered. His voyeurism or his unexpected desire?

'Edward, I forgive you.'

He slid his arm gratefully through hers. 'Come on, let's go for a coffee,' he said, leading her to a nearby café.

Without any protest, Florence slid into her seat, her stick resting against her leg. With the table dividing them, Edward relaxed. There was now a barrier which separated them and, having abused her privacy, he felt relief at the enforced distance. His tone was light when he spoke.

'You can tell me to mind my own business . . .'

She smiled distantly.

'But I wondered how you and Aubrey Taverner met.'

Her mouth opened as though she was about to speak and then she closed it again. Her hair, quietly red, was buoyant with health, her skin pink and unlined. Edward realized suddenly that because of her handicap he had thought her unlovely, but her face was exquisite, as was her body.

He swallowed, unnerved by the memory, and pressed on. 'Do you mind my asking?'

'It's very simple,' she replied, leaning back as the waiter placed a coffee in front of her. Carefully she felt for the sugar and emptied the contents of the sachet into her cup. 'I met Aubrey when we both hailed the same taxi. It was on Gloucester Road. I was waiting on the corner and simply raised my stick.' She smiled. 'It's very easy for a blind person to get a taxi in London . . . Well, I was just opening the door when someone opened the door on the other side of the cab. I could hear the conversation and realized straight away that there had been a misunderstanding.' She paused. Her eyes looked down. Her eyebrows were narrow, fox-coloured. 'Aubrey insisted that I take the cab, but I thought we should share it. So we did.'

'And?' Edward prompted.

'I was going to look at a flat. I'd only recently come to London and he offered to go with me.'

'He did?' Edward asked, incredulously.

'He's kind,' she replied. 'You forget that, or maybe you haven't fully appreciated his kindness.' Her head tilted to one side. 'He pays you a good wage, a wage which allows you to gamble, doesn't he?'

They had been talking about him, Edward realized. His gambling had been discussed, picked over.

'He *is* generous with you, isn't he?' Florence persisted.

'With money, yes.'

'What else do you expect, Edward? He's only your employer.'

'I know, but it's as though I don't exist for him. I just do the work and that's it. I thought that after a while he might show some interest in me.'

'Why should he? Because you're interested in him?'

Her perception caught Edward off balance. 'Anyone would be interested in their employer.'

'I don't think so. Most people find their bosses terribly dull.'

Florence sipped her coffee carefully. Her lipstick left a sticky crescent on the rim. 'But Aubrey isn't dull, is he?'

Edward hesitated. What reply did Florence want from him? She knew the man, she had made love to him – what *could* Edward say about Taverner that wouldn't sound ingratiating or antagonistic?

'He's a fascinating man.'

Her smile was hollow.

'But very secretive . . .' Edward hurried on. 'What do you know about him, Florence? Do you know where he comes from? Why he's writing that book?'

She glanced up. At him, through him.

'What's he up to, Florence? Why collect experiences? What for? And where does he get the money to pay for them?'

Edward stared into her eyes. The pupils were clear. Dead marbles.

'He pays out a lot to the clients, sometimes too much. The cash has to come from somewhere, but where?'

'I don't know,' she replied coldly. 'I've never asked him about his background or his work.'

'But you must be curious.'

'Evidently not as much as you are.'

Edward had the grace to blush. 'Don't you *want* to know anything about him?'

'I'm blind. I don't *see* like normal people,' she replied, her left hand stroking her temple. 'But inside my head I have a life of my own, and because I can't see I'm free to imagine what I like. In my mind I see a man I love, I see Aubrey as I want him to be. Reality plays no part, because details would only take him away from me. I don't want to know about his past, because he might one day have reason to return there and I don't want to consider his going. For the same reason, I've no interest in his work. If I did, I might start asking questions. What will happen when he has all the experiences he needs? Will he leave me then?' Her voice, its tone husky, intimate, fell drowsily. She seemed to be turning pictures over in her head. 'I see him as everything I ever wanted. In him, I see all the men I desired, with all the talents in the world. I see strength and gentleness, kindness and tenderness. I don't see disappointment or boredom. Thank God, my blindness saves me from some of life's worst cruelties . . . Besides, the things I've wanted to know, I've discovered. I've felt his body, I know certain things about him.' She smiled languorously. 'But not enough to make him attainable. I know he may leave me and that knowledge makes me careful.'

Her passivity infuriated Edward. 'He couldn't leave you. It wouldn't be fair.'

'If I wasn't blind, we wouldn't be having this conversation,' she replied sharply. 'Do you think he seduced me, Edward? Is that what you think?'

The question gagged him.

'Well, he did. And I wanted him to,' she admitted triumphantly. 'I *ached* for him to make love to me. I longed for it. I pored over the image in my brain. Day after day, night after night.' Her voice hummed with carnality. 'I had this vision of how it would be . . .' Her tone swooped downwards suddenly, Edward straining to listen. 'But the reality bore no resemblance to what I'd expected. Aubrey was not callous or kind. He was indifferent.'

The words slapped down on the Formica table-top, falling noisily like loose change.

'It wasn't cruelty on his part,' Florence went on, reaching out and touching the back of Edward's hand, as though he needed comfort. 'It was disinterest. He had performed a function, that was all.'

An image of Taverner's white sleeping form flashed up before Edward. The long limbs, the white frost of his hair. Cold to the heart.

'I don't think you should see him again, Florence.'

She laughed unexpectedly. 'Oh, Edward, you're so naïve!' she said. 'What can he do to me that I can't do to myself? He can't destroy me, only I can do that. He can't abuse me, I gave myself willingly.'

'But he doesn't love you!'

'He doesn't love anyone,' she countered, 'so I can't grieve for that loss. If he loved another woman, that would be hard, but in loving no one he gives me no competitors to envy. And besides, there's always the hope that one day he may change.'

Edward shook his head. 'He won't.'

Florence leaned back against the bench, her eyes closing. 'Did you talk to your sister this way, Edward? Did you try to protect her too?'

'She was tougher than you.'

'You mean she wasn't blind?'

He nodded, then realized she couldn't see the action.

'No, she wasn't blind,' he agreed. 'And I did try and help her. Just as I want to help you. I'm worried about you, Florence. I don't think Taverner's the kind of man you should rely on. You know nothing about him.'

'And what do I know about you?' she retorted, opening her eyes – dead eyes, doll's eyes.

'You can ask me whatever you want. I'll tell you anything.'

'But, Edward,' she said quietly, 'I'm not interested in you.'

The words should have been cruel, but they were merely honest.

'I was thinking about his clients this morning,' Edward said, changing the subject. 'They've nothing obvious in common. Different personalities, different backgrounds. Some are poor, others well off. Some have handicaps. For instance, you're blind—'

She winced. 'I'm not a client.'

'Hear me out,' he said, hurrying on. 'Glaxman's deaf, Alan Painter's a depressive—'

'Does that count as a handicap?' Florence asked. Her tone was arch, but she was obviously curious.

'You'd think so if you met him,' Edward replied. 'Taverner's interested in handicaps – loss of sight, loss of hearing, loss of hope – and then there's the others, who aren't handicapped but who've experienced things outside the normal, like English. He's involved in the supernatural. And at the other end of the spectrum we've got Martin, a street kid helping a man dying with Aids. The paranormal versus reality.' He paused, marshalling his thoughts. 'Taverner's not curious about one thing, he's curious about *everything*, Florence. Handicaps, fear, death, love—'

'Love?'

'Well, Martin has a kind of love for the man he's helping,' Edward paused, choosing his words carefully, 'and now Taverner's got a new experience from you.'

Anger fluttered in her voice. 'I've told you, I'm not a client.'

'No, but he still got an experience from you, without paying for it.'

She leaned forward quickly, her hand raised to strike him, but Edward had seen the blow coming and caught her arm. Gently he settled her back in her seat.

'Listen, I didn't mean to hurt you, I just wanted you to be warned and see the situation as I see it.'

'I don't want to!' she snapped, her eyes filling, her voice falling away, 'I want to see it in my mind, I don't want reality.' She struggled to keep her composure, but the tears had started and ribbed her cheeks. 'You say he has no pity, Edward. Well, you're wrong. He shows me the pity of indifference. *You're* the cruel one.' Her voice shook with distress. 'I don't want you to care about me; my life has nothing to do with you.'

He was horrified by the pain he had inflicted. 'I just want to help you.'

'Then let me be!' she said pitifully. 'I walk in a blind world, Edward, down my blind alley. I don't know what's before me and I don't care. If Aubrey Taverner destroys me, it's with my blessing, and perhaps, just perhaps, I'd even be grateful to him.'

Chapter Nine

THE DISPLAY cabinets had been emptied, Taverner laying each object on his desk. He worked deftly, quickly and silently, dusting each object and brushing the green baize on which they had lain. Then, equally carefully, he replaced the red ribbon, making a grid, each portion the same measurement, the tape pinned meticulously back into place. From the door, Edward watched him, saw him wipe the piece in his hand, the small head of a humming bird mounted on a faded gilt cushion.

'Where did that come from?'

'A client,' Taverner said evenly, placing the object in its designated place. 'People give me things and I display them.'

'Someone gave you that mask?' Edward asked, pointing to a death head.

'One of my first clients. Yes.'

'Who is it?'

'I don't know,' Taverner replied. 'Is it important?'

Edward shrugged. 'It just seems an odd thing to keep, that's all.'

'Not to me.'

'No.'

Taverner straightened up. 'I like unusual things, Edward. I like to feel them, touch them, pick up feelings from them. You must have things you value.'

'Only memories.'

'Ah . . .'

*

The air had been heavy that day, Edward remembered, and there had, for once, been no sound of insects as they ran across the field, Hennie calling to him. They ran in the long grass, feet pounding the ground. The first slash of lightning broke through the cloud in the distance and Hennie stopped running, her face turned towards the horizon. Edward hurriedly caught up with her. The distant village darkened, houses outlined against the inhuman light, the church spire glowering. Together they waited, counting. As they reached fourteen the thunder shuddered behind them.

'Fourteen miles!' she said eagerly. 'The thunder's fourteen miles away.'

Her face was white under the clouds, her dress hanging listlessly in the thick air.

'We should go back, Hennie. We can go to the village tomorrow.'

'Go back,' she repeated scornfully. 'Never!'

'But—'

She turned, moving towards the gloomy village, and he followed. As he always did.

'Hennie, it's raining. Let's go home.'

She ignored him and hurried on, her legs striding defiantly through the lush grass.

'*Hennie, I said it was raining!*'

'I know,' she snapped impatiently. The material of her dress was already wet along the shoulders. 'Stop moaning . . . I'll race you.'

Immediately another bolt of lightning crashed over them. Hennie waited for the thunder and then turned triumphantly to her brother.

'The storm's only five miles away now, Edward. It's coming for us . . . Come on, Edward. Run! *Run*!'

Her long legs covered the earth quickly, her whoops of laughter shattering under the crashing thunder as Edward ran after her. She seemed exhilarated, over-excited, and he found himself falling behind, his right foot suddenly turning under him as he fell to the ground. In an instant, the high grass folded over his head, the wetness clutching at his body, the sky moving down to smother him.

Although she had not seen him fall, Hennie turned immediately, pushing her wet hair away from her eyes. But there was no sign of Edward. All she could see was high, wet grass, green as water weeds, deep as a drowning pool.

'Edward! Edward!' she screamed, her skin slicked with rain. '*Edward!*'

She began to run back, looking for him, her voice high over the thunder. The grass shivered around her, the dark sky poisonous, a spiteful wind slapping her flesh. Deserted, she ran abandoned in the open field, sobbing as she called for her brother, her cries getting weaker, panic making her a child again.

Suddenly she saw him. First one arm waving, then the other, the top half of Edward's body emerged from the shaking grass as he struggled to his feet. With an animal cry of relief she ran towards him, catching hold of his right hand, her fingers digging into his flesh. She faced him, her eyes wild, her face unrecognizable, and for an instant she frightened him.

Then together they began to run. Under the thunder, they ran, side by side, their feet in unison, their hands clasped. Silent, wet with rain, they spoke without words and in that instant knew what they meant to each other.

'What are you thinking about?' Taverner asked curiously, breaking into Edward's thoughts.

'A memory . . . About Hennie.'

'I envy you,' he said simply, turning back to the cabinet and closing the glass door. The airlessness of the room was heightened by the dull day outside. No light penetrated the drapes and when Taverner turned back to his employee, he seemed oddly lethargic.

'Talk to me. Tell me a story, Edward.'

'What!'

'Tell me about Hennie.'

He hesitated, remembering his sister as she was dressed for her first date, her hair held back with a band of spring flowers, her eyes for once apprehensive.

'You're lovely,' he had said, violently jealous of the boy who was coming to take her out, wanting to go in his place. 'You'll have a good time.'

'No, I won't! I wish it was just us, Edward,' she had answered.

I wish it was just us.

'I thought you were going to stay in your room and refuse to come down to see me off,' she had said. 'I thought you were sulking. What kept you, Edward?'

What kept you?

'Tell me what you're thinking,' Taverner urged.

But Edward refused. He had grown cruel and withheld the memory, knowing how much Taverner wanted it. My memories and experiences are my own, he thought defiantly. You have no place there.

They faced each other, Edward obstinate, Taverner almost pleading. The doorbell broke into the moment and forced them apart.

'He said he'd thrown some boy over the bloody banisters,' Martin said indignantly, sitting down in Aubrey Taverner's office. 'He's bleeding crazy.'

'Edward is a very good assistant,' Taverner replied calmly. 'What have you got for me today, Martin?'

'But he said—'

Taverner's eyes fixed on the boy harshly. 'What have you got for me today?'

'OK, OK,' Martin said, shifting his position in his seat. 'It's about this kid—'

'Not Geoff?'

'Geoff's fine.' Martin said hurriedly. 'He's fine, O bloody K? He's coping. This Aids thing, it's not so bad. Well, it's bad, bloody bad, but he's coping . . . He *is*.' His voice was anxious and he kept his eyes averted. Taverner realized immediately that the experience he was about to hear was untrue. Martin needed money badly and had come to milk him, or so he thought.

'So who's the child?'

'He's a she.'

'Wait a minute,' Taverner said, turning on the tape-recorder and leaning back to listen.

'Go on.'

'Well, it's like this. This girl lives near us – my dad and me – and she's only fourteen, but she's pregnant. Can you believe it? Pregnant? Well, my dad goes and sees her father and tries to give the family some kind of bloody guidance. Well, it seemed a bleeding daft idea to me, so I thought I'd go along with the old man, and we arrived at this place, some tower block, and knocked on the door. The girl's father, taking one look at my father holding the Bible and wearing a holier-than-thou look, tells him to piss off and slams the door in his face.

'So Dad tries again. You've got to give him credit, he's a trier – he's a bloody nut, but he's a trier. So this guy opens the door again, and stands there with a McEwans in one hand and a TV control in the other. Seeing his chance, my dad then starts saying that he'd heard about his daughter.

' "What about her?" the guy asks.

' "Her difficulties," my dad replied, a bit stiffly, 'cos he could see he was getting into difficulties himself.

' "What kind of 'difficulties'?"

'"Can't we talk inside?" my dad asked, looking round and seeing a group of women listening.

'"I don't want you inside. Now bugger off," the man says, then tips the contents of the beer can all over my dad's shoes. Now that really pissed him off, 'cos he was really proud of those shoes. You see, he'd bought them when he wanted to impress some woman and he got them from Russell and Bromley and they cost him a fortune, all ponced up in blue tissue paper . . . Anyway, my dad looks at his feet and freaks out. I mean, he really freaks out. I've never seen him like that before. He's a man of God, a lay preacher, and all that, but he sees those soggy shoes and goes ape . . .

'So he grabs hold of this guy's shirt and says, dead menacing, "You can pay for those."

'Well, the guy tries to shake him off, doesn't he? But my dad holds on, and the women on the landing all watch, and the girl in the flat – the pregnant one – comes to the door and she watches, and we're all shouting and cheering my dad on – 'cos he's the good guy – and then he suddenly gets hold of this bloke and hurls him over the railings . . . You should have seen it! I mean, it was only the first floor, so the bloke didn't have far to fall, but it surprised him, you could see that.'

'Is that it?' Taverner asked.

'Well, it's interesting,' Martin said defensively, 'especially as my dad's a lay preacher. A man of the cloth isn't supposed to go around throwing men with pregnant daughters off bleeding balconies.'

'There seem to be a lot of people falling off balconies and banisters lately. Apparently Edward also has some experience of this phenomenon,' Taverner replied thoughtfully. 'It's not true, is it, Martin?'

'It is!'

'No, I don't think so,' he said. 'And you can't expect me to pay you for a lie.'

'It wasn't a lie!'

'It was, Martin.'

'All right, all bloody right!' the boy admitted fiercely. 'So it was. But it could have been true – my dad *did* go and see the bloke and he *did* have half a can of McEwans poured over his Russell and Bromleys.'

'But he didn't throw the man over the balcony?'

'No. He gave him a Bible instead.'

'Then what happened?'

There was a long pause before Martin answered. 'Then the bloke threw the Bible over the balcony.'

Aubrey Taverner laughed, and, still laughing, took the tape out of the machine. 'You can have fifty pounds.'

'Bloody hell, thanks.'

'It's not for the experience, Martin, it's a loan against the next experience you bring me. You need the money now, so you've got it, but make sure you bring me something good – really good – next time.' His voice had no humour in it any longer. 'Don't forget to pay the loan back, Martin, and don't let me down.'

'I know about some woman who passes herself off as a duchess and writes porn.'

Taverner's face was impassive. 'Tell me about it next week, Martin. I have another client now.' He stood up and walked the boy to the door. 'And don't lie to me again. I don't like people underestimating my intelligence.'

Noting the warning tone in Taverner's voice, Martin left without saying another word.

The next client was already in the waiting-room, sitting in one of the chairs with a bag of books next to him. He was a man of about fifty, with protruding teeth so large that his lips did not meet and a goitre which was clearly visible at the collar of his open-necked shirt. Obviously preoccupied, he was reading avidly when Taverner walked in.

'Mr Cummings?'

'Gummings, Dr Gummings,' the man corrected him, one finger on the page to keep his place.

'Dr Gummings, would you like to come through?'

'I wanted to have a word with you first,' the man replied. He appeared to be smiling, but it was difficult to tell, the formation of his teeth forcing a perpetual grin. 'Are you Mr Aubrey Taverner?'

He nodded. 'Yes.'

'Well, it's like this. I saw your advertisement and I thought, that's interesting, and so I rang you to make this appointment.' Taverner stood, listening patiently. 'This appointment,' he repeated. 'But then I started wondering, you're nothing to do with the occult, are you?' He smiled, or appeared to.

'No. I'm collecting experiences for research.'

'For a book?'

Taverner nodded. 'As it said in the advertisement.'

'But it's not an occult one? Occult one?' Gummings asked again, echoing the last two words.

'No.'

'Good.' He moved his finger and closed the book, pushing it into the bag next to him and getting to his feet. 'I wanted to make sure first, before I told you my experience,' he said, possibly smiling and hauling the bag on to his left shoulder. 'Well, you lead the way.'

He walked into Taverner's room and glanced round uneasily, his eyes fixing on the glass cabinets.

Taverner reassured him immediately. 'They're relics . . . objects given to me. They have nothing to do with the occult.'

Gummings's eyes flicked back to him. The rigorous grin was strained. 'The occult frightens me, you see.'

'Is that what you've come to talk about?'

Gummings glanced up, then shook his head and undid his jacket. A faint whiff of liniment snaked across the desk towards Taverner as the man rubbed his left shoulder.

'No, I want to talk about my dreams.'

'Dreams aren't strictly experiences,' Taverner said at once.

'Oh, I agree,' Gummings said, 'I agree. But I'm talking about lucid dreaming.'

'Go on.'

'You know about this?'

'No.'

Gummings was definitely smiling now as he stooped towards his voluminous bag, took out a book and pushed it towards Taverner. 'This tells you something about it. Go on, go on,' he insisted, nudging the volume across the desk. 'Have a look.'

'I don't want to read about it, Dr Gummings, I want you to tell me your experience.'

'But it would help you to understand—'

Taverner's voice hardened. 'Just tell me about your experience, Dr Gummings.'

He didn't seem in the least discouraged by the chilling tone and leaned back in his seat.

Automatically, Taverner turned on the tape-recorder,

'Go on, please.'

'Well, it all began a while ago – about a year. I'd been over to the States on a trip and had met up with these doctors who were doing some research into dream patterns. I'm a doctor, you see – not a GP, a psychiatrist . . . a psychiatrist, and I've always been interested in sleep. You know, how much is good for you? Well, anyway, these Americans told me that they had done some research into lucid dreaming. Now, this is a field in which I have some interest . . . some interest. For years no one believed in it . . . Oh, I'm not making myself clear, am I? Dear me, perhaps I should.'

'Take your time. Relax, Dr Gummings.'

'Oh, I never could do that . . . never could. That's always been my trouble, not relaxing . . . Anyway, lucid dreaming occurs after REM sleep—'

'REM?'

'Rapid Eye Movement – it's the time during sleep after the first initial deep sleep, when the sleeper is coming into a lighter period of rest. The eyes move under the lids – under the lids – as the dreamer is actually watching *their dreams, as we would watch a play. Hence the Rapid Eye*

Movement . . . Well, after this period of REM sleep comes a time when dreamers can enter into lucid dreaming.'

'Which is?'

'Dreaming when the brain is partially lucid, so that the mind knows *it's dreaming. You know the kind of thing – you're dreaming, but you* know *you're dreaming, not like other dreams when you think you're living the events. Well, during this time of lucid dreaming we did some experiments. We then did some double-blind trials, so there were no means by which we could cheat, no means at all, and the results were incredible. We practised for months – we would go to sleep, dream, then reach that part of the night when we knew we were lucid dreaming. Ittakespractice—'*

'Pardon? Can you speak more slowly?'

'I said, it takes practice, but we did practise and after a while we could easily reach that point where we knew we were lucid dreaming. Lucid dreaming.'

'Go on.'

'Well, then we realized we could control what we dreamed. If we wanted to dream about a lake, we could . . . or a house, we could. And, if we were woken by the examiners, afterwards we could go back to where wehadbeeninthedream—'

'Pardon?'

'Sorry. We could go back to where we had been in the dream . . . in the dream. Don't you see what I'm saying, we could control *our dreams? Even when people disturbed our sleep, we could go back to sleep and back to the dream . . . So then we realized that because we had mastered the lucid dreaming, we should be able to master the dream world. Not only that, but we should be able to meet up with each other in our dreams.*

'So we tried other experiments. We concentrated before we went to sleep and decided that we would report our experiences to the examiners independently, so there could be no mistake about the outcome. For a week the three of us – three of us doctors – went to sleep in three different rooms, all set up with monitors. The examiners knew from the way our brain-wave patterns altered when we had fallen asleep, when we entered REM sleep and when we entered a phase of lucid dreaming. They monitored our

heart-rate, breathing, blood pressure and, as I said, our brain-wave patterns.

'Then, after the first night, we reported our dreams. But theywereall-different—'

'What did you say? Please, speak slower.'

'Sorry. I said that our dreams were all different. It was a terrible disappointment, but we persevered and the next night there was a slight matching. I and one of the other doctors dreamed we were on a boat – but that was all, nothing more detailed. Well, it wasn't good enough. Which was when we realized that we had to setthescene – sorry, set the scene – ourselves. So we all agreed to dream about being in a museum. We were to meet in this particular room, full of Roman fertility masks and busts, masks and busts, but that was all we knew. The rest, the details, what we wore and what we said, were unknown. That was what we had to dream and then report back independently to the examiners.

'So that night I went to sleep and went into lucid dreaming. I went to the room in the museum and waited for the other two doctors. It was sunny and the light fell in through a skylight, and there were two unknown women there looking at the exhibits. I wore a black jumper and trousers. Well, after a little while the first doctor walked in.

'We were so pleased to see each other – he was wearing jeans and a white shirt – and we talked in detail about one particular mask which was cracked across the nose. We waited, so certain that the third doctor would come . . . would come. But he didn't, and so the two of us finally parted, and later woke.'

'Then what?'

'Why, we told our stories independently to the examiners and then tried to match them. The doctor who had met up with me in my dream could describe exactly what I was wearing and the fact that there had been two women in the dream, but hecouldnotrememberthemask—'

'Slower, please.'

'He couldn't remember the mask. It was a partial success. After all, we had met up with each other in our dreams *and held a conversation, but the third doctor could only report that he had gone to the room in the museum, waited for us, but we hadn't come.*

'Still we persevered – you have to, in this kind of work – and then we had a success. Only a few months ago the three of us tried to meet up in a dream which would be prearranged. We agreed to meet in an art gallery – that was all we told each other, nothing more – and then we went to sleep. I was the first to arrive, then the second, then finally the last doctor came in. We'd done it! We were so excited that we embraced each other and held a long conversation about the paintings and about the people who came in and out of the gallery. It was so real that we couldn't believe we were dreaming. But it was a reality of a kind unknown in normal life. Speech was effortless, effortless, and time was altered. The people who came into the gallery walked round, looking at the paintings, but some left aged and some left younger. We laughed about that and wondered how, in the space of what appeared to be minutes, people went forwards or backwards in time.

'There was one girl so lovely that we all stared at her. She was glorious . . . Anyway, she came in and looked at one painting and began to cry, so naturally we went over to her. She talked normally, but as she talked she became older and started getting angry, asking us what we were doing there. By the time she left us she was old and ugly, but when we turned around a little later, she was just walking into the gallery, young again . . . It was so tremendous that we didn't want to leave. It was incredible, and we all knew it would make our names all over the world. We would win the Nobel Prize, we would be fêted – and we could just imagine the possibilities of what we had discovered. People meeting up in their dreams, people thousands of miles apart coming together at night and talking easily, so easily. Easily. People travelling without problems, people attending meetings, people giving advice – no planes to wait for, they would be there as you closed your eyes. The potential was gigantic.

'And what about the ageing? What was that? Had we inadvertently uncovered the "secret of life"? Was it in dreams? Could wetelltheworldhow-tocheatdeath? What comfort it would be for people to think that they could age like that girl, and then walk in and start again . . . young again.'

'What happened then?'

'We went back every night for a week. We met up in our dreams. We

did more talking and thinking in those seven days than we had ever done. We were brilliant. Then . . .'

'Then?'

'Three weeks ago we met in our dreams once more, the two doctors and myself. We talked, and then we woke up and reported what we said to our examiners. Everything matched, except for one thing – the third doctor had wanted to stay in the dream. *He had argued with us, but the first doctor and I had insisted that he return. Dear God, how he had wanted to stay! He had even fought us. When we woke, we all had marks on our hands and faces to indicate the fight, and we told the examiners all about it. But we thought he had come back. He seemed to be back, he seemed to be as he always was, but there was something different.*

'The other doctor and I knew he had gone, that he had somehow managed to stay, but we were afraid and said nothing to anyone. After all, it would have been seen as our fault. And instead we decided that the following night we would bring him back ourselves.'

'And?'

'We went to sleep as usual and met in the same gallery, the first doctor and I, and we waited for him. We waited a long time, even in the dream the day faded and night came in. The visitors came and went, they aged around us, they re-entered, they kept coming, but each time the door opened we were looking only for him, only for him. But he didn't come.'

'So what happened next?'

'We both woke up, frightened, afraid for him. But the next night when I fell asleep, I found myself in a room I had never visited before, and after an instant the first doctor joined me. He was in a terrible state, as confused as I was. You see, we hadn't agreed to meet there, and we didn't know the place. *It was a dark place, cold, without people. We tried so hard to wake ourselves up, but we couldn't. So we waited. Then, after a while, the third doctor came in. He was angry. He said that we were in* his *dream and that we had to leave. We tried to reason with him, but he just kept insisting that we leave. We tried to bring him back, bring him back . . . Honestly, we did try, but he wouldn't come. He wouldn't come.'*

'I don't understand. Where is he?'

'We don't know. His body's in hospital, in a catatonic state. He comes out of it now and again, perfectly reasonable, then he slips back. We know he's just visiting, that he's actually living *in his dreams, but no one else knows that. And now . . . now the first doctor's gone too, and I don'twanttobenext.* I don't want to be next.

'I won't go, you know. I won't! I left America last week. Ran away, I suppose you could say, and now I stay awake all I can. I read a lot. A lot. And I make sure when I do sleep I sleep in quick snatches so they can't get me. I make sure I've tied my hands to the bed or the chair. I put the alarm clock next to me and set it. I only sleep for half an hour at a time, no longer. Not long enough to go into REM sleep, then lucid dreaming. I worried about the clock, though, worried it might not go off. So I bought another. Well, I bought four actually. They sound loud at night, ticking . . .

'I'm not mad, believe me. In a little while everyone will know all about lucid dreaming, it will be commonplace. But not now. If I told them now, they would commit me.

'SoIkeepreading. Sorry. So I keep reading. There must be something in these books which will tell me what to do. I'm a clever man . . . a clever man, a medical man. I'm cleverer than they are. After all, it was my idea in the first place. I'll outwit them, both of them.'

'Why are you telling me all about this? Why don't you tell the examiners?'

'I've told you, the examiners would have me committed, and besides, I need money. You are going to pay me, Mr Taverner, aren't you? Aren't you? You are *going to pay me?'*

'Only if you promise me to come back.'

'Oh, I want to come back, Mr Taverner, believe me. I want nothing more than to tell you I'll be back. Don't worry, I'll do all I can to keep my promise. I just have to be careful, that's all. Restrict my sleeping, keep reading, keep reading . . .

'I'll be back.'

Chapter Ten

AUBREY TAVERNER rose to his feet and walked down into Cook's Alley. The girl at No. 3 glanced over to him, then looked away, her eyes returning to the doorway of No. 6 as she waited for the printer's boy to come out for lunch. Slowly Taverner turned his head in her direction. He saw a girl with a sullen look and the easy seductive movements of someone used to men. He watched her, and she, thinking he was interested, sat down on the stone steps outside No. 3 and crossed her legs. Her calves were muscular, her thighs over-exposed, as she leaned back on her elbows and turned her face up to the reluctant sun.

Frowning, Taverner glanced away. No. 8 and No. 10 sported TO LET signs, although No. 12 was busy. He could hear the sound of phones and faxes, and see a thirtyish woman walking out hurriedly with a mobile phone pressed to her ear as she slid into her car. He watched her as she negotiated the gears, the sports car easing out of the alley and into Greek Street, then his attention moved back to No. 3.

The girl was still sitting there, trying to get his attention, her gaze holding his fixedly. She smiled languorously, studying him. He was a strange one, she thought; too old, of course, but interesting, and smart. Her eyes ran over his suit, the long line of the navy jacket, the white shirt and silk tie. She worked out quickly the cost of such clothes and decided that maybe he wasn't that old after all. And Taverner just kept staring at her . . . He was unusual-looking, the girl decided, tall and slim. Maybe his eyes were a little sinister . . . She shivered with the realization of what that might mean as the word took on a sexual connotation. But he was rich, he had to be. That suit must have cost hundreds.

She swung her right foot idly in the building heat, and Taverner watched it swing. Backwards and forwards, its shadow black on the cobbles. Back and forth. In and out, Swinging, swinging . . . He smiled slightly, knowing how she watched him, and then she leaned forwards, her T-shirt falling forwards, the deep V of her cleavage dark against the pale skin. Across the alleyway they studied each other, the sun heating up, the rhythmic banging of the printing press seeping out from under the door of No. 6.

Taverner's eyes never left the girl, but when she realized that he was not going to approach her, she rose to her feet and walked slowly across the cobbles.

Leaning against Mrs Tunbridge's railings, Taverner watched her approach.

'Nice day,' she said simply.

'Yes,' he replied, folding his arms.

'You work here, don't you?' she asked, gazing up at him.

'I have my offices here, yes.'

'I work over there.' She jammed one thumb across the alley. 'I'm a seamstress. Well, I work on a machine actually.'

'Making what?'

'Clothes.' Her hand snaked out and touched his jacket. 'Not like that though. We're not in the same league as St James's, more Oxford Street really.' Her fingers lingered against his jacket and then fell away. She was irritated by his lack of interest and tried to provoke him. 'You've got that good-looking guy working for you, haven't you?'

Taverner's face was impassive. 'Edward Dadd?'

She nodded. 'Yeah, he's quite something. All the girls think so.'

'And what about you?'

'Well . . .' Her head tilted to one side. 'I prefer older men myself.'

Taverner's eyes narrowed momentarily, then his attention wandered to the small figure walking down the alley. He straightened up immediately, dismissing the girl from his thoughts.

She saw how he watched the approaching woman and felt a savage nudge of jealousy.

'She's blind,' the girl said spitefully.

'And you're a slut,' Taverner responded coldly.

She took in her breath with shock. She even thought she had misheard and stood rooted to the spot, her eyes fixed on the tall man in front of her.

'What did you say?'

'You heard,' Taverner replied, walking away.

Florence heard his feet on the cobbles and smiled, knowing instinctively that the smile was returned. In an attempt to make herself more attractive she had asked her landlady to help her to choose her prettiest clothes and had gone to the hairdresser's to have her nails painted. They shone, poignantly cheerful, against the dark wood of her stick.

'You look well,' Aubrey Taverner said, taking her arm. 'Are you?'

She sighed. She had been worried about how he would greet her, and her voice was mellow with relief.

'I'm fine,' she said, holding on to his arm. 'Just fine.'

'We're on our own today,' Taverner continued, passing the machinist without so much as a glance in her direction. 'Edward's gone out. He seems a little . . . preoccupied.'

She felt only minor interest. 'Why?'

'He had a phone call this morning. Apparently his mother's ill.'

'I'm sorry,' she said softly, as they walked up the steps of No. 6. 'And surprised. I've never heard him talk about her.'

'But he does talk to you about other things, doesn't he?' Taverner asked.

'Sometimes,' she replied cautiously, unwilling to talk about Edward; unwilling to be reminded of what he had said, and the warning he had given her.

Up the dark stairwell she followed Taverner, without question. The stairs were ice cool, the sun not having yet passed over the rooftops and lighted this side of the building. As she walked, a mixture of excitement and anxiety drummed in her chest, and for once she lost hold of her stick, stiffening as it fell down the long lapse of the stairs. It seemed to take an age to fall, endless moments passing before it struck the floor of the hallway below. And when it did, she jumped as though she had not expected the sound.

'I'll get it for you. Wait there,' Taverner said quietly, leading her through the reception area and into the waiting-room beyond.

He was gone only for a moment, and when he came back he was carrying the stick. Instinctively Florence extended her hand to take it, but he held it back, tapping the tip of the cane against the floor, then the wall, then gently, almost hesitantly, against the back of her legs. Surprised and startled, Florence turned round, and kept turning blindly in the direction of the tapping cane, her hand outstretched. Tap, tap, tap, went the cane. Tap, tap, tap . . . then silence. Stillness. She waited in the quiet for a sound, some clue to tell her where he was, and then winced as he walked up behind her and looped his arms over her head, the cane pressing against her stomach to hold her body against his.

She panicked. 'Don't, don't . . .' Then she heard the cane fall to the floor again.

His hands ran down towards her breasts hurriedly, his palms spread out against them as he leaned down and laid his lips against her cheek, his mouth moving quickly, his tongue flicking against the pulse in her neck. Sighing, she closed her eyes and leaned back against him, without realizing that his gaze had already moved towards the window, his thoughts with the girl at No. 3. The memory of her swinging foot unsettled him, and he pushed his hands roughly into Florence's blouse, his fingers gripping her nipples.

Startled, her eyes opened and she tried for an instant to move away but couldn't, Taverner's right arm folding across her chest and holding her body against his own, pressing her to him tightly. Then suddenly he dropped to his knees, taking her with him, and she cried out, not understanding what was happening and incapable of seeing it, the floor hard against the skin of her knees. Quickly he pulled off her clothes and turned her over, looking curiously into her blank eyes.

In response, she looked and saw nothing, and automatically reached out, her hands searching for his face as he entered her. She had the scent of him and she could feel him inside her, but he kept moving, his face held back, away from her, so that she had no clues to his expression and no comfort from him. Frantically, Florence's hands grasped upwards, her fingers closing on nothing, and as he climaxed she cried out, the long grief of her blindness taking root in the scent of dead air.

'It's inconvenient,' Taverner said shortly.

Edward winced. 'Illness is always inconvenient.'

'Don't be impertinent!' his employer replied, turning away. Slowly he ran his left hand over the top of the display cabinet under the window, his eyes resting momentarily on the earring he had just added to his collection.

'I can't spare you at the moment. We're too busy.'

'Listen, I don't want to go to France, but I have to . . . She's my mother.'

'What's wrong with her?'

'She's sick.'

'You said that.'

'I won't be gone long,' Edward persisted. 'I'll just make sure she's being looked after. A week should do it.'

'Hah!'

'I have to sort this out. She's my responsibility!' Edward snapped.

'My, how you're changing,' Taverner said slyly. 'You know, I've been watching you, Edward. You're losing your sense of humour. You used to be so light-hearted – delightfully irresponsible. Now you seem distant, withdrawn. Why is that?'

Edward refused to be provoked. He was a slow learner but was gradually discovering how to handle his employer. Barbs which would have reduced him to fury before now merely irritated him; his feelings, normally close to the surface, were more controlled. Wanting to remain at Cook's Alley, he had adapted to Taverner's ways and, in adapting, had strengthened his own position.

He was determined to keep his job and stay with his employer, and knew that the only way to ensure Taverner's interest was to be less open. Friendliness had done little to intrigue his employer; indeed, a willingness to please had alienated the one man he wanted to impress. So now he held back, offering little, and in doing so he made Taverner come forwards. The more Edward withheld of himself, the more his employer wanted to know. The more he stood up to him, the more Taverner respected him. Little by little, the diffident Edward Dadd was changing.

'I have to go.'

'So, go!' Taverner snapped, exasperated. 'You have one week. Stay longer and you'll have no job to come back to.'

The following day, Antoinetta Dadd awaited her son in the house at Misérie, tensing as she heard Edward drive up to the front door and park. The paintwork was faded, the roof open to the sky in parts, the outhouses half demolished. The central area of the building was still sound, but years of neglect had taken their toll and the house was now urgently in need of repair.

He'd have to send money home, Edward thought guiltily. Money to restore the house. After all, if he didn't do it, who would? Not his father, he'd gone long ago. Guilt jolted Edward. He too had run away, left his mother and Hennie, left all the memories – and when he had gone, he had forgotten. In Cook's Alley he earned a considerable wage and spent it, or gambled it away. He had never thought to send some of it home. He had not wanted to be reminded of Misérie. He had abandoned his home, his mother and his memories.

Uncertainly, he walked through the front door and headed for his mother's room, although when he reached it he changed his mind and climbed up the stairs to Hennie's red and gold chamber instead. The room winked at him when he walked in, the windows looking out towards the village, the church roof steel blue under the sunlight. As ever, her things remained in place. The clothes in the cupboards, the drawers untouched. Curious, Edward slid open the top drawer of the dressing-table. A pair of tights, still in their wrapper, looked back at him, a black velvet hairband next to them. He reached out, his forefinger running over the band, then he closed the drawer and sat down on the bed.

The red quilt was still there. It glowed in the sunlight, the dark crimson breathing with life, and for an instant Edward caught the scent of his sister – not a perfume aroma, but the deep alkaline scent of warm flesh which was typical of her. He knew the smell, he had noticed it on her clothes long after she died, her body leaving an indelible imprint on everything she had ever worn.

Slowly he rose to his feet.

'Well, I'm back.'

There was no reply.

'I know you're here, Hennie.'

No reply.

He paused, then clicked his fingers three times. There was no response. Disappointed, he walked to the window. She *was* there, he knew it. Maybe sulking, maybe waiting, but she was there. His gaze moved out to the field where as children they had been caught in the storm. His eyes fixed on the moving grass – and then slowly, incredulously, he saw a figure making its way to the village beyond.

She walked quickly, head held up. She walked without looking back. But he knew her and, crying out, pressed his hands against the glass, his mouth forming her name repeatedly.

'Thank you so much for seeing me. I'm so glad to meet you, Mr Taverner. What a lovely room, so interesting, and all those delightful things you have in your cabinets. Very exciting. People don't collect objets d'art *so much these days, they haven't the patience. Oh, is that a bone? How remarkable, and this? A death mask! Goodness, you* do *have a wide variety. My mother used to collect books. I know it's not the same, but she was very clever and knew all about first editions and such like.*

'Forgive me, I'm rambling on, aren't I? I do that sometimes when I'm nervous. I must apologize. It must be very tedious for you. Well, what do I do now, Mr Taverner?'

'Talk.'

'Just talk? I see, just talk . . . Very well.

'I'm a secretary. I'm sixty years old, and I work – worked – at St George's Hospital in the Pathology Department. That was why I was interested in your lovely collection. I don't suppose many people like bones and such things, but I've been working amongst them for so long they seem quite normal. Oh, I didn't mean that your collection was abnormal . . . Forgive me, I hope I haven't offended you. Sometimes I do that without realizing. It's shocking to be so tactless, especially when I don't mean to be.

'Anyway, where was I? Oh, yes, I'm sixty and I have many good

years in front of me. My brain is as agile as it always was. Professor Clements used to say that I was "remarkably adept" – those were his very words – "remarkably adept". The girls who call themselves secretaries now don't know the meaning of the word. They have no shorthand and type so slowly. Some of them can't even answer a phone – you should see the kind of girls we get as temporaries. And the way they dress! Goodness, it's shocking. Short skirts and so much make-up.

'You would never have got away with it in my day. When I started at St George's we wore black office dresses and no make-up. Soap and water was good enough for us. And in a hospital environment you have to look clean. Don't you think so, Mr Taverner? Well, anyway, I took my secretarial course and went to St George's. I was very lucky, there was a vacancy in the Pathology Department and, although I had no experience, they hired me! You can't imagine how thrilled I was. I lived at home then, with my parents, and every Friday gave my wages to them. I had spending money, of course, they were very kind, but we pooled our resources. Shared the finances, so to speak.

'Do you know, Mr Taverner, within a year they had given me a rise, and a bonus at Christmas! I loved the work. Oh, I dare say that some people thought it was a bit odd, and we did see some terrible things . . . I worked for Professor Clements, as I said, and when he did a post-mortem he would dictate to me. At first I must confess I was a little queasy! I saw sights that most people never see, but I have a very strong faith in God, so I was never repelled by what I saw. I pitied the dead, Mr Taverner. I did not despise them.

'They say that there is a smell attached to anyone who works in a Pathology Department. Forgive my being so personal, but it's important. Well, I don't know if there is an . . . odour, but I must say that every night I came home and bathed, putting a few drops of Dettol in the water, just in case.

'It was difficult telling people what I did. Not that I went to many parties – I'm not a very sociable person, the night life's not for me! But when someone did ask, you could see it surprised them. Other people were very curious, unpleasantly so, I'm afraid. They asked all manner of provoking questions and sometimes I'm afraid I was quite rude.

'But I believe in God, as I said, and I know that He wanted me to work there, so I was quite willing to obey Him. Besides, my church friends never gave my job a second's thought. Boyfriends did, unfortunately – in fact, the only man I really cared for refused to see me again after he found out where I worked. I was upset. In fact, the experience rather altered me. You lose confidence, Mr Taverner, when people are cruel. Especially when a man is cruel, a man you love . . . Oh dear, listen to me! What a fool you must think me. After all, there was nothing wrong with the job, and I really can't think that it would matter in this day and age. People do some terrible things now, but in the early 1950s it did matter. It mattered very much. He said that his friends had laughed at me, and called me "The Ghoul".

'I was very upset, but if you believe in God's word, you have to abide by it, and my friends at the church said he wasn't good enough for me, and that he had been seeing someone else all the time he had been courting me. I think they told me that to make it easier, but it didn't. In fact, I rather wish they had kept it to themselves.

'But it was God's wish, so I put it behind me. Put on a brave face and smiled at the world. That's the spirit! No one likes a misery, do they? I concentrated on my work after that, and became very proficient. We saw terrible things, murder victims, burn cases, children. Sometimes you could hardly believe you were looking at a human body. It was sad really, although when the corpses came in decomposed it could be rather nasty.

'We had masks, of course. Even good old St George's provided those. But they could only keep out some of the smell, not all of it. Decay has a sweet, sickly odour, and yet it's bitter too. You can taste it . . . Oh dear, that sounds terrible. Forgive me, but it's true. You can. It lingers long afterwards in the nostrils and at the back of the throat. But a gargle with TCP soon clears it up and besides, someone has to do the job.

'I only thank God that I had the ability, and, as Professor Clements said, no one could run the department as well as I could. The notes were very precise, I insisted on that, and when I was promoted, I had a girl to take over that side of the work so that I could go out on calls with the Professor. Oh, Mr Taverner, you can't imagine what it was like. Sometimes we were called out to murders or suicides – I remember one young woman

had thrown herself under a train at Charing Cross and had been trapped in the undercarriage and dragged for three hundred yards. Even her mother couldn't recognize her.

'That was where my faith came in. You can't see all that human misery without knowing that there is a God looking after us all. There has to be, otherwise it makes no sense . . . There was only one part of the job I really disliked. One place. A corridor off the Pathology Laboratory. It was cordoned off from the main body of the hospital because you wouldn't want someone coming across it unexpectedly. It was a long, narrow passageway between the laboratory and the old file room, and on either side were shelves.

'They had to keep exhibits, you see. It was important for the students. So they kept them there, in jars, suspended in formaldehyde, so they wouldn't decompose. They floated in this solution and after a while they all became the same colour, a kind of soapy pale yellow. We had all kinds of specimens. Organs, limbs, heads and embryos. Some were more developed, they were real babies. Well, not real, not like any babies you ever saw. Some had two heads, some had their intestines on the outside and one had no head, just a sexual organ there. A penis. Forgive me for being so blunt, Mr Taverner, but it's the truth. I forget how alarming this must sound to an outsider – one gets used to anything.

'Anyway, I'm not fanciful, but I have to admit that this corridor upset me. And when I had to go down there at night, it was terrifying. I used to cross myself, and even though I knew I was protected, it was still awful. I used to run. Unprofessional, I know, but still, everyone has their Achilles' heel, don't they? I couldn't help wondering about those exhibits, who they belonged to. I was glad that the mothers never saw their babies. They probably don't even know that their dead children are there, swimming in formaldehyde for ever in that dark place.

'Dear me, I do sound silly. Anyway, I was made redundant a little while ago, Mr Taverner. Made redundant! *Can you believe it, after all those years? Professor Clements had died, so in came the new men and their new secretaries, and they didn't like my way of doing things. They wanted computers in there. Why, I don't know. After all, what can a computer do that I can't? But that was the way they wanted it. In came all the over-made-up girls with their short skirts and soon I was being edged out.*

'They tried to force me to leave. You know what I mean, they tried to make me feel uncomfortable – wouldn't talk to me, and laughed at me. They humiliated me! But they couldn't find anything wrong with my work, so I hung on. I wanted to work until I was sixty-five, that had been our agreement, Professor Clements and I, and besides, I needed the money. I'd been there all my life – it was all my life – *and now all these new brooms were trying to sweep away all my years of effort.*

'I clung on – and I had my faith, remember. I knew God wouldn't let me down. They did what they could to make me uncomfortable, but they couldn't make me leave, whatever they did. Until . . . until they found out about Margaret. She's a friend of mine, a good friend. You know what I mean, Mr Taverner? A good friend . . .'

'You were friends. Yes, I understand.'

'Close friends.'

'Friends?'

'Lovers, Mr Taverner. Goodness, how difficult that is to say. We loved each other, really loved each other. We had a great deal in common and we made each other happy. God approved of it. He must have done, otherwise He wouldn't have put those feelings there in the first place, would He? I really loved her. Really. And she loved me. She did! We thought no one knew about us. We were very discreet – two spinster ladies sharing a flat – but someone found out. After all those years, someone found out.

'They laughed at me, nudged each other when I went past. Made it seem dirty . . . I couldn't stand it! Couldn't bear the jokes and the way they looked at me. What we did wasn't wicked, it was God's will . . .

'I had *to leave then. I took redundancy pay and left. They all thought it was a huge joke.*

' "Who would have thought it of her?" they used to say.

' "What a turn-up!"

'The humiliation nearly killed me. You can't imagine how I felt, how I hated them all.'

'Margaret left me soon after. She met someone, she said. Some man she wanted to marry. But I didn't believe her. So I was left without a job and without Margaret, and all I could think about was the Pathology Laboratory and all those years I'd spent there. It had ended, just like that.

Spiteful people had ruined me. Ruined me and *my reputation. I could still hear the giggles when I left, and see the looks on their faces. The girls had called me a freak! A* freak, *because I loved someone.*

'So I made a copy of the Pathology Laboratory key and a few days after I left I went back at night. It was very quiet – no one uses that part of the hospital after midnight, no one dares – but I dared. I opened the door and went in. It was very cold, I remember that, and dark, and as I walked past my old office my anger nearly choked me.

'I found the passageway and paused. I didn't dare to turn on the light – that would have been too risky. Instead I used the torch I had brought with me. The light shone on the bottles and the exhibits. A freak, they had called me! A freak! And here they were, surrounded by real freaks. They had to be shown what a freak really *was . . .*

'I knew it was wrong, but I couldn't stop myself, and I lifted the umbrella I had brought with me and brought it down on the first bottle. But nothing happened. The bottle shuddered on the shelf, the horrible little figure in it bobbed in the formaldehyde, but it didn't break. So then . . . so then I reached out and pulled *it off.*

'It fell with a terrible crash, the bottle smashing on the floor, the smell of formaldehyde overpowering in that narrow space, the dead body slipping across the tiles like a nasty little worm. I couldn't stop then. I just kept pulling the bottles off the shelves, and they kept falling, one after the other, until the floor was covered with yellow bodies, or bits of bodies, swimming about in the spilt liquid. I slipped once, but it didn't stop me, and by the time I reached the other end of the corridor all the bottles were broken . . .

'It was very cold in there . . . I stopped and shone the torch on the floor. A freak, they'd called me. Well, soon they'd see what freaks really *looked like. It took all my courage to pick up some of those specimens. They were ungodly, some of them, and the smell . . . They felt greasy in my hands, slippery, but I'd no choice. It took me nearly half an hour to place them where I wanted them, and when I'd finished they were propped up against the computers, leaning against the screens for everyone to see when they came in the following morning. They had called* me *a freak! Well, now they were going to know what a freak* really *was . . .*

'It took me days to get the smell off my hands.

'They wrote about it in the evening paper. Said it was an act of unbelievable vandalism. They never said what they did with the bodies – if they buried them or put them back into other bottles.

'But they never suspected me. Who would?'

EXPERIENCE TAKEN FROM *Miss Joan Warbeck*
FEE PAID: *£700*
SIGNED: *Aubrey Taverner*

Antoinetta waited. She had been bathed by the nurse and dressed in her finest négligé, the high cream fluting of the neckline flattering the slackening line of her jaw. She lay unresponsive, heavy against the mattress, her eyes fixed ahead as Edward walked in.

'Mother, it's me, Edward.'

She remained staring ahead. 'So you've come home, have you? It's good to know that all I had to do was break my arm to get a visit from my son.'

He laughed without malice. 'It's good to see you too, Mother.'

Her eyes turned to him and her intelligence flickered: 'I'm ill.'

'You've only broken your arm.'

'It's more than that,' Antoinetta snapped. 'I don't remember things. I'm getting older.'

'You're getting lazier,' he said evenly. 'You're under-occupied, Mother, that's all. You should make some new friends, go out.'

'That's easy for you to say. You don't live in the wilderness.'

He sighed. 'So move.'

'This is my home!'

'So stay!' he retorted angrily, then sat down on the end of

the bed, immediately contrite. 'You have a good brain, Mother, you should use it.'

She watched him, concentrating. This was her son. If Edward was here, everything would return to normal. All she had to do was keep him with her.

'We were very happy when we lived together, weren't we, Edward?'

He said nothing, knowing she would continue.

'You could come back.'

'No, Mother. I live in London now. I'm not coming back.' He softened the blow. 'I don't want you to worry though, I'll make sure you're looked after.'

She threw up her hands with irritation. 'Don't inconvenience yourself. I'll cope on my own!'

'You're not alone. You have the housekeeper and the nurse.'

'And who will pay for them? Your father?' Her eyes sparked with fury.

'I will, I promise.' Edward said patiently. 'I'll send money home. Don't worry.'

'I've been thinking about the past,' Antoinetta said listlessly. 'About Theo, your father . . .'

Her thoughts drifted. Edward watched her, wondering how much she was exaggerating her condition, using her illness to make him stay.

'When we were married we lived on . . . we lived . . .'

He said nothing, just waited. He didn't know if she was really losing her mental faculties, but having been manipulated by her before, he was suspicious.

'The rue de Grenelle!' she said triumphantly, her recall apparently coming back, a quick flash of colour on the dry cheeks. 'On the rue de Grenelle!' she repeated. 'The rue de Grenelle.'

Edward's tone was cautious. 'Well done, Mother. You see what you can do when you try?'

She said nothing else, just gave her son a long look and then closed her eyes.

He spent the afternoon working, clearing out the drawing-room to occupy his thoughts. The Hoover was pressed into service and a cloth employed on the windows, the accumulated grime making the bucket of water murky in seconds. Working quickly but methodically, he cleaned the display cabinet, the tarnished silver trophies, polishing and then re-arranging them in regimented rows, whilst the mirror over the fireplace, fly-blown and mottled but free of its dust, reflected the room avidly. Edward then laid out a small side-table, setting two dining places by the french windows. In the dying afternoon, the breeze fluttered the table-cloth, an early moth settling briefly on the arm of one of the chairs.

Satisfied, he moved into the kitchen and thoughtfully regarded the food on the table, uncertain of where to start.

He could almost hear Hennie's voice . . .

Oh, do get on with it.

Then he smiled to himself and, picking up the lettuce, sliced it down the middle with one easy stroke.

The light faded as he worked and he turned on the lamp over the table, the shadows in the kitchen scurrying back. The salad made, Edward then took the chicken out of the oven and tested it, easing a fork into the breast, the pink juices running down the skin. The aroma leaned against him, it nuzzled his skin and made lazy inroads into his clothes as he basted the fowl and then returned it to the oven. Only then did he light the candles in the drawing-room and walk upstairs to his mother.

She sat in front of her dressing-table in a dated Givenchy dress, the left sleeve large enough to accommodate the plaster cast on her arm. She turned to greet him as he walked in. The scent of the lighted candles and the aroma of the cooking chicken came with him. They coaxed her and, although she was still angry with him, she found herself unexpectedly hungry.

'Ready?'

'I suppose you left a mess in the kitchen? You always did.'

'Oh, you remember!' Edward replied wryly. 'You're making progress already, Mother.'

She rose to her feet, impressively tall. 'You're changing, Edward, and you're growing cruel. You were never cruel before.'

He made no comment, merely extended his arm to her, and she took it, walking down the stairs and into the drawing-room with him. Attentively, Edward seated her by the partially opened french windows and studied her. He had never trusted her; knew she had resented the bond between brother and sister, and remembered too clearly what she had said about Hennie. Cook's Alley was educating Edward. He was no longer prepared to take life at face value and had found the advantage of caution.

The candlelight was kind to Antoinetta. It flattered her carefully made-up face and cheated her age, lending her some semblance of the glamour she had taken for granted when young. Kindly, Edward arranged a jacket over her shoulders and then gave her a glass of Madeira.

'Welcome home,' she said simply.

'Good health,' he replied.

'Will you stay?'

'No.'

She hesitated. 'Not for a little while?'

'You ask too many questions, Mother,' he replied, and then remembered Taverner having once said the same to him.

They ate and talked. Remembrances were sometimes imperfect on Antoinetta's part but Edward ignored her hesitancy and talked of London, skirting the subject of Hennie and thereby avoiding the argument her memory always provoked. Outside the breeze changed direction. It fluttered quickly in the garden as the night came in, skittering amongst the untended apple trees and whispering down the unlit chimney, and the candles burned on.

They burned steadily as Edward helped his mother to her feet, and they burned on as he danced with her, the strains of

Sinatra's torch songs dipping their blues into the blue of the night outside. Under the song they danced, Antoinetta's head against her son's shoulder, the dark scent of her clothes and the heavy weight of her hand in his curiously tender. They danced in each other's arms, a lonely saxophone talking for them, all acrimony suspended, their desires for each other expressed without words.

And then, under the song and under the candlelight, a sudden cold brush of air hurried into the room. Surprised, Edward moved to the window and hurried to close it. The shutter escaped his hand and rapped three times on the wall outside.

Chapter Eleven

FLORENCE couldn't see the bruises, she could only feel them when she touched her knees and pulled her skirt down further. If she could feel them, other people must be able to see them, and if they could see them, they would guess what had happened. She blinked sightlessly and calmed herself. No one knew except her, and Aubrey Tavener . . . The bus jerked along, the conductor calling out the stops, the exhaust fumes building in the Easter air. They shuffled through Oxford Street and hiccuped past Marble Arch, Florence holding her bag on her lap, the child next to her sniffing loudly with a cold.

She hadn't been in touch with him for over a week. Usually they would meet every few days, but now, now . . . What was she expected to do? She didn't know. In thirty-four years her sexual adventures had been limited to timorous couplings with a blind man and a brief affair in Italy – the result of a week's package holiday booked at the last minute. Otherwise she had been perceived as a blind woman, and, as everyone knew, the blind had no libido.

Smiling bitterly to herself, Florence thought of Aubrey Taverner. What had he wanted from her? A sexual partner, some grateful, unseeing vessel into which he could empty himself? Some woman who would not expect too much and be flattered? God, how she hated herself for her stupidity. How *could* she have thought he would have felt anything for her? She was neither beautiful nor clever. Edward had been right: Taverner had simply collected another experience from her – without payment.

Florence's fists clenched as she remembered what Edward had said, how he had warned her – but she hadn't listened. She had even muttered some rubbish about not caring about Taverner's indifference, about how he might change . . . Well, she had lied. She *did* care. She cared because she was human and because she needed affection; because, although she couldn't see, she still felt the desires and anxieties of the sighted.

Distraught, her hands went up to her eyes and she rested her fingertips against the lids. Blind! Blind to reason, to sense. Blind . . . The sound of her own stick tapped into her head. He had tapped the stick around the room, teasing her, reminding her of her vulnerability, embarrassing her. Then he had hurt her. Why? she wondered. Why?

Oh, Taverner was extraordinary, she knew that. Extraordinary and unique. She winced as though she felt his hair against her hair, or the pressure of his body on hers. But what did she know of this extraordinary man? Only his voice and his mannerisms and his kindness – that limited kindness which had apparently been exhausted. But why? Why now? What had she done to make him alter?

You've done nothing, she told herself, the fault isn't yours . . . Florence's mouth was firm, her lips pressed together. She had endured humiliation before. Being blind was humiliation enough for anyone. But this was different, this was humiliation of the soul and the deep wounding of the heart. A bitterness lodged inside her. It found its footing and straightened up, unhealthily aroused, and it turned its face to Taverner.

She had tried to dissuade Edward from prying into Taverner's life because she had wanted to protect the man she loved. But not now. If Aubrey Taverner was anxious to conceal his past, he must be hiding something . . . In that instant Florence's heart lurched not with love but with the quick snap of revenge, and as she tapped her way off the bus and down to Green Park, her thoughts were no longer with herself but with the man in Cook's Alley who worked on the second floor of No. 6.

*

'It's Edward.'

'Edward.'

He sighed down the line 'I'm just ringing to say—'

Taverner cut him off in mid-sentence. 'When are you coming back to London?'

'That's what I'm phoning about,' Edward replied pleasantly. He had no desire to provoke his employer: he needed the job to pay for his mother's care and the upkeep of the farmhouse. Good money. Regular money. 'My mother's better.'

'I'm delighted for you both. So when are you coming back?'

The line was muzzy with interference. 'Next week.'

'No sooner?' Taverner countered irritably.

'Can't you manage until then? I have to get things sorted out here.'

'I need help,' Taverner said coldly. 'You were hired as my assistant, if you can't—'

'All right, I'll be back on Friday,' Edward replied, giving in before his employer had time to issue the threat.

'Good. I look forward to seeing you,' Taverner replied, pacified. 'We have some interesting new clients. A lady who came to see me yesterday had a fascinating experience to relate, and Alan Painter's developing nicely.'

Edward's interest was quickly awakened. 'Really? That's good . . . How's Florence?'

The line crackled with static for an instant before Taverner replied. 'You're asking questions again, Edward. Don't do that. You know how it irritates me.'

As Edward talked on the phone upstairs, the housekeeper prepared the vegetables for dinner at Misérie, her heavy legs planted firmly on the cement floor, her forearms deep in the cold water. Above her head a clock ticked, the window displaying the unchanging view of the bleak yard outside. She worked in silence, then dried her hands and sank wearily into one of the kitchen chairs and looked round.

The brass hood over the cooker was dimmed, the calendar two months out of date, but the plaster animals on the window ledge were the same as they had always been and there was still a bunch of dried herbs hanging by the door. Her thoughts moved upwards as she heard the phone click and she remembered the conversation she had had with Edward the previous night. They had been talking about Antoinetta and then paused, both of them hearing something – some unexpected sound from above.

'What was that?'

'A cat,' she replied quickly.

Edward heard the tension in her voice and watched her curiously. She had been with the family since his childhood, had known Hennie, had been in the house when she died.

'Do you hear her sometimes, Jeanne?' he enquired. 'I've often wanted to ask you that.'

The old woman scratched the back of her right hand and shrugged. 'I don't believe in ghosts.'

'But you think Hennie's still around?'

She had a dark look of suspicion. 'I pray for her and light a candle after mass.'

Edward raised his eyebrows. 'She didn't care much for religion.'

'I don't care what she thought! It's for her soul,' Jeanne replied sharply. 'I ask the priest to remember her too. And I put flowers on her grave. I ask for her to find peace, and rest . . .'

Edward leaned towards the old woman. 'But do you ever *feel* her around?'

Startled, Jeanne crossed herself and rose to her feet. 'No, she's dead.'

Not yet, Edward, not yet.

Chapter Twelve

On arriving back in London Edward's first port of call was Ladbrokes. He tried to resist the temptation but hurried in at the last moment before the race, putting five pounds on a horse called the Frenchman. He thought the name was an omen but he was wrong, and the animal came in fifth. The torn pieces of the betting-slip dropped from Edward's fingers and skipped down the road to Ealing Common. Dispirited, he walked on back to his flat, only to find a message waiting for him – from Florence.

Curious, he dialled the number quickly and her melodious voice answered on the third ring.

'Edward, thanks for calling. How's your mother?'

'Better,' he said, still baffled. 'She's making some progress but she's as difficult as ever.'

'I'm sorry. I didn't realize that you didn't get on with her.'

'We shadow-box around each other,' he replied truthfully. 'We don't trust each other. She doesn't even like me, she just wants me to look after her . . . In fact, she wants me to stay in France.'

'Will you?'

'No,' Edward said quickly. 'And I've told her that. Not that it makes any bloody difference. She'll try anything to make me stay. She seems confused at times, but you never know with her. She's always trying to manipulate people.' He paused, uncertain of how to continue. 'How are you?'

'Fine,' she replied. 'No, not fine at all. I've made a fool of myself, Edward, and I owe you an apology.'

He raised his eyebrows. 'For what?'

'For not taking your advice.' Her voice seemed outlined,

harsh, like a tune pitched a key too high. 'I know you want to find out about Aubrey . . .'

His name danced on the line.

'Well, I've thought about it and I want to help you. I think we *should* find out more about him. About his background, I mean.'

Edward's suspicions were immediately aroused: 'Why now?'

She hesitated momentarily. 'His behaviour is getting more and more . . . erratic. "Changeable" was the word you once used.' She paused, picking her way carefully. 'After I talked to you the other day, I began to wonder about him, and after . . . after . . .'

'After what?'

She was torn between embarrassment and the desire to be truthful. 'He's not the man I thought he was.'

Edward sighed. 'He hasn't hurt you, has he?'

'No, I hurt myself,' she said, the lie coming easily, a protective response. 'Listen, Edward, I want to understand him, I *have* to know about him. I just can't accept the situation otherwise.'

'But how can I help?' Edward asked. 'I don't know any more than you do – unless you're holding something back.'

'No,' she said firmly. 'I've told you everything I know. Aubrey *was* ill but he never told me what the illness was, but I suspect it had something to do with his nerves – which was why I overreacted when you asked if he had had a nervous breakdown. I could have asked Aubrey more, but he seemed so eager to avoid the subject, and I didn't want to push him.' Her voice fell. 'But now I want to know what's the matter with him. I *need* to know.'

'I've been trying to find something out myself,' Edward admitted, 'but the hospitals have no record of his even being admitted, let alone treated.'

She laughed unexpectedly. 'How curious you are, Edward!

Aubrey would be so angry to think you had been checking up on him.'

'And how do you think he'll feel if he finds out that you're prying into his life?' Edward queried. 'Anyway, all my detective work came to nothing.'

'Nothing?'

'Nothing.' He paused before asking the next question. 'Are you sure you don't know any more, Florence?'

'I only know what I told you,' she answered, then added quietly, 'but that doesn't mean that I *couldn't* find out more.'

Edward shifted in his seat uncomfortably. 'How?'

'Edward,' she said simply, her tone implying a mixture of humour and incredulity. 'Think that one out for yourself.'

A van was blocking the entrance to Cook's Alley. Edward squeezed past the side of it as the driver carried on a heated argument with a biker on Old Compton Street, his voice rising over the traffic as Edward stopped and, cursing, noticed a smudge of dirt on his jacket. Rubbing off the mark with his hand, he glanced up when he heard a window opening and, seeing him lean out, waved to the printer's boy.

But the boy ignored him and turned his head, looking over the alley. The ash trees were listless in the still air, although a cat basked on a high branch and someone had stuck a cinema poster on one trunk, its colours already fading. The same slow humming of sewing-machines came from No. 3, and yet their rhythm seemed slower, as laborious as the day itself.

Having been away for a while, the melancholic atmosphere of the alley struck Edward forcibly on his return. Working there, he had grown used to its suspended tension and had ceased to notice it, but now the mood unsettled him and he felt a peculiar reluctance to continue.

Slowly he walked on. The cobbles were uneven under his feet. The windows of No. 14 were boarded up, the door criss-crossed with wooden planks. Another business had folded, another inhabitant gone. The listless day hung over the buildings, a phone ringing mournfully from an open window. He glanced over to No. 6. A red glove hung limply from the railings, the fingers empty. His gaze fixed on the article, his vision momentarily blurring, the crimson dancing in front of his eyes.

Yesterday, today and tomorrow swung uneasily together, the sky darkening, clouds moving over the sun, the PR man from the far end of the alley getting into his car. Edward stared at him, thinking for an instant that he was watching someone in another time, and that he was invisible; that somehow he had strayed into a different existence and was not part of his surroundings. A terrible loneliness entered him at that moment, a dismal sense of foreboding, as he realized that he was not participating, only looking on.

The thought disorientated him, but then the moment passed, the printer's boy seeing him and waving, the PR man nodding his head in acknowledgement as he passed in his car.

Aubrey Taverner was standing in the doorway of his office with his arms folded when Edward walked in. The room was gold behind him, a sudden sun making the walls shimmer so luminously that for an instant a halo appeared around his head.

'So the wanderer's returned,' he said, walking into the office, Edward following. He paused by his desk, then slid easily into his leather chair. 'How's your mother?'

The question startled Edward. 'She's making some progress.'

'Has she a nurse?' Taverner asked, his tone lucid with interest.

'Yes, I've just hired one.'

'They cost money.'

Edward nodded.

'Have you enough money to pay for her nursing?' Taverner asked pleasantly, one hand fingering his tie. 'I could help you out with your finances, you know. Especially as you don't seem to be able to keep a firm grip on your salary.' He met Edward's eyes. 'You're still gambling, aren't you?'

'Now and again,' he admitted reluctantly. 'But I can handle it.'

'I'm sure you can,' Taverner replied smoothly. 'But for how long? Medical expenses are always high, and I would hate to think of you worrying unnecessarily.'

Edward hesitated. The interest he had longed for was finally there. At long last his employer was finally expressing some curiosity. Edward was no longer merely a machine to work to order but a human being with a family and responsibilities. The sun dipped unexpectedly, making the room cold.

'It's expensive to hire a nurse, yes. But my mother needs one.'

'So you need a rise?' Taverner asked eagerly, and smiled. The smile pooled in his eyes, it warmed them, and forced a return smile from Edward.

'That would be marvellous,' he answered cautiously.

Taverner wrote a cheque quickly and passed it to Edward across the desk. The writing was quick but clear. He was still smiling.

'I've missed you, you know. Perhaps I have been too busy to compliment you on your work for a while. My error, forgive me.'

Edward was finding it hard to respond. The change in Taverner was so unexpected and so out of character that when he rose to his feet and walked towards him Edward had the sudden ludicrous desire to step back.

'We make a good team,' he said, tapping Edward briefly on the shoulder. The touch was territorial. 'I've grown to rely on you, and the clients like you. You see, Edward, I don't want you to leave, especially if money can make your situation easier.'

'That's very good of you,' Edward said, his tone stilted.

'No, it's only what you deserve,' Taverner retorted, smiling again. 'Welcome back.'

Puzzled, Edward wandered out of his employer's office and into the waiting-room, pausing by the doorway with the cheque in his hand. He read it several times, stunned by the amount, and by the conversation he had just had with Aubrey Taverner.

A voice broke into his thoughts and made him jump.

'You bleeding sick or something?' Martin asked, sitting on the couch with a duffel-bag on his lap. 'Every time I see you, you're always in a flaming daze.'

Edward blinked. 'Martin,' he said, beckoning the boy to him with his forefinger.

The boy rose to his feet reluctantly, his expression fierce. 'I thought you'd gone for ever.'

Edward's face was impassive. 'I trust that that's the only thought we'll ever have in common,' he said, opening the door of Taverner's office and ushering him in.

When he returned to his own office it seemed even narrower than he remembered it. Narrower and hotter. The window was jammed and it took him several minutes to open it. The cat regarded him from the nearby tree and yawned as he leaned out for some air. So Taverner had finally realized his value, Edward thought, as he slid a tape into the machine and pressed the REWIND button. After so long, he had finally admitted that he had grown to depend on his assistant. The thought should have comforted Edward, but it puzzled him instead. Oh, yes, Taverner wasn't quite as arrogant now, but how long would *this* mood last? There was always tomorrow to think of. And yet . . .

Pulling the cheque out of his pocket for the third time, Edward read it and smiled. Half to France to cover the medical expenses, half in the bank, ready for when it was needed. The white cheque tickled his palm, nestling against his flesh luxuriously. With this cheque and his regular salary, he could afford to take a little out for himself . . . Just a little, to while away the time. Just one visit, as a reward. After all, it was his money, he had earned it. The paper sighed up at him. He could go to the casino again – just once – and play a little roulette, a little blackjack. Just once.

But then . . . Angrily, Edward pushed the cheque back into his pocket and turned to the tape. But the recorded words jumped over each other and made no sense, the slip of paper suddenly becoming heavy, dragging the material of his jacket downwards, clamouring for his attention as insistently as a child tugging a sleeve. Struggling to keep his mind on his work, Edward rewound the tape. Dr Gumming's voice came into the room. It hurried in, telling its story, fighting to hold Edward's attention, whilst the cheque fidgeted in his pocket.

Finally Edward rose to his feet, pushing the chair back crossly. The afternoon light was fading, rain making the cobbles shine; two desolate pigeons were fighting for space on the windowledge of the basement at No. 3. He leaned his forehead against the cold windowpane, trying not to see the recurrent image of a spinning roulette wheel, trying to obliterate the sight of the quick sweep of cards on green baize. But the images persisted, the cards pooling into the wheel and spinning together, the pigeons on the windowledge becoming picture cards, birds metamorphosed into paper kings and queens. And the wheel kept spinning, turning, turning, taking Cook's Alley downwards under Soho, sucking it deeply into the green baize . . .

Edward snatched at his coat and began to run down the steps, hurrying towards the bank, the cheque heavy in his pocket. He arrived as they were about to close and waited in the queue, a paying-in slip in his hand. The people inched towards the cashier. Creeping forwards, Edward gripped the cheque, his breathing laboured.

When he finally reached the front of the queue the CLOSED sign went up solidly before his face, like a factory gate. Anxiously Edward rapped on the glass but was ignored. He rapped again and the cashier turned round, reluctantly taking his cheque and filling in the paying-in slip. Edward could feel the skim of sweat on his top lip and wiped his face with the back of his hand, watching the man in front of him.

'You want to put all this in the bank?'

You want to put all this in the bank?

Edward hesitated. His voice seemed to stretch his mouth as he spoke.

'No, half.'

'So you want fifteen hundred pounds to take with you?'

Edward's eyes fixed on the man. Was he stupid? What did he *think* he wanted?

'Yes, I want to take the fifteen hundred with me now,' he said, his heart hurtling, the vein in his neck pulsing. 'Now.'

The cashier counted out the notes slowly. Then recounted them. The images shuffled before Edward's eyes like a pack of cards and when he took the money his hand was shaking.

Chapter Thirteen

PUSHING open the tinted glass double doors of the casino, Edward was immediately confronted by a reception desk manned by two dinner-jacketed men, a leather-bound book in front of them. The taller of the men, hair white and layer-cut, slid from behind the desk, his hand extended.

'Mr Grubeck . . . And you, sir?'

'Dadd, Edward Dadd,' he replied, feeling the pressure of the man's hand and the faint scent of Eau Sauvage. 'I'm a member, a new member,' Edward continued, aware by this time that several people playing inside the casino were looking at him through the second set of glass doors. 'It's my first time here.'

Grubeck smiled, touching the heart area of his dinner shirt as though checking for signs of life. 'I'm in charge of the PR,' he said, smiling warmly. 'Perhaps I could show you around?' he offered, sliding Edward towards the casino, the double doors opening smoothly, without the help of human intervention.

Embarrassed, Edward followed him. The room was healthily busy and unhealthily warm, four roulette tables manned by dealers, the ubiquitous inspector sitting on his stool at the end, a series of blackjack tables set against the outside wall. There were no windows and no clocks.

'Do you have a favourite game?' Grubeck asked, then signalled to a girl in a black off-the-shoulder dress. 'Drink?'

'Mineral water,' Edward said quickly, too quickly.

'Do you prefer roulette or blackjack?' the PR man persisted, 'or perhaps punto banco? We do have a table here.' He touched his shirt front again. 'We like our customers to be relaxed.'

Stiffly, Edward smiled. He had wanted to leave the betting-shops and the race-tracks, had dreamed of visiting casinos, and had already experimented with some of the less select clubs. But this was different. In the most affluent area of London, this was a club where people could afford to lose; to experience the frisson only loss could give. In the perfectly gauged atmosphere of weary appetites, Edward nursed his mineral water and began slowly to perspire.

'The tables are all different, of course, sir. Some have higher stakes than others. For instance, on this . . .' Grubeck waved his hand. '. . . we have twenty-pound chips, on that one . . .' Again, the arm waved across the casino. '. . . the chips are two hundred.' He smiled, nodding briefly to an Oriental man playing blackjack. 'You choose whichever is the most agreeable to you.' He paused again, steering Edward towards another roulette table.

Edward knew he was being watched and that the casino floor was being filmed. The thought made him uncomfortable and he glanced towards the door, the glass of water warming in his hand. He felt too young and too inexperienced, and had the unwelcome impression that he was being laughed at.

Yet the longer he stayed and listened to Grubeck, the more Edward realized that although the casino staff might be interested in their new member, the customers hardly noticed him. Their eyes were fixed on the wheel, all attention focused on the chips and the revolutions which dictated winnings or losses. There was little conversation. Even people who were obviously couples exchanged few words, and the dealers were seldom looked at – their attraction was limited to their hands, nothing else. Edward paused by the roulette table, where two Middle Eastern men were jostling to place their bets opposite him.

'This table, sir?' Grubeck asked, with some surprise.

Having forgotten the man was with him, Edward turned hurriedly and, unwilling to lose face, nodded. 'Yes, I'd like some – ten – chips.'

Grubeck nodded to the dealer. The chips were counted out, harmless plastic chips. Not currency at all, just little disks of plastic – counterfeit, Monopoly money.

His hands damp, Edward placed three of the chips on red 24

and then stood back. Cautiously he waited for the other bets to be laid, then watched the wheel spin, his tongue running quickly over his lips, his guilt lifting as the roulette wheel turned. It turned quickly and yet unendingly; it whirled, taking in the farmhouse at Misérie and an image of Hennie in the storm. It turned on, taking only an instant, yet it seemed to anaesthetize Edward, his anxieties and insecurities all blessedly obliterated by the repeated rotation. Then it slowed, and the serenity inside Edward altered to excitement. Now he leaned forwards, watching. The ball moved, jumped, hesitated and landed in the wheel at red 24.

It took him a second to respond. He looked at the ball in the roulette wheel and then at the chips, and then he heard Grubeck's voice congratulating him and telling him he had won three hundred pounds. Breathing unevenly, Edward frowned and turned to the man. His voice seemed buried, distant.

'Three hundred? But the stake is only two pounds on this table, isn't it?'

The PR man frowned, then smiled, his eyes liquid. 'No, sir, this is the hundred-pound table,' he replied, seeing in Edward the first look of surprise, followed by the second look of understanding and the third of greed. 'It's obviously your lucky night.'

It was. It was a lucky night in Knightsbridge, lucky for Edward, who multiplied his pounds, swelling them, a monetary reproduction taking place without a period of gestation or a twinge of labour pain. He lost all sense of guilt – after all, he was making money, not losing it – and he lost all sense of reason. This was better than betting on the horses, he told himself, as the moon swung over Hyde Park, much better. Anyway, he had always lost on the horses. Maybe he was meant to frequent casinos, maybe this was his *métier*. As the night wore on, he found himself feeling less foolish and less gauche. What did it matter that he was the youngest and least experienced person there? He was winning. People would watch and envy him; they would think he was a natural.

And as he continued to play, Edward found a peculiar camaraderie with the other players. They didn't talk to him, but the odd smile was exchanged, and the waitress was pleasant. Even the pit boss walked past him and nodded briefly when he looked up. By two in the morning Edward was comfortable, like a man experiencing the euphoria of the second drink before the third strikes home. The casino folded its walls around him and he relaxed. This was better than the greasy flat in Ealing; better than the steady deterioration of the house in Misérie. This was all-consuming excitement. When he was playing nothing mattered any more; all life was concentrated like the will of God into the revolving, hypnotizing world of the wheel.

After another half an hour there were no more thoughts of Hennie or his mother, although Edward did remember Taverner and was agonizingly aware that his generosity was the reason why he was now enjoying his present state of grace. The wheel spun again, Edward's heart pulsing, his hands gripping the two remaining chips. I shall win and keep winning, he thought. I shall win and win and win. I'll send money back to France and move out of Ealing. I'll be what I want to be.

What is that, Edward? Hennie seemed to ask.

He kept his eyes on the wheel and answered her in his head. *I want to be at peace, Hennie.*

Oh, she replied, laughing, *is that all?*

That's all, Hennie, that's all.

In a world where there are no windows and no clocks, Edward lost his grip on time, and when he was told the casino was closing he blinked, without understanding. He had walked in with fifteen hundred pounds and walked out with seventeen hundred. The night had been a lucky one. The chips jingled in his hand, they clicked against each other and chatted in his palm as he walked towards the cashier. It was only when he saw the money counted out that he realized it was *cash* – real, living money. Not plastic, not Monopoly money, but real notes with real value.

He walked out into Knightsbridge with the wad in his wallet and a giddy sense of satisfaction dancing in his head – yet as he continued to walk down Brompton Road, the feeling evaporated and he was left with only a numbing sense of anticlimax. His feet quickened, almost as though he could run from the feeling, but it pursued him relentlessly, and when he arrived back at his flat Edward was breathing heavily, his shirt sticking clammily to his back.

'I don't suppose you thought you would see me again, Mr Taverner. I bet you thought old English was finished. You can admit it, I won't mind. I thought the same myself, I can tell you. I bet when you heard what I had to say you thought I'd gone mad. I think I did, for a while.

'It was the waiting that did it. I didn't get used to the thoughts in my head. No one could have done, but the waiting was the worst. She said she would come back you see. Well, of course you remember, you know all about it. You know about Timothy, everything. You came to his funeral . . .'

'Go on, Mr English. Please.'

'It's still hard to talk about him. Even now. But he was a good boy . . . Anyway, the woman did leave to go on holiday, and she left me to look after all those consciences. It was hard work; I was up day and night. I don't sleep well, even when I'm drugged; they still get through. My wife went to live with her sister after a while. I don't blame her, she couldn't understand, even when I explained it to her. She thought I was crazy, that I'd tipped over the edge because of Timothy. Even when I told her about the boy I'd bullied in the Army she couldn't take it in. Even then she didn't understand.

' "That was war time," she said.

' "You had to keep discipline."

' "Everyone knows that."

'I tried to tell her that I had driven the boy to suicide, but she wouldn't understand.

' "That was war."

'"You did what you had to do."

'"Now, don't dwell on it."

'"Get yourself out in the garden."

'"What you need is good fresh air."

'Funny how stupid women can be. They talk about feminine intuition but I don't believe it. My wife hadn't the intuition to know when it was raining . . . Still, that's not important, is it? You want to know about "the woman". Well, so did I. I waited for her to come back, and clung on to the thought of her return, whilst day and night all these sights and sounds kept screaming in my head. But she didn't come back. Wouldn't come. I think she liked being free of her work. I think it pleased her so much that she didn't want to come back, and who could blame her?

'I could. I could blame her, and I did. I cursed her, Mr Taverner. Whilst all these bloody images kept pounding in my head, I cursed her and damned her to hell. I shouted the words so loudly that they almost drowned out the noises in my brain, and then I remembered the address. You know the one? The one she had given me, the one I couldn't write. The one I asked you to write for me.

'Well, I remembered it and I wrote a letter to her, begging for news. I was careful in the letter, careful how I phrased it, but I was firm. When I'd finished writing it, I picked up an envelope and nervously began to write the address. Her address. The one I could never write, the one which altered even as it touched the paper. But do you know what happened this time? I'll tell you, Mr Taverner, because you would never guess. I could write it! Yes, I could! I could write it perfectly. The letters glided on to the envelope, clearly and precisely, bold as brass.

'Oh, God, how wonderful it felt! I was going to be free! Completely free, at last. All the hideous images would go. She would take them away. She would get the letter and come and release me . . . I posted it that morning, and all that day I walked around the house. The noises and scenes were still in my head, that terrible despair was still there, but I could almost cope with it. After all, when she got the letter I would be freed. It was only a matter of time, after all. Only a matter of time.

'I'd posted it first class, so I knew that she would get it the next morning. I could have an answer the following day. It wasn't too long to *wait, not really, not when you considered what was at stake. Just two days, that was all . . . Imagine how it felt, Mr Taverner, waiting to be set free. Waiting to be released from that horrible punishment.*

'Well, I got an answer. Yes, I did. Just as I'd hoped. It came the following day, as expected. I saw the envelope and the sender's address on the back. Her address. *And I felt such relief that I could hardly open it. My hands shook so badly I couldn't focus on the writing, so I laid it on the table.*

'She had written back, I was to be freed.

'Only it wasn't a letter from her. It was from some man writing on behalf of her. He said that he'd received my letter that morning and thanked me for it. Then he said he had some bad news for me. He said sorry . . . Sorry, that was the word. One little word, Mr Taverner. Sorry . . . He said that he was sorry *to have to tell me that the lady I had written to had been killed in a car accident only the day before. If only you had written sooner, he said.*

'If only.'

Experience taken from *Mr Michael English*
Fee paid: *£500*
Signed: *Aubrey Taverner*

Antoinetta's voice was calm, serene. 'I saw Hennie, Edward.'

The words struck out at him.

'Hennie's dead, Mother,' he said quietly, his own voice faltering.

'No, I don't think so.'

'She is dead,' he persisted, his tone a little sharper than necessary. 'Hennie died over two years ago. You must remember that.'

'Don't treat me like a fool, Edward!' Antoinetta snapped. 'I know what I saw, and I saw your sister. I would have thought that would have pleased you. Hennie is here, Edward. *Your*

Hennie. That should be a good enough reason to come home. After all, you always said you loved her so much.'

Her manipulation was crude, obvious. Yet Edward hesitated. Had she really seen Hennie? Or was she just using his sister to force his return?

'She's dead,' Edward repeated again, almost angrily.

She was dead.

He gripped the telephone tightly, steadying himself. He had loved Hennie above everything and everyone. No one had ever matched his sister in beauty or talent. They had been together in the womb and in the heart. No other two people on earth had had such a nexus. And yet Hennie, *his* Hennie, had returned to Mrs Tunbridge in Cook's Alley. She had chosen to visit a woman to whom she meant nothing, a woman who had never known her; had chosen an old lady instead of her brother . . .

The knowledge had rattled against his nerve endings, had ground into his heart; and now to be told that his beloved Hennie had returned to their mother, the woman who had always tried to come between them. No! She wouldn't do that. His mother had to be lying.

'Hennie has gone,' Edward said finally. 'Gone.'

'But—'

'It's over. She's dead.'

'Very well,' Antoinetta replied coldly. 'If that's what you want to believe, Edward. I just thought I should tell you. I thought you would like to know. After all, you two were so close.'

He put the phone down then, severing the connection.

Antoinetta walked back into the drawing-room, her eyes fixed on the ceiling. Maybe it *was* simply imagination. Old houses creaked; it was summer and the wood dried out. That was all. Nothing more. There could be nothing more, could there? Her left hand idly fingered the crucifix around her throat. People didn't come back from the dead, she told herself. I laid flowers on her grave. I know she's dead. The priest said so. The dead stay dead, Unless . . .

'You're a wicked girl, Hennie,' she said out loud, her tone artificially light. 'You're making a fool out of me. I thought you would bring Edward home. I thought that was your purpose. But I was wrong. You're just teasing me, and I won't have it. Do you hear me, I *won't* have it!'

Silence.

'I don't believe in you,' Antoinetta continued, her voice firm as she glanced round the room. 'I won't believe in you. Haunt Edward, if you must, but leave me alone!'

Silence.

'I'm not well, you must know that. Besides, you and I never cared for each other.' Her tone rose, suddenly shrill. 'I don't want you, here, Hennie! Go away. Go to your brother, but get away from me.'

Silence.

'I never meant you any harm, you know that. I just wanted to keep Edward with me. Just the two of us together. You know what that's like, you wanted him too. You can't say you didn't.' Her eyes narrowed suddenly. 'I was wrong to think you would help me. You never did, did you? You never gave a damn for me. Well, I never cared for you either, Hennie! So you can go elsewhere for comfort. Leave me alone. Do you hear me? *Leave me alone!*'

Exhausted, Antoinetta paused to listen. The silence in the room seemed intensified. It hummed in her ears. And then, without knowing why she did so, she turned.

There was a hand at the window, a small, quick hand. One, two, three, it rapped. One, two, three.

Chapter Fourteen

'So, I made my appointment, didn't I? I was rather afraid I wouldn't . . . rather afraid. I'vegotsomenews – sorry, I've got some news for you, Mr Taverner. Something interesting. Well, I thought it was interesting, I hope you will too.'

'I'm sure I will. Tell me about it.'

'I don't sleep any more. I've not been sleeping at all. I don't need to. Apparently I've managed to delay my rest so much that I no longer need sleep. Need sleep. Oh, I know what you're thinking – everyone sleeps, even if it's only to dream. I know what you're thinking. People work out their subconscious in dreams. We dream about jobs, travel, lovers; we do in our dreams what we fear to do in life. We can kill in dreams without punishment, Mr Taverner. We can love without fear of rejection, achieve without effort and enjoy the smile of the world . . . In our dreams, we inhabit our wishes and make a world of our desires. Well, I have cordoned off this area.'

'What?'

'I know how to reach the bliss of sleep and dreams and how to stay there. Peoplewillbeatpeace – sorry, people will be at peace. At peace. Do you know what that means? No rejection, no insecurities. Heaven without God. Without any payment, religious or otherwise. I can do it. I can.'

'I don't understand. You'll have to explain.'

'I can escape to the other side. We thought for years there was life after death. There isn't, only will. Only will. Desire. The force of belief. I can imprison you if my desire is stronger than yours. It's an eternal conflict, a psychological game. Those I love, I can win. Those I hate, I can dismiss. Ifellasleeptheotherweek – sorry, I fell asleep the other week, just after seeing you, and realized at once that the two doctors I spoke of had come to take me with them. But I resisted, I made my will picture them gone – and they went! I pictured myself handsome and I was. I touched my skin and it was firm – no ugliness, no buck teeth, no anxiety.'

'Imagination, Dr Gummings.'

'Yes, that's exactly it. My imagination is my life. My life. Imagination takes us where we desire to go. You know the story of Cambuscan's horse? You don't? Well, there was this brass horse of the gods. You got on its back between sunset and sunrise and whispered into its ear to take you where you wanted to go, then, when you arrived, it disappeared. Well, we don't need Cambuscan's steed any longer, we need only our minds. The imaginative will inherit the earth, Mr Taverner. Do you understand? Those who can see themselves surviving, loving, achieving, they will do these things. Those who accept reality will not. Here we accept ageing, we die as we live. From the womb to the tomb, no more. But there is *more, a life between lives, believe me. Come with me, I'll show you.'*

'I don't believe you.'

'Of course not. Neither would I, a while ago. But it's true. People will come to see imagination as a gift beyond money. There will be imagination banks, imagination advisers, imagination agents who are specialists in their own fields. The imagination will take you to this other life. Only that. Not money nor power. Only imagination . . . And so many people will want to go, Mr Taverner, and not be able. So they will pay imagination couriers to take them . . . You think I'm crazy, don't you? YouthinksoIseeit – sorry, you think so, I see it.'

'I think you're tired, that's all.'

'I see more than you imagine. Don't forget, Mr Taverner, I have nothing to lose. I am between living, death and understanding. There is no home for me. Remember that . . . If I choose I can take you with me. If I choose. But you have your own route, don't you?'

'I live my life my way, yes.'

'Tonight, when you sleep, you will go into lucid dreaming. I will come to meet you then. Together, Mr Taverner, you and I will go into this life I speak about. Then you can see what I mean. Then you will choose . . . The imagination will succeed. My will against yours. My images against yours. No more. If I see it, it is. Whatever I see, exists. If I see chaos, there will be chaos . . .'

'Unless someone else sees peace more strongly.'

'That is your choice, Mr Taverner. Are you stronger than I am or not?

I have nothing to lose. How about you? Take the chance and come with me. I'd pit my wits against yours any day, so how about you? Will you dare, Mr Taverner? Will you? Or are you afraid? Is that it?'

'I don't feel afraid.'

'Are you never afraid?'

'Not that I remember.'

'So will you come? If Icallforyoutonight – sorry, if I call for you tonight, will you come? Will you? Will you?'

EXPERIENCE TAKEN FROM *Dr George Gummings*
FEE PAID: *£200*
SIGNED: *Aubrey Taverner*

'So did you go?' Edward asked, looking at his employer.

'No. He never came for me,' Taverner replied, leaning against Edward's desk, his arms folded. He seemed placid, curiously still.

Edward glanced back to the tape-recorder. One line had lodged in his head: *a life between lives*, Dr Gummings had said, using the same words Hennie had uttered that day at Misérie. *There is a life between lives, Edward,* she had said with such certainty, and now this man had repeated it. Coincidence? No, he didn't think so.

'Do you think he's sane?'

'What's sanity?' Taverner retorted, smiling down at Edward. His hair was pulled back into its usual pigtail, his tie secured with a pearl pin. The white roundness of the gem shone opalescently in the afternoon light. 'He might be mad or not. I'm not an expert on sanity.'

'But what do you think?' Edward countered, surprised by the ease with which his employer was talking.

'I think that Dr Gummings believes in what he is saying. Whether that makes him right is another matter.' Taverner paused, then tapped the computer screen in front of Edward. 'You're doing well, you seem to have caught up with the backlog.'

The compliment caught him off guard. 'I'm getting used to the work.'

'And you're not worrying too much about your mother?'

'A little.'

'But she's being well looked after. You have enough money to see to that.'

Edward glanced away. Taverner saw his response and pursued the matter. 'Still gambling?'

'A little.'

'But you have enough to cover your mother's medical fees?'

'I'm not a fool, I won't let her down.' Edward replied testily. 'Sorry. Yes, I've enough. You've been very generous.'

'I can afford it.' Taverner responded, glancing out of the window down to Cook's Alley. 'I don't want you to leave. I've grown used to you,' he said simply.

Edward felt a rush of emotion – a quick beat of relief, followed by a sense of power. He was now invaluable and his triumph glowed in him. He knew he needed the approval of this man as much as he needed the money; just as he knew he needed the job as much as he needed the relationship. He needed to feel that there was a place for him in Cook's Alley, away from his mother's dependence and his longing for Hennie.

'You've helped me a great deal,' Taverner said quietly.

'I don't intend leaving.'

Taverner smiled faintly, turning his back to the window. His dark suit emphasized the white blond of his hair and when he smiled the expression was one of unexpected sweetness.

'Tell me about your sister, Edward.'

'She . . .' he paused, keen to keep Taverner's interest and yet unwilling to share Hennie. 'We were very close.'

'Twins usually are, I believe.'

'Yes,' Edward agreed, 'but we were closer than most.'

'Even as a boy and girl?'

'Perhaps *because* we were different sexes.'

To his astonishment, Taverner pulled up a chair and sat down. His interest was obvious, his eyes alert. 'Did you love her?'

'Of course,' Edward replied, frowning.

'In what way?'

'In the way that all brothers love their sisters.'

'Not all brothers love their sisters, Edward.'

He smiled in reluctant agreement. 'All right, I loved Hennie more than I loved myself.'

'Ah . . .'

The words had surprised both Taverner and Edward. They had been spoken without thinking – words expressed from instinct, not intellect.

'To love someone more than yourself could be dangerous,' Taverner went on. 'Because if anything were to happen to that person, you would feel doubly bereft. You would feel a loss of the loved one and a sense of loss in yourself. What purpose do you then serve by living without loving? When the person has gone, you must feel not only grief but an overwhelming desire to find a substitute.'

'You do,' Edward agreed hurriedly.

'So what is your substitute?'

'I haven't found one.'

Taverner gazed at him for a long moment. 'Poor Edward, ' he said kindly. 'Do you think you will ever find one?'

He glanced away. 'I don't know.'

'Do you search for someone?'

'I don't think I could find anyone to replace Hennie.'

'I wasn't talking about her. What about other people?'

The question caught Edward off guard and he hesitated. 'I can't imagine loving anyone as much as I loved her.'

'But women, Edward,' he persisted, 'what about other women? Is there none in your life?'

He fidgeted, suddenly threatened. 'Sometimes.'

Taverner's interest faded. The alert look dimmed in his eyes and his thoughts moved on. 'Apparently I've annoyed Florence,' he confided unexpectedly. 'She hasn't come to see me for over a week. She hasn't even phoned.' He stared at Edward. 'Why do you think that is?'

'I don't know.'

'But you talk to her, Edward,' he said firmly. 'You must have some idea.'

'She hasn't said anything specific,' he replied, suddenly on his guard.

'But if you asked her, she might,' Taverner urged him. 'You see, I would like to understand her, and you seem to have the one thing I lack – a rapport with women.'

Edward hesitated. He remembered all too well what Florence had said, and had seen the interest with which the machinist at No. 3 had watched his employer. Around Aubrey Taverner there was always a sense of repressed sexuality, a frosting of intense desire. As an attractive man, it seemed incredible to Edward that Taverner was unaware of his effect on women and yet he seemed oddly bemused.

For an instant Edward wondered if he was teasing him.

'Women seem to like you.'

'Do they?' he queried, frowning as though he was considering the words. 'I wonder.'

'Well, Florence cares for you.'

He turned his gaze on Edward, studying him. For a long moment, two pairs of grey eyes matched each other, then he glanced at his hands.

'I want to ask you a favour,' he said slowly.

Edward felt a sudden rush of warmth. That the enigmatic Taverner could want something from *him*.

'I want you to talk to Florence. See what she feels about me. I would like to understand.' His left hand extended towards Edward, then he paused, resting the tips of his fingers on the edge of the desk. The nails glowed whitely. 'Find out what you can, will you?' he said, his tone light, without body. For one instant he had the transparency of a ghost. 'Help me with this, Edward. Please.'

It had seemed a strange place to meet, but as soon as Edward walked into the Brompton Oratory he saw Florence sitting in the right-hand section of the church, facing the Lady Altar. His shoes tapped noisily on the floor and a cleaner glanced up at him as he passed, a duster suspended over the branches of a candelabra. Automatically Edward raised his heels off the floor, passing the figure of St Peter and pausing beside Florence.

'Edward?' she asked, her face turned to his.

The candles flickered over her skin and made flames in her eyes.

'Yes, it's me,' he said quietly. 'Did we have to meet here?'

She smiled mischievously. 'I thought you were a Catholic, Edward.'

'My mother is,' he replied, 'but my father's Church of England.'

'So you're a lapsed Catholic?'

'I don't think you can lapse from something unless you believed in it once,' he said, glancing around uncomfortably.

'Will you light a candle for me?' she asked, waving her hand in the direction of the altar. 'Here's the money.'

He closed her hand over the coin and dug into his own pocket, slipping the money into the cash box and taking up a candle. It spluttered quickly before lighting, the flame taking hold only as he placed it in the metal tray.

'Who's it for?' he whispered, sitting down beside her.

'Who do you think?'

'Aubrey Taverner?'

'No,' she said firmly, 'someone altogether different.' Her face turned towards his. 'Aren't you lighting one?'

'I don't think so,' he replied, his glance moving towards the altar again. The inlays of lapis lazuli, mother of pearl and agate shimmered in the candlelight, the statue of the Virgin looming above.

'You could light one for your sister.'

Edward laughed softly. 'Hennie wouldn't approve,' he said. 'Besides, if I lit a candle to her she would probably knock it out of the tray and ignite the whole church. The first *auto da fe* from beyond the grave.' He unfastened his jacket and leaned back in the pew. 'She had no time for religion. In fact, she had all the instincts of the born heathen.'

The word came back to him – heathen. The word his mother had used to admonish Hennie when she was a child.

'I don't believe you,' Florence answered, smiling. 'I can't think she was bad.'

'Oh, she wasn't bad, just irreverent. She mistrusted authority in all its forms.'

'She was lucky she didn't live long enough to be forced to change.'

'Hennie would never have changed,' Edward said simply. 'She wasn't open to alteration.'

'Everyone is, in time.'

Something in her tone alerted his interest and Edward glanced curiously at the figure next to him. Florence sat with her hair covered, a creased headscarf masking her light red hair, her hands on her lap.

'Aubrey misses you.'

'*Aubrey*?' she countered. 'Since when have you called him Aubrey?'

Unreasonably embarrassed, Edward flushed. 'He asked me to.'

'So you're friends now?'

Her tone was judgemental, irritated, the deep musicality of her voice striking a dead note.

'No, Florence, not friends. We just talked, that's all.'

'That's how friendship usually begins,' she replied fretfully.

Torn between his loyalty to Florence and his debt to Taverner, Edward hesitated, uncertain of how to reply. Beside him, Florence reached into her bag for a handkerchief and raised it to her face. It took him a moment to realize she was laughing.

'What's so funny?'

'You are,' she said without malice. 'I thought you wanted to find out about Aubrey, all his little secrets, but because he's suddenly shown some interest in you, you've drawn back from me. Who has your loyalty now, Edward?'

You can't ride two horses with one arse.

The phrase came back to Edward almost as though Hennie was sitting beside him, leaning forwards from the pew behind to whisper it in his ear. He turned expectantly.

'What?' Florence queried.

'I was just remembering something my sister used to say,' Edward replied, smiling. 'She always had a way with words.'

'I wonder what she would have made of Aubrey?'

'She would have been curious. More than that, she would have had to know all about him. She hated mysteries.'

'You sound angry with her,' Florence said, her instincts alerting her.

'A little,' Edward replied cautiously.

'Why?'

'She . . . Nothing.'

'Oh, Edward,' she admonished him. 'Tell me what's the matter.'

'Before she died,' Edward began, the candles spluttering before the altar, 'she said she would come back. She made a promise.'

'And she hasn't kept it?'

Edward sighed noisily. 'Oh, yes, she's come back. To everyone except me.' His tone hardened. 'My mother's seen and heard her. I think our housekeeper in France has too. Even Mrs Tunbridge—'

'At Cook's Alley?'

He nodded, then realized that she couldn't see the gesture. 'Yes, even old Mrs Tunbridge. Apparently Hennie paid her a visit one night.' He dug into his pocket and brought out his wallet, laying the faded newspaper cutting in Florence's hand. 'She even left something with her, just to prove she'd been.'

Carefully, Florence's fingers ran over the page. 'What is it?'

'Aubrey's advertisement, entered in *The Times* the day Hennie died.'

The candles spluttered. They fluttered in the still air, then steadied themselves.

'So you're angry with her for not coming to you?'

'I loved her the most. She *should* have come to me first.'

'Sometimes things don't work out the way you expect,' Florence said, handing him back the newspaper cutting. 'Perhaps she's trying to tell you something.'

'Well, she never had any trouble making herself understood before,' he said bitterly.

'You'll have to be patient.'

'Why?' he countered.

'Because that's all you can be,' Florence said soothingly. 'She'll come when she's ready.'

Irritated, Edward changed the subject. 'So, what about Aubrey?'

'What about him?'

'Do you still want to find out about him?'

'Do you?'

He frowned, considering the question. What was there to gain by turning over his employer's past? If Aubrey found out, Edward would lose his friendship, the thing he valued above everything. But his curiosity pushed him on. He didn't need to know, he *had* to know.

'I want to go on with it,' Edward said. 'What about you?'

'Yes.'

'So we try and find out more?' he asked.

She nodded. Her headscarf fluttered.

'He was asking about you this morning,' Edward volunteered.

Her expression was steady.

'He thought he'd offended you.'

Her mouth tightened. One hand automatically extended towards her knees, tugging her skirt down.

Edward saw the gesture but didn't remark on it. 'He wants to see you. He asked me to help.'

This time her face was not calm. Her eyebrows rose, her mouth opening then closing again noiselessly.

'Well, will you see him?'

'He's got you working for him, Edward,' she said, her tone shocked. 'Be careful, please, be careful. You're not dealing with a stupid man. Aubrey is very adept, very clever. He is not what he appears.'

The warning slid over Edward like a shroud. 'He seemed genuinely upset.'

'Upset!' she sneered. 'Aubrey Taverner is *never* upset. He doesn't know how to be. It's not in his make-up to be distressed. Remember that, Edward. He can't feel for people. He can only ask and pry and learn. He can't feel.'

'He seemed upset.'

'You're so stupid!' she snapped furiously. 'Stupid, stupid! You think that because he's been kind to you there's some bond between you.' Her blind eyes turned to his. The pupils were constricted. Tight. 'Do you really need his approval so much? Is there no one else who can give it to you? Don't try and make him into something he isn't,' she said, calming down and taking Edward's hand in her own. 'Don't look for him to fill your emptiness. He can't, and he won't. If you rely on him he might even damage you.'

'Damage me?' Edward echoed incredulously.

'Yes. Some people give. They give automatically, without thought or need. Others give to receive. He gives only to learn. Think about it,' she said, pressing his hand. '*He buys people's experiences*. He *buys* into their lives. He doesn't take chances, doesn't take the time to understand and love people, doesn't risk. He simply buys a place in their lives.' Her tone was bitter. 'Oh, and how they grow to need him. They all begin by thinking that they have the upper hand. That they can walk into Cook's Alley and sell him their stories. They become bloated on their own conceit. Everyone thinks their own life is important and interesting, and he feeds that. He listens, which is the most dangerous thing anyone can do. And we all need to talk. Every one of us. So we do. We talk and he listens – and then he rewards us. He is our eternal mother. Only with Aubrey Taverner there is no breast to suck on, just a payment, a monetary reward for the baring of our souls.'

Her voice had faded, all animation gone. In her blindness she had seen more than Edward ever would.

But he didn't believe her. 'I think you're being too hard on him. Maybe there's a reason why he acts as he does.'

'The reason is fear,' she said chillingly. 'Beware of people who are afraid, Edward, they have no conscience. Aubrey is afraid of himself. I don't know why, but that terror is his motivation. He sees fear in you too, just as he saw it in me. I'm afraid of my blindness, of having to rely on people. You're afraid of your loss, the emptiness inside you. And he's the most afraid of all of us. It's no coincidence that the people who come to see him are all running away from something.' Her hand gripped his, her fingers reddening. 'Think of the clients, Edward, think.'

'Gummings, English . . .' He began to remember, and in remembering her words seemed to take on sense.

'Who else? Edward, who else?'

'Alan Painter . . .' He thought of the depressive with the white scar marks at his wrists. He thought of the numerous hospitalizations. 'But Martin isn't afraid.'

'Martin was the exception, I grant you,' Florence said quietly. 'At first he didn't fit into the pattern at all. But now he's afraid too. Look how he relies on Aubrey, how he comes to see him, to sell him stories. Martin's looking after a sick man. He *needs* Aubrey's money, so now he's afraid that he will fail to amuse, and that at any time the money will cease. And if it does, how will he cope? God, Edward, think! Can't you see how they all fall into the same pattern? Even Martin?'

'But the deaf man,' Edward persisted, 'Glaxman?'

'He is afraid of loneliness,' Florence persisted. 'Edward, who comes to Cook's Alley who's whole? Who's happy? At peace? *Who?* Is there one person who visits Aubrey who isn't faulted? You said so yourself, Edward, when you talked about my blindness. You know what I'm saying is true.'

'But he's just collecting research.'

'For what?'

'A book!' Edward retorted sharply. 'He needs to get together stories for a book.'

'And who will read this book?' Florence demanded. 'A book about fear, loss, loneliness. Who will pay money to buy the misery they can see on the streets any day? No, Edward, there's far more to this than we understand – and we've got to find out what.'

For a long moment Edward stared into Florence's face. She knew that he was scrutinizing her and yet she did not turn away.

'But why do you need to know about Aubrey *now*, Florence? What did he do to make you turn against him?'

She hesitated. The candles shuddered, their light unsteady.

'Is the candle still lit, Edward?'

He glanced over to the altar. 'Yes.'

She nodded, then left.

Chapter Fifteen

THREE months passed. The summer came limping in with intermittent showers and long, overheated nights. In the offices at Cook's Alley Edward arrived at noon and worked on until midnight, the hours filled with spinning tapes, voices pooling over the second floor of No. 6, long after the other buildings had been vacated. Although the capital quietened in August, the procession of clients did not falter. There were always people phoning for appointments, always a selection of feet on the stairs.

Some came hurriedly, running up; others held back and still others came breathlessly, pausing under the skylight at the top of the house. They came with their experiences, wearing them like medals to prove that they too had fought their battles; all ages and all appearances – and they kept coming.

And Aubrey Taverner kept listening. As sultry Soho hung limp in the aftermath of yet another storm, he welcomed Martin, recording the boy's words on the inevitable tape. Apparently Geoff was failing, the disease taking its rapid course, the listless air of London making sleep difficult. True to his word, Martin told Taverner about the upper-class matron who wrote erotica under an assumed name; he even presented his listener with a book to prove what he said. When he had gone, Taverner glanced at it, read a few words and then threw it to the back of his desk drawer. He seemed one of the few who was relaxed in the heat, his suits light-coloured silk, his hair always perfectly in order, whilst Edward sat sweltering in the outer office.

'Get some proper ventilation,' Taverner said, standing by the door, a look of concern on his face. 'You don't have to suffer.'

Listlessly Edward fanned himself with a copy of that day's *Times*. 'I will, when I can find the energy to go out.' The sun swamped the window suddenly, the heat making molten inroads into the narrow space.

Idly, Taverner glanced around. 'You need a better office, Edward,' he said, 'and some nicer furniture.'

His employee's reply was guarded. 'Thanks.'

'Oh, don't thank me, it's only what you deserve,' he said, smiling.

The months had passed evenly, the two men cementing a hesitant friendship, Edward welcoming his employer's interest, Taverner confiding in snatches. At first they didn't socialize, but after a while Edward was lunching with Aubrey Taverner – and sharing an element of Florence's role.

'What did he talk about today?' she would ask when she knew Edward had broken bread with Taverner.

He was cautious on the phone, even though he knew that his employer was engaged with Alan Painter and unlikely to overhear what he said.

'Nothing much. He was talking about the clients most of the time.'

'Nothing more?'

'I'd have told you.'

She was surprised by his tone. 'Would you, Edward?'

'Don't you trust me?' he asked, with faint irritation.

'Of course. It's just that I don't want him to turn you away from me.'

'Why would he?' Edward queried with open astonishment. 'What purpose would that serve?'

'Who knows?' she replied listlessly.

He imagined her in her flat, and even though he had never seen it, he had the impression of lightness and of high windows. Surprising for a blind woman.

'Florence, you and I are in this together, you know that,' he assured her, and then changed the subject. 'When are you seeing him again?'

'The day after tomorrow.'

They both thought of Taverner. Florence thought of his love-making and Edward thought of the image he had seen, the figures on the couch. Both hesitated, unable to keep the flow of the conversation going.

'I just thought . . .'

'What?' she queried.

'Maybe you shouldn't see him.'

'What about our plan?'

Edward glanced over his shoulder out into the corridor. Taverner's office was off limits and not a sound bled out from behind the closed door.

'I don't want you to put yourself into danger.'

'Danger?' she echoed, laughing. 'What danger is there?'

'Well, perhaps danger is too strong a word. But I don't want you to be used, Florence.'

She was touched by the words and paused before continuing. 'You worry too much.'

'You don't worry enough,' he answered protectively.

They talked for a little while longer, but their conversation was forced, their ease with each other strained. Her repeated warnings about Taverner had jangled Edward's nerves so much that after a while he had convinced himself that her animosity was, in fact, jealousy. But as he thought it, he felt guilty, knowing he was judging her unfairly.

Something had happened between them that he did not understand, some incident which had altered their relationship and alienated Florence. She still loved Taverner, Edward was sure of that, but now she disliked him too. He could see the alteration in her manner, the diffidence which came over her as soon as she was in Taverner's presence. Yet she still gave off a sexual need in his company, a form of longing which was palpable – at least to Edward.

But not, it appeared, to Taverner. He treated her in the same way as he always had. Attentive, courteous and yet peculiarly unaware of the desire which emanated from her. As an intuitive woman, Florence tried to disguise her feelings but failed. She knew that her desire was apparent. Yet knowing that didn't make it easier to control, and her tone when she spoke to Taverner was a heady amalgamation of flirtatiousness and provocation.

Which didn't affect him in the least, Edward realized, suddenly wondering if he was misreading the reason for Florence's irritation. Perhaps it had nothing to do with her love affair. Perhaps it had more to do with the growing bond between the two men, a bond she might well resent. Before she had been Taverner's sole confidante. She had listened to him and drawn him out, and she alone had been privy to his thoughts. How distressing, then, to suspect that she was being usurped, that Edward was now encroaching on the territory of which she had thought herself the sole occupant.

For a woman who was handicapped, such a shift in circumstances must have been threatening, so Edward was careful with her. He told her everything that passed between him and Taverner. Her reassured her about their pact and constantly restated their agreement, but as the summer hauled on their friendship shifted and they found that, instead of sharing Aubrey Taverner, they were in constant competition for his attention.

Of course Taverner noticed the unease between them and questioned Edward about it.

'Do you still talk to Florence?'

'Yes.'

'But she doesn't seem so friendly with you any more,' he said, his fine head tilted to one side. 'Why, Edward?'

'Who knows with women?' he had countered, wincing as the words left his lips. 'Maybe she has things on her mind.'

'Like what?'

Edward shrugged. 'Money worries, or maybe she's not well.'

'No,' he said firmly, 'she would have told me. It must be something else. Find out for me, Edward, would you? She talks to you.'

The words lodged in his head and, caught between the two of them, Edward found himself again in the situation of onlooker – and resented it. Their plan was not working. Neither he nor Florence was uncovering more about Taverner, except for the odd scrap he threw out when his guard dropped. *If* his guard dropped. Perhaps he was merely scattering his thoughts like largesse, feeding their curiosity as a tourist feeds pigeons – without thought.

But Edward doubted that. His employer never did anything spontaneously. He was well aware of Edward's interest and Florence's. He was aware of it, he used it – and he needed it. Just as Edward needed Taverner emotionally and financially. So the peculiar *ménage à trois* waltzed around each other with the perpetual motion of clockwork figures. They all followed the steps and all heard the music, but Taverner controlled the rhythm of the dance.

In Misérie, Antoinetta was recovering in snatches, the plaster cast removed from her arm, her mental state altering daily. At times she pretended to be indifferent to the world; then she would be fiercely alert. Mystified by her condition, the doctor frequently summoned Edward back to France, and for a while she would rally – only to relapse as soon as he made plans to leave. Caught up in her manipulations, Edward was frequently irritated and would cajole or bully her as he saw fit. But the effort exhausted him and he always returned to London depleted.

Not that Aubrey Taverner complained. Edward felt an unexpected rush of gratitude towards his employer. Who else would have endured such behaviour? Who else would silently leave cheques in an employee's desk – money willingly given and urgently needed? But not just for Antoinetta. The money was also needed for the upkeep of Edward's new flat in Holland Park Avenue and the small hired BMW. It was needed for the membership fee to the casino and to pay off Edward's gambling debts. Without complaint, Taverner moved into the role of indulgent father, paying for his son's excesses, whilst retaining the status of employer. And what did Edward do to reward him? Why, he became gradually blind and deaf. He exchanged his curiosity for the affection of Aubrey Taverner, and his integrity for the money he needed to absolve the guilt such behaviour inspired in him.

He had not the inclination or the insight to see the circle in which he so readily spun. Like the roulette wheel, he was activated by an outsider, the dealer's hand replaced by that of Aubrey Taverner, but he could not see it. As his employer flattered and relied on him more, Edward believed that he held the trump card, and foolishly never considered how he was being played along. Hennie would have seen it immediately but Edward couldn't. Wouldn't. He saw only what he wanted to see. The affection and approval he had longed for were now his, and he would do anything to avoid losing them.

In his limited way Edward was happy. Being a man who appreciated happiness, he could make a little affection seem boundless. That was his talent. But it was also his failing. As a child he had always had his sister's perception to protect him; now Edward had only himself to rely upon. It was not enough.

'Taverner's using you.'

'Oh, Florence, not again.' He sighed. 'We've been through this before. I owe him.'

'You're immune to reason!' Florence said, her voice, freed of its melodious tone, turning suddenly savage. 'He's eating into you and you don't see it.'

'Florence, he's *helping* me!' Edward said with irritation. 'How else could I pay for my mother's treatment?'

'And your flat, and your car, and your gambling,' she reminded him.

He resented her interference. 'It's nothing to do with you.'

'Since when?' she countered. 'We were friends, Edward. We still should be. Why do you allow yourself to be taken over by Taverner? You didn't *need* the flat or the car, and you don't need to gamble. You could be free of him. Free of any debt to him, if only you'd see the situation as I do. You don't need *him*; he needs *you*.'

His tone was cold. 'As a secretary?'

'No, not as a secretary. It is far more complicated than that,' she responded quietly. 'Aubrey Taverner needs your adoration and your dependency. Don't ask me why, I don't know. But I'll find out, Edward. In time, I *will* find out.'

He hesitated before he said the next words. 'Maybe I don't want you to.'

'Never refuse help, Edward. The time will come when you may need it.'

But Edward ignored her advice and, as he moved further towards Taverner, his world shrank into the tiny kingdom of his own making. He moved between Misérie, his flat, the casinos and Cook's Alley. He had no friends other than the one he valued above all others, and he had no thoughts other than those which were in line with Taverner's. It did not seem to Edward that he had lost anything. He had always loved with total absorption and his temperament was constant; it was only the object of his love which altered.

So summer drowsed on, vicious storms rattling the windows of Cook's Alley – Dr Wells barking hoarsely from the basement below as Alan Painter's steps sounded on the staircase.

'I like women. All sorts. Can't get enough of them. And they like me. They all like a bastard. True, just like all women are stupid. Only good for one thing. Up North you don't get feminists. Feminists! Ugly cows. Can't stand them. Can't stand clever women. Not that there are any.

'I met this one at a pub. Picked her up. They're all willing. Then they act so bloody surprised when you make a move. This one was OK. Not

thrilling. OK. She didn't say much. Makes a change. Just drank. And smoked. I don't like women smoking, the smell stays on them. But what can you say? I wanted to sleep with her, not reform her.

'She said she was a hairdresser. Not that you'd have known from looking at her. We went to a club. Not expensive. Well, I don't splash out until I know I'll get something in return. But it was all right. She danced a bit. Not bad. Had a tight skirt on and a black top. A bit overweight, but busty. So that was OK. She danced like I wasn't there. All wrapped up in herself. Which was a bit thick, since I'd paid to take her there. The least she could have done was to make up to me a bit. But she just danced, like she was in a daze.

'I gave it an hour. After that, I'd make my move. Offer to drive her home. Take her to my place instead.

' "Like a coffee?"

' "Well, I shouldn't, it's late."

' "Not that late. I'll drive you home afterwards."

'Then they act surprised when you try it on! Like every woman under fifty's a virgin. Verging on the bloody ridiculous, if you ask me . . . But this one was different. Drinks the coffee, then goes into the bedroom. Just like that! Didn't say a word. Just got on with it. Well, I put the dog out, like I always do when I get romantic. Out into the yard. He howls a bit, but I can't have him indoors, he puts me off.

'But to get back to the woman . . . I couldn't believe my luck. An hour or so later she's up and dressed. Walking to the door.

' "Thanks for the coffee. I'll be seeing you."

' "You don't want a lift?"

' "No, thanks. I'll walk."

'And off she goes. Then I let the dog in. He's sulking, like he always does, but that's life. He should be used to it by now.

'Anyway, next night she comes round with her girlfriend. Yeah, Mr Taverner, she comes round to my flat with her friend*! And the same thing happens. I put the dog out. He howls. They go through the routine. Coffee, bed, out. I can't believe my luck! All this is costing me is a tin of Nescafé. Nothing else. Oh, and extra dog food, to make up to the flaming animal for sticking him in the yard.*

'So the next night she comes with two *girls! Imagine it, well, try to . . . Always the same – put the dog in the yard, then coffee, bed, out. None of that phoney love stuff. Just in and out. Well, you can imagine, this was some way to live. I was beginning to think there really was a God when the girl stops coming. Nothing for a week. Then she's back on the doorstep and we go through the whole scene again. First her, then the other girls, then on the third night she brings this woman.*

'I don't want to be cruel. But you've got to be honest. Ugly – that wasn't the word for this one. She could have turned milk. And there's the girl expecting me to perform. No way! I mean, there's a limit. So she starts crying and saying that this lump's her friend. So what? I'm not desperate, even if she was.

'So she got mad. Real mad! She said I'd insulted her friend. Insulted her*! What the hell had she done to me? Anyway she storms out with this gargoyle and the next day the dog's gone.'*

'The dog?'

'Yeah, my dog, Tyson. The one I put out in the yard. She'd kidnapped my bloody dog! Anyway, I went to the police. They thought it was a great joke. Laughed like hell. Said maybe the girl had paired the dog off with her friend. Very funny! I loved that dog. Only thing I ever loved. I adored that dog. It went everywhere with me. Walks, ran by the bike, the works. I was never lonely with that dog. He was my only friend. D'you know what that's like, Mr Taverner, losing the one thing you love? He was my world, and even though he used to get mad when I put him out, he always forgave me later. And because I'd told that ugly bitch to get lost, they took my dog!'

'So what happened then?'

'I slept with her, didn't I? I mean, it was the only way to get the dog back, and love's love, isn't it? Isn't it? I mean, I'd like to think he'd have done the same for me. The dog, that is. But life's a bitch. The dog didn't want to come home. *It liked her better. Her! That ugly cow. He* stayed with her, *and wouldn't come home.*

'So now she brings the dog to see me when she visits. We share custody of the bloody animal, and the dog just sits there, looking at me, probably thinking about all the times I put it in the yard, and laughing to itself.'

EXPERIENCE TAKEN FROM *Mr Alan Painter*
FEE PAID: £450
SIGNED: *Aubrey Taverner*

Edward heard the tape and leaned back in his seat, frowning. He knew Alan Painter, and knew that this experience had been for his benefit. It might be true, it might not. That wasn't important. What was important was that Painter knew he would *listen* to it. He would hear about the women and wonder, he would think about the women and wonder, he would imagine the scene in his head and wonder.

Impatiently Edward took off his headphones and tried to dismiss the images, but he knew that Painter was baiting him. Taverner wouldn't realize it. In fact, he would be amused, thinking of the dog. He wouldn't have the sour taste in his mouth that Edward now had. How could he? He was buying the experiences, he was in control. He wasn't sitting in a narrow, airless little office, listening.

It took a while for Edward to shake off the feeling of unease, and only when he had typed up several more pages did it finally lift. His thoughts drifted. He forgot Painter's story, thinking of the casino instead and the gambling he looked forward to that night. He typed automatically, listening to the voices in his headphones, their stories sliding from the tape to the screen. He typed without thinking, without considering what he typed. He stood back in his head and kept his thoughts to himself, putting forward no judgements to risk Taverner's anger. He watched and he listened. No more.

Some clients visited regularly, others disappeared, like the medical secretary from St George's. She never came back. All that was left of her was her experience on the computer. That, and the umbrella she had left by mistake, an umbrella which had pride of place in Taverner's cloakroom. Otherwise there was no trace.

In her place came others, like Chloë. Pretty, clever Chloë, who wanted Taverner; pretty, clever Chloë about whom Edward and his employer laughed late in the night. Not unkindly, not really, only with amused detachment. She was tall and came in on the first day wearing a short linen dress and flat shoes. Her legs were brown, her hair long, down her back, and she wore a pair of sunglasses rimmed in gold and a watch with the face of Mona Lisa on the dial.

'I hope you won't think I'm being silly, but odd things happen to me, Mr Taverner. I was born in Holland. My parents were quite well off and I was sent to school in England, in Berkshire. I never got homesick . . . never. The others did, but not me. Well, anyway, after a little while I found that I liked to steal. Not just that – I needed *to steal. I stole everything I could: pens, books, food . . . I didn't need it, I just stole it.'*

'Go on.'

'Well, I got caught, of course. You always do in the end. I was expelled and sent home to Holland, but I ran away – I was seventeen at the time – and I met up with this man in London. Did I tell you I came to London? Well, I did. At seventeen. I wasn't what you think, Mr Taverner. I wasn't a prostitute, just a thief. That counts for something, doesn't it?

'I stole for him. You know, we would go out to some show and I would steal from the women in the toilets. They left their bags around, but more, they used to take off their jewellery to wash their hands. Rings like you couldn't imagine, all left there. Claridges was the best. The women just went into the loo there and got so busy talking and powdering their noses that they forgot to be careful . . . And I was always that. I stole from them and of course no one suspected me because I was as well dressed as they were, and I had jewellery as good as theirs.'

'So then what happened?'

'I stole one woman's bag one night at the opera. She'd left it on the

bar stool and I took it. She never saw me. In fact, when all the brouhaha broke out, I helped her look for it. She was very grateful to me . . . Anyway, in this bag there was a card, a business card, with the name of my man friend on it. So I got to thinking, and when I kept seeing this woman in the same places as I was working, I finally realized that he was running both of us! We were both *stealing for him. There was a character in Dickens like him – Fagin – only difference was that* he *wasn't sleeping with the Artful Dodger.'*

'Go on.'

'So this woman and I got together. We got rid of our man friend and recruited some other girls. We got clever, dressing the part. After all, there's no point going into the National Gallery in an Armani suit or attending Ascot in jeans. We slid into our roles so well that no one suspected us. We stole and pickpocketed and it was marvellous. Then one of the girls suddenly discovered that she wasn't criminally minded. She wanted to drop out. Fine, we said, but that wasn't all. She wanted to make a clean breast of it. Confess all. Including our *part in the story.*

'We had to stop her, naturally. But how? How, Mr Taverner. You tell me. You can't kill someone, that's just for the movies, but we had to find a way to stop her talking. What better way to make someone feel less guilty about what they have *done than by making it look as though they have done something worse?'*

'Pardon? I don't understand.'

'Listen, I'll explain. She wanted to be respectable, so we obliged. What's the most respectable thing anyone can do? Why, get married! So we married her.'

'What?'

'We were in Las Vegas when we plotted it. We took her out for a meal to say goodbye and to tell her that we completely understood that she was going to expose us. And she believed it! She fell for it. We then gave her a couple of drinks, drugged one of them, and when she passed out we slipped a ring on her finger, left a fake marriage licence in her bag, took her to a motel and left her unconscious to wake up the following morning as the blushing bride – sans *bridegroom, who had apparently regretted his hasty action.'*

'I don't understand. Why would that silence her?'

'Because she's already married! Well, she came to and went berserk. She thought she was a bigamist and was terrified that her husband in England would find out. Or the police. She said she couldn't remember a thing, and kept asking us about the man she had supposedly married. Well, we went along with it, didn't we? We made up some dumb story about a Lebanese waiter at the Sands who had fallen head over heels in love with her, married her and then disappeared, having apparently had second thoughts. We hinted that he was also the worse for wear that night. You know, been drinking heavily. Well, she kept asking questions and got into a terrible state. Naturally this little incident took her mind off going to the police – stealing seems nothing compared to bigamy.'

'Is that all?'

'No, that's only really the beginning. You see, this woman is a little . . . intense . . . and it turns out that she wasn't really in love with her husband in England and so now she wants to find her phantom spouse! She's crazy for him, and everything we said about him she believed. She's been back to Las Vegas, asking about this ghost and searching for him. She's in love with a man who doesn't exist!

'Sorry, I shouldn't laugh, but it's just so ridiculous. Can you imagine anyone being so stupid? He doesn't exist Mr Taverner, our Lebanese waiter doesn't even exist!'

EXPERIENCE TAKEN FROM *Miss Chloë Farrier*
FEE PAID: *£420*
SIGNED: *Aubrey Taverner*

The story stunned Taverner. He admitted as much to Edward when Chloë left, watching her as she walked down the alley, her bag swinging cheerfully against her right thigh.

'There goes a clever, pretty woman,' he said.

Intrigued, Edward leaned out of the window for another look. 'But tough.'

'Do you think that's a failing in a woman, Edward?'

He shrugged. 'Depends. It's not good for a woman to be hard.'

'So what makes Chloë hard?'

'Stealing,' Edward said flatly, 'and playing a cruel joke on someone helpless—'

'But the other woman was also a thief.'

'But she wanted to stop.'

'And punish the others at the same time,' Taverner reminded him. 'We shouldn't sit in judgement over our clients, you know.'

Edward let the barb pass. 'Do you think she'll be back?'

Taverner nodded thoughtfully. 'She won't be able to help herself.'

He was right. The lovely Chloë returned weekly, with a variety of stories to tell. She was always well dressed, always light-hearted, always funny. Her footstep lingered on the stairs, and something of her – some amoral scent – loitered about the offices long after she had gone. Without truly liking her, Edward looked forward to her visits, seeing some vague recollection of Hennie in her. Not that he thought of his sister much any more. Inexplicably disappointed in her, he turned his attention to the living, no longer listening or looking for the dead. Hennie was gone, that was reality. Never had any man wanted so much to be haunted, and when the ghost refused to oblige, it was forgotten. Until Edward saw someone like Chloë, and thought about Hennie again . . .

But other clients were not blessed with Chloë's down-at-heel charm, and remained permanently tedious. Like Mr Glaxman. He had had a long summer. The heat and rain had swamped the colour out of him and when he came to Cook's Alley he climbed the stairs slowly, wearing a summer shirt, the flesh-coloured wire of his hearing-aid hanging listlessly in the torpid air.

Edward was already waiting for him on the landing. 'How are you?'

'I've never had it.'

Patiently he repeated the question. 'I asked you how you were.'

Mr Glaxman shot him a dire look. 'You should speak up. I can hear every word Mr Taverner says. You mumble. I can never catch a bloody thing!'

Edward sighed. 'It's hot today.'

'Well, you got that right, at least,' Mr Glaxman said, panting for breath. 'Is he ready for me?'

'Ready and waiting,' Edward replied, exasperated as he showed the old man in.

He had just finished English's last tape when he heard a familiar sound outside and rose to his feet. She came along the alleyway in the same way she had always done, only this time her appearance seemed altered. Wearing a loose white dress and shoes, Florence looked at first oddly diminished and yet there was an unsettling physicality about her. Slowly, she tapped her stick along the railings, striking every third one, the sound sidling up to Edward's open window as it had done the first time he met her.

Hesitating only momentarily, Edward ran downstairs. Dr Wells was already rushing up from the basement to greet the visitor.

Florence's head was bent down towards the dog, her hand on its back. 'Oh, hello, boy, how are you today?' she asked, her voice so low and sensual that the hairs rose on the back of Edward's neck.

'Florence,' he said simply. 'It's good to see you.'

She did not glance up. Instead her hand worked along the dog's back, the heat of the summer's afternoon dragging on the limp cotton of her dress.

'Won't you come in?'

She still continued to stroke the dog. Her hands spoke for her.

'Are you angry with me?'

Lifting her head, she finally turned her face towards him. If she could have seen him she would have been surprised by the change in Edward in only a few weeks. He was as finely handsome and blond as he had ever been, but his expensive suits were now carbon copies of Aubrey Taverner's and his hair was longer than before.

'Florence, please say something,'

'I wondered if you would be here,' she answered.

'And you're sorry that I am?'

'Don't pick a fight with me, Edward,' she said, chastising him. 'I haven't the stomach for it.'

'I didn't mean to argue with you,' he replied, glancing across the alley. On the steps opposite the machinist sat with her latest admirer. The printer's boy had long gone and her attentions now were fixed on the fat PR man from No. 2.

Edward dropped his voice.

'Come up. He'll want to see you.'

'I don't think so,' she replied, jumping when she heard the basement door open.

'How are you, dear?' Mrs Tunbridge asked, struggling up the steps towards Florence. 'I was only thinking of you this morning. There was a programme on the radio about the blind.' She tugged on the dog's tail. 'Radio Four, I think it was, but I can't be sure. They're all pretty much the same, all going on about babies or germs in the food. You know what I mean – bugs.' She paused, putting her head on one side. The heat made her hair limp, flat against her head. 'You look different. Is everything all right with you?'

'Fine,' Florence answered.

'Well, you don't look fine,' Mrs Tunbridge replied briskly, turning to Edward. 'You want to take her indoors and give her a nice cool drink.'

'I was just about to do that.'

'Lemonade would be nice,' Mrs Tunbridge went on, staring hard into Florence's face. 'You take care of yourself, girl. You have to. No one else will.'

They climbed the stairs in silence, Florence's stick tapping out her way. It seemed to have a melancholy sound to Edward's ears and he realized for the first time how his behaviour must have wounded her. They had kept in touch, saw each other when she visited Taverner, and spoke several times a week on the phone. But the urgency of their pact had dwindled. Each assured the other that they still wanted to uncover Taverner's history, but the words lacked conviction and sounded hollow in their ears.

Edward knew he had rejected her, that his allegiance to Taverner had edged her out, and he knew that she felt it also. *I walk in a blind world, Edward*, she had once said. A blind world without the comfort of sight; a world where so much guesswork and trust were exchanged for knowledge. A world which relied on others, and on others' integrity. An uncertain world.

Edward's manner was stiff. 'If you don't mind waiting,' he said as he ushered her into his office, 'Aubrey should be out in about ten minutes.'

She sat down, resting her hands on the top of her stick. 'I'm in no hurry.'

'Listen, Florence,' he said aimlessly, 'I feel as though I've let you down.'

'Why?' she asked simply. 'Because your first loyalty is to Aubrey and not to me? Well, what should I say to that? That it doesn't matter?' Her eyes turned to his. Without expression. Dummy eyes. 'Well, it does. I wanted to help you, Edward, and I thought you wanted to help me. But I was wrong. He has the upper hand – as usual.' Her voice shattered, and she dropped her head. 'I'm tired, Edward, so tired.'

He leaned towards her.

She didn't see the movement, only sensed it, and drew back from him.

'Don't!'

'Listen, Florence—'

'No, Edward! I don't want to listen to you, or to anyone.'

Her distress rode the walls. It slid long, listless arms across the desk; it laid its head down wearily. Her voice seemed to be drawn from her. Not spoken, but pulled from her body. 'I can't think clearly any more.'

'Tell me what it is. Tell me what's troubling you.'

Her hand moved over her chest. It hovered in the hot air and then came to rest on her abdomen. Through the white dress, her breathing came rapidly in the stillness.

'Will he help me?'

'Who? Aubrey?'

She nodded. 'Will he?'

'Yes, of course,' Edward assured her.

'You never told him what I said about him?' she asked, her voice tremulous. 'You didn't, did you? Not even when you and he became friends?'

Her anxiety touched him and he reached out, his left hand covering her own, both lying on her stomach.

'I'm so afraid.'

'Why?'

'Everywhere I go there's darkness . . .' She stopped, breathing in brokenly. 'I was never so lost before. Never. Even blind, I never felt like this.'

He was genuinely distressed. 'What is it, Florence? What is it?'

There was no expression in her eyes. 'I'm pregnant, Edward.'

The confession left him without words.

'It's Aubrey's child. Of course, who else's?'

An image of the two of them in the waiting-room came back to Edward. Florence's form under the sleeping Taverner, her face turned against the white frost of his hair.

'You'll have to tell him.'

'Yes.'

'He'll help.'

'Yes.'

'He'll see you have the best care,' Edward went on blindly. 'Or something . . .'

The implication darted between them like an arrow. Or . . . Or what? Abortion? Edward swallowed.

'I won't get rid of it.'

'No.'

'I won't!' Florence insisted. Her hand fluttered under his. For an instant he had the impression that he had felt the child move.

'You don't have to make any decisions now.'

'I won't get rid of it!'

'No,' Edward repeated lamely.

Florence pregnant with Aubrey Taverner's child. The thought whirled in his head. Pregnant with Taverner's child. How could she? He felt sudden anger towards her, an unexpected jealousy, then a rush of remorse as he clutched her hand.

'We'll help you. Don't worry.'

'I suspected it for a while before I knew for certain,' she went on. 'That was one of the reasons why I had to find out about him. He's the father of my child. *The father.* I *should* know about him. I should. Who is he?' she said, her voice rising. 'Tell me, who is he?'

'Sssh! He'll hear you,' Edward said hurriedly, glancing towards the door of his employer's office. 'Calm down, Florence, please. He's just Aubrey, Aubrey Taverner. That's all.'

'That's *all*!' she repeated incredulously. 'God, you're stupid, Edward.'

He flinched and said coldly, 'If you want to know about Aubrey, ask him. You're carrying his child. You have a right to know.'

'What if he already has a family?'

'I doubt it,' Edward said drily. 'I doubt that any man could work the hours he does and still have a wife to go home to.'

'He might have children.'

Edward frowned. 'No, I can't believe that.'

'So, if he has no one, do you think he might be *glad*? Do you think he might want this baby, Edward? Do you?' Her voice pleaded with him, begged for a reassurance which was not his to give.

'I don't know. He might . . . You have to ask him.'

She bent over suddenly, as though winded, and rocked herself. Edward could feel his hand against her breast and tried to withdraw it, but she held on to him.

'Stay with me when I tell him. Please.'

'I can't.'

'Oh, God, Edward,' she said fiercely. 'You owe me that much.'

They waited for the office door to open. They waited, the hands of the clock moving through the seconds and the minutes. The sun hummed on the roof tiles, the sky cloudless, the far-off sound of a sewing-machine coming in through the open window. They waited. And Mr Glaxman continued to talk, continued to hold Aubrey Taverner's attention long after he should have done – an old man with tiresome memories talking on and on whilst Florence sat in the office rocking herself unceasingly in the humid air.

Chapter Sixteen

SLOWLY and luxuriously, Antoinetta prepared to meet the day. Without disturbing the housekeeper, she got out of bed and padded quietly to the bathroom. The water spluttered noisily into the deep tub, a sponge bobbing on the surface, pummelled by the heavy gush of the inflowing water. With effort, Antoinetta pulled off her nightdress and lowered herself into the bath, her long legs bent slightly at the knees, her arms floating. She closed her eyes, shutting out the sight of the slack flesh of her stomach and the heavy fall of breast, and in her mind she savoured her course of action.

Her hands moved listlessly under the water, her hair piled on her head, the warmth lapping at the nape of her neck. Gradually the window in the bathroom steamed up, as did the mirror, the heavy dripping of the old tap hitting the water between her feet.

Suddenly a memory jolted her and her eyes flickered up to the ceiling. The night had been disturbed by dreams, sounds unexpected and distorted, footfalls in the morning before dawn. She smiled, her expression cunning. The telephone conversation she had had with Edward the previous night had been illuminating. Oh, he might say that he didn't believe her, might insist that Hennie was dead and that his mother was just imagining things, but she knew her son well enough to realize that he would worry, and in worrying he would think about Misérie and long for his childhood, and in longing he would return . . . She sighed with satisfaction. If Edward came home, she would be looked after, would have company, attention. *If* Edward came home.

It annoyed her that she wouldn't be the reason for his return; that Hennie had, even in death, more power than she. But if that was the way it had to be, she would adjust. After all, the result was the important thing, not the method of achieving it. She had to get her son home. That was all that mattered. If that meant creaking floorboards became the walk of the dead, so what? If it meant that she allowed her imagination to see and hear things that might or might not be there, so what? Hennie might be a ghost at Misérie, or not. What did she care if it brought Edward home? All that mattered was that *Edward* believed Hennie was there.

Antoinetta smiled, roundly confident. Edward could always be manipulated, always persuaded to help, always made to feel guilty. Oh, yes, he could be enticed home. In fact, she was going to use every means at her disposal to *ensure* that he would . . . There was always a solution, she thought contentedly, climbing out of the bath and drying herself. Edward might resist now, but he *would* return. She would slowly and certainly draw him back, baiting the way to Misérie with Hennie's real or imagined help.

Parking the car, Edward glanced into the back seat, frowning. Asleep, Florence lay on her side, her legs curled up, her head tucked towards her chest. He had never considered her age before and found it difficult to gauge. She could have been twenty-five or forty. Her skin was bland, without the lining which dictated ageing, but there was a definite tightness around the mouth which suggested the passing of thirty.

Yet as Florence slept on, the tightness relaxed and now she seemed hardly more than a teenager. She breathed regularly, as she had done on the boat, although he knew she was apprehensive. Not frightened – all Florence's fear had been exhausted, her meeting with Aubrey Taverner taking her well beyond anything she could have anticipated – but she still breathed narrowly and the sound made quick catches in her throat. Edward sighed, winding down the window and taking several deep breaths of French air.

Whilst Florence had waited to tell Aubery Taverner her news, Glaxman had outstayed his welcome. He had remained long after it was necessary and even hesitated on the stairs before walking away. Edward had seen him go from the doorway of his office, then slipped in to see his employer, leaving Florence in the office outside. Taverner had been bent over one of the display cabinets, a piece of ornamental carving in his hand, his pigtail as white as a bone.

'Florence is here,' Edward said simply. Too simply, as though there was nothing extraordinary about her visit.

Taverner had hesitated, then straightened up. 'Is she well?'

'Fine,' Edward replied half-heartedly. 'She wants to see you.'

His eyes had narrowed, his face suddenly feral. But the look lifted as he sat down behind his desk, one hand on the tape-machine.

'Mr Glaxman had something interesting to say—'

Edward interrupted him impatiently. 'Florence wants to see you. She *needs* to see you.'

'I want this tape putting on the computer.'

'Didn't you hear me!' Edward snapped, walking towards the desk. '*Florence is here*. She's waiting to see you.'

'Why?' he said simply, the word dense with suspicion, as though he already suspected something.

'She has to talk to you.'

'What about?'

'*She* has to tell you that.' Edward insisted. 'Listen, let me bring her in.'

Taverner raised his hands as though to stop him. To Edward's astonishment, his eyes were full of tears.

'No. I can't see her.'

'You have to.'

'I *have* to do nothing,' he said quietly.

'Please see her,' Edward pleaded, thinking of the distraught woman in the other room, waiting and rocking herself. 'You have to see her . . . Aubrey, what do you want me to do? Aubrey?'

There was no answer.

Angered, Edward backed out of the room.

'Come on, you've got to face him,' he said gently, taking Florence's arm. 'I'll stay with you.'

She nodded, turning blankly towards him. 'Is he in a good mood. Is he, Edward?'

'He's . . . OK,' he blundered. 'Come on, I'll help you.'

She stumbled into Taverner's office, unusually clumsy as Edward helped her to a seat. The draped walls threw up the colour of the hot day and the warmth seeped dangerously over the three of them. In silence, Taverner regarded his visitor, her face tight with anxiety. She had stopped rocking and her hands were now still on her lap, the white dress tinted yellow in the strained light.

'Well?'

Taverner's voice cut through unexpectedly and she jumped. Her reply was clumsy. 'Are you all right, Aubrey?'

'Yes. I'm fine,' he answered, glancing over to Edward standing protectively by Florence's side. Their allegiance unsettled him.

'I wanted to see you,' she said lamely.

'Why?'

'*Why?*' she echoed hollowly.

Edward stared at his employer, repelled by the callousness of his voice. The tears had gone. He even wondered if he had imagined them.

'Why?' she repeated. 'Because I'm having a baby, that's why. Yours.'

There was only a momentary pause as the words fought for space in Taverner's understanding, then he reacted. Rising quickly to his feet, he moved round the desk and raised his hand.

She didn't see him, but she anticipated the action and ducked, her body twisting away as she lost her balance and fell heavily off the chair.

'Christ!' Edward said disbelievingly, lunging forward and knocking Taverner back against the desk. 'You bastard!' he shouted, turning away from his employer and kneeling down next to Florence.

Her face was expressionless, her right hand extended in front of her, her fingers grappling for her stick. Dumb with pity, Edward tried to lift her, but she resisted.

'Go away!' she hissed, finding the stick and getting awkwardly to her feet.

'Florence, let me help you . . .'

But she pushed his hand away and turned to Taverner.

His face was dead, without expression. All his anger had been concentrated in the attempted blow. But it wasn't his employer's face which startled Edward, it was Florence's. She stood only feet from her lover, her eyes fixed on him with such loathing that a heat came from her. In that one instant Edward believed she could *see* Taverner, that her hatred had returned her sight.

'I'm carrying your child, Aubrey, and I'll give birth to your son.' Her words chilled them both. 'And one day, one day, that child will pay you back in full measure for what you've done.'

'Get out!' Taverner screamed.

'Stop it!' Edward said warningly, squaring up to his employer. 'Stop it now, I warn you.'

'I don't want a child!' Taverner said viciously, then turned away, his tone altering. 'I'm sorry,' he purred, sliding back into his seat and breathing in deeply. 'I was unkind, wasn't I?'

Edward watched him without speaking – unable to speak – and when his employer calmly untied his pigtail, he shook his head in disbelief. Slowly and methodically Taverner combed his luminous hair, it fanned against his shoulders like ice, then just as calmly he replaited it. His face was transformed. There was no anger. In its place was bewilderment. Only his fingers seemed to function normally, his emotions concentrated entirely in his hands, the clever fingers plaiting the ethereal hair.

'Florence,' he said finally. 'Forgive me.'

She had not seen the bizarre ritual, she had merely waited

for his next words. And when she heard them, she turned to the door, tapping her way with her stick.

'You have to go,' Taverner continued. 'Get away from here. I can't help you. I can't have children,' Taverner went on calmly. 'I just can't look after a child.'

She hesitated, her back to him. 'This is your child.'

'I can't have children,' he repeated.

Edward's voice was hard with contempt. 'Don't keep saying that, Aubrey.'

Taverner's eyes dilated. His hands rapped on the edge of the desk twice and then stopped.

'All right, I don't *want* children, is that clear enough?' he asked, turning back to Florence. 'You should have used something.'

'Jesus . . .' Edward said incredulously. 'This is your responsibility, Aubrey, and you're going to pay for this child. For its birth and its upkeep.'

'What business is it of yours?' Taverner asked coldly.

'Florence is blind,' Edward replied hoarsely. 'She relied on you and you let her. You made it seem as though you cared for her. You took advantage of her and now you'll have to look after her.'

'Really?' Taverner said archly.

'Yes, really,' Edward replied, his voice thick with disgust. 'You use people, but you're not using Florence any more. I can't think why I've stayed with you, why I liked you, why I wanted you to think well of me . . . I despise you now.'

Stung, Taverner rose to his feet and faced his employee. Ignoring Florence totally, his eyes fixed on Edward; the old gentleness was there, the expression of ineffable sweetness.

'Don't say that. I need you. I've behaved badly . . .' His hand touched Edward's shoulder. 'I was wrong. I've treated Florence cruelly,' he said, continuing to talk as though his lover was not in the room. 'I need your help. You don't know how much I need you to help me. Tell me what to do, tell me how to make things right.'

'I'll manage on my own,' Florence snapped.

'You can't,' Edward replied, glancing back to Taverner and hesitating.

One part of him wanted to be gone, to take Florence away, but the other wanted to remain, the bond between Taverner and himself impossible to sever. In that sultry moment his wish was being granted, his mentor was finally relying upon him. If Edward helped him now, he could control Taverner and secure the limitless affection and gratitude of the one man he admired above all others. He knew then the absoluteness of love, and the tie of obsession.

'Edward, I need you,' Taverner pleaded, his eyes begging.

'Florence needs help and she'll need money for the baby,' Edward said, clearing his throat. 'You have to support them.'

'Yes. Yes . . . All right,' Taverner agreed, leaning towards his employee earnestly.

'You have to give her money. She'll need money,' Edward repeated, damning himself for ever with his next words. 'I'll sort it all out for you, Aubrey, but you'll have to do as I say.'

Taverner's eyes flickered, then stilled. The room, swamped with its yellow glare, made his skin waxen, unliving, his hair the colour of church candles. He seemed unearthly. His helplessness was gone, snuffed out in the moment Edward had pledged his allegiance.

Edward didn't see it, but somehow Florence did, and with her last resource of courage she cursed Taverner.

'Be careful, Aubrey, because one day your child will come for you,' she said, with a dreadful stillness. 'Watch everyone, be suspicious of everyone, trust no one, because one day he'll come for you, I swear it.'

Her words shattered him and in that one instant all three of them saw a fate they could never deflect.

*

Carefully Edward helped Florence downstairs, taking the route slowly out of No. 6 as Mrs Tunbridge was sunning herself on the basement steps. She called out, but neither of them replied. Dr Wells ran down Cook's Alley and then paused to watch their progress along Greek Street. Under the white sun, Edward half walked, half carried Florence, whilst her head hung forwards, her stick trailing uselessly on the pavement. All her courage had gone. In cursing Taverner she had exhausted all her reserves of strength and now despair folded in on her.

People watched them go, passers-by curious as Edward belligerently forced a passage for them between the pedestrians. The sun melted into his clothes; his hands were moist as he gripped Florence's side and kept walking. He knew that he had taken on responsibility for her, had made a private contract with Taverner which only they fully understood. But he hadn't thought about the reality of his actions and now walked without knowing where he was going. He could take Florence to her flat, or to his, but neither seemed the right solution. She needed care, long-term care, of the kind he was not qualified to give.

They stumbled along the pavement, a blind woman with a tall blond man, walking nowhere. Edward began to panic, his thoughts leapfrogging over each other. What had he done? Why had he taken on the responsibility of a child which wasn't his? Out of pity? Out of some perverse belief that through such an action he could control Taverner? He stopped suddenly. Florence leaned against him. Dear God, where could he take her? Where could they go?

Home, you idiot.

Edward blinked. The sun shuddered on the road, rose in a heat haze, distorting the oncoming traffic.

Go on, go home.

The words seemed to vibrate in his ears, as did the noise of an oncoming taxi. In the hot afternoon, the road swam with heat, the shiny black-bodied cab coming towards him as he stood transfixed on the corner. The engine hummed, the smell of diesel and the hot tar on the road making him dizzy as he left Florence and stepped out directly into its path.

And still the taxi kept coming.

Go home, Edward, go home.

'Hennie?' he cried out, moving towards the cab, running frantically into the middle of the road. '*Hennie?*'

The vehicle swerved. It skimmed over the melting road, plunging through the heat haze; it floated for an instant in Edward's vision, then blasted its horn and passed him.

But as it pulled away into the traffic of Charing Cross Road, Edward saw a woman sitting in the back seat – a young blonde woman, wearing a black jacket, the collar of her white shirt turned up.

Chapter Seventeen

'Do you know about goodness, Mr Taverner? I do. I know about real goodness. I had a brother who was as good as an angel.

'I'm an old man now. Eighty-five, to be exact, and I never thought I'd live this long. I hope you can understand my accent. I know it can be difficult at times, but, you see, I came from Poland many years ago and I've found that the older I get, the more pronounced my accent becomes. Going back to one's roots, I imagine. Not that it has been a handicap. To a writer an accent is irrelevant. On paper there are no dialects, so the author is curiously free of any defect in language.

'We were a small family, my parents and my brother, and we were always encouraged to achieve. This beneficial upbringing was a godsend, and when I showed some promise as a writer I was supported and applauded at home constantly. No child, Mr Taverner, had a more secure background. My brother was encouraged too, but he had little academic prowess. His achievement was his appearance.

'I have seen an angel, and loved one. How many can say the same? My brother was still, placid, without malice, and yet not without spirit. His head was oval, his face with its olive skin, perfectly symmetrical. Large-eyed and a little above medium height, he was always bright-hearted and concerned. No one's troubles went unnoticed. He never heard of anyone's anguish without sharing it. Yes, he was exceptional and everyone loved him. They treasured his every word and an artist even painted him, the portrait being exhibited and then passed on to me.

'He wore such idolatry lightly. I know for certain that he took no kindness nor affection for granted. He was as perfect in his heart as in his physique. And I despised him.

'Yes, I know I said before that I loved him. I did, and that was what was so difficult. I loved and *despised him. Look at me, Mr Taverner, and what do you see? An old man, shuffling. I even needed help from my driver to get up the stairs to your office. I'm a gnarled old man, ugly through age.*

No, that is not true. I was always ugly. Age has simply made me seem more acceptable.

'To be forever compared to a brother of such infinite quality is a cruel burden, and one which would test a saint. I was no saint, and had little goodness. All the world's gifts were my brother's, apart from the gift of intelligence. That was mine, and I employed it to its fullest extent. No man ever put his peck of wisdom to such good use. Whilst I was ugly, I was clever.

'But I still resented him. Whilst I worked, he was entertaining the vast number of people who visited him. Whilst I longed for a lover, he effortlessly fascinated women. And whilst I looked at myself and loathed myself, he saw only the reflection of his inner kindness in the glass. I was deformed – not greatly, but I had one shoulder higher than the other, and chose to see it as a hump. A hunchback, I thought of myself, exaggerating the handicap because it seemed so much greater by comparison with the perfection that daily confronted me. I resented my ugliness, although my brother never saw it as such.

' "You have an angel on your shoulder."

' "He said."

' "An angel."

' "And he goes with you everywhere."

'But it made no difference. I saw myself as a hunchback, nothing else. And gradually I gave in to that image of myself. More and more humped I became as he seemed to become more and more handsome and tall. My brain was the only part of me to retain any quality, and in my ugliness I punished myself and grew jealous of him.

'My envy corrupted me. It bore down on me. It doubled me up. It was the burden which grew on my back. Not an angel but a devil, pushing my head between my shoulders and forcing me to look downwards, always downwards, until I saw each flagstone of each pavement, and each gutter, and every crack and jagged edge of the city on which the world passed daily. My whole existence was beneath my feet, and my future was written there.

'For me, there might have been no sky and no trees. What did I know of such things? I had no right to look upwards, no expectation of beauty. My brother might belong to that upward world, but I did not, and daily I

grew more rounded, and more certain of my fate. The hump on my shoulder stayed with me, and grew. Indeed, it seemed to enjoy my company, and we were inseparable.

'But misery is not inexhaustible and, as my academic reputation grew, some part of me felt gradually at peace. Not that I found love, nor real affection – not that I expected to – but my intelligence gave me some standing in the world and it was almost enough.

'My brother and I grew apart. My bitterness estranged us, and yet he never ceased offering affection, no matter how often it was rejected. I was a poor friend and was unable to respond as he deserved, so when he was taken ill I was the last to visit him and always the first to leave. He was patient, endlessly so.

' "You have an angel on your shoulder."

'He said it, again and again, as though to comfort me, even though he was the one in need of comfort. And I never believed him, never believed that anyone would love me or accept me, and blamed my appearance for my own shortcomings.

'He died within weeks. Died in full beauty and grace. He died and I took his portrait and kept it with me in my study. I worked then as no man has ever worked before, day and night I read and studied, and I wrote more fluently than I had ever written before, and every time I paused I glanced up – and saw him watching me.

'But I could not escape myself or my despair. Could not escape the hump on my back and the steady fall of my spirit and confidence. And then suddenly, for some inexplicable reason, I began to talk to him. Yes, Mr Taverner, I talked to my brother in a way I had never talked to him before. I spoke from the heart, from that part of all of us which carries the world's hopes and despairs. I talked so long that the room was soon full of my anguish. The windows were hung with it, the furniture sagged under its weight and the carpet was stained with it.

'Then one evening I talked until my voice failed, until I lost all words and fell into a dark silence and a darker sleep. When I woke it was still night. The world was not ready for morning. I woke and rubbed my eyes and glanced up at the portrait of my brother. I stared at it, startled, then

looked again. It had altered, *his perfection shifting, the outline of his form changing as I watched him.*

'And I was afraid, I admit it. I saw what was happening and I was afraid. The outline of his shoulder lifted, it grew upwards, it moved on the canvas, whilst his wonderful head looked out at me, perfectly serene.

'Terrified, and yet ridiculously hopeful, I moved to the mirror and tore off my shirt, running my hands over my shoulder. The hump was less! I tell you, Mr Taverner, the hump was less.

'From then onwards, at night, whilst the world slid under its covers and slept, I talked to my brother. Night after night I talked, and night after night he took on a little of my deformity. Each morning there was a change in the canvas, each morning there was a change in me. I straightened up, I looked up, I saw the sky in all its bewildering brightness, and saw what I had missed. The air was intoxicating, and I breathed like a child, new-born.

'It took seven weeks, Mr Taverner. Seven weeks for my brother to take on my burden, seven weeks for the painting to change and release me. And after seven weeks I was no longer the pitiful cripple I had always seen myself as. I was whole. My brother had taken the hump from my back, he had taken my ugliness upon himself.

'I kept the painting in a room where no one visited. I hid it, kept it secret, and I also grew to love my brother. I saw then his goodness and felt protected by him, and as my life transformed itself, I thanked him daily. But now I have reached a crisis – for all this happened a long time ago – now I'm old and know that I will soon die. Time was good to me, and life was eventually kind, but it will all be over within weeks. What my brother did from beyond the grave released me, and made possible a happiness I would otherwise never have secured.

'So now I want to repay him. The painting is still with me, as I said. His image is there, his shoulder still carrying my deformity, the hidden canvas bearing witness to his act of kindness. Yet lately I feel a sensation of my own back, a pressure of the type I remember from many years ago. Last week I felt the skin move. Sometimes now it wakens me as it shifts, and the first nub is reappearing.

'You see, I know what I have to do. I have to take the burden back. But time is very short now. I want to die, I have no fear of it, but when I go I want the world to see my brother in all his beauty. Not spoiled, not minimized in any way. It is the very least I owe him. So I must return the portrait to its previous state. When I am gone, I want everyone to see him as he was: as good and perfect as any man could ever be. In my coffin it will not matter how I appear, but my brother's image and his memory must be restored. It is my duty to him, and my last gesture of love.

'So I wondered if could leave you the painting, Mr Taverner, for reasons I will explain. I am still talking to my brother, as I have done so many times before, but I worry that I will run out of time before I have accomplished what I set out to do. Therefore I ask this of you – that I might return weekly and tell you of my progress, and then, if the transformation is not complete when you hear of my death, I ask that you look at the painting.

'If my brother is not perfect, not wholly perfect, then burn it, Mr Taverner. But if he is, if *I have completed the task and he is restored, then please keep the portrait, and sometimes look at him and remember what I said.*

'You see, I have seen an angel, and loved one.'

EXPERIENCE TAKEN FROM *Mr Leon Kowalski*
FEE PAID: *£500*
SIGNED: *Aubrey Taverner*

Edward glanced away from Florence and stared out of the car window. The road ahead led to the hill and the village beyond, the tip of the church spire bolting upwards to the afternoon sky. The fields were drying, the succulence of the earlier crops giving way to the winding down of a long, hot summer. Far in the distance a man whistled, whilst in the back of the car Florence slept on.

It had been Hennie, of course. Finally and certainly she had made contact. When he had most needed her, she had been there. Edward sighed and leaned his head back against the seat. A fly landed on the windscreen and inched its way down the hot glass. She had told him what to do, as she had always done when they were children. She had been quick to see the situation *and* the solution.

Go home, Edward.

And as soon as he had heard her, he had acted. In the suffocating heat of that afternoon, Edward had made his plans, phoning his mother and telling her to expect him that night. He had then packed some of Florence's clothes, whilst she sat silently on the edge of her bed. The flat had surprised him – a poor, shabby little home, probably far worse than she realized – and when they left, Edward drew the curtains, closing off the place. She walked with him without asking questions, unusually compliant as he took her to his flat and collected some belongings of his own. He did not know if she was beyond suspicion or simply trusting. She indicated nothing other than a catatonic obedience as he led her to the car.

They travelled throughout the afternoon and into the evening, the crossing on the boat uneasy, Florence refusing food although, when Edward insisted, she accepted an ice-cream. He watched her eat it, knowing that she did so only to please him, and as it melted, some of it dribbled on to her skirt, spreading greasily over the thin material. He wiped the stain away with a paper tissue, whilst she sat unresistingly and pitifully embarrassed, her arms by her sides.

Finally, when they reached Calais, Florence moved into the back seat to sleep. Her lack of curiosity was absolute. She had no interest in where she was or where she was going, and simply curled her body up, her hair falling over the sleeping cheek. Edward had no words of comfort. He tended her and protected her, but beyond that they were silent. What they had shared, and would share, was beyond words.

Finally, in the late summer evening, Edward stopped the car

on the bank of the hill – just as he had done so many times before – and shored up his courage for the last lap home. He knew Hennie was there, knew that she had travelled with them and had watched them. He had even thought he saw her in the queue at the self-service restaurant, tapping her foot impatiently, and later he thought he had caught a glimpse of her figure looking over the side of the guard-rail.

An old memory had returned to him.

Jesus, I hate boats! she moaned, queasy, her usually tanned face khaki-coloured. *This is the last time I ever cross water. Ever.*

Well, Edward thought, you never did sail again, did you? Until now . . .

Wearily, he leaned his head against the car window whilst, in the back seat, Florence stirred, then slowly awoke. Her white dress was crumpled and one shoe had fallen off. Her eyes widened as though, for an instant, she could see. In the confined space of the car, her voice hummed drowsily, and when she reached out her hand towards Edward, her skin smelled of the darkness of sleep.

'Are you all right?' he asked.

Her face was without colour as she nodded. 'Where are we?'

'Home . . . France.'

She expressed no surprise at all, only an awful stillness. He wondered then if she was frightened.

'It's a place called Misérie. It's where I was brought up.'

'Why did you bring me here?'

'Because it's safe,' Edward replied, leaning over and smoothing a hair away from the side of her mouth.

Touched by the tenderness of the gesture, her eyes filled and she rested her head against his seat. 'I don't know what to do.'

'You don't have to do anything,' he replied. 'I'll take care of it.'

'But—'

He placed his fingers over her mouth, repeating the gesture she had used once. 'Don't worry. Everything will be all right.'

She smiled faintly. 'Do they know I'm coming?'

Edward hesitated. 'I phoned my mother.'

'And told her you were bringing me?' Florence paused. 'Oh, Edward, you didn't tell her, did you?'

He squeezed her hand quickly. 'Listen, there's nothing to worry about. It'll be all right, I promise you.'

But he still waited for another half an hour before making the final stage of the journey. The light faded, the sky darkening, a sudden flurry of bats skimming the bank of apple trees. Across the field, lights went on in the windows of village houses, a late cat crossing the road, the growl of a van muffled in the distance. Still Edward hesitated . . . The car cooled down as the evening did, Florence's hand resting in his, her eyes closed.

She thought of Aubrey Taverner and he thought of Hennie, but neither thought of what was to come. For an instant there was no future, no anxiety, no need to leave that one particular moment in time. There was only a complete understanding between two people which could never be as perfect again.

'Ready?' he whispered finally.

And she nodded.

'Let me in!' Martin shouted, kicking the door at No. 6 Cook's Alley in frustration. 'Come on, you bloody sod, open up! I've got an appointment!' Martin howled. 'You've *got* to let me in.'

His voice was powerful and soon drew Mrs Tunbridge out of the basement.

'Hey, what's all this noise about?'

Martin ran to the railings and looked down, eager to find an ally. 'That bloody man—'

'Watch your mouth!' Mrs Tunbridge said harshly, interrupting him. 'I won't have that kind of language here.' She glanced at the dog next to her. 'We don't like it, do we, Dr Wells?'

The boy looked at the dog balefully and then pointed up to the second-floor windows.

'I saw a light on before. There *was* a light on up there. I saw it!' he said furiously. I bl— I did. He turned it off! He saw me coming and turned it off. Pig!'

Mrs Tunbridge frowned disbelievingly.

'Who turned it off? Mr Taverner? Never! You're all mixed up, dear, he would never do anything like that. He's a gentleman, he is. He never lets his clients down.' She paused, glancing up at the dark windows. 'Stands to reason that he can't be there now – unless he's working in the dark, and that's silly.' She pulled her cardigan around her. 'You must have the wrong time, dear.'

'I haven't!' Martin shouted furiously. 'I made the appointment yesterday, and he said eight-thirty, and it's eight-thirty now.' His voice was high were frustration. 'I want to see him. It's important . . . It's *vital*.'

'Nothing's that vital it can't wait until morning.'

'How do you know, you stupid cow?' the boy exploded, running away and then stopping to shake his fist uselessly at the second-floor window. 'I'll get you for this, you see if I don't, Mr Bloody Taverner. I'll get you for this!'

As the sound of his feet died away, Mrs Tunbridge glanced up at the second floor, frowning. It was unlike Mr Taverner to finish so early, she thought, but with Edward being away maybe he'd decided to call it a day and go home . . . She stepped out into the alley to get a better look, but there were definitely no lights burning upstairs and, after another moment, she went back into the basement.

Above, Aubrey Taverner stood by his office door in the darkness. His body shook, his eyes burned, his arms were wrapped around himself; the pale silk suiting looking for an instant like a straitjacket.

He had hardly heard Martin, had hardly noticed the boy's cries from below. That afternoon, after the old man left, he had watched the Daimler draw out of Cook's Alley and then, startled, had seen the figure watching him from the pavement opposite. The woman was standing, leaning against the railings opposite, her hands in her pockets, her head tilted upwards to the window where he stood.

She was wearing a short skirt and a white blouse, her jacket over her shoulders, her hair shifting in the slight breeze which blew down from Greek Street. Her poise was absolute and for an instant he thought she worked as a machinist in the building behind her and was merely returning from her break. But the longer he looked the more he realized that there was a quality about her which was disturbing, and when her eyes fixed on his and she smiled, he found himself unable to respond and he stepped back, rigid with unaccustomed fear.

But she kept smiling, drawing him towards the window again, pulling him towards her. And when he was transfixed by her, mesmerized by her, only then did she stop smiling. Only then did Hennie raise her right hand and point directly at him, her mouth forming the words:

I'll be back.

The terracotta pots outside the front door of the farmhouse in Misérie were heavily full of flowers, their voluptuous faces caught momentarily in the car headlights as Edward paused and parked in the yard. He had no sooner turned off the engine than Jeanne came out, walking with her arms extended to him. He responded eagerly, embracing her and then pulling back when he felt her stiffen in his arms.

'Who', she said quietly, looking into the car, 'is that?'

'Florence Andrews,' Edward replied, opening the door and helping her to her feet. Carefully he performed the little rituals she would normally have done for herself, smoothing her dress and passing her her stick. She stood in the cooling night, half lighted by the kitchen window, her face turned to Jeanne.

'This is our housekeeper, Jeanne,' Edward said quietly in English, then turned to the older woman, 'and this is Florence. She's coming to stay for a while.'

Jeanne blinked, then folded her arms, cordoning off any further show of affection. Her eyes were quick to assess the stranger, and even quicker to find fault. Who was this little scarecrow? she wondered, and why, after never bringing any women home, did Edward have to bring this wretched little scrap?

Her glance was so intense that it grazed Florence and she felt, rather than saw, the animosity.

'Edward, perhaps . . .' her voice, although plaintive, still had its melodious quality and a curious power. It was not a voice which lacked character, and the older woman responded to it.

'Are you hungry?' she asked in French, then repeated the question in stilted English.

'I would like a little something. Thank you,' Florence replied, Edward helping her into the kitchen.

Jeanne walked into the kitchen before them, noisily laying out a breadboard, a knife and some cheese. Resentfully she cut into a new loaf, only glancing up in surprise when Florence banged into the side of the table. She was about to rebuke her and then paused, studying her for a moment. Slowly she realized that Florence was blind. As though to confirm her suspicions, she glanced over to Edward and pointed to her own eyes. He nodded without speaking and guided Florence to a chair.

'Is bread and cheese all right for you?' Jeanne asked, her glance fixed on the slight figure in front of her. 'I could get you some soup.'

'I don't want you to go to any trouble.'

'No trouble,' Jeanne said eagerly. 'I made it for my husband this morning,' she volunteered, mesmerized by the stranger and unusually loquacious. 'He likes soup when he's been working all day. Just like Edward – he likes my soup too. Even when he was a boy he ate it.' She glanced at him. 'You must have some too. It's good.'

Surprised by the change in her mood, Edward sat down. There wasn't a sound from any other part of the house.

'How's my mother?'

'Asleep. She waited for you, but after a while she dozed off in the drawing-room. She was so looking forward to your coming home,' Jeanne continued, repeatedly stirring the soup in a pan on the stove. 'She was talking about your return all day.' The spoon stopped moving, Jeanne's hand poised, as she glanced over to Florence. 'Your coming is quite an event for us. We don't have many visitors any more, since Madame was ill.'

Florence winced, understanding the implication in the words and turning nervously to Edward. 'Listen, maybe I shouldn't have come here. Maybe it wasn't a good idea—'

'It was!' he said, glancing at Jeanne warningly. 'My mother's fine now. Besides, she needs some company. You'll get on.'

'But—'

'Soup,' Jeanne said flatly, laying a steaming bowl in front of both of them. 'When you've had that, I'll wake Madame.'

But it was not Jeanne who woke the sleeping woman. Sitting stiffly erect in a high-backed chair, Antoinetta did not appear to be asleep, more like someone who had closed their eyes for a second to facilitate concentration. She was wearing a navy silk suit, the pleated skirt falling luxuriously over her legs, a large pearl and gold brooch pinned to her left shoulder.

She slept on, without stirring, as Edward entered and looked around him. The drawing-room wore its familiar expression of magnificent exhaustion, but although there was little evidence of restoration, the silver was clean and some of the curtains were newly lined. To Edward, the partial recovery seemed to mirror his mother's condition and, finding himself momentarily freed from anxiety, he bent down to kiss her cheek.

'Edward,' she said automatically, opening her eyes. 'Hello, darling.'

He smiled. 'You look *impériale*.'

She rose on the word, her height as impressive as ever, her eyes on a level with her son's.

'I did it for you,' Antoinetta said, flushed with the compliment. 'I've been waiting so long. I wasn't asleep when you came in, just resting my eyes. When you called, it was so good to hear from you. We argue too much, Edward, we should be friends.' Her head tilted to one side coquettishly. 'You said you needed my help. You know I'd do anything to help you, darling. What is it?'

He paused, unwilling to test her, knowing that she thought he had returned alone.

'Sit with me,' she went on, regaining her seat and motioning for Edward to take the chair next to hers. The lamplight shaded one side of her face, her shadow thrown high on the wall behind. 'We have so much to talk about.'

He knew she was feeling triumphant and that she believed she had won. Her son was back; her one wish was granted. Her skin was flushed with victory. For an instant he felt almost sorry for her.

'What can I do for you?' Antoinetta asked eagerly. 'You tell me and I'll do it. I've always had your interests at heart, Edward, you know that.' Her hands became animated, her excitement extending along the length of her fingers. 'Is it to do with work? Your work?' Again, she tilted her head archly. 'Or perhaps it has something to do with your employer Mr . . .' she faltered. It seemed to Edward that in struggling to remember the name she rocked mentally, like a cat almost losing its grip on landing. Was she acting or was her memory *really* failing her?

'Don't tell me the name, darling. You mustn't.' She frowned, then smiled winningly, 'Taverner! Aubrey Taverner.'

The cat had cleared the jump.

'Yes, that's right,' Edward said cautiously. 'Well done.'

He felt cowed by the damage he was about to inflict. When

his mother knew the reason for his visit, everything would change. The two of them would become three – with all the implications such an addition meant.

'Well, is it about Mr Taverner?' Antoinetta asked, still smiling.

'In a way,' Edward admitted. 'You see, I've brought someone home with me.'

The expression on her face fixed. The flirtatiousness was gone, cold suspicion replacing it.

'And I'd like you to meet her.'

'*Her?*' She made the pronoun sound poisonous.

'Yes, she's called Florence,' Edward said quietly. 'Florence Andrews . . . And she needs help.'

Antoinetta stared at her son unblinkingly. 'Help?'

'She's in trouble.'

Her hand rose, palms facing him, warding off further information. 'I don't want to know—'

'You have to!' Edward said hurriedly. 'You're the only person who can help her. She's pregnant.'

'Dear God!' Antoinetta cried, turning away and walking to the window. 'I can't imagine what you want me to do. Pregnant . . . Dear God, Edward, are you mad, bringing her here?'

'I had nowhere to take her.'

'This is not a refuge and I'm not a charity!' Her anger flared violently. 'You bring some woman here and tell me she's pregnant, and you expect me to help you.' Her eyes narrowed. 'Is the child yours?'

The question surprised him. He had never considered the obvious conclusion to which his mother would jump and replied quickly. 'No, it's not my child.'

Her eyes were hard with temper. She had been cheated and lied to. She had thought her son was coming home to stay with her, and instead he was bringing trouble to her door. For an instant, she genuinely despised him.

'If it isn't your child, why are you involved?'

'Florence can't look after herself,' Edward explained carefully. 'She wants to have the baby, but she can't manage alone.'

'So I am supposed to look after her!' Antoinetta snapped. 'Well, you're mistaken, Edward. I won't do it.'

Edward heard the spite in his mother's voice and loathed her. He detested her then for every act of unkindness and selfishness. He resented her for her jealousy, her constant undermining of Hennie, and his temper broke.

'I should have known better than to expect help from you.'

'I'll help *you*, Edward, but not some woman I don't know. You expect too much from me.'

'I expect nothing from you, because that's what I usually get – nothing.'

She winced at the words. 'How dare you talk to me like that! I love you.'

'You *use* me,' Edward retorted. 'You wanted me home, you've begged me to come back. Well, now I've returned. You should be pleased.'

'Of course I want you back, but not some stranger.'

He was stubborn, unyielding. 'Florence needs help.'

'Then let her go to her own family!'

'She *has* no family.'

'There are places, people who help,' she said, pacing across the floor furiously. 'I've been ill. I can't do anything for her.'

'Yes, you can. You just don't want to. You have nothing in your life, Mother. Your daughter's dead, your husband left you, you've no interests, no friends – just a house which is far too big for you.' His voice was cold. 'You have nothing else, Mother.'

'You're cruel!' she said, her face rigid with anger, 'and you're wrong if you think you've outsmarted me.'

'But I don't,' Edward replied incredulously. 'And how like you to think of it in those terms – that I've outwitted you, cheated you. You've spent too long manipulating people, Mother. You judge everyone else by your own standards.'

Furiously, Antoinetta clutched her son's arm. 'Take that back!'

'Why? It's the truth.' Edward insisted.

'I'm not looking after a slut,' she said savagely. Her face was pale, without colour.

'She's a better woman than you are.'

She struck him once on the side of the face. The slap rocked him and he stepped back.

'What the hell was that for?' he asked fiercely. 'You don't love me, Mother, you just want a companion, someone to keep you company and run around after you. You never forgave me for going away, did you? And all you can do now is plot, trying to find a way to get me back into this bloody house.' He was hoarse with fury. 'You even tried to bribe me back, turning yourself into a little old lady whose memory was failing.'

Her grip on his arm tightened. 'I was ill.'

'Oh, come on, Mother!' he snapped. 'Let's be honest for once. It didn't work, did it? I came home, but I left again, so now what? Now you're trying to use Hennie to make me return—'

'I've heard enough!'

'But I've got a lot more to say, Mother. You see, I'm beginning to understand how your mind works. I'm not as stupid as I was, certainly not as trusting. You really thought you could use Hennie to bring me home, didn't you?'

She was enraged and surprised that he had seen through her.

'Your sister *is* here.'

'Maybe,' he said, 'but I doubt it. After all, why would Hennie come back to you? You never cared for her.'

'I loved her!'

'No, I loved her!' he shouted back. 'I miss her every day. I miss her every minute. She was the best of me. We did everything together, shared everything. When she died, I died.'

'*You* died? And what of me?'

'What of you? You again, Mother?' Edward said sharply. 'Is it always to be you? What about *her*? What about Hennie? You resented her enough when she was alive. You owe her something now she's dead.'

Antoinetta stared fixedly at her son. '*What* do I owe her?'

'It was Hennie who told me to bring Florence here,' Edward said quietly. 'She told me to bring her home. Florence has no family, no money, nothing. She's been used and now she's only her child left. She's determined to keep it. She'd never think of getting rid of the baby.' He gave the words time to have an impact. 'Hennie sent Florence here and if you send her away, I'll go with her – and I swear I'll never come back. Never.'

'That's blackmail.'

He nodded. 'Yes, I know.'

Antionetta stared at her son for many seconds and then glanced away to gather her thoughts. His attitude astounded her. The subservient Edward suddenly having the upper hand! She had thought she could control him and now found that he was controlling *her*. If she rejected this woman, she would lose her son, lose the one person upon whom she had constantly been able to rely. The ultimatum angered her, but at the same time she was thinking ahead, considering the future. If she accepted Florence, she could regain control over Edward in another way. There was always a solution.

Her eyes softened. 'Forgive me.'

The words sounded like a plea, but the emotion behind them was insincere and, suspicious, Edward took an instant to respond.

'Can I bring Florence in now?'

'Of course,' his mother replied, stretching up to her full height.

She was ready to hate her rival and, as she stood waiting in the drawing-room, she felt belittled and ashamed of the shabbiness around her. Clenching and unclenching her fists in controlled fury, Antoinetta thought of the house's crumbling decline and the lack of money which was obvious to anyone. Humiliation gagged her. This woman that Hennie had sent, would she be judgemental? Would she look at her and be critical? Would she look at her and see not a *grande dame* but an ageing, selfish old woman?

Her eyes fastened on the door, knowing herself about to be judged, measured and possibly held up to ridicule. Who was this interloper, this stranger coming uninvited into her life? she wondered angrily. Her eyes widened momentarily as the door finally opened and Florence walked in.

She came in on Edward's arm. She came in small and silent. She came in blind.

Antoinetta glanced at her, realizing in an instant that she could not see, and then she took her hand.

'Florence, come in, my dear. Come in and sit by me.'

Chapter Eighteen

It had never occurred to Edward to ask how far Florence's pregnancy had advanced and he was incredulous when told that the baby was due at the end of November – a winter baby, born into the chilling time of year. Watching Florence in the poor little garden beyond the yard at the back of the farmhouse, Edward found himself trying to picture the child but he could see only a repeated image of Aubrey Taverner, his spectacular hair loose around the mesmerizing face.

Almost as though she knew she was being watched, Florence turned. She had been in France for only three days, but in that time Antoinetta had found a companion in Florence, and Florence had found a confidante in Antoinetta. She admired the Frenchwoman, and for once in her life her blindness was seen as an asset – what greater ally could any vain woman have than an unseeing, uncritical friend? With Florence, Antoinetta could return to her halcyon days; with Florence she retained her youth and looks and her lost admirers. She wanted to impress the little Englishwoman, so she charmed her and attended to her, making her welcome, the *grande dame* again.

Perfectly attuned to her needs, Florence was more than willing to fulfil Antoinetta's requirements in return for the stability of her new home and the constant concern for her condition. Even Jeanne was cajoled into helping the visitor. At first she resented the newcomer, but a blindwoman was no threat and before long Jeanne found herself pitying Florence. In fact, she oozed pity, extending it in ladlefuls, her voice soothing, her compassion constant and inexhaustible – although she found the idea of Florence's pregnancy disconcerting, and hardly referred to it.

But Florence was immune to her feelings, her confidence

returning rapidly, the French soil offering a refuge from the horror of Cook's Alley. In her mind she replayed the last scene with Aubrey Taverner, seeing as a blind woman, recalling not images but sounds and senses. She felt again the impact of her fall from the chair and the scramble for her cane, the bitterness of his words spitting down on her head. She could remember in minute detail the touch of the carpet, and the smell of the leather chairs. No love remained, only the terrible desire to injure the man she had once idolized.

She had cursed him, throwing out the words blindly, yet intuitively knowing their power and the way they would cling to their victim. And she had meant every word. The day *would* come when she would cease to be dependent, and through this child she would repay Taverner measure for measure.

'When I first came to London it was different to how it is now. Especially Soho. There used to be greengrocers and booksellers around here, long before the sex shops came in and the girls.'

'Go on, Mr Glaxman.'

'Well, there was something that came to me last night in bed and I thought it might interest you. I suddenly remembered it – the monkey.'

'The monkey?'

'Yes, it was a little chap, all dolled up in a little red and gold suit, with a little fez hat – the way they used to dress them before these do-gooders insisted that it was cruelty. It wasn't cruelty, not at all. The monkey was as happy as you like and it just sat on the man's shoulder while he played the accordion. It just sat there and when he finished it held out a cup for the money.

'People loved it. They gave the bloke money because they liked the monkey, not because they liked his playing. He was a rotten musician, and he only knew three tunes. Over and over he played them, until someone came up and asked him about the monkey.

'He'd stop then and tell them the story. Well, you see this little monkey had come over on a boat. The man wasn't sure from where, but he knew it was a long way away, Africa, or somewhere like that. He had come into the docks sick to death and one of the sailors had taken pity on him and taken him to a pub – one where the musician played at nights. Well, the man really took a fancy to this little monkey and kept him, and nursed him back to health. He trained him too, and bought him a little suit, and after a while he and the monkey were really good pals.

'He used to say that the monkey understood him and that he understood the monkey. Well, it sounds daft, but you had to wonder when you saw them together, because they really seemed to know what was going on in each other's mind. If the thing was hungry, he knew. If it was thirsty, he knew. If it was unhappy, he knew. It was really clever the way they got on, and that monkey became real fond of its owner.

'The musician loved the animal too. He'd tell you that every time you stopped to talk to him, and at the end of the day he'd count out the money he'd made and put it in a purse and give it to the monkey! God, that little thing was smart. Later, the musician would take it to the pub and offer to buy someone a drink, and if the monkey didn't like them, it'd shake its head and hug the purse to itself! And God help you if you tried to take the money off it – it bit like a lion.

'And d'you know, the more that man taught that monkey, the more it learned. It could count, could dance and *keep the money. A better companion than most wives . . . Well, after the man had had it for about two years, he went into the pub one night and the monkey saw someone at the end of the bar, and to the musician's amazement it ran over to the man and jumped on his shoulder.*

'It knew the sailor, you see. It recognized him. Only the sailor denied ever seeing the monkey, let alone knowing it. The musician didn't believe him, though. He knew the animal and knew that the man was lying, and he got angry as hell. Before long there was an argument between them, and some harsh things were said, but the man still denied knowing the monkey, even though the animal was sitting on the bar watching him, its eyes following every move the sailor made.

'Well, the musician couldn't force the sailor into admitting anything.

But d'you know something, that sailor kept coming into the pub every night, and the animal kept going over to him, and trying to make friends with him. Every night, it got all excited when he walked in and ran over, chattering to him. It was pathetic, real sad, to see the little thing so upset. The musician was upset too, because he loved the creature and he knew that it was hurting – and that hurt him too. But the sailor was a hard man and he kept ignoring the animal, just as the animal kept trying to please him.

'It lost weight, that little monkey did, and lost heart, and after a while it didn't dance any more. It just lay on the musician's shoulder and only came back to life when they went to the pub and the sailor came in. The musician worried about it, wondered if he shouldn't stop going to the place, but when anyone suggested it, he said that it was the animal who wanted to go – and you couldn't argue with that. After all, he understood the little fella better than anyone else.

'Then one day the sailor stopped coming. A week passed and the little monkey looked for him every night, but he didn't come. Someone said his ship had left London, but the animal keep waiting, its eyes fixed on the door, waiting for the sailor to come in.

'Finally, after nearly three weeks, the musician arrived late at the pub one night with the monkey. It was in a real state then, its coat matted, its little jacket dirty and its face pinched like a child's. He tried to play with it, but it wasn't interested. Then, at eleven o'clock, it suddenly began to sit up and take notice.

'It also began to dance. I tell you, it's true, I was there and saw it. It danced and danced, and the musician played, and it doffed its little hat and did somersaults, and when it'd finished everyone clapped and put money in the cup. But then, only minutes later, the little thing just keeled over! It fell dead – just fell off the musician's shoulder and into his lap.

'I remember it as if it was yesterday. The musician crying as if it was his child that had died, and the monkey lying with its eyes closed, its little hands still round the purse. But that wasn't all there was to it, Mr Taverner. You see, the next day we had word that the sailor's ship had gone down and all hands had been lost. They'd run into a storm and sunk – just at the time the monkey had died.'

EXPERIENCE TAKEN FROM *Mr Jacob Glaxman*
FEE PAID: *£800*
SIGNED: *Aubrey Taverner*

'Her figure is still very small, considering,' Jeanne mused, watching Florence through the kitchen window.

'It's because she's so tiny,' Antoinetta said magnanimously, secure in the knowledge that her visitor lacked her elegance and height. 'She's actually carrying the baby very well. Dr Vallant said so this morning.'

Amazed by a summons from Edward, Dr Vallant had arrived to find a vivacious Madame Dadd and a frail Englishwoman sitting on a battered wicker couch in the back garden, a tray of coffee in front of them. The late afternoon sun was warm. A straw hat shielded Florence's face and her hands were folded over her stomach. When he approached her, she glanced up, one finger brushing a speck away from the corner of her eye.

'Dr Vallant!' Antoinetta said happily, rising to her feet and extending her face to be kissed.

Surprised, the doctor kissed both cheeks. 'Madame Dadd, you look well.'

'I am, Dr Vallant, and no little thanks to my guest.' She gestured to Florence as though introducing a celebrity. 'This is Florence Andrews from England. She's a friend of Edward's – and now a friend of mine.' She smiled with triumph. 'Little Florence needs your help, Doctor. You see, she's having a baby.'

Immediately Dr Vallant glanced over to Edward. He was leaning against the side wall of the house, out of earshot, and looked altered, his hair longer than usual, his features more defined, the last lingering traces of extreme youth gone. There was also a difference in his movements, Dr Vallant realized, a firmness in his manner which had never been evident before. So

Edward was to be a father, he thought wonderingly, glancing back to his new patient.

'Florence is blind, I'm afraid,' Antoinetta said without embarrassment, and with a palpable relief. 'That's why she's staying here to have the baby. Oh, and she'll remain afterwards, of course.'

Florence looked up. 'Madame—'

'Call me Antoinetta!' she chastened her. 'We are friends now.'

'Antoinetta. I can't expect to stay for ever.'

She said the words quietly, but the doctor was not immune to the richness of Florence's voice and found himself suddenly taking an interest in the little Englishwoman.

Gently Antoinetta touched Florence's arm. 'This is your home now. You can stay for as long as you wish, remember that.'

By the side of the house Edward stood watching, thinking of the time he and Hennie had talked whilst leaning against the same wall. So this is to be your replacement, he thought, studying Florence and feeling a deep and unexpected affection for her. Oh, Hennie, it was clever of you, clever and cunning . . .

Antoinetta laughed quickly. Florence rose and took the doctor's arm. She wore a print dress, typically country style, and flat shoes that a child might wear, the rounding of her stomach hardly apparent. The three of them stood on the grass together, perfectly complementing each other, unaware of Edward watching them and performing as actors do when unable to see the audience beyond the footlights.

Edward turned and moved back into the cool house, dialling the London number and waiting.

'Hello?'

'It's Edward.'

'Good, I wanted to talk to you,' Aubrey Taverner said eagerly, taking a sip of the water next to him and leaning back in his seat. In Cook's Alley the temperature was mounting, the thick webbing of London streets preventing a free passage of air. The room smouldered, the smell of dry wood milking the atmosphere.

'How's Florence?'

'Fine, she's at my home.' Edward paused, then hurried on. 'We're in France.'

'France?' he echoed.

'She's fine, Aubrey. The doctor's seen her and the baby's due at the end of November—'

'Don't tell me any more!'

Edward's voice tightened. 'It's your child.'

'I know. I know . . .' He trailed off, then brightened almost immediately. 'Listen, I'm very grateful for everything you're doing to help, very grateful indeed. I'll make it up to you. You see, I couldn't cope with the idea of a child, Edward. I just couldn't.' He shivered, suddenly chilled.

The coolness seemed to swim over the phone line to France.

'Are you all right?'

'Fine. It's just difficult trying to cope here on my own. I need help. The clients are so demanding.' Taverner's voice rose eerily. 'They ring up all the time, asking for appointments, then they turn up and stay. They stay for so long. They spend hours and hours talking.' He paused, lifting one hand to his head. His skin seemed to peel as he touched it. 'Chloë came yesterday and Alan Painter. He told me that he had injected himself with mercury.' His voice swooped into a low dive. 'They are all quite mad, you know.'

Edward frowned. 'Why don't you cancel some of the appointments? Don't take on too much when you're on your own.'

'I wouldn't *be* on my own if you were here.'

'And I wouldn't be away if it wasn't for you!' Edward said angrily. 'Jesus, what *is* the matter with you?'

'I'm tired, that's all,' Aubrey replied, his tone perfectly pitched, refined and cool. 'Not that I should have taken it out on you. You've been splendid. Do you need any more money yet?'

Edward thought of the goodly sum he had already been given and shook his head. 'No, money's the one thing Florence has plenty of.'

'And your mother? If either of them needs money, Edward, just ask.'

The offer was inviting. Having shouldered Taverner's responsibilities, Edward found himself tempted to claim monetary recompense for his efforts.

'Everything's all right *here*.'

'But what about you?' Taverner asked, quickly alerted to the phrasing of Edward's words. 'Do *you* need more?'

'Well, perhaps we could talk about that when I get back,' Edward replied cautiously.

After all, what harm was there in being rewarded? He'd done a good job, he'd saved his employer aggravation, surely that was worth something?

Oh, Edward, he seemed to hear Hennie say.

'Listen, Aubrey, I just phoned to let you know what was going on. I'll get back when I can.'

'When is that?'

'In a week or so.'

'So long.'

He stiffened. 'You asked me to help you,' Edward said coldly, 'so don't start placing conditions on that help or I'll withdraw it.' His own tone of voice shocked him, as did his employer's response.

'You take as long as you need, Edward. I won't push you again.'

Edward put down the phone and leaned back against the table. He felt a taste in his mouth, a bile which was unfamiliar. His actions shamed him. That he could consider taking money for helping Florence! What was he thinking of? he wondered disbelievingly. It wasn't in character for him. He was always eager to help without ever looking for reward. He was changing, his moral standards blunting. Time was when he would never have thought of such a thing. Time was when he would never have considered a friendship worth any form of moral compromise. Time was . . .

Disturbed, Edward glanced out into the garden again. Florence was in the house with Dr Vallant. Only Antoinetta was still walking around, her tall figure throwing its formidable shadow, her fingers busily pulling off the heads of dead roses. Obviously concentrating, she gestured quickly to M. Délange, the gardener, who hurried over to listen to her liturgy of complaint. Edward could see her white arms move and imagined the conversation.

I want the lawn tending, and some new bushes . . .

I want the apple tree shaping . . .

She would continue to dictate her terms until the old man would say he couldn't do it all alone, and then Madame Dadd would grandly tell him to hire help. After all, she had the money now.

She had the money. Whose money? Aubrey Taverner's money. Money from a man who bought experiences for a living. Taverner's money. Money from a man about whom little was known. Money offered and taken readily, money to provide necessities, money to secure undreamed of luxuries, money that had made a flat possible and a car, money that supported a habit which was expensive and indulgent. Taverner's money.

Edward's eyes fixed on his mother, his thoughts accelerating. But where did the money come from? he wondered, surprised that he hadn't considered it before. He had taken it without question, wanting it so desperately that his need had overridden his good sense. The cheques had been pushed over the desk or slid into his pocket, pieces of paper materializing effortlessly from Aubrey Taverner. But where did he get his funds from? All that money his employer passed over the desk to the clients, whose was it?

Carefully Edward calculated the amount paid out by Taverner over the last eleven months and then breathed in, shocked by the sum. He thought of the cash he'd been given to pay off his debts, the money to help with the rental of the Holland Park Avenue flat and the BMW – but *why* had it been given so readily? And for *what*?

Oh, yes, Taverner paid the clients for their experiences, but for what was he paying his employee? Loyalty? Was any amount of loyalty sufficient compensation for such largesse? No, Edward thought, it made no sense. The return was pitiful for the money invested. He shook his head in disbelief, suddenly alarmed as he looked at his mother again. He had *needed* the money before, needed it for her medical care; she had been sick and had required help. But Florence wasn't sick. Florence was impregnated with Aubrey Taverner's child. Not an invalid, not ill, only pregnant . . .

A queasiness settled in Edward's stomach as he suddenly realized how skilfully he had been manipulated. He hadn't seen it, but he had been very adeptly used. Aubrey Taverner had relied on Edward's admiration to extract himself from a difficult situation; he had played him to perfection, giving him enough funds to support his gambling and make possible the upturn in his lifestyle – an upturn Edward had wanted so much.

He had hated the Ealing bedsit and resented having no car and no money. The despair of the house in France and the loss of Hennie had left Edward emotionally bereft, ready and eager to be washed up on the fruitful Taverner shore. How he had wanted that man's approval; how he had wanted him to take over the role of his absent father and make compensation for his mother's dependence and Hennie's death. How he had strived to secure his interest, and how he had rejoiced when their friendship finally began.

What *friendship*? Edward wondered suddenly. Oh, yes, he had confided in Aubrey Taverner, but what had his employer ever confided in return? What information had ever been handed out about his family, his friends, his background? What of his hopes, his desires? Nothing, Edward realized, suddenly angry with himself for his own blindness.

The word jarred on him. Blindness. More blind than Florence. She had an excuse for her actions. She had loved Aubrey and needed him. Her disability had merely cheated her, withholding information which could have saved her. Edward had no such excuse. He had his sight, but had chosen not to use it. He could have seen what his employer was, but didn't choose to. Instead he had gratefully accepted the friendship, expecting it to mean as much to Taverner as it did to him, revelling in it, needing it so much that whatever his friend asked of him, he did.

Edward felt trapped, cornered. He had been played for a fool and resented it, seeing Taverner's actions as an extension of his mother's manipulations. His eyes narrowed and his thoughts ran on, the threat of panic retreating under the serene wash of cold rage. There was only one way to escape from the situation. He would turn the tables on Aubrey Taverner: he would demand something in return for his help and loyalty. Not merely money, but something infinitely more precious: the thing Taverner valued above all – his own story.

For years he had bought into people's lives and paid for their experiences without exchanging any confidences of his own. He had moved through the world without leaving a past and without seeming to dream of a future. No one had challenged him or come near to solving his enigma. Not even Florence. But *he* would, Edward promised himself. He would go on and on, and play whatever game it required, until it was all over.

He was a gambler, used to taking risks, a man with a reckless streak, a man who had been humiliated. The realization made Edward dangerous. Taverner had been clever, as clever as Edward had been stupid. But in the end his stupidity would be his greatest weapon. His employer would not know that Edward had changed. He would not suspect perception on Edward's part but would see him as he had always seen him – pliable and eager to please.

He would continue to take him for a fool, and that would, in the end, be his downfall.

Chapter Nineteen

SHE FELT around the edge of the door, then walked in, tapping her way with her cane. The smell of warm dust rushed out to meet her, the long hot night leaving its mark, the sound of a bird scuffing the windowledge. Unable to see, Florence could distinguish only lightness and darkness, and she moved towards the window, knowing that the french doors led out to the garden beyond.

Edward walked in to find her there, her expression alerting him. 'What is it?'

'I had a dream,' she said tonelessly. 'It was about Taverner.'

Edward noticed how she used his surname. 'Do you miss him?'

She was amazed that he had misunderstood her and was suddenly irritated. 'No, it's not that!'

Her indignation surprised him. 'I just wondered if you did,' he replied, adding cautiously, 'I spoke to him yesterday and he asked how you were.'

'Yes, he would be polite,' she said with real bitterness. 'Everyone always says what good manners he has.'

Edward persevered. 'He's given me money to make sure you have everything you need, you and the baby.'

She did not reply, simply touched her eyelids. The action was tentative.

'He said—'

'I heard!'

Slowly he walked over to her. 'Are you all right, Florence?'

'I'm fine,' she said, her fabulous voice distorted with fury. 'I've been dumped by my lover and I'm pregnant. What *could* be wrong?'

Edward breathed in deeply. He had seen many of Florence's

moods and took her courage for granted, but bitterness was something he had not suspected.

'It'll be OK.'

'Of course it will!' she hissed. 'We'll have everything, won't we, Edward? All medical bills paid, all the child's needs seen to. I mean, you'll see to that, won't you? You always clean up after Aubrey Taverner.'

The words struck out at him and he winced.

'Listen, Florence—'

'Listen to *what*?' she asked savagely, turning to him. 'You'll sort it all out, won't you? You'll make sure I'm all right so your friend will have nothing to worry about. You'll see I'm looked after.'

'This isn't fair, Florence,' Edward said warningly. 'I brought you to my home—'

'And I expect you'll be well paid for your kindness,' she snapped.

'That was a vicious thing to say.'

'I feel vicious!' she replied without remorse. 'I feel sick with spite.'

He reached out to her, but she pulled away, bumping into a chair and cursing under her breath.

'Florence, calm down!'

'I want a name.'

'What?'

'A name!' she repeated, her hair falling over her forehead, a thin film of sweat on her skin. 'I want a name for this child.'

He didn't understand. 'You want Taverner's name?'

'Why not?' she countered fiercely. 'He's the father.'

'I don't think he'll agree to it.'

She smiled coldly. 'No, I don't suppose he will. And you should know, shouldn't you? After all, you know him best.'

'There's no point attacking me,' Edward replied, struggling to keep his temper. 'I'm trying to help you.'

'Help me!'

'Yes, help you. We have to make the best of this situation.'

'Why?'

The question, asked with such venom, wrong-footed him.

'Because that's the way things are, Florence. You're having a child and we have to think of the baby now—'

She cut him off. 'And a baby should have a father. Especially when it won't have much of a mother.'

'You're a remarkable woman, Florence.'

'Bullshit, Edward!' she flashed. 'I'm an embarrassment and you know it.'

He was staggered by her anger.

'No child would be proud of me. And what will it think when it's old enough to understand what happened? Will it wonder why I gave birth to it? Or will it wish that it had been aborted?' she went on relentlessly. 'Will it be ashamed of its fumbling mother, when it looks at all the other happy parents standing at the school gate?'

'Stop it, Florence. This is doing you no good.'

'Don't patronize me!' she howled. 'I'm a drag on you and I'll be a drag on my child. I have no skills, no money, nothing. I worked as a switchboard operator tucked away at the back of a factory where no one could see me, and I lived in a mean little flat, always *so* grateful for the time people could spare me. I was *endured*.' She paused, her voice marbled with bitterness. 'So when Taverner wanted me *I was flattered*. Isn't that terrible, Edward? But you see, I was frustrated. I never got used to living without sex, even though most of the time I had to. Men don't find blind women much of a turn-on.'

He touched her shoulder, trying to make her stop, but she shook him off.

'I was grateful that Taverner wanted to sleep with me. *Grateful*. I even thought he cared for me. Hah!' Her sourness blistered the walls. 'But I was kidding myself. He felt nothing for me, not even pity. Maybe I should thank him for that at least. I hate to have people pity me.'

'You pity yourself enough,' Edward said evenly.

She flinched. 'That was cruel,' she said, smiling without warmth. 'You have such an unexpected capacity for cruelty, Edward.'

'You deserved it,' he said calmly. 'You're not helpless, Florence, and you're not on your own.'

'Ah, the value of friends.'

He caught hold of her arm tightly. 'Don't sneer at me. Remember, I'm the one who's helping you.'

'By proxy.'

His grip tightened. 'Do you still want Taverner, Florence, is that it? Is that what this is all about?'

She stiffened. 'No.'

'I don't believe you.'

'It's the truth, Edward.'

'You still want him.'

'No! I want to forget him, that's all.'

'You won't.'

'I know that,' she said, her voice losing its bitter tone, her anger lifting. 'I'm sorry for what I said. I've been a bitch. Sorry.'

He let go of her arm, accepting the apology without comment. 'What about the baby, Florence?'

'*What* about it, Edward?'

'Do you really want a name for it? Does it matter to you so much?'

'Yes,' she said with conviction. 'I want a name for my baby.'

He nodded, knowing she couldn't see him.

Aubrey Taverner knew she was out there, knew she was waiting for him to go to the window, but he would not go. He listened instead as the client talked on, the tape reeling beside him, the atmosphere in the room cloying. An electric storm rattled the windows at Cook's Alley, pelting the skylight overhead and making gurgling sounds down the gutters.

But he knew she would be there. In the rain, under a porch or ducked into a doorway, she would be there.

The client talked on, monotonously, incessantly, pouring out his story as the rain poured down from the heavens. And the tape kept running. It twirled and took on the man's tale and kept it safe in the recorder. It heard every word and listened far more eagerly than Taverner did, and when the man rose to leave, it took down the details of his departure – the scraping back of the chair and the opening of the door, even the distant sound of descending footsteps on the stairs.

Taverner waited until he heard the front door close and then walked into Edward's office. The rain ran down the windows, bounced off the old sills, dived into the basement and pooled in the alleyway as slowly he walked to the window, not wanting to, but unable to resist.

She was there, just as he knew she would be. But she hadn't taken cover in a doorway or a porch and stood, defiant, under the worst of the storm. She stood *untouched* by the weather, her hair and clothes dry, an entity unaffected by the elements. In her *own* element Hennie stood, and when she saw him at the window she smiled, then waved briefly and walked away.

Antoinetta was already impatient with the boy from the village, waving her hand vigorously and keeping up a stream of orders in French as he replanted the laburnum in the steaming soil. It had rained during the night and now the noon sun was drying the earth, vapour rising mistily as his foot dug into the yielding ground. She stood with her head on one side, a large azalea by her left foot, her face protected by a white linen hat, her hands gloved.

The garden was beginning to look as it had done in its heyday, Antoinetta again the demanding perfectionist, her autocratic tones ringing out stridently when the men lapsed in their work, the bushes planted in meticulously ordered rows. If they were even inches out of alignment, they were dug up again, Madame Dadd standing over the careless gardener like an unhappy spirit. Naturally they called her names behind her back, and soon it was the talk of the village that Antoinetta Dadd had fully recovered.

Not that her recovery made her husband return to her, some said spitefully. And why she was affecting her old regal ways with such a house guest – such *une petite dame* – it was preposterous. Who was this little English scrap? they asked themselves. Blind and *pregnant*, and who was responsible for that? Why, Edward Dadd, of course, they decided, although what a handsome young man like him could see in a woman like that was unthinkable. . . .

Dr Vallant tried gallantly to stem the rumours, although he too suspected that Edward was the father of Florence's child, despite Antoinetta's repeated denials. After all, why would he look after the woman if it *wasn't* his child? And why would he bring her to France, to his mother and his home? Dr Vallant frowned. Even when he had first met Florence he had been fairly certain that the baby was Edward's, and now, with the latest news to come from the farmhouse, it was a certainty.

It was a certainty because Edward Dadd was about to marry Florence Andrews. Or so went the local gossip. In the village they talked of little else, although confirmation was slow to come from the Dadd house, Antoinetta volunteering nothing and ignoring the curious glances. In fact, she had been told only two days beforehand, the information ricocheting around like a stray bullet.

Her reaction was violent, her voice hysterical, as she faced her son.

'Are you insane?' she demanded imperiously. 'Why would you want to marry the woman when it's not your child?' Her eyes narrowed with suspicion. 'Or is it?'

'I told you before,' Edward said simply. 'It's not my child.'

'So why?' she asked, her tone needle-edged.

'The baby needs a name.'

'But not yours!'

'Why not?' he countered evenly. 'I like Florence.'

'People do not marry because they like each other!' she bellowed furiously. 'They marry for love.'

'Do they?' Edward replied. 'Did you?'

'You're not the one to judge me!'

He ignored her and continued. 'Florence needs me.'

'And so you have to help her?'

'Why not?' he answered. 'Isn't that what we're supposed to do, to help?'

'You are my son, not a priest.'

'There's no point arguing about this,' he said firmly. 'You can't stop me, you can only tell us both to leave, and what purpose would that serve? You'd just be alone again.'

'You're behaving like a fool!'

'I've often thought the same of you,' he replied unemotionally.

Stunned, she regarded him for a long instant, realizing that the son she had borne was no longer the character she remembered. There was a steel in him which had never before been apparent, a violence of feeling which had been obvious in Hennie but not Edward. Not in kindly, slightly malleable Edward.

'I think you're making a mistake,' she said carefully, feeling her way. 'I like Florence, but she's not the kind of wife who'll bring you credit.'

'Bring me credit?' he repeated. 'Is that the best basis for marriage?'

'You have a future, Edward.'

He shrugged his shoulders. 'Of a kind. Listen, Mother, I'm

not brilliant. Hennie was the clever one. All I have is a well-paid job, which could end any time.'

'So do something more with your life!' she snapped. 'Don't squander it. You're well educated, you could do more.'

'I don't *want* to do more,' her son replied steadily. 'I like the way I live. I've a good job, a good flat and a good car, and—'

'Now you want a blind wife?'

Her tone scratched him.

'Florence needs me.'

'*I* need you.'

'You had me!' he retorted angrily. 'You've had your share.' He softened his tone. 'You've got the chance of having a grandchild—'

'Who isn't my flesh and blood.'

'Well, you were never that close to your own, Mother, so maybe this one will have an advantage from the start.'

Her eyes flickered. 'Are you going to keep bringing that up? Will you never forgive me?'

He had the grace to be ashamed. 'I told you that I brought Florence here because of Hennie.' He glanced at his mother. 'My sister wanted it.'

Antoinetta said nothing.

'Why are you looking so surprised? You told me that you saw Hennie here. You *did* see her, Mother, didn't you?'

Impatiently Antoinetta turned away. She wanted to hurt her son, to punish him for his waywardness. 'Maybe I just thought I did.'

'You did. Why deny it?'

'I'm not denying it!' she responded angrily. 'I just imagined something because I *wanted* it to be true. That's all.'

Edward shook his head incredulously. 'You never give up, do you? You'd twist anything to suit your own ends. Well, I *know* Hennie's here. She was also in London, and she came to me when I needed her. She's helping me, Mother. She might even help you if you could only just accept it.'

'What a remarkable woman my daughter was,' Antoinetta said icily, folding her arms, her hands clasping her elbows. 'I always admired her so much, Edward. Not just because she was attractive, but because she had such courage. Always such courage.' She smiled without warmth. 'They say there is always jealousy between mothers and daughters. Well, I was certainly jealous of Hennie.'

The admission was not unexpected.

'She was so determined, always *so* certain she was right. I think of her and wonder what she would have done if she had lived, what astonishing things she would have achieved.' She paused, but there was no response from Edward so she continued. 'She was never truly in love with anyone, was she?' her eyes fixed on her son, searching for the truth. 'Not any one man. Apart from you.'

'She wasn't in love with me, she loved me.'

Antoinetta smiled closely. 'Really? I always thought there was more to it than that.'

The insinuation lay festering between them.

'Poor Edward, you don't understand, do you? I did wonder how much you knew, but now I realize. Have you never wondered why you haven't found your ideal woman? Have you never been curious to know why you haven't fallen in love and stayed in love?'

He felt threatened, but held his mother's gaze.

'You *still* don't understand, do you?' she queried. 'Think, Edward. Why would you want to marry Florence so much? For honour or for escape?'

'You're talking nonsense.'

'I am talking perfect sense, if you would just listen,' she retorted coldly. 'You are marrying Florence for a variety of reasons, some of which I don't understand. But I do know that by marrying a woman you don't love you can continue to love the one woman you wanted above all others. Your sister.'

He was outraged and reacted hotly. 'You don't know what you're talking about.'

'I'm talking about love,' she replied evenly. 'What are you so afraid of? You loved your sister, you still do. So, why not admit that it was – *is* – there in your heart? It's nothing to be ashamed of, only accepted.' Her tone implied anything other than understanding. 'Your great good fortune in life was to be Hennie's twin; your great misfortune was to lose her. Believe me, Edward, no woman can live up to her ghost. Whatever a woman says, or does, or thinks, or feels, can never match up to the sanctity of what Hennie did and felt.' Her tone was soothing, though the words were poisonous.

'She had such power alive, but I never realized that she would increase her power after death. That surprised me, and it still does. Her memory is stronger now than it ever was. I feel it, yes, of course I do, Edward. I go to her room and look at her things and expect to feel sadness, but I *can't*. There is no sadness about Hennie. She was too powerful, too sure of herself. You cling to her as she clings to you. But you're alive and should distance yourself.' She tilted her head to one side, watching her son carefully, choosing her words. 'I've told you before, she was always selfish, Edward. Always selfish and greedy—'

'She was not!'

Antoinetta laughed resignedly. 'You see how you defend her? Even now, how you protect her from every angry word.' Her hand shot out and gripped his, all pretence suspended. 'Listen to me, Edward. Until you learn to control your sister's memory, she will always be the first woman in your heart.'

His eyes narrowed with suspicion. 'You're still jealous, aren't you, even now?'

To his surprise, she nodded in agreement. 'Yes, I still am. But now it's a different type of jealousy. When you were children I used to resent the bond between you and feel angry that you excluded me, but now I feel only a pity for you, Edward.' She picked at his confidence, destroying the memory he prized above all others. 'I can grieve for my dead child, but you are *absorbed* by Hennie's memory and your sorrow persists.' She leaned towards him. 'Remember, you don't see yourself as I do. You don't see how you walk around the house, how you glance upstairs at every sound, how every inch of this place is turned over by you constantly in search of some part of Hennie. Your walks are conditioned by her. The back yard, the lawn, the drive – all bring back memories, and *how* you want them to . . . But, my dear, Hennie is not your guardian angel, she is your leech.'

The word shattered him. 'Rubbish!'

'She is your *leech*,' Antoinetta repeated, drawing up to her full height, her face implacable, 'and like a leech she will cling to you and leave you dry and bloodless. Do you know why? Because she understands your *weakness*. She knows that she was always the stronger one, that you relied on her utterly. So now she plays on that weakness. You miss her and are haunted by her because you *wish* to be haunted, and she knew that was how you would react. You make a ghost out of a memory and a living woman out of a buried girl.'

'I know what you're trying to do,' Edward snapped, squaring up to his mother. 'You're trying to separate us. You wanted to use Hennie to bring me back, but it didn't turn out the way you planned, so now you're trying to make me doubt myself. Well, it won't work. I saw Hennie in London. I saw her as clearly as I see you now. And it wasn't just me. Mrs Tunbridge, an old woman who had never even *heard* of Hennie, saw her and took a piece of paper from her. She even spoke to her.' His eyes were calm with certainty.

Antoinetta paled. 'I still say that it's only your will that's bringing her back. That and nothing else.' She touched her throat quickly. 'Hennie didn't want to die and she'll come back if she can, *if you let her*. I warn you, Edward, you are putting yourself in grave danger if you go on with this.'

'Grave danger?' he repeated disbelievingly. 'No, I don't think so. My sister would never hurt me, I know that for certain. She always protected me, and she always will. Hennie is helping me, not injuring me.'

'She is dead! You should let the dead rest.'

'I can't, it's out of my hands now.'

They both felt the same chill in the same instant.

'I can't *stop* her, don't you realize that, Mother? Hennie's done what she set out to do. She's found that *life between lives* and she's found a way of coming back.' He glanced upwards momentarily, towards the empty bedroom. 'When she was dying, she promised she'd return, and I believed her, so don't expect me to stop believing now. Don't try and divide us. We were together when she lived, and we'll stay together now she's dead. I will *never* abandon her.'

'You are risking more than you know,' Antoinetta said softly, her energy dampening, 'and I'm afraid for you. Edward, truly afraid. Don't pursue this, please. Let your sister die, let her rest. After death, no one knows what there is to come.'

'Hennie is to come,' he said softly. 'Hennie is to come.'

Chapter Twenty

'I've changed haven't I? Yes, of course I have. No one would recognize me now. I used to be a big man, with a military bearing – Sergeant English – a man in his prime. But I've changed now.

'I don't know how to live and I can't die. The noises in my head are growing, like the sounds. I thought I'd go mad when I heard the woman had been killed, but I didn't, that would have been too easy. There's nowhere to escape to, not now. Maybe not ever.

'So I had to find a way of coping. Some way I could handle all the images and the sounds, because no one was going to take them away from me. The woman could have done, but she's gone. Or maybe she knew she would never come back . . . I don't know. I can't think about it too much. Besides, what good would it do? I have to find a way of coping alone.

'My wife's gone and I've moved back into the house. It's very quiet and I keep the curtains drawn most of the time. I only go out to shop, get some bits and pieces for myself, otherwise I see no one – apart from you, that is. I still come here, and it's not just for the money, Mr Taverner. I feel comfortable here. It's about the only place I do feel comfortable now.

'You see, you're a little like me, I think. You're not a part of this world. I know that. I would have laughed at such an idea not so long ago, but now I don't. Now I know better. I think you're a bit of an outsider, like me, and you have the same atmosphere around you. You're doomed, and you carry a deadness with you—'

'You're not here to talk about me.'

'No, but whilst I'm talking about my fate, I'm talking about yours. Not that your experience is mine, but there is something coming for you that will be similar.'

'Go on with your story.'

'If you insist . . . Well, I had to find a way to cope with all these pictures in my head. All these consciences suffering day and night. You

can't believe what I saw, and what I will see. Think of your worst imaginings, Mr Taverner, and double them, treble them, and you will still come nowhere close to what I suffer every moment.

'There is no end for me. Only an exhausting litany of distress. I can offer no help, can do nothing constructive, only listen . . . Like you listen, Mr Taverner. Just like you . . . And then again, not *like you. You have your hours of business, you can close up shop and walk away from your work. I can never escape.*

'When I found out the woman had died I locked myself away. I didn't sleep, and in the mornings I would be crouched in the corner of the bedroom with my hands over my ears. Not that it did any good . . . The sounds were still there, and if I closed my eyes, the sights were still there too. My punishment is to be unending, eternal. I am not even to be blessed with the comfort of madness.

'I walk around the house all day and most of the night. I doze sometimes, but wake quickly. It seems that when I do sleep, the noises increase in volume to wake me, and when I shut my eyes they burn – burn *– from the scenes running constantly in my brain. I have no hunger left, I eat little, which is why I've lost weight. I don't wash any more either, unless I'm coming to see you, Mr Taverner. Somehow I feel I should make the effort, even in this state, when I see you.*

'Give me some paper.'

'What?'

'Some paper, Mr Taverner.

'Thank you. Now watch me carefully and see what I do. I'm one of the damned, I know that now. I walk in my own darkness and everyone else's too, but I'm developing ways to cope. Now watch me . . . See how I spread out the paper on your desk? See how I look at it? I'm concentrating, Mr Taverner, I'm thinking about the scene going on in my head.'

'Dear God!'

'You see it, don't you? You see the image coming on the paper. It's horrible, isn't it? And that's only one of the pictures that I see daily. Touch it, Mr Taverner, touch the paper. Go on, touch it!

'Feel how it burns*? Now look at your hand, Mr Taverner, see how*

the paper's blistered your hand. Watch it, feel it burn you! It burns in me all the time like that. All the time . . . But look, it's all gone now. The paper's clear again. It's all gone.'

'Where? Where did it go?'

'Who knows? I used to try and keep *the pictures after I'd thought them on to the paper. I used to try and file them. I tried to put them into alphabetical order, A to Z, Mr Taverner, filed like Army records. Only every time I put them into the filing-cabinet they would burst into flames. And afterwards nothing remained. No ashes, no scorch marks, nothing.*

'They go on in my head, though. Look at me, watch me. Watch the wall. Look at the picture there—'

'Stop it!'

'I can't. I won't! *See the figures moving? See them? See how they come to life? They're on your wall, Mr Taverner, I've let them out of my brain to play with you. How's that for an experience? You're watching the damned. Maybe I could even convince some of them to stay with you.'*

'Mr English, I think you should go!'

'Yes, of course. I'm frightening you, which isn't fair. But you see, you're such a strange man I thought maybe you'd enjoy what I had to show you. You want to know so much, don't you? Well, be careful. I tell you as a friend, take care. I see something in you which I see in myself, something I cannot avoid, but you still might. For me, all hope is gone. For you, there's still a chance.

'I'll take the picture back now, Mr Taverner. There, you see, the wall's bare again, they're back in my head. All cosy, all safe. I'll think of you. When I have a moment – if *they give me a moment to myself – I'll think of you . . .'*

EXPERIENCE TAKEN FROM *Mr Michael English*
FEE PAID: *£750*
SIGNED: *Aubrey Taverner*

*

It was a Saturday when Florence and Edward married in the little village church at four-thirty on a steamy afternoon. The heat was fierce, falling through the crude stained-glass windows with an angry insistence, the altar mottled with colour, a pool of ultramarine spilling over the single arrangement of white flowers. Edward looked round, thought of Aubrey Taverner's office in Cook's Alley and of the coloured drapes, and then glanced towards his mother.

Having realized that her son was not about to change his mind, Antoinetta had accepted the inevitable, and to everyone she expressed effusively warm feelings for Florence and for the baby, speaking vividly about her coming grandchild and working the gardeners into a frenzy to repair the neglected garden in time for the wedding. Aubrey Taverner's money was never so wisely spent.

For a wedding which should by rights have been his, there was much preparation. The faulty roof was restored, the few remaining summer birds dismissed from the dry rafters, their nests abandoned as the smell of new paint and the banging of hammers replaced their singing. Workmen hired by Edward repaired the chimneys, ropes hanging over the gable ends and along the drainpipes. The pointing was renewed and paintwork glistened after two applications of burning white.

The house came back to life, the four boarded-up windows of the outhouses were finally replaced, the glass winking blindly in the hot light. Galvanized by all the exterior activity, Jeanne hired two young girls from the village and began a rigorous cleaning of the interior. Carpets were beaten and curtains washed, the three women working upwards, floor by floor, until, on the third day, they reached Hennie's room.

'Look at this!' one of the young girls said wonderingly as she stood transfixed by the door. 'What a place.'

'Leave it alone!' Edward said suddenly, materializing at her side. 'I'll see to it.'

The girl shrugged and moved away as he walked past and

closed the door behind him. The room smelled of Hennie, and of heat, as violently red and gold as it had always been, and when he sat down on the crimson quilt his hand rested momentarily where his sister had lain.

'I'm marrying Florence tomorrow,' he told her softly. 'I know that's what you want.'

Silence.

'I'm taking Aubrey's place by marrying her, Hennie. It should be his day.' He glanced at the bedside table and the clock which had stopped three hours after Hennie's death and had never been rewound. 'I don't love her, you know that, but she needs me.'

He remembered talking to Hennie years earlier, and the way she had chided him for wanting to marry a divorced woman with children.

You shouldn't take on someone else's children, you should have your own, she had said, and yet she had brought Florence here. Pregnant Florence, who needed a name for her child.

'This is what you wanted, isn't it?' he asked her, glancing around him. 'I wish I could hear you. I need to hear you, talk to you, Hennie? Hennie?'

The room was silent, no sound of anything, no sign, no marker.

'Am I doing the right thing?' he begged, pleading for reassurance, aware that he was about to take a step which would alter his life for ever.

'Am I doing the right thing? Tell me.'

Again silence.

'She needs me, Hennie. You never did. I needed you instead.' He rose to his feet, pacing restlessly. 'You *have* to tell me that this is what you want . . . Tell me, Hennie!'

The weight of the responsibility fell over him heavily, the pressure unwelcome.

'If you'd lived, none of this would have happened. If you'd been here now, our parents would have stayed together and I would never have gone to work for Aubrey Taverner.' An image of Cook's Alley flashed into his mind and his resentment rose. 'This is his child and his lover. His, not mine.' Edward's hands went up to his head, and he found himself shaking. 'I don't know if what I'm doing is right, Hennie. I don't know any more. Tell me, please.'

Silence.

'I need you!' he shouted. 'I need your help. Just tell me I'm doing the right thing. Just tell me that.'

Nothing.

'I *shouldn't* be marrying her. I'm not Taverner. I'm not supposed to be living his life.' The thought seemed macabre. Unreal. 'For God's sake, Hennie, you can't just make things happen and then walk away. You have to see it through with me, you have to let me know what I'm doing is right.'

His hands gripped the quilt, his fingers plucking at the blood-red satin.

'Hennie, don't ignore me. Talk to me . . . Let me know you're there.'

Outside, one of the workmen on the roof lost his grip and let go of a rope. It uncoiled almost languidly. It unwound in the heavy air, tightening as it reached its full length. Then it swung heavily against the house – and against Hennie's window. It swung once, twice and then again.

Edward jumped, then turned, lifting his left hand and clicking his fingers three times to answer her.

Florence walked the few steps as though she wasn't blind, as though some inner sense of sight guided her up the aisle towards Edward, her walk full of grace, her head held high. No longer the little scarecrow, in her mind Florence was as beautiful as any bride hoped to be, and had seen no reflection in a mirror to deny the fact. Her feet and her intuition guided her to Edward and, as she reached him, his hand moved out to touch her arm and she glanced up smiling.

Having been reassured by Hennie, he was prepared for the step he was about to take and returned Florence's smile immediately, knowing that if she could not see it, she could sense it. She was dressed in an azure blue suit, her fine red hair held away from her face with a coronet of cornflowers, her skin hesitantly tanned from her time spent in the garden. Her poise was at once inspiring and poignant, the swell of her stomach hidden by the bunch of late summer blooms she carried, her hands without rings or bracelets.

She came to him in all her sweetness and all her courage, and he responded with all his kindness – a man who was kind because kindness became him. In the first row Antoinetta stood smiling determinedly, and when Theo Dadd arrived just as the service began, he hesitated for an instant before slipping into the pew beside his wife.

In surprise she glanced at him, seeing a worn man and the shell of a lover. But her mind ground into gear immediately, her old instincts returning, her old desires struggling up to the surface. In time he too would come home, she told herself, *in time* he too would return.

Instinctively Edward glanced over his shoulder and saw his father. He was not surprised by his ageing, and simply nodded to acknowledge his presence. In response, Theo Dadd smiled stiffly, then stared at his son, mesmerized by the blond hair and seeing a memory of his daughter mirrored there.

But Hennie was dead, and this was Edward's time. Theo scrutinized his son, spellbound by his blondness and all his beauty, transfixed in a small village church on a sweating afternoon in summer – a country summer made steamy with late crops and flocks of cawing, indolent birds. He stared at him and wondered about the woman who was about to become his wife.

Edward wondered about Florence too, and knew in his heart that his reasons for marrying her were twofold. It was true that he wanted to protect her, but it was also true that he wanted, through her, to get closer to Taverner. He disliked admitting the callousness of his behaviour, but would not deny it, even to himself, and besides, how could Florence be injured by his actions? She would have the protection and the name she wanted, and he would have one more overpowering reason to maintain his relationship with Taverner.

Florence did not read his thoughts. Her own were too complex to allow another's to intrude. She stood at the altar and thought of Aubrey Taverner and her heart twisted. She had no sense of triumph on her wedding day. Gratitude, yes – she knew what Edward was doing for her – yet she suspected that his loyalty was divided, and that he was still bound to Taverner more strongly than he would ever be to her.

Side by side they stood, both thinking not of each other but of a man in an alley in London. Even then, as they prepared to marry, Taverner absorbed them; even then his absence was more powerful than the reality of the congregation. He was in their minds so forcefully that they *willed* him into that church, and each thought the other loved him, each misunderstanding the other as they married into their own revenge.

'I'm going back up North. I've had it with this town. And you. This place, it's creepy.'

'I didn't ask to you come, Mr Painter. You made the appointment.'

'Sure . . . Well, I sold the saxophone, bought a new bike instead. After all, you can't ride a bloody instrument. I'm going back.'

'You said that.'

'Yeah. Up North, that's reality. Not like here. People like you wouldn't exist up there. They'd sniff you out good and proper. Have you stitched up in no time. They don't like phonies . . . Anyway, I've got an experience for you. My mother's actually. She works in a launderette in Salford. Does the service washes.

'Well she told me that this bloke had come in the other week with a set of towels. Good ones, Kendal Milne, you know. Big fluffy ones – the ponce! He said he'd had an accident – they had blood on them, you see. Said they needed two washes.

' "That'll be three quid," my mother said.

' "Three quid, that's steep!"

' "You see if you can get it cheaper anywhere else. Well, d'you want them doing, or not?"

'So he leaves them. And she put them in the washer. With the powder. Leaves them to soak. Then she relaxes. It's late, so she sits down with the Manchester Evening News, *reading. Now and again she looks up. Sees them going round. Then reads some more. Because they needed the two washes she's there long after closing. Watching these bloody great towels. Going round. Round and round.*

'She fell asleep at one point. Who wouldn't, watching washing? You know, that place is spooky, next to an estate. All the other shops boarded up. But she's still there, working late for three quid. It gets hot in there, what with the washers and the dryers on, but she'd locked the door so she felt safe. Safe as anyone feels in Salford at night. When she woke, her neck's stiff, but the towels are done. So she takes them out. Starts folding them. They're clean as you like. But then she sees a mark on one.

' "Bloody hell," she said.

' "Two washes, and still dirty."

' "It's the powder."

' "They don't make it like they used to."

'Her eyes aren't that good, so she gets her glasses. For a closer look. The mark's not dirt, its a diagram! Rough-drawn street map. But no names on it. Can you believe it? Well, she's mystified and starts scrubbing at the thing. But it doesn't come off, and so she's just about to put the thing back into the washer when she thinks, Bugger it.

'Time to go home.

'I'll only get paid for two washes whatever I do.

'But she's curious, my mother, so she copies this diagram. Like a rough map, she said it was. She draws it on the back of her pension book

and tucks it in her bag. Thinks she'll show her friends at bingo. Something to talk about. A street map on a towel!

'"Well, you see plenty," she said to me.

'"In a launderette."

'"But not street maps."

'She folds the towel carefully, so that the markings don't show, so that he'll never know when he picks them up. He comes in the next day, when she's not there, and he takes them. Never noticed any marks. Just picked them up and left. She never saw him again.

'She saw the police instead. They asked her questions about the washing she'd done and showed the towels to her. Did she recognize them? Sure, she said, she'd washed them. Had blood on them, she said. Yes, they said, the man had killed his wife and then committed suicide. In Central Manchester, they said.

'"So why did he bother to have the towels washed?"

She asked.

'"If he was going to bump himself off?"

'"What a waste of three quid!"

'They didn't have an answer for that. They showed her a photo instead. And she identified him. Then she remembered the street plan. Got all excited. Hadn't remembered it before because it wasn't on the towel any longer. *And they were the same towels. She knew that. Anyway, she told them all about it, and showed them the map she'd copied.*

'"Look at this."

'"Was this the place he did it?"

'"Yes, I know there are no names on the streets."

'"But it must be somewhere."

'"It must mean something to someone."

'"Mustn't it?"

'But they weren't interested . . . I was, though. She showed it to me the other night. The copy she made on her pension book. The copy of the place she didn't know. But I knew where it was.

'It was here, Mr Taverner.'

'What?'

'Yes, that's right. Here. I copied it myself and laid it over this area in

the A–Z. *Right over Cook's Alley. And it matched. Now that's odd, isn't it? That the murder and suicide took place up North, and yet the map fits here. It made me wonder, Mr Taverner, about places and people. It made me wonder if the man was a client of yours, or if he had seen this place and it had affected his mind. Because it does, after a while. I know that. I know how this stinking little pit gets to you.*

'They're only buildings. You say. Only old houses and railings. Only an alleyway over an old church site. But it corrupts, Mr Taverner. And you *corrupt.*

'You frighten me. And I don't frighten easy. But I know when I'm out of my depth. So I'm going back home. Up North. I don't understand you. I don't want to. I think I'd lose something by getting too close to you . . . I can't think here. I want to go where it's safe. To get away. No, I don't want your money. Give it to someone else. I'll give you *money instead.'*

'What!'

'I've saved nearly five hundred quid.'

'What for?'

'To buy my experiences back from you, Mr Taverner. I want them back. Every one of them. And I want to forget I ever saw you, or spoke to you, or gave you any part of my life. Let me have them back, Taverner. Please.'

EXPERIENCE TAKEN FROM *Mr Alan Painter*
NO FEE
SIGNED: *Aubrey Taverner*

'Is it done?'

'We're married, yes,' Edward replied, frowning.

'Thank God.'

Edward's tone was sour. 'God had nothing to do with it actually.'

Taverner had the grace to be abashed. 'I didn't mean it like that. You've done me a great service.'

'I did it for Florence more than you.'

'So now you hate me?'

Edward considered the question. 'No,' he replied. 'I don't hate you, Aubrey. I am simply mystified by you.'

'When can you come back to London?'

'Soon.'

'When?'

'Next week.'

'Good.'

'How is everything?'

Taverner sighed. 'Chloë came yesterday.'

'Chloë?'

'Yes. She's as handsome as ever and twice as outrageous. I think she's making her experiences up, Edward. In fact, I'm sure of it.'

'But you're still paying her?'

'She makes me laugh.'

'Are you sleeping with her?'

'Edward!'

'Well, Aubrey, are you?'

He smiled icily. 'No, I have no desire for her.'

'But she's lovely,' Edward persisted. 'You made love to Florence, so why not Chloë?'

'You can't expect me to answer that, Edward. Florence is your wife now.'

'Don't bullshit me!' he snapped suddenly. 'I want to know the truth. Why did you make love to Florence and not to Chloë?'

Taverner paused for a long time before answering. 'I wasn't afraid of Florence.'

'That's the first honest thing you've said to me,' Edward replied calmly. 'Thanks for that at least.'

There was a long pause before Taverner spoke again.

'Are you happy with her?'

'Florence?'

'Yes.'

'She's kind and sweet.'

'But does she make you happy, Edward?'

'As a child would, yes.'

'But not as a wife?'

Edward hesitated. After the wedding there had been a few cursory celebrations, a late supper laid out on the lawn, a haphazard mingling of guests picking listlessly at the exquisite food and wine. The evening remained light until ten, the last guests slumping into wicker chairs, the sky darkening and mottled with a flurry of pipistrelles. Lights shone out from the windows of the farmhouse and a few lamps hung in the garden, one suspended from the low branches of an apple tree.

Standing beside it, Edward watched the guests, seeing Florence talking animatedly to his mother and wondering when his father had slipped away. A smooth breeze hustled the hot day away, the lamp humming languidly as he studied his wife. *His wife,* he thought, looking at Florence and seeing the new wedding band on her hand. Shiny, unused, a circular ring of gold which encompassed her world, her man and her child. Slowly Edward glanced at his own hand, then thoughtfully turned the wedding ring round on his third finger. The flesh underneath seemed suddenly to itch, and after another moment he slid the ring off and dropped it into his pocket.

Around midnight, Antoinetta retired, and Jeanne, kissing both of them, pressed a small present into Florence's hand. She blushed hotly with delight and stumbled over a few words in French. The old woman squeezed her arm before she left.

Finally alone together in one of the previously unused upper rooms, Edward sat down next to Florence on the edge of the bed.

'So, how are you feeling?'

She smiled distantly. 'I don't know what to say . . . except thank you, Edward.'

He nodded, realizing too late that she would not see the response.

The lamp by the bed was muted, leaving the room in semi-darkness. It dimmed Florence's hair and shadowed her eyes, and for some inexplicable reason Edward suddenly remembered her naked body under Aubrey Taverner's sleeping form, and the erotic longing it had excited in him. He knew the image should have repelled him, but it stimulated him instead, and he found himself suddenly wanting her.

'Florence,' he said simply, putting one hand behind her head and pulling her towards him.

Her lips parted slightly as he ran his finger over her bottom lip, the red inside exposed for an instant before his mouth moved hurriedly over hers.

'Relax,' he coaxed her, studying her face and pulling off the coronet of flowers which still encircled her head. Longingly he weighed her hair in his hands. 'You look wonderful . . . wonderful,' he crooned, knowing that he wanted to make love to her, and yet knowing at the same time that she was heavily pregnant with Taverner's child.

'Hold me, Florence, please,' he said. 'Hold me!' he repeated, his arms wrapping around her, his weight pushing her back against the bed, his head filled with the image of Taverner and the white hair fanning out around the pale face. Hurriedly he kissed her, ignoring her obvious discomfort, immune to her distress as his mind replayed over and over again one constant series of pictures – the cold waiting-room at Cook's Alley, the white flesh of Florence's breasts, and the long winter limbs of Taverner nakedly exposed in the chilling light.

'Florence, want me,' he begged, tugging at her clothes, her hands fluttering helplessly. 'Want me . . . please.'

Then suddenly he stopped. He sat up on the edge of the bed, mortified with shame. His face was flushed, his hands shaking as he hung his head for an instant and then slowly turned back to her.

'I'm sorry . . . sorry,' he mumbled, pulling the white counterpane over her protectively. 'I didn't mean to upset you. I wasn't thinking.' He took her hand anxiously. 'Florence, this won't happen again. Ever. I'll leave you alone. I promise. Nothing like this will ever happen again.'

Her relief and embarrassment were obvious, her voice heavy with kindness when she answered him.

'Thank you, Edward.'

He nodded only once, then left the room.

'Geoff's in hospital, but I suppose you'd bloody guessed that, hadn't you, Mr flaming Taverner? I know you were there the other week when I came. You should've answered, you know you should. It wasn't bloody fair to sneak off like that and leave me on the doorstep. I felt a right frigging idiot.'

'I had to go away.'

'Sure you did, just like Geoff's had to go away – only he *won't be coming back. If you'd been there, I would have sold you something and got some money, and then I could have kept him a bit longer. I could . . . I could have kept him on the boat. Kept him comfortable, bloody comfortable . . . But you didn't care, did you? Not you, not Mr bloody Taverner. You don't give a shit for anyone.'*

'Have you got something for me today, Martin?'

'Sure I've got something for you. It's about my friend, Geoff. He can't breathe too well any more and he can't talk. He's in the Royal Middlesex now and no one visits him, and he wears bloody nappies because he craps himself. He cries a lot too . . . I could have looked after him a lot longer if I'd had the money. I could have kept him.'

'Geoff wasn't a pet. He needed treatment.'

'Nah! You've got it all wrong. He didn't need treatment, because he's going to die anyway. He needed affection; needed to feel that someone cared for him. Now he's a leper like all the rest. A frigging leper . . . I didn't want to see him like that. He deserved better. He's failing fast now because

he's frightened and bleeding embarrassed. Bleeding embarrassed! He doesn't want to be a nuisance. Jesus, how could he have been a nuisance?

'He used to sit on the boat on the river and wait for me, and I'd come along in the afternoon and play cards with him. He was a good player. Real bloody good. He was a good man too. He never seemed to be in that much pain – not really – and when he was up to it he'd talk of his creeping bloody family, and of his old girlfriend. Silly tart, running off like that.

'He said he wasn't afraid of anything – and I believed him. I never saw anyone – bloody anyone *– who was as brave. Brave as a lion.* Two *lions. He used to whistle when I left – you know, dead loud, that French tune—'*

'The "Marseillaise"?'

'Yeah, maybe . . . Anyway, he'd whistle dead loud so I could hear him on the bank and know he was saying cheerio for now. Sometimes, if he felt really good, he'd wave through the window, too, but lately he wasn't bloody up to it. I just needed more money to keep looking after him – but you weren't here when I called to see you. Or rather, you bloody were, but you wouldn't answer. You're a shit, Mr Taverner! You let them take Geoff away. It's your *fault, and I just hope you can bloody live with that.'*

'Geoff's condition is not my fault.'

'It is! He could have had an easy death. A comfy one . . . He could! Now he'll die quick, in bloody hospital – which was just what he dreaded. You'll die afraid too, Mr Taverner. You'll die frightened and alone. I swear you will. You'll have no one. No family, no friends—'

'That's enough!'

'No! No, it isn't! You're going to have a terrible death, Mr Taverner, and you'll die alone and howling.'

'Get out!' Taverner bellowed, suddenly losing control and jumping to his feet. Frightened, Martin ran out of the room, making for the staircase. Taverner leaned over the banisters and screamed down at him.

'Don't you ever come back! Don't ever come back here!' he shouted violently.

When Martin reached the ground floor, he turned and looked up the stairwell, his voice high with spite.

'I curse you! I damn you to hell, Taverner! I don't know who you are, or what you've done, but you'll bloody pay for it. You will . . . You'll pay for everything.'

His face chalk white, Taverner began to run down the stairs. Martin hurried out of the front door and past Dr Wells, barking hysterically at the top of the basement steps. Taverner's long legs carried him quickly, but Martin had the advantage and kept his lead, hurtling along Cook's Alley, still shouting over his shoulder, the corpulent PR man from No. 2 coming out to watch.

'You're going to die, Taverner. To die! And no one will care. No one will give a damn!' His voice began to fade as he ran on, Taverner stopping, standing in the middle of the alley, breathing heavily.

But Martin kept running, and shouting, his last words skimming over the cobbles and reverberating in Taverner's head.

'No one cares about you. No one! You're no one. You're already a dead man because no one gives a shit for you. You could be dead already . . . No man! No man!'

Transfixed, the PR man glanced over to Taverner in open astonishment. He knew little of him, other than that he was an enigmatic, solitary figure with considerable style, and he couldn't help feeling momentary pleasure at his obvious mortification.

'What was all that about?' he asked with mock sympathy.

'Fuck off,' Taverner replied coarsely, his voice altered, the words coming as a surprise to both of them.

Chapter Twenty-one

EDWARD returned to London the following week, arriving at Cook's Alley just after midday, his steps echoing as he mounted the stairs, the building ominously quiet. Cautiously he moved towards the office, glancing with surprise into the empty waiting-room before knocking on Aubrey Taverner's door. There was no reply. He walked in – and then stopped, rigid on the threshold.

In his chair Taverner sat motionless, his hair unfastened and hanging over his shoulders, his face white. He seemed frosted, a hoar mist freezing him into immobility, his eyes fixed ahead, unseeing.

'Aubrey?'

There was no response. Hurriedly Edward felt for a pulse at Taverner's wrist.

He stirred when touched and drew back.

'Edward?'

'Yes. Are you all right? You look awful.'

Taverner nodded and staggered to his feet. The desk was covered with torn papers, half-emptied coffee cups and a stack of used cassette tapes. Beside his left hand was the inevitable ledger and next to it his discarded tie, the pearl pin blinking luminously against the dark silk.

'I'm not well.'

Edward moved around the desk, trying to help Taverner to his feet, but was shaken off impatiently.

'Don't touch me!' Taverner, his usually refined voice blunted, like the voice of another man. 'I need help. You shouldn't have gone away, Edward, I needed you.'

'You know why I had to go.'

'I know nothing!' Taverner howled, his white hair falling forwards over the bleak face.

'Aubrey, calm down,' Edward said quietly. 'I'll get you a drink.'

Taverner's hand shot out and gripped Edward's arm savagely. His fingers were mortally cold.

'Get me some coffee. Coffee, Edward.'

The kitchen was sour with dirty plates and half-eaten meals, a maze of bloated flies hovering greedily over the remains. The air was rank, and for an instant Edward gagged before moving towards the window and throwing it wide open. The flies droned lazily into the fresh air. Disgusted, he tipped the decaying food into a bin-liner and filled the kettle, wincing as he moved a greasy dishcloth and saw a scattering of silverfish dart for cover.

That the fastidious Aubrey Taverner could let himself and his surroundings deteriorate so far and so rapidly stunned Edward. Only illness could have effected such a drastic change, he thought, filling the sink with hot water and then opening the cupboard underneath.

'Jesus,' he murmured, turning his head away and gingerly lifting out the slimy bin.

Mrs Tunbridge was sitting on the basement steps and smiled hesitantly when she saw Edward.

'Oh, Mr Dadd, Thank God you're back. Have you seen him?' she asked, getting to her feet, her usually well-tended hennaed hair fading, a grey parting beginning to show at the roots. 'He wouldn't let me in to clean. He just shouted behind the door for me to go away.' Her gaze travelled upwards to Taverner's window. 'I think he's been sleeping here – but not eating. He wouldn't let that Kirovski man in either.' Her hand went out towards Dr Wells and she absent-mindedly stroked the dog. 'He's gone all funny . . . odd.'

'Why?' Edward asked. 'Something must have triggered it off.'

'That boy came and they had a row about something.'

Edward frowned. 'Who? Martin?'

'Yes, that's the one,' she agreed. 'Mr Taverner ran after him. He looked like he could have committed murder, honestly he did. Not like himself at all. Always so polite usually . . .' She tugged the dog's tail thoughtfully. 'Is he all right? He's usually such a gentleman.'

'I don't know what's the matter with him,' Edward replied impatiently, dropping the stinking rubbish into the dustbin at the base of the steps.

'Oh, let me do that! That's my job!' she said quickly. 'I've always looked after him, Mr Dadd. I can't understand what's happening,' she said brokenly. 'D'you think I've done anything to upset him?'

Edward touched her shoulder. 'No, you've done nothing, Mrs Tunbridge. He's just been ill, but he'll be all right now I'm back.'

'Oh, I do hope so. I don't like to think of him up there alone.'

Edward frowned. 'Haven't there been any clients lately?'

She shook her head. 'None for over a week.'

'And he hasn't left the office in all that time?'

'Not that I know of,' she replied, 'and Dr Wells always tips me off to people's comings and goings.' She shook her head again. 'No, I think it would be true to say that Mr Taverner hasn't been out for a week.'

After begging some food and milk from Mrs Tunbridge, Edward went back upstairs and made a sandwich and a coffee, taking them into the office and placing them in front of his employer. Taverner regarded the food thoughtfully for a long moment and then began to eat, his usual manners abandoned as he began to devour the sandwich, tearing at the bread and swallowing it down hurriedly with gulps of coffee. Repelled, Edward turned away and started to tidy the room as his employer ate, emptying the waste-paper bins and removing the plates before finally taking the cassette tapes into his own office.

He returned a moment later. 'So what was the matter with you?'

'I was ill.'

'With what?' Edward pressed. 'A nervous illness?'

Taverner bit into the sandwich again, but said nothing.

'Aubrey, what was the matter with you?'

'I have a problem,' he said finally, finishing the food and sucking his fingers. The action seemed hopelessly out of character. 'I get moods sometimes. I can't help it. I just do. So then I keep away from people. I think instead. I think about all kinds of things. Anything.'

'So it's happened before?' Edward queried.

'Sometimes.'

'Why don't you go and see a doctor?'

'Doctors can't help,' Taverner replied, pushing the white hair away from his face. His hands shook violently.

'They must be able to,' Edward persisted, pressing his advantage and sensing that Taverner was about to confide. 'How long have you had this trouble?'

'For many years.'

'What started it?'

Taverner's ash-coloured eyes glanced upwards, his body relaxing and sinking back into the leather chair. He lost all his anxiety suddenly, as though the food had pulled him back into reality.

'I don't remember.'

'You must!'

'I don't, Edward, I really don't,' he insisted, then smiled and began to toy with his hair. But his hands still shook too much and he couldn't plait it properly, his actions jerky and unexpectedly pitiful.

'Let me,' Edward said, getting to his feet and walking behind his employer's chair.

He expected Taverner to resist, but the man sat motionless

as Edward lifted his hair. It was light in his hand, weightless, and when he began to braid it, it was oddly cool to his touch.

'I used to do Hennie's hair when she was little,' Edward confided, intoxicated by the intimacy of the memory and the closeness of Taverner. 'But she used to wriggle all the time and I could never do it as neatly as I wanted to.' His fingers worked deftly, the plait lengthening, the mesmerizing banks of white making a queue down Taverner's back. 'Your hair's longer than I thought, even longer than Hennie's was,' Edward said, securing the plait with an elastic band and stepping back to admire his handiwork. 'How does that feel now?'

There was no response. Surprised, Edward glanced into his employer's face. His eyes were closed, his lips tightly pressed together as he breathed regularly – deeply asleep.

That afternoon many of the clients called at Cook's Alley and were relieved to find Edward back in charge. He explained repeatedly that Aubrey Taverner had been away – not ill but away from the office – and apologized for the inconvenience his absence had caused. Most seemed quick to forgive, too glad that Taverner was back to grumble further. But some were fiercely belligerent.

'He should have let me know. I phoned repeatedly. I thought he'd died or something,' one complained. 'Besides, if he was away, he should have had someone there, holding the fort. After all, that's your job, isn't it?'

Edward dodged the question. 'It won't happen again, believe me . . . Now, do you want to make a new appointment?'

So the afternoon passed, Aubrey finally waking and walking aimlessly into his bathroom and locking the door. Soon Edward could hear the shower running and half an hour later a shaved and dressed Taverner re-emerged, his suit brushed, a clean shirt and fresh tie restoring his composure.

Apparently fully recovered, he leaned against the door of Edward's office, arranging his gold cuff-links.

'I'm glad you're back.'

Edward nodded curtly, answered the phone and then turned back to his employer. 'It's Chloë.'

Aubrey shook his head. 'I can't talk now. Tell her to come tomorrow at five.'

Edward spoke quickly into the phone and then replaced the receiver.

'She's relieved to know that you're back,' he said, smiling. 'She said she's missed you.'

'Missed me,' Taverner repeated, his tone vacant. 'I'm glad . . . Martin cursed me, you know, Edward. He said that no one cared for me. That I was a "No man", and that I was already dead.' His voice accelerated. 'He said I'd die alone and howling.'

Edward could hear the sudden rise in his employer's voice and looked up anxiously.

'Martin has a very vivid imagination. You know that. He also has a very colourful way of expressing himself.'

'But he meant it!' Taverner replied, touching his forehead with the tips of his fingers. 'I think he's cursed me.'

'People can't curse other people,' Edward said calmly. 'Don't let some bloody kid worry you.'

'But he *has* worried me,' Taverner replied, leaning heavily against Edward's desk. 'He cursed me.'

'Martin couldn't curse the Devil,' Edward said dismissively. 'He hasn't the power. He's just mad at you, that's all . . . Anyway, what happened between you two? Didn't you pay him for something?'

'I didn't let him in one night,' Taverner admitted. 'You'd just gone to France and he came over – and I didn't let him in.'

'Did he have an appointment?'

'Yes!' Taverner snapped. 'But I didn't want to see Martin. Not when I was thinking of you and Florence, trying to make sense of what had happened . . .' His thoughts wandered. 'Is she all right? Florence, I mean. Is she well?'

'She's happy. At least, I think so. My mother's looking after her. Well, they're looking after each other actually. They :e both looking forward to the baby being born, even though everyone thinks the child's mine.'

Edward paused, wondering how much more to say and surprised by Taverner's lack of response. His employer was obviously struggling to hold his thoughts tog ther and was evidently frightened of something. What *was* it that Martin had said to provoke such a response? he wondered. What *could* he have said to have had such an effect?

'Aubrey, I said that everyone thinks the baby's mine.'

'It is,' he replied, surprised. 'Isn't it?'

He asked the question so innocently that for an instant Edward was too stunned to respond.

'What the hell are you talking about?' he snapped finally. 'You know it's your baby.'

'But if everyone thinks it's yours—'

'Thinking doesn't make it so! Thinking doesn't make a lie a truth,' Edward retorted heatedly. 'You slept with Florence, not me.'

'Yes,' he said, suddenly reverting to his normal manner as he straightened up and smiled elegantly, his voice assuming its previous tone. 'Of course I'm the father, Edward. You and I both know that. But it's our little secret, isn't it? And it's going to remain secret, isn't it?'

The vulnerability had gone and in its place was the Taverner of old. Poised and faintly venomous. For an instant, Edward hated him.

'Yes, it's our secret,' he agreed reluctantly. 'But secrets are expensive,' he went on, thinking of Florence – and of his own security. 'She'll need more money.'

'Then she'll have it! As much and as often as she needs,' Taverner replied, unruffled as he took out his cheque book. He wrote a generous figure and passed the slip to Edward, then filled in another cheque. 'And this is for you,' he said softly, passing it across the desk. 'My thanks for what you've done.' He paused, then stared hard into Edward's eyes. 'There's just one more thing,' he said. 'Something I have to ask you to do for me.'

'Ask.'

'I don't want you to sleep with Florence.'

The words swam upwards in the dull air. Edward hesitated, wondering how to respond. He had already made the decision not to consummate the marriage, but Aubrey Taverner didn't know that. He simply wanted to prevent any intimacy between the two of them, and was prepared to buy Edward's agreement.

The cheque lay on the desk between them ominously.

Finally Edward picked it up. His palm was sweating.

'All right, Aubrey. I agree.'

Over the next three weeks Edward restored Aubrey Taverner. He cajoled him, forced him to see clients, ordered his meals and generally nursed him. He also watched him constantly and was rewarded when his employer confided little snippets of information – which left much unanswered and served only to excite Edward's curiosity further.

Aware of Taverner's unbalanced state, he dared not press him and decided to bide his time. Whilst he waited, he gambled, his losses always exceeding his winnings, and Taverner would pay off the debts without demur, without question. As Edward supported him emotionally, so he supported Edward's addiction – as that was what it had become, an addiction. Because money was available, there was now no curb on Edward's gambling. He played wildly and lost, he played carefully and won; then he staked everything on the turn of a card or a spin of the inevitable wheel.

Before long, he lost the pleasure of gambling, but he couldn't stop. He would leave Cook's Alley at midnight and turn his steps to SW1 and the blessed anaesthetic of the wheel. As Taverner grew to depend on him more, Edward found playing no longer a thrill but a therapy, the only escape from Taverner's shadow. Even when he lost, he knew he was secure – the debt would always be paid. But some part of him was sacrificed to Taverner in return. Taverner leaned on Edward, and Edward allowed him to, needing the dependence and resenting it at the same time – too addicted to the friendship and the gambling to call a halt to either.

Daily the dependency and the anxiety increased, Edward feeling an overhanging sense of danger and wondering what Hennie would have said.

Get out, you bloody fool. Get out, before it's too late.

Yes, he thought, she would have said that. But he ignored her advice and continued to gamble, jubilant when he won one night and sent most of the money to France the following morning.

The letter came a few days later.

Dearest Edward

Antoinetta is writing this for me, as I wanted to have it written down, rather than phone. It's more personal that way, isn't it? Thank you for the money, your mother and I are so grateful to you, but please don't overwork yourself to provide for us – and don't take too much from Aubrey.

I've explained everything to your mother, Edward. We have no secrets now. She knows that he is the father. I suppose I should ask how he is, but I have no curiosity – not like you. Just be careful. Be *very* careful. Don't let him use you, but don't let him escape his responsibilities either. You are not supposed to live his life for him. Remember that. You took over his problems, but *not* his destiny.

We both miss you and look forward to the baby being born soon.

Come home when you can,

Florence

Irritated, Edward tossed the letter aside. With one breath Florence told him to free himself; with the next she reminded him to secure Taverner's continued interest. *Don't let him escape his responsibilities.* Edward gazed blindly out of the window and thought of the first time he had come to Cook's Alley . . . He had returned to England, missing Hennie, a poor young man without a wife or child, with only the memory of a lost sister to cling to.

Yet now, only a year later, he had a family, money – and problems. With a sudden flash of insight, Edward admitted to himself that he was a hopeless gambler, and that his weakness of character had tied him to the gaming-tables as securely as it tied him to the man who provided him with the means to play.

If Taverner had planned everything in advance, he realized, it couldn't have worked out more smoothly. He had carefully stacked the odds against Edward, supporting his mother, then transplanting his own family on to his employee, knowing full well that Edward would never be able to turn his back on Florence. With formidable skill, Taverner had assessed his character and exploited it, winning Edward over by offering the rare gift of his friendship, then the irresistible attraction of his dependence, and finally had secured Edward's continued presence with the bait of his ever-open cheque book.

But if Taverner disappeared suddenly, how could Edward support the two women dependent upon him? How could he run his flat and his car, and continue to gamble? The thought made his skin clammy. He had hoped to exploit the situation, but it was getting out of control. Taverner still had the whip hand, and he was still indebted. His employer might need him whilst he was ill, but for how long afterwards? If Taverner disappeared, what would happen to him? What? Edward's suspicions escalated, his head buzzing with panic. Perhaps his employer wasn't as dependent as he pretended to be. Perhaps he hadn't really been ill, after all. Perhaps . . .

Immersed in his thoughts, Edward jumped when Taverner walked into the office.

'God, you startled me!'

'Why, what were you thinking about?' Taverner asked, his

head tilted to one side. 'I was watching you from the door. You looked worried.'

'I was daydreaming—'

'No, I don't think so,' Taverner interrupted deftly, pulling up a chair next to Edward and sitting down. 'We get on well, don't we?'

'Yes.'

'And I rely on you a great deal,' he admitted, 'but you see, that's because I never found anyone else I could trust, Edward. No one ever did anything for me before. I was always the one who sorted out people's lives and listened to them, and I got so tired of it all . . . so tired. I've walked alone for too long, with no friends, no ties, nothing. Only the clients, and even they are turning against me now. I think that was why Martin alarmed me so much – he seemed to *know* how my life would end. That I would die alone and howling. Like the priest.' He smiled suddenly, a smile which had all the kindness of the ages in it. 'Do you remember what I told you about the priest when you first came here?'

'I remember.'

'I still think I hear him at night. Howling. Or maybe I'm just hearing my own future.'

Edward shivered involuntarily.

'Don't worry about the future, Aubrey.'

'But I do! Just as I worry about the past.' He seemed about to continue, finally to confide, but then he drew back. 'I need you, and you need me. I can help you in certain ways and you can help me in others. You do see that, don't you?'

Edward nodded automatically. 'Yes, I see that.'

'I'm tired of pretending, of being someone I'm not.'

'So who are you?'

He blinked slowly. 'I want to find my home, Edward. I want to belong somewhere,' he said at last. 'I want to rest, to lay down my head and stop running.'

'I don't understand,' Edward said quickly. 'What are you running from?'

'The past.'

'Why?' he persisted. 'What happened to you?'

Aubrey Taverner studied Edward for a long moment. 'No,' he said finally. 'Now is not the time. Not yet.'

Elegantly he rose to his feet, his full composure regained. 'I'll tell you everything in time. Be patient a little longer, Edward. As much for your sake as for mine.'

But patience was the one thing that Edward had exhausted and when he finished at Cook's Alley that night just after twelve he left the back window of Taverner's office unlocked. He then waited on Greek Street until he saw his employer's tall form emerge from the alley and move towards Charing Cross Road. For a further twenty minutes Edward hovered in the dark street, until he was certain that Taverner would not return, and then he retraced his steps and climbed up the fire escape at the back of No. 6.

The building was in darkness, the only sound coming from a late sewing-machine in No. 3, the rhythmic hum droning over the sloping rooftops. Carefully Edward lifted the unlocked window and climbed in. His hair prickled on the back of his neck as he felt his way into Taverner's moonlit office, the draped walls making the room shadowed like the inside of a sumptuous coffin. Inching his way along the floor, Edward's eyes gradually adjusted to the light and he moved confidently towards Aubrey Taverner's desk, pulling open the middle drawer.

There was nothing remarkable there, merely a collection of oddments which meant nothing. Hurriedly he moved over to the display cabinets, but although the death mask stared eerily up from the baize, the humming bird lay unmoving next to its neighbour and the solitary earring glinted in the dim light, the contents said nothing about the owner, and Edward felt only a mounting sense of disappointment as he moved on to the bathroom. Checking that the window was shuttered, Edward flicked on the light and then opened the medicine cabinet. Only the usual motley assortment of toiletries looked back and he was just about to leave when he noticed, under a box of tissues, the corner of a photograph.

Carefully he lifted the box and took down the picture. It shuddered in his hand, it fluttered like a trapped bird, and then fell with a heavy slapping sound into the basin beneath.

But it fell facing upwards, and Edward could see the image clearly and began suddenly to sweat. The picture was of *him*. It was his own image, his own face and yet not his face. Something had gone from it, and something had been added. His eyes fixed on the shiny print. It had been skilfully altered, some adept colourist adding years by the application of a few facial lines, changing the whole look of Edward Dadd by bleaching his blond hair a shade lighter – and adding a white pigtail.

The photograph was of Edward but *not* of Edward. It was a photograph of Edward becoming Aubrey Taverner, the older man superimposed over the younger image.

Get out! Get out now! Hennie said.

Panicked, Edward dropped the print, hurriedly bending down to retrievc it before rehiding it under the tissue box. Then he slammed the bathroom cabinet closed.

The noise reverberated loudly, the mirror on the door juddering for an instant before it reflected the darkened room behind.

Get out! Get out now!

The sound came into the silence unexpectedly, loudly, the whirr of a cassette tape clicking into place.

Chapter Twenty-two

THE BABY would not come. It clung on in the womb and refused to be born. It held on to its safety, and all through the night of 29 November, Florence struggled to give birth to Aubrey Taverner's child. Previously confident, Dr Vallant had believed that the labour would be easy, but as the time passed his doubts increased and he found himself telephoning the hospital to warn them of a possible Caesarean.

But Florence also held on. Grimly she closed her eyes and saw only redness, the blinding pain of a lingering birth coming near to the agony of death. In her blindness, she was spared others' anxiety, but her isolation intensified, her world confined without the comfort of sight and reassurance. So on the bed in the farmhouse – the same bed where Edward and Hennie had been born – she struggled to bring another child into life.

And she waited between pains for the footsteps she knew so well. She waited for the step on the stair, that one step known before all others – Edward's step. When the pain came again, she breathed hard and forced her mind back to Cook's Alley – not to Aubrey Taverner but to the young man who had first helped her, the man who had warned her later at the Brompton Oratory, and later again taken her away from London and brought her to safety. Florence had no visual memory, so she relied on sound and scent and sense and she heard again Edward's feet and the bark of Dr Wells, and the shuffle of kneeling worshippers at the Oratory; she could smell the candle wax, and the salt air on the Channel crossing and the hot tremulous evening in Edward's car.

'Ready?' he had asked her.

And she had nodded.

The pain increased, but she didn't cry out. She wasn't going to give anyone the satisfaction of showing weakness. Oh, she might have to rely on them in her day-to-day life, but she was going to do this alone. This baby was going to come into the world *proud* of its mother . . . Florence's thoughts wandered again, back to Cook's Alley and the hum of the sewing-machines at No. 3 and the high voice of the printer's boy as he ran past her down the steps. He wouldn't be a boy any longer, she realized. By now his voice would have broken and he would be showing the first shadows of a coming beard.

Gently she smiled to herself and Dr Vallant exchanged curious glances with Antoinetta. Oh, yes, Florence thought, the printer's boy would be grown up and gone, as all children grow up and go. As Edward and Hennie had left Misérie . . . She thought of Hennie suddenly and unexpectedly, thought of all the things Edward had ever said about his sister – about her laugh and her jokes, about her failed love affairs, and about the bitterness of her dying. He *loved* her, she realized with an aching heart, far more than he will ever love me.

Yet he *married* me . . . Again she smiled, lost and drifting between receiving pain and giving birth. Maybe after the child was born Edward would learn to love her, perhaps he would even *make* love to her. Her thoughts spiralled uneasily as the red waves of pain swamped her. But she held on silently. Blind and quiet. When everything was over, when her son was here, then she would relax, and Edward *would* grow to love her, Florence swore. In time, he would grow to love her. After all, she wasn't the woeful little scrap she had been when she first came to France. She was learning from Antoinetta, mastering the language and improving her appearance. She would never be a beauty, she knew that, but there were other things a woman could be for a man . . .

If he would just come home, she thought longingly, if Edward would just come home. Then she could forget Taverner and concentrate on the present, because her son would resolve the future for her. If only Edward would come . . . Her head moved on the pillow, turning towards the door as though to catch the sound of his approaching footsteps more easily. She had dreamed the other night of him and had been alarmed, wondering why he hadn't been in touch, why only cheques had come through with a brief typed note. But no phone calls for over a fortnight – nothing direct or personal. Florence knew she should have phoned herself, but she had lacked the courage to call Cook's Alley – too afraid that Edward would not be there and that Aubrey Taverner would pick up the phone instead.

She could have shared her fears, but that would have been selfish. Antoinetta had been kind to her and needed no further anxiety. So Florence had hugged her worries to herself and believed that somehow, by some process of telepathy or instinct, Edward would return when the baby was being born. But she had been wrong and he hadn't come home. The step hadn't sounded on the stair and the phone hadn't rung. When Antoinetta called Edward's flat, only the answering-machine replied, and that was a poor substitute.

Longing for him, Florence clung blindly to the thought of her child and hurried to force it out into the world. She wanted that part of Aubrey Taverner delivered from her, separated from the body in which it had been conceived, so that she could think of the baby as a person in its own right, without Taverner as its father but with Edward Dadd as the man taking the father's place. But he wouldn't come home, she thought despairingly, or maybe he *couldn't*.

Florence turned in the bed, but remained silent. The pain screamed inside her and she tilted her face upwards, the room above her the red and gold shrine where Hennie had died. She travelled in her head, swimming through bloody agony, towards her own crimson daylight, and in moving she seemed to lift upwards, her body weightless as she slid from consciousness into semi-trance. She floated, blistered in pain, a burning throughout the length of her body, and then for an instant she had a brief restoration of her lost sight.

It fluttered in her head and threw up images – of Edward, of Aubrey Taverner and of a young woman she had never known. A blonde woman who glanced over her shoulder at Florence and then turned.

'Where's Edward?' Florence stammered, the words indecipherable, although the girl seemed automatically to understand.

I'm trying to bring him to you.

'Please, help him,' Florence begged. 'Edward needs help.'

I know, but I can't get through, the young woman replied impatiently.

'Try! Please try! It's Taverner, he'll stop him coming.'

Hennie laughed suddenly, then began to fade.

Trust me, Florence, I know all about Mr Taverner.

'I'm having this experience delivered to you. My sister will bring it. I can't, for reasons which will soon be obvious. I liked you, Mr Taverner, fancied you. I bet you're laughing now, thinking of me, thinking of Chloë and all her stories. I always amused you, didn't I? Always made you laugh, even when you didn't believe what I told you, which is not surprising, considering how I sometimes lied.

'The money you paid me was useful, I'll give you that. I needed it and you were always generous. I wondered about that, wondered if you were as generous with all your clients, used to imagine that you had a soft spot for me. Yeah, a bog in Ireland! – isn't that how the joke goes? but I'm past it now, bloody tired, and so you'll have to forgive my last experience coming this way.

'I thought about it for a long time. Wondered how to impress you. Wondered why I wanted to. I'd never had any trouble attracting men before, but not you. Now, why was *that? I know you're not gay, I can tell that much, but whatever I did you didn't respond. So I thought I'd seduce you with my stories!*

'Scheherazade, wasn't she called? That woman who told stories to save her life? I tried that, kept telling stories to try and win you over. But it didn't work, and after a while I wondered if you held what I told you against me. I've done some pretty crummy things, slept around a bit, thieved a bit, run with a rough crowd. I don't deny it, I can't deny it, and now I wonder if that was why you didn't want me. I blotted my copybook good and proper, didn't I? For a man like you, at least.

'You see. I know now that the stories worked against me. The more I told you, the less you responded. The more I gave, the less I had. And when I repeated these experiences of mine, they seemed so much worse and they played on my mind afterwards, although they never had done before. Having to talk about them made me think about them, made me think about what I'd done and what I'd become. And I didn't like her – Chloë, that is – I didn't like her at all.

'After a while the experiences didn't seem so funny any more. But I couldn't stop coming to Cook's Alley and to you. Couldn't stop trying, even when I saw how cheap I must look to you. Even then, I kept talking. Gradually I saw myself as I really was – as you must see me – cheap and cheerful, an expensive tart. Clever and hard.

'Well, my life wasn't too clever once it was laid out and picked over, not too clever at all. Empty, bleak, without hope. And we did pick it over, didn't we? Well, I did, you said little. Just recorded all the experiences and put them on tapes. Lined them up like the row of sordid little tales they were, one after another, like the black railings outside – the life of Chloë, in all its rotten gloss. Funny how, in trying to impress you, I learned to hate myself.

'Oh, it's not your fault. I fell in love with the wrong man. Enough said, we always want what we can't have. It's not your fault. Maybe it was inevitable. My mother said I'd never make old bones and I suppose she was right, the old cow.

'So, this is my last experience and hopefully it will have more of an impact than the others. It's a little gift to you, Mr Taverner. A free one too! After all, I can't leave you a forwarding address . . . I hope you're getting this loud and clear, because I'm going to sleep soon. But I'll keep talking just as long as I can and tell you what I see. Some experience, hey?

Suicide. I like to think that you're here with me, but I know you're not. Still, you'll hear it when you have this brought to you.

'I only hope it'll be worth it. Oh, don't get me wrong. I'm not killing myself because of you. I was never that much of a fool about any man. I'm killing myself because I can't see where I could possibly go from here. Petty crime, prison, prostitution? No, enough is enough, Mr Taverner. This is where I stop.

'I'm very tired now. The time is four-fourteen and I'm lying on the bed in the flat. There's a dripping pipe outside the window and the radio's on. They're playing Elton John – I like him, he reminds me of when I first came to London. In fact, they were playing one of his records the first day I came to Cook's Alley.

'I don't like that place. It gives me the spooks. God knows how you stand it day in and day out. Still, that's not important. I'm tired, but it's a nice tired, sort of dreamy. I can't say that there's anything happening yet, but I'll keep talking . . .

'When I was a kid I was the prettiest girl in school and the boys fancied me. All of them. I slept around a bit – well, a lot actually! But I enjoyed it . . . The rain's stopped now, but I think it'll begin again in a minute.

'Four-twenty – slow, isn't it? I want so much to give you a real experience, something no one else has given you. You'll remember me then, won't you? I can't keep my eyes open now, it's like falling asleep . . . When I was little we went house-hunting, my parents and I, and we walked all day. Then my father drove us home and I slept in the back of the car, all safe and warm. Going home.

'It's the same feeling, Mr Taverner. When you come to die I hope it's the same for you. Going home . . . Four-twenty-one. God! I can hardly read my watch. It takes so long to live and such a little time to die. I think . . . I think there were trees at home, apple trees . . . and the first boy who kissed me was called Jim . . . Ah, here we go, here we go . . .

'Sorry, Mr Taverner, but there's nothing to see . . . At least, not yet . . . nothing at all. I can't tell you anything, and I so wanted to . . . wanted to impress you and make you remember me. I bet you're glad you're not paying for this. After all, it's nothing but an anticlimax!

'I'm sorry, but it's nothing. It's just sad and silly . . . Hardly an experience at all . . .

EXPERIENCE DELIVERED
NO FEE
SIGNED: *Aubrey Taverner*

'How is she?' Antoinetta asked Dr Vallant, her face creased with worry, her hands clenched together.

'She's having a difficult time.'

'But she'll be all right, won't she?' Antoinetta queried frantically, her head turning towards the bedroom door as they stood talking on the landing outside. 'She's not that strong.'

He raised his eyebrows. 'She's a good deal stronger than she looks,' he replied firmly. 'But I think she's worried. She wants the father here.'

Antoinetta winced at the word, her tone icy. 'The *father* is not likely to come.'

Discomforted, he shuffled his feet. 'My apologies, Madame, I meant Edward.'

She gave him a slow, penetrating look.

'My son will be here soon. I left a message for him as soon as Florence went into labour.' Her voice sounded confident, but as the hours passed she did wonder why her son hadn't arrived. Reliable Edward, always available to help. So where was he now?

'He's probably travelling at this minute and hasn't had time to phone.' Her eyes moved towards the landing window as though she half expected to see his headlights in the drive outside. 'But he'll come. Edward is always there when you need him. Always.'

Rigid-backed, she returned to the bedroom, her dignity fully restored. She then sat in a chair by the bed and wiped Florence's face and hands with a damp cloth, the semi-conscious woman hardly noticing what was being done for her. The repeated ministrations kept Antoinetta calm, although she was always straining for the sound of Edward's car, realizing again just how much she relied on her son. He *had* to come, she thought angrily. This was his wife, and the child was his responsibility; *she* couldn't manage on her own. It wasn't fair, she thought self-pityingly. After all, she hadn't asked him to bring Florence to her home. She hadn't wanted all these problems. She had been ill herself, horribly ill, and now she had been left to cope alone.

Absent-mindedly, Antoinetta wiped Florence's forehead. Edward had been selfish, she decided. Oh, yes, he provided for them well, sending all that money home – enough money to have the house restored – but he had been wrong to leave his family with her. Wrong and selfish. What did she need with a blind woman and a child? Not even *her* grandchild, but some other man's child . . . Antoinetta's self-pity accelerated rapidly. How much better it would have been if Edward had returned home alone. Together they could have lived as they used to, and they could still have restored the house – but not as a nursery! They could have brought it back to its former glory and enjoyed it themselves, Antoinetta thought with irritation. Alone, they might even have coaxed Theo back . . .

Disturbed, Florence moved in the bed beside her, Antoinetta's hand lying for an instant on the heated skin of her forehead. It wasn't Florence's fault, Antoinetta decided magnanimously, that things had gone so wrong. The poor girl had done her best, but Edward should be there to help them; he should be looking after them. What good was money, she thought wretchedly, when it was used only to solve troubles and deal with responsibilities? Money was like life: it should be enjoyed, not used to cope with a succession of mundane problems . . . Distantly Antoinetta continued to watch over her charge, her mind choked with a mixture of anxiety and self-pity, her thoughts, as usual, predominantly concerned with herself.

The moon shuffled indolently behind a high cloud, then blinked, running out again into the night sky over Cook's Alley. The cobbles, silver-marked, were still cooling from an earlier shower, the rooftops streaked, a night cat crossing the skylight of No. 6. In the basement, Mrs Tunbridge stirred in her sleep, Dr Wells growling softly at the foot of her bed.

She turned over, disturbed in her dreams, and the dog sat bolt upright, beginning a low howl. It began softly, then rose in volume, the dog's hackles lifting as it suddenly jumped to the floor and began to scratch frantically on the bedroom door.

'What is it, boy?' the old woman asked drowsily, struggling to find the light switch and then flicking it on. The worn little bedroom came into view, as did Dr Wells, growling hysterically at the foot of the door.

Alarmed, she pulled on a dressing-gown and hurried over to him. 'Come on, lad, there's no one there . . . No one. Come on, boy.'

But the dog would not be consoled. Hesitantly Mrs Tunbridge opened the bedroom door, and the animal rushed past her, hurtling down the corridor towards the basement door which led outside. She followed timorously, the dog's head turning in her direction as though to encourage her, his eyes showing their white rims as he began to whine softly.

'What is it?' she asked, at once frightened, her hand cautiously lifting the tired yellow curtain on the back of the door. 'There's no one there. There's no one out there.'

She seemed hardly to believe it herself and yet the moonlit yard looked back at her – empty and quiet. There was no sign of a person or a straying animal, only the black outline of the bins standing, ominously dark; and the steps leading up to the street, streaked with silver light, the shadowed space under them impenetrably black. Beside her, Dr Wells kept growling, the sound deep in his throat, ears now flat to his head.

Cautiously Mrs Tunbridge continued to peer through the window, a sudden noise outside alerting her.

'Who's there?' she snapped fiercely, her heart racing. 'Who's there?'

Silence.

The dog howled twice.

'Who is it?' the old woman asked again. 'I'll set the dog on you!' she shouted, opening the door. Dr Wells threw himself into the yard, barking frenziedly. 'Who's there?' she shouted again. 'Get them, boy!'

But the animal had already crossed the yard, his barks increasing as he took the basement steps two at a time and then paused, standing on the pavement above, a black dog silhouetted against the moonlit sky. Then he lifted his head and, under the shuffling moon, howled at the unlit windows on the second floor.

Edward could not move. From below he could hear Dr Wells howling, the sound raising the hairs on his arms, the noise ungodly in the listening night. The tape whirred on. In a moment he knew the talking would begin, some experience would bleed out from the machine. He tried to move again but couldn't. There wasn't a sound from the room beyond, although he knew that someone in the outer office must have turned on the machine. The darkness beyond the door was absolute, whilst below Dr Wells contined to howl.

'What are you doing here at this time of night, Edward? And how did you get into my office?'

Taverner's voice cut through the darkness.

'I left a window unlocked,' Edward replied hoarsely. 'I waited until you'd gone and then doubled back.'

'Did you find what you were looking for? By the way, what were *you looking for?'*

'I don't know,' Edward answered stupidly, still standing by the wash-hand basin and peering frantically into the dark office only yards away. He could almost smell his own fear, the howling of the dog below scratching at his nerves. Where was Taverner? Edward asked himself. He must be in the outer office, but he couldn't see him. He could only hear him, Taverner's voice composed, baiting him.

There was no one else in the house, Edward realized with terror. No one knew they were there. If he called out, no one would hear him. Certainly not old Mrs Tunbridge. Only Dr Wells would hear, and the dog was already barking . . .

'I was wrong to do what I did,' he stammered. 'I'm sorry, Aubrey. I just wanted to know more about you. I wanted to understand—'

The voice interrupted him.

'I told you I would explain in time. But you would rush it. You have no patience, Edward, and far too much curiosity. That was always your greatest failing. You know, I would have explained everything to you in my own time.'

'But, Aubrey—'

The voice rolled over his, and in that instant Edward realized that he was listening to a tape of Taverner's voice. The man wasn't talking. His voice was. He was explaining on tape, just as all the others had done. Disembodied, the voice continued. On the street below, the dog howled, the sound swinging up through the moon-heavy air. Edward's shirt stuck to his back, his hands shaking.

'I suppose you've found the photograph. Well, I knew you would. I expected it of you. I planted it for you to find. And now you want an explanation. You want to know all about me. Strange, how fascinating I've become. Ready, Edward? Are you ready now?'

The voice paused. Edward imagined the strip of plastic coiling through the machine.

'Now, let me think, how do the clients do it? Oh, yes, they just talk. Streams of consciousness. Chat, chat, chat . . . Well, here's my experience, Edward. After all, that was what you wanted, wasn't it? I do hope it will live up to your expectations.

'I was ill. With a mental problem. I had a fall which resulted in some injury to the brain, some damage to certain areas . . . I lost parts of my memory. Not all, of course. I remembered the basics – how to wash, eat, go to the toilet – but it took a while, and a lot of effort, for the other parts to return, and my emotions never did. I do not feel as others do, Edward. But I'm jumping ahead in my story, forgive me . . . Immediately after the illness I could recall nothing. I did not know where I came from, who my family was, if I deserted a wife or children. I did not know if I was successful or talented. My memory was wiped. I existed in limbo. Other people would talk of their lives and pasts. I had none. I had no references, nothing to guide me, reassure me. I walked like an alien in another world, where everything was threatening. People spoke of their childhood; I had none. People talked of their schooling; I had none. People grieved and dreamed; I had no griefs and no dreams. History meant nothing to me. I was the only person who couldn't remember where they were the day Kennedy was shot!'

He laughed on the tape.

'I tried to trace myself – to find out where I belonged – but there was nothing. It was as though I had arrived fully grown into the world. No past, no memory, no experiences against which I could map out my progress or plan my future. I floated – a No Man. That was why Martin upset me

so much. He knew, *you see, and more than that, he prophesied my death – the thing I fear above everything, that I will die alone and howling . . . You're thinking now that my malaise is due to amnesia, but you're wrong. It's much more complicated than that. You see, I didn't realize it, but the gods had blessed me when they wiped out my life. They had allowed me to forget the stinking existence I had once led.* But my memory came back. *Yes, Edward, it did. It hiccuped back in snatches and then I* really *suffered. The wish I had begged for was granted. The thing I had prayed and prayed for eventually occurred.*

'I remembered who I was and, in remembering, recalled my childhood and the man I had become. I saw myself, a man unloved, with parents who had abandoned me, a wife who had deceived me, a child who had died. As I had tried so hard to remember, now I longed *to forget. But I couldn't, I could only come back, become again the man whose life had been empty, without hope. A dull life, full of terrors, a life in which I had burned with distress and knew the true poverty of my own existence . . . My misfortune was not in* forgetting *but in* remembering *the man I had been.*

'You see, there is no hope for me. I want no part of my past, and have no true belief in my future . . . Tell me, Edward, how could I confide that to anyone? And for what reason? To have people pity me? No, I don't think so. I don't like to be pitied. So I decided that there had to be a way out. I had means, plenty of money. I changed my name and my appearance, but it wasn't enough. I knew that there had to be another way to escape – a means of escaping my old life and giving myself a new life.*'*

Edward backed away from the voice. The sink pressed into his thighs, the window was bolted behind him.

'Yes, I decided to give myself a new life. Do you see now why I bought all the experiences? I had to buy knowledge, Edward. I had to educate *myself about life, investigate my options. I couldn't beg for help, couldn't get people to confide in me spontaneously, so I* bought *their experiences and, by doing so, I bought parts of their lives. I paid for it all, and they were all only too willing to sell. I have to say that their experiences were astonishing. Love, death, murder, betrayal, sex, jealousy, loneliness, envy . . .*

the list went on and on. I suppose you're wondering about Florence now. Well, that's easy to explain, Edward. I told you I have no emotions, so I had to know about love. But I only found out about sex, and I believe the two are different.'

His voice was without hope.

'That's been the most unbearable thing for me – not to understand love. To listen to people talk of love, to see how their faces change, to sense and smell the odour of that emotion . . . I wanted to love, Edward. So I chose Florence. Because she was sweet and because she was needy. I could have picked a prettier woman, like Chloë, but I was afraid of her – as afraid of her as I was of that petty-spirited little machinist at No. 3.

'I wanted to love Florence, I did truly. I didn't want to hurt her. I never thought she would get pregnant. Dear God, Edward, how could I *be a husband or father?* How? *With all you know of me, how could it be possible?'*

Edward glanced round, wondering if he could get out, run past the voice in the outer room. Perhaps there was no one there, after all. Perhaps Taverner had just turned on the tape and left . . .

'You don't know how difficult it has been for me. I thought I could learn, understand, but I couldn't. I bought experiences, not life. The experiences gave me a false impression of the world. They weren't reality; they were extreme stories about extreme emotions. Most of life is sad, Edward, I know that now. It's horribly mundane, ordinary, useless, but that's my point! The life I want isn't going to be mundane. I don't want to be ordinary. Oh, yes, I want to be a part of the world, but a part of my *world. On* my *terms.'*

His voice took on a different tone, one voice shifting amongst many.

'So I kept investigating other people's lives. I learned how intensely people felt about their families and their lovers, their pains, their injuries, and, in the end, their deaths. They educated *me through their own agonies and anxieties. I gave them money, and they gave me life.'*

Automatically, Edward stepped further away from the door.

'You're afraid of me now, Edward. But then, you should be. You've been cocky, with all your prying and poking, and all your wretched curiosity. You wanted to know everything, all the time. Whereas I wanted to listen – that was the secret of my success, my ability to listen. They all educated me – Martin, Dr Gummings, Chloë, Florence, Mr Glaxman, Alan Painter. But the education was limited. What I had paid for was part of their lives, but what I actually needed to find was my own. *So I searched for a new life. I looked for the life I wanted. A new life.'*

Edward's head seemed full of noises. Hushing sounds.

'Yours.'

His legs buckled and he slumped against the basin. Taverner's voice sounded distant, almost as far away as the dog howling below.

'I waited for such a long time for you, Edward. And you played into my hands so nicely. You followed my every lead, and did everything I could have hoped for. You have no need to be afraid of me. I'm not going to harm you. I just want to make a deal with you. A gamble, if you like. And you do *like, don't you? You interest me so much. You're reliable and yet reckless. An intriguing man, a complex man . . . You have weaknesses, but those I can eliminate. Believe me, Edward, if you give me your life, I'll make a much better job of it than you ever could.*

'Neither of us would lose by the arrangement. We would be changing places, that's all. You would take over Aubrey Taverner and I would become Edward Dadd . . . It's perfectly possible. Think logically, Edward,

without emotion. Look at your life. You've always been a crutch for people. You supported your manipulative mother, then Florence, and now her child. You work to earn money from me to send to them – your dependants. You are, at the age of twenty-eight, weighed down with problems and people who need you and lean on you. People who look to you to provide for them and support them. Only once in your life did you have any real joy in a relationship – and that was with Hennie. And what happened? She died. You have been abandoned by your one ally, used by your parents, and yet here you are, still looking after them . . .'

Edward stood immobilized. As Taverner described it, his life seemed bleak, hopeless.

'You resent your situation, but you won't admit it. You would like to walk away from your responsibilities and escape, but you can't. The nobility of your nature ties you. So what do you do to find relief? You don't find forgetfulness with a woman, but at the gaming-tables. You gamble your sorrows away. You concentrate on the roulette wheel, or the cards, because they are the only means by which your whole attention is absorbed, and whilst you play you forget the mean drudgery of your life.

'Don't fool yourself into thinking that people need you. They need your support. *They don't want your love. Florence isn't in love with you, any more than you are with her. Your mother and father have little feeling for you. Love went out of your life with your sister. All your dependants need is your money. But it isn't even your money, is it? It's mine.'*

He paused, allowing the words to take effect.

'Admit it, Edward, you want to be free of them all. To enjoy your flat and your car and your gambling – and I can give you the means to do just that. I can give you the money to keep you happy for ever.

'I only ask for your life . . . Oh, I know I have made it sound hopeless, a worthless existence, but I could make it much more. If I became Edward Dadd, I would move away. I would keep myself apart from my responsibilities. Oh, yes, I would support your mother, Florence and the

child – but from a distance. They would have security without anxiety, and I would have the freedom to be the Edward Dadd you only dream of . . .

'A man who can indulge himself. A man who has the security of a family at home, but the freedom of an unrestricted life. A man who, if he died, would be mourned – if not deeply, at least decently. A man no longer alone in the world. Money will assure distant devotion from my family, whilst I can pursue a life apart. I would make a fine job of being Edward Dadd. I would, *Edward, trust me.'*

His voice plummeted on the tape.

'I'm tired of being Aubrey Taverner. Tired of listening to the constant stream of whining clients. I have heard all I want now. I have gathered all I need to know. I am weary of absorbing woes. I too want to escape . . . And think of what you *would have, Edward. You would become Aubrey Taverner.'*

Edward's eyes flickered.

'Oh, I know how that appeals to you. I understand you very well. You've often wanted to sit in my chair and enjoy the adoration I inspire, haven't you? You want to know why women are attracted to me and why men confide in me. Why they all seek to interest and amuse me. You've wanted my freedom, my clothes, my money. You've pictured yourself with my power many, many times in your mind's eye, I know you have. You've lusted after it, tasted it, wanted it, been jealous of the fact that I made love to Florence and that the child she is carrying is mine . . . Don't curse me, Edward. Admit the truth to yourself and you'll resent me less.

'You've had no power in your life. None at all. No power over your circumstances or your loves. People have rejected you, left you or needed you. But never chosen *you. The world has buffeted you and you've resented it, and when you met me you saw in me the one thing you had never had, and wanted above everything – control. The power to control my life was the thing you admired in me, Edward. That was what tied us. You wanted to learn from me, as I wanted to learn from the clients. You wanted to pick*

your way into my head, to understand how I was as I was. You wanted my secret. So now I give you that secret – and the chance to live *that secret.'*

Slowly, hypnotically, Edward put out his hand, reached for the photograph and studied it. His eyes fixed on the image as he swung eerily between logic and fantasy, between the reality of his life and fear of the unknown. He longed to escape his ties, to throw off his responsibilities. But he was afraid, aware that in taking over Aubrey Taverner he might take the first step into a life no man could live.

'It's impossible,' he said out loud.

'No,' Taverner replied.

Edward jumped violently and turned. His employer stood in the doorway. The taped voice had ended, the experience related. Reality had taken over. It was standing in front of him. The darkness in the outer office haloed Taverner, made his head ethereally beautiful. And terrifying.

'Look at the photograph, Edward,' he crooned. 'Look at it carefully. You and I are alike. We could be brothers, and we could so easily change lives. All that's needed is a little adjustment.' He hands moved, unfastening his plait. Languidly he reached into the bathroom cabinet beside Edward and took out a pair of scissors. 'Watch,' he commanded, cutting off his hair in one quick movement, the white mass falling on to the tiled floor at his feet. 'Now look in the mirror.'

Transfixed, Edward turned as Aubrey Taverner pulled back his hair and held it tightly at the base of his neck. His grip was fierce, tugging.

'You just lighten your hair a little and plait it and you begin to be me . . . You see how easy it is? People only remember the obvious, Edward, I learned that much. They will remember a tall man with a white pigtail, no more. People have no eye for detail.' He stared fixedly at Edward, his pupils dilated. 'We'll have to plan everything very carefully, of course, and move away from Cook's Alley. But Aubrey Taverner can go anywhere else. Anywhere he likes.'

His voice was soothing. Edward looked into the mirror and saw himself turning, adopting the appearance of the man behind him. Petrified, he continued to stare, seeing Taverner altering, his shorn hair making him younger, more like Edward. Together they faced the glass, two men shifting into each other's space and lives. They shuddered between each other's existences, Edward held in Taverner's grip, his mind swimming, seduced by desire and terror.

Softly, Taverner talked on.

'Agree, Edward! You have a chance to be powerful, to be what you wanted to be. People will tell you their secrets. They'll talk to you.' His voice was quiet, hypnotic. 'Look at yourself in the mirror. Look!'

The reflection hovered, Taverner becoming Edward, magicking himself into the other man. Suddenly Edward felt himself falling, the tiled floor beneath his feet widening, his body weightless.

'Give in, Edward! Give in!' Taverner urged, his mouth pressed against Edward's neck. 'I am you and you are me.'

I am you and you are me.

Edward struggled against the words. Wasn't that what Hennie had once said? he thought, fighting hopelessly against a dark wash of terror.

Still Taverner held on.

'Edward, let go! Let go. Relax. Give in . . . Agree. Agree. I am you and you are me.'

His breath soaked into Edward's skin, his hands dropping to Edward's shoulders, the weight of his fingers sliding into the younger man's flesh. Clumsily, Edward tried to move, turning drowsily like a sleepwalker, bumping into the wash-hand basin, treading the white hair underfoot.

'I can't,' he stammered, his mouth filling with the stickiness of fear, the words balling up in his throat. 'I can't.'

Taverner's voice intensified. 'Agree!'

'I can't . . . can't.'

'Agree!' Taverner repeated again, loudly, the word making a black shape in Edward's head.

'I . . . can't.'

'You can!'

'No . . .'

'Agree! Agree! Agree!'

The word shuddered in the cool air, the bathroom swelling under the sound, the distant whirr of the tape-machine still humming malevolently in the outer office.

'I agree,' Edward said finally.

And the tape clicked off.

Chapter Twenty-three

FLORENCE's bed was full of red. Red as blood, as damask roses, red as pain. Swimming in red, deep as veins, full as the heart of blood. She moved fretfully on the bed, the child inside her suspended, hanging in a womb of blood, not yet ready, still there, still waiting . . . Taverner's child. The pain gobbled her. It had a noise, a sound, dark and oily; it growled inside her. And still the child wouldn't be born. The night ground on – and the baby stayed out of the world.

As rhythmically as breathing, Florence drifted in and out of consciousness. She no longer wondered where Edward was; she no longer had the strength to listen for his footfall or the sound of his car. Her thoughts left the world of men and slipped into the space between pain and birth, lingering on that step between life and death. And there she stood – sightless, unhearing, unfeeling, her whole being centred on the coming of her child.

But the baby still would not be born, and 29 November ended, passing its midnight deadline and slipping over the wall of the thirtieth day.

Mrs Tunbridge was irritable. Having had an interrupted night she was not in a mood to be pleasant and cleaned Aubrey Taverner's office hurriedly, for once too dispirited to read his mail, her head thumping with a dull, unrelenting ache. Having howled for nearly two hours, Dr Wells had finally fallen silent around three in the morning, leaving his post on the pavement outside No. 6 and slinking back down to the basement, his tail between his legs.

The dog had slept fitfully, Mrs Tunbridge waking often to

find a pair of watchful eyes on her, and when the morning came the atmosphere of the night had overworked her senses to such an extent that she could hardly raise herself. But slowly she pulled herself together and did the usual round of chores, finishing early, the pervasive depression of the house attacking her nerves and making her unusually reticent.

So when the footsteps sounded on the steps outside at noon she never even looked up, and when another pair of feet followed soon after she ignored them. Only Dr Wells ran to the door, but instead of howling he wagged his tail sadly for an instant and then returned to his bed.

'Who is it, lad?' Mrs Tunbridge asked. 'A friend?'

The dog's eyes followed hers, but he made no movement. It seemed as though he had thought he knew the feet then changed his mind.

The world was wicked that day.

'It's good to see you. Thank you for giving me an appointment so quickly.'

'Don't I know you?'

'Maybe . . . I have something very interesting to tell you, Mr Taverner, an experience no one can have described before . . . I can see you're going away. Well, I'm glad I caught you. But then, everything in life is timing, isn't it?

'But back to my story – sorry, experience. I want to tell you about this girl I knew very well. Very well indeed. She was everything people wanted and envied. Good-looking and clever, articulate, and sufficiently streetwise to survive anything. This woman of whom I speak had a good life. A bloody silly one too, at times. But who hasn't made mistakes, Mr Taverner? At times we all believe we're cleverer than everyone else, don't you think so?

'I see you do, even though you won't admit it. A man of few words, but then, it's quality that counts, isn't it? Anyway, to get back to my tale. This woman I know travelled a great deal. Gone everywhere you could imagine, and places you couldn't. She's clever, knows all about magic,

could tell you a thing or two about myths as well. Sees into the heart and into the future. Even the past . . . Ah, I see that interests you, Mr Taverner, I thought it might. I just thought it might.'

'I do know you, don't I? I've seen you watching me.'

'Maybe . . . But let me continue. Her travels are extensive and exhaustive. And she moves alone. Time means little to her, because she has no limitations in her head. No home and therefore no reason to return. She travels light, this woman, takes taxis when she needs to and moves around the city at night. And no one ever bothers her. I thought that was strange – pretty women have a habit of being bothered – but not this one. She carries her own protection with her, you see.

'I hope I'm not boring you, Mr Taverner. I'd hate to outstay my welcome, especially as I can see you're waiting to leave, so I'll be brief. This woman has gone somewhere no one living has ever gone . . . Yes, Mr Taverner, do let the tape keep running, I want you to get every word clearly and accurately. It's so important to keep records. You see, she has passed into another place and moved through the grave. She died, and yet did not die. Instead she carried her death with her and now occupies a life between lives. I see you follow me . . . Well, Mr Taverner, would you like to follow me now? Why don't you come on your travels with me? I could take you somewhere no one has ever gone before.'

'You're Hennie, aren't you?'

'Yes, I'm Hennie, and I have a proposition for you, Mr Taverner. I want my brother's life. I don't want you *to have it. I want it to remain his. All his life, for all his life. I have seen the future and I know what is right. You have no control there. Don't fight me, because you will lose. I do assure you of that. You are up against more than you know, Mr Taverner.*

'You're a clever man. A very clever man. I understand your problems, believe me. You lost your life, only to find it again and discover that it was the thing you least wanted. You have a madness in you now, but although your story's tragic, you can't get your revenge by cheating Edward out of his life. He would be so *lost, and that would be cruel . . . Oh, no, I can't have that. I spent a lot of time trying to get through to him, but it was very difficult. More difficult than you could possibly know. And he was so stupid at times. I could even get through to that old crone in the basement more*

easily than I could reach him. But I love him, you see, so I persisted. Besides, I don't want you to take Edward's life away from him because yours would be such a poor substitute.

'So I'll do a deal with you, Mr Taverner, because I know what a wicked man you are, and how you're open to temptation. I see the evil in you already, long before it shows on the outside. Let my brother go and I'll give you the experience of a lifetime. I'll take you to a place no one has ever been before. When you get there – if *you get there – you will have power, Mr Taverner. More than even you dream of. And the fee for this little trip? Edward's life. That's all. Not much really. I know, I can see the future and it would never have worked out for you, being Edward Dadd. You would have soured and corrupted your chance. Let him go, Mr Taverner. Let my brother go, and I'll reward you, I promise you . . . I'll reward you. It just takes courage, that's all, and you don't lack that. Think of it. You'll be the first man* alive *to go where the dead go.*

'But then, that won't be so bad for you, will it? You are already half dead. Come with me and I'll keep my promise. Come with me . . . come with me. I ask only for my brother's life. No more. Not even a payment. You don't have to give me any money for this experience. Leave the money for Edward. He'll need it. You shouldn't hesitate, Mr Taverner, you have nothing to lose. If you steal Edward's life, you will never have a moment's peace, and you will, believe me, die alone and howling.

'There, I see you've made up your mind. You see how easy everything is in the end? Giving in isn't the same as giving up, Mr Taverner . . . Now, you just follow me, that's all. That's right, I'll tell you what to do. No, don't write anything, the tape will tell the story.

'Just give me your hand. There, you see how easy it is? Do you see how easy it all is in the end?'

As Hennie's feet moved down the steps of No. 6 Cook's Alley with Aubrey Taverner following, the child finally broke through from Florence's womb into the outside world. It came in screaming, howling into life as two others left; it came in covered in blood, white-haired, angry, its fists flailing – a winter baby. It opened its eyes briefly without focusing but with full sight. It gulped at the air and filled its lungs, and turned towards its mother with urgency.

And Florence held on to her son. She crooned to him and felt his face and knew him, and drew a picture with her fingers and held on to it in her mind. In the deep bed in which Edward and Hennie had been born, she held her child and in her mind the memory and pain receded. They ebbed back from her, taking Taverner and the long retching of agony out on the bloodied tide.

'I know this place.'

'Of course you do. It's the white room. One of your clients told you about it a long time ago. The white room where we all come in the end. Look, Mr Taverner, look at the white walls and the white windows, and now look through the window. It's a white landscape out there – white trees, white sky, white grass. Only the clock is coloured, the photograph clock. You just wait here until your picture comes up on the face. Then they'll come for you.

'You mustn't panic. The machine's waiting for you and it doesn't pay anyone to panic. Not now . . . They'll take off all your elegant clothes, Mr Taverner, before you go in. And they say that it hurts less if you don't struggle.

'Relax, there is *no door, and no escape . . . Come on, sit with me here. You look shaken, Mr Taverner. Well, you shouldn't be. You chose to come and you have many friends here. Many, many old friends. You remember Mr English, don't you? And Chloë? And all the others? See, they remember you, they're waiting for you. They're all at the window, looking in, waiting. Waiting to see how you get on. You can't let them down, can you? You can't panic. Not you.*

'You see, they don't expect it of you, Mr Taverner. Not Aubrey Taverner, not after they gave you so much . . . Stop looking at the

photographs. It's easier if you don't look. I know that the noise is unnerving, the clicking does get to you after a while. Click, click, click, . . . on and on.

'It's odd how you resented Edward's curiosity, especially as you have so much yourself. Your curiosity is what brought you here, that and nothing else. Stop looking at the picture clock. You'll know when it's time. We all do . . . every one of us.

'It's funny, Mr Taverner, how you've ended up. It seems such a long way to come, just to get back to the start.'

Spellbound, Edward stood at the doorway of Aubrey Taverner's office. The place was abandoned, although the kettle was still warm and a tap dripped idly in the kitchen sink. The rooms smelled deserted, as though no one had lived in them for a long time, and as Edward moved towards the desk he felt the mixture of disappointment and grief so strongly that his legs almost failed him.

He saw the tape and automatically rewound it, pressing the PLAY button and listening as the first words came over the speaker. At the sound of Hennie's voice, his eyes filled and he glanced down, her laughter coming like a firecracker into the gloomy room. He listened, and in listening came finally to understand. The tape ended, the machine clicking off loudly in the abandoned room.

He sat unmoving whilst the daylight grew heavy with London rain, the draped walls darkening, swallowing up their Egon Schiele painting, the display cabinets shaded, their malignant trophies staring up sightlessly through the weighty glass. Taverner had gone. The one thing Edward had dreaded had finally happened. The man had gone, gone on, gone past him. Gone. And taken his magic with him. All that remained were his ledgers and the rows of tapes.

They had decided to change lives that afternoon, Edward

surrendering to Taverner at last. He was supposed to have arrived at quarter to one, when they were to exchange documents and Taverner was to have paid him. Then the transfer would have been complete.

Edward tried to move, but the effort wearied him and he remained slumped in his seat. There was to be no exchange, the man he was was the man he was to remain. The responsibilities were still his, the dull weight of his future was his own. Without Taverner, without the sweet terror of escape.

He had wanted to go. Had, in the end, *longed* to go. Only Hennie had saved him. The room seemed to grieve with him, Edward finally rising to his feet and opening the drawers of Taverner's desk. Slowly he pulled out the tapes, weighing them in his hands. They were real. Even if Taverner no longer existed, their stories were fixed on the plastic spools.

Mindlessly Edward began pushing the cassettes into his pockets, stealing Mr English, Mr Glaxman, Chloë and all the others, taking them away with him – to remind him of what had once been.

Chapter Twenty-four

THIRTY YEARS LATER

EDWARD stood at the entrance of Cook's Alley, where it meets Greek Street. Under the cloud-lapped sky a sullen shower began and then stopped, throwing the rain aside like a discarded glove. Two women passed him without showing any interest. His hair had thinned, he had even begun the hint of an early stoop, and all his platinum beauty had dissolved like a bar of soap left far too long in water. He was still Edward, still the Edward Dadd of earlier years, the man who had learned too much and loaned too much – but he could still be kind, because kindness became him.

He hesitated on the pavement, then walked slowly into Cook's Alley, surprised by what the passing of time had done. The bellied houses still jutted out, the rooftops uneven, a selection of old bills and posters lining myriad windows. But the machinist had gone already to her council house in Brixton, and was now no doubt swinging her leg at a recalcitrant son, not to lure a lover. And the printers had moved on too, following the printer's boy and the winding summer of sex and hot sun, taking their routes from the capital to where? The lonely security of Southend? Or the stagnant lure of sheltered accommodation in outer London? To what little emptiness of hearing-aids and supplementary benefits?

No. 2, where the corpulent PR man had once worked, had, like the printers, closed up shop. The PR man had left no trace either – only an oil slick on the cobbles and a faint memory which Mrs Tunbridge could have told him about had he come only six years earlier. But not now. Now she was with Mr Tunbridge in a joint grave. And as for Dr Wells – he had developed cataracts and breathed his last under the vet's anaesthetic years earlier. So now the basement steps were unswept and no one sat on them, not in summer, nor on the first warm morning of spring. In fact, no one ever came any more; all had gone and left no trace, and the alley, its pockets emptied of people, waited, boarded up and blinded, for redevelopment.

Mesmerized, Edward walked on, his gaze travelling upwards to the windows of No. 6 as he remembered. The memories came back sharp-pointed, acute – Aubrey Taverner sitting on the bench on the Embankment, Florence tapping her stick along the railings, Martin calling up from the street below, and the dark nights when the procession of clients walked up the stairs, coming to talk and sell. He shivered on the cobbles, looking up again at the windows on the second floor and remembering the deep-gutted mystery of it all. The tapes, the ledgers, the experiences, and the shadow of his sister. *One, two, three*, said Hennie, clicking off the switch on the machine. *One, two, three.*

Edward's eyes filled. Not in sentiment – he wasn't old enough for that kind of sentiment, only in his fifties still – but time had been sour with him and all his failings had, like the best of his life, been conquered. Edward no longer gambled; and he no longer dreamed. He had married Florence for kindness and now loved her – for kindness. The passion which tormented others had missed him. Dodged him like a speeding car, missed him like a mis-aimed bullet; passed by like a stranger in the street whom one wants to know but lacks the courage to confront. He had conquered himself, but had found in that courage of discipline no reward. Nothing, only a gentle love from a grateful wife – and from Aubrey Taverner's child.

It was enough, he told himself. He assured himself. He insisted, when he woke as blind as Florence – only his blindness was forced and rooted in his body; flesh blindness, the negation of passion and the refusal to risk injury. So now he stood on a winter's afternoon in the middle of Cook's Alley and wondered about what might have been. He wondered as a middle-aged man might wonder about a lost love, with the breaking realization of what had gone and what would never return . . . And he found in that wondering such pain that it made him dizzy, and he gasped involuntarily.

And it was then that Edward realized that in the last thirty years nothing had equalled the year spent in Cook's Alley, and that in the next thirty nothing else would. *His life had been here.* Before and after there was only the pedestrian filling in of time. The disappointment beggared him and left him standing helplessly in an empty alleyway, a few pigeons skirting the jagged roofs, the memories of old sounds reverberating in his ears: the slam of the printing-press, the hum of the sewing-machine, a sports car starting up and the bleep of a portable phone. He turned around, half expecting to see the scene recovered, but the windows remained boarded up and empty. No faces calling out, no man in shirt sleeves eating an apple under the London sun. Nothing – only a blank arena from which the competitors had long gone.

And then he saw him.

Edward blinked, then stared. Oh, yes, it was him, Aubrey Taverner, high and tall and slim and white-haired as Gabriel, walking past him towards No. 6. Edward saw him and tried to call out, but nothing came from his lips. And Taverner walked on, straight-backed, no older, no greyer, no different, walking into the ruin of a dream. Transfixed, Edward gazed at the familiar figure and wanted suddenly to return – *longed* to go back to the past, far away from thc steady dejection of reality; far away from a woman who no longer needed him, a woman who had a son who could so easily fill his place.

Taverner walked on, then pushed open the swinging front door of No. 6.

He was going to work! Edward thought with a rush of pleasure, hurrying towards him. He was going to make out his list of clients and Edward would welcome them as he had always done – Chloë, back from suicide, Martin, grown up, Mr Glaxman, back from the grave . . . Thirty years moved over in an instant, turned like a lover in bed. But they were no longer coming, Edward realized suddenly with blistering disappointment. They were gone for ever, and in their going Edward knew that the best of his life had gone with them. His glory days had been at No. 6 Cook's Alley, and all that was hopeful in him had found a place there. Nowhere else. Not in France, only there.

Hurriedly Edward took the stairs upwards, following Taverner. The steps rocked under him, unsafe steps leading to the magic of Taverner's rooms, steps which juddered as his feet moved over them. But Edward kept running, following the unaged figure who compelled him onwards. The walls ran with damp, the banister rail was rotting and fell outwards as he touched it, but he kept coming, calling out to the man who moved before him.

'Aubrey! Aubrey Taverner!'

His voice came back in the empty house unanswered, but he kept running. His wife and son were well provided for, there were no responsibilities left to meet, nothing, only a chance to go back, to return . . . Up the dim stairs Edward went, blindly, wildly, towards something beyond reason. Or merely that – the end of all reason.

Then, on the second-floor landing, he stopped. The office door looked back at him, closed, barred, the name AUBREY TAVERNER barely decipherable on a brass plaque. Compelled, Edward knocked in the name of friendship and weariness; he knocked to absolve the image of a man he had wanted to be; he knocked to escape the sadness of a good marriage and an easy death; and he knocked as a gambler and as a curious man.

The world went on PAUSE – just like the tapes he had stopped so often. PAUSE. Hold it there. Just there. Just for a while – and then what? Why, reality, that was *all* there was . . . Edward knocked again, and then slowly he began to push open the door.

He expected Aubrey Taverner, white-haired and as wicked as a fallen god, but there was no evidence of his mentor in the room. He had been the messenger, no more. He had enticed Edward home, no more. As always, he had played his part to perfection, drawing Edward into a deserted alley where the ghosts walked. Where Taverner had gone that hot summer day thirty years ago, and where he now was, would be explained – but not by him. The answer was available to Edward only if he followed in his footsteps. The beginning and the end suddenly dovetailed into a moment of complete clarity, and finally Edward understood.

In Aubrey Taverner's seat sat Hennie. She seemed as cunning and clever as she had always been, and smiled as her brother walked in.

'Oh, come on, Edward. What kept you?'

What kept you?

Chapter Twenty-five

HOURS LATER, THE SAME DAY, NEW YORK

THE YOUNG man stood outside the phone-booth and cursed his luck. He dipped into his pocket as though this time he would find some money, even though he had repeated the action without success several times already. Irritated, he then drummed his fingers on the glass hood, his blond hair white under the hard daylight, sunglasses shielding his pale eyes.

He could reverse the charges and call home to France, he knew that. But that would result in arguments and questions, his father demanding to know what he had done with his allowance. A reasonable question, demanding a reasonable answer – and he didn't have one. After all, how could he admit that his money had been wasted, gambled away? He knew that Edward Dadd, his father, would be unsympathetic. Having conquered his own weakness, he would be appalled to see his son following in the wake of his own addiction. And as for his mother . . . the young man smiled. No one had a better mother. So what if she was handicapped? he thought. She might be blind, but she was also charming and loving and could handle his father. No, he thought, shaking his head. She was too kind and too trusting. It would be taking unfair advantage.

What he needed was a job. That was the solution. So instead of calling home for help, the young man turned back to the phone and put in a reverse-charge call to the number listed in the advertisement in the Personal Column in the paper.

He then leaned back against the glass hood and read the few lines for the third time.

WANTED Intelligent young man
to assist in research for author.
Excellent salary in return for loyalty
and integrity.
Tel: —

The number rang out several times until someone answered, talking to the operator and agreeing to accept the call. Finally a cultured English voice came over the line.

'Can I help you?'

'Listen, I'm sorry about asking you to pay for the call, but I've run out of money,' the young man explained, hurrying on, eager to make a good impression. 'I'm phoning about the advertisement in the paper this morning.'

Taverner frowned, a sudden memory stirring at the back of his mind.

'Don't I know you?'

The young man hesitated. 'No, I don't think so . . . Anyway, I'd like to come and see you. That is, unless you've already hired someone for the job.'

'Oh, no,' Aubrey Taverner replied cautiously. 'I'm new to the city and the notice only went in today.'

The caller smiled with relief. 'So you're a stranger to New York?'

'Yes,' Taverner replied patiently, 'but I intend to settle here now.'

'That's great,' the young man replied eagerly, 'because I need a secure job. You see, I want to settle down. I've been moving around far too much for far too long.' He paused. 'Have you been travelling too?'

'You could say that I've been on a long trip,' Taverner responded drily, 'and I've only just found my way back.'